A Witch's Journey

by

Tena Stetler

The Lobster Cove Series

A Witch's Journey

Cover Art by *Kristian Norris*

The Wild Rose Press, Inc.
PO Box 708
Adams Basin, NY 14410-0708
Visit us at www.thewildrosepress.com

Publishing History
First Black Rose Edition, 2016
Print ISBN 978-1-5092-0820-3
Digital ISBN 978-1-5092-0821-0

The Lobster Cove Series
Published in the United States of America

She hopped out of the truck

and took a deep breath. The ocean breeze brought a mixed scent of brine, sand, sun, and kelp. Seabirds whistled and screeched through the air diving into the white crested waves, proudly emerging with dinner. Turning her attention to the land, she noticed beyond the barn the pond was still there, even a bit bigger than she remembered. Caught up in the smells, sights, and sounds, she didn't hear someone approach.

"Ms. McKay?"

"Sssshit," she yelped and whirled around to see a muscular man, well over six feet, with surfer blond hair nearly to his shoulders, tousled by the ocean breeze. Rounding the corner of the cabin, he waved at her as he approached walking with a slight limp. Deeply tanned, he appeared to spend a lot of time outdoors.

"I'm Lathen Quartz. Glad you made it before dark. The road up here can be treacherous at night if you don't know where you're going. I finished up the enclosed aviary and was getting ready to leave. But now that you're here, I'd be happy to show you around. Help you get settled."

"Pepper McKay, call me Pepper." Extending her hand toward him, she met his gaze. His large aquamarine eyes were mesmerizing, set above the high cheekbones, full lips, and a butterscotch five o'clock shadow. She gave her head a shake. "Wait. You built an aviary?"

He shook her hand and smiled, shoving his hands in the pockets of his jeans and rocking back on his heels.

Praise for Tena Stetler

Dedications

To my family and friends, who are so supportive.
My husband, Bruce, who rocks!
And my editor, Lill,
who makes my books the best they can be.
To my readers, thanks so much!

Chapter One
Sometimes You Have to Slam a Door
Before Opening a Window

A loud knock on the apartment door broke her concentration. The scrying crystal connected to a delicate gold chain that seconds before floated in the air, dropped and bounced once, then came to rest on top a dog-eared map of the United States. Pepper cursed, shoved at the map spread across the glass-topped, oak coffee table, then closed her eyes as her mind's third eye opened. At her apartment door stood a stocky young man with short dark hair, dressed in business casual attire. He shifted from one foot to the other and held a large white envelope along with a business card.

He leaned his ear to the door, listened, and knocked again, louder this time. "Ms. McKay...Pepper McKay are you in there?"

Not wanting to acknowledge the visitor, Pepper sat still, opened her eyes, and rested her head in her hands. The last thing she needed tonight was a visit from another process server with more legal papers telling her she was no longer welcome in Salem. Or at least in this quaint, cozy apartment building she'd called home for the last ten years. It was within walking distance to the wildlife rescue she worked for as a licensed rehab specialist. The rescue was more than a job. It was her life's work. But her continued employment now

1

endangered the grants and funding the center depended upon to stay open. Even though Gwen protested, Pepper resigned, came home, packed up her apartment, and prepared to leave by week's end. All thanks to the landlord who had a vendetta against witches. *Gee, imagine that, discrimination against witches in Salem, Massachusetts.*

In her heart, she knew she could win a lawsuit against the manager and the corporation that owned the building. But she was also aware a legal battle against a large corporation would take money, lots of it. The costs would gobble up the small inheritance she'd received from her paternal grandmother and probably cut into her modest income from the rescue. But it was a moot point, she had resigned.

All this happened due to the magic storm that hit the town a month ago on the anniversary of a Bishop witch's burning during the Salem Witch Trials. The magic climate was always unstable around the anniversary, but this year, buildings were damaged, sidewalks buckled, mortals became disorientated, and chaos reigned for almost forty-eight hours. She had put up a magic barrier around the rehab center, so there was no disruption, but it had drawn attention and couldn't be explained away. If she had it to do over again, she wouldn't change a thing. Her boyfriend's big mouth didn't help matters. She'd given him the boot shortly thereafter. Bad taste in men, her downfall.

She shook her head and blinked away the tears. She wouldn't cry anymore. Straightening her shoulders, she pushed up from the couch, swiping at the crumpled eviction notice next to the map, which went flying across the room. Her elbow caught the edge of the lampshade sitting on the end table beside the couch, send the lamp crashing to the floor. *Great. Now whoever was at the door knows I'm here.*

In the darkness she stumbled over one of the boxes, and fell against the oak table, hitting her head on the floor. She sat up, flicked her wrist, and a ball of light hovered in the center of the room. Getting to her feet, she rubbed the bump on her head, walked to the end of the couch, and turned on the other table lamp. What a mess. *Where the hell did I pack the dustpan?*

Another series of knocks on the door pushed Pepper's temper to the end of its tether. All the hurt, anger, and frustration of the past weeks boiled over. She flung the door open and screamed, "What the hell do you want? I'm leaving." Her cheeks warmed as she stared at the stranger.

The young man took a step back, eyes rounded, he looked through the doorway into the room stacked with boxes and said, "I think you have me confused with someone else. My name is Jack Kelly. I am a private investigator for the Fairbanks Law Firm in Bar Harbor, Maine." He extended his hand, with the white envelope in it, toward her.

Pepper stared at the envelope and business card attached. *Was this some kind of joke? What would a law firm in Maine want with me?* She took the envelope and gave the young man a rueful smile. The heat in her cheeks continued to burn. "I'm sorry, I've had a rough week or two."

"That's all right, I think your luck is about to change. Have a good night."

As Jack turned to walk away, she leaned against the door frame and let the envelope flutter to the floor, too tired to care anymore.

Just before Pepper closed the door, Jack turned around and asked, "Did you know an Ashling Connor McKay or Colleen Denton?"

Pepper's eyes went wide. Ashling was a favorite aunt. She'd loved spending summers in Maine working with her aunt rehabbing harbor seals that had gotten caught in boat propellers, fishing nets, or worse, barely escaping the jaws of an orca. Her aunt had been instrumental in helping Pepper get her certification, once she graduated from college with a degree in Marine Biology.

After the funeral, Colleen, Ashling's companion for over twenty-five years, was devastated. Pepper's mom kept in contact with Colleen, but Pepper threw herself into her work trying to fill the void her aunt's death left. She'd talked to Colleen by phone on holidays, but hadn't returned to Lobster Cove since the funeral.

"Ms. McKay?" Jack asked, jolting Pepper back to the present.

"Yes, Ashling McKay is…was…my aunt. She passed away five years ago. Why? What does this have to do with her?" Pepper wanted to know.

"Well, I don't know all the particulars. I was only hired to find you." Jack peered through his wire-rimmed glasses, his forehead wrinkled, and paused for a couple of beats. "But it's my understanding that Colleen Denton gave notice that she would be vacating the premises she had shared with Ms. McKay and moving in with a brother and his family." He shrugged. "Guess upkeep of the place got to be too much for her. That terminates the life estate Ashling set up for

Colleen."

At Pepper's quizzical look, he explained. "A life estate is where Ms. McKay's Last Will and Testament allowed Colleen to live on the property they shared until she died or chose to relocate. At that time, the property reverts to the estate. Therefore, since you are the sole beneficiary as set out in Ms. McKay's will, the property and the rest of the estate now go to you. It's all explained in the letter." Jack nodded toward the floor where the letter had fallen,

"What? Are you sure?" Pepper gulped in air as her heart thundered in her chest, hoping the room would quit spinning. She put her hand on the wall beside the door frame to steady herself and closed her eyes for a few seconds. When she opened them again, the room was stationary, and a trickle of sweat ran down the side of her face.

"You didn't know?" Jack asked raising an eyebrow. "Maybe you should sit down. You don't look so good."

"I'll be fine," she said taking another deep breath and feeling better. "Just give me a minute or two." Pepper directed her gaze toward him. "Now you were saying?"

"I've probably said too much. Anyway, Mr. Fairbanks asked that you call him right away. All his contact information is in the packet. Mine is the business card attached to the outside."

"Thank you." Pepper bent over, scooped up the envelope, ran her fingernail under the flap and turned her attention to the contents. She pulled out the papers and glanced over them. "Appears I've all the information needed." She looked at her watch. "He's probably gone for the evening. I'll contact him tomorrow."

"Okay," Jack said and started down the hallway, then pulled his cell phone from his coat pocket.

Pepper watched him put the phone to his ear, closed the door, and leaned her back against the solid surface. If the PI was to be believed, at least now she had a place to go. She considered calling her parents and decided against it. A better idea was to finish packing her stuff in the trailer she'd rented, then drive up to Lobster Cove. See what the attorney had to say and take it from there. She tapped the envelope against her leg, thinking.

As she started out the door with the last box, her knee caught the strap of her backpack sitting on the little table beside the entrance.

"Shit." She'd left it unzipped, and her wallet, keys, phone, and pepper spray skittered across the floor. Setting the box down, she stuffed all the items into her backpack, and a membership card to the gym fluttered to the floor. Although she spent long hours at work, hitting the gym afterword seemed to ease the day's stress and helped her sleep better. She picked up the card, tore it up, and tossed it in the trash. *Crap, I was paid up for three months.*

When she bent over to pick up the box again, her phone rang. She pulled her cell out of the backpack and checked caller ID. "Hi, Gwen."

"What ya doing?"

"About to put the last box in the trailer. I'm headed to Lobster Cove in the morning."

"Lobster Cove? What's up there?"

"The strangest thing happened tonight," Pepper

said and proceeded to tell Gwen about Jack and the conversation they'd had.

"That's great news. I hate to ask, but would you be willing to take Kaylee with you? She's been out of control since you left yesterday. Kept the other birds up all night with her sharp whistles. This morning she wouldn't eat and continued with her frenzied noise."

"Won't relocation stress her?"

"Not any worse than she is right now. We can crate her for you and pack fish on dry ice for the trip."

"No—don't crate her, I'll do it when I get there, but appreciate the fish. I'd planned to leave before dawn tomorrow, but I can wait. What time will someone be there tomorrow morning?"

"I'm staying the night, to try to calm everyone down. So the earlier, the better."

Gwen's jaw-popping yawn came over the phone, and Pepper paused. "How about I come over right now? That should calm her down and in turn the others, so everyone can get to sleep. I'll stay tonight then feed and crate Kaylee at first light, and we'll be off when you arrive."

"I'd be grateful. See ya soon. "Gwen blew out a breath and disconnected the call.

Pepper tucked her phone in the backpack, picked up the box, and took one more look around, then closed and locked the apartment door. A few minutes later her truck rolled to a stop in front of the center. She hopped out and sprinted toward Kaylee's enclosure. The sound was deafening. Kaylee had all the birds in an uproar.

Gwen waited at the gate, her short dark brown hair wild as usual, sporting new pink highlights. She unlocked the enclosure. Pepper did a double take at her friend's new color and slipped her arm in the leather protector. On the way through, she grabbed a portable perch made for Kaylee, stepped inside the area, and raised her arm. The four pound, twenty-four-inch-tall osprey wobbled through the air and touched down gripping tightly to Pepper's arm. In a quiet voice, she calmed the bird and transferred her to the perch. With the ringleader quieted, the rest followed suit.

Gwen shook her head. "She's a far cry from the nearly dead osprey chick from eight years ago. She was your first rescue and rehab, wasn't she?"

"Yeah, vet said with Kaylee's busted-up wing and mangled foot, if she survived, she'd never fly or perch well. Yet, she is doing both. The vet did a good job putting her back together."

"Yep. Thanks for coming. It's almost like she knew something was wrong."

"Seems everything is going to be all right. Go get some sleep."

Pepper crashed on one of the cots used for emergencies, Kaylee's perch positioned next to the bed.

The horizon was a magnificent yellow with orange tentacles spreading across the dusky sky before Pepper said her goodbyes with promises to keep in touch. Kaylee's crate was secure in the back seat of the truck with her cooler of fish on the floor. After five and half hours on the road, Bar Harbor's welcome sign came into view.

Pepper followed the navigator's directions to the Law Office of Fairbanks and Fairbanks. With the prevailing winds, the spring day was cool, and dark clouds threatened an afternoon storm. During her early morning call, Brandon Fairbanks said he could meet with her early afternoon to discuss the estate and answer any questions she may have. He was reluctant to discuss the case over the phone, which she felt was understandable.

She locked the doors, but left all four windows cracked in her maroon crew cab pickup, covered Kaylee's crate, and hoped she'd be quiet. Before pushing through the sparkling glass doors to the upscale law firm, she wiped her sweaty palms on her jeans. Once inside, her steps were hushed on the plush tan carpeting as she walked to the circular desk in the center of the lobby. The receptionist greeted her with a smile and put a call on hold.

"May I help you?"

"Yes, I have a meeting with Brandon Fairbanks," Pepper said quietly, noting from the name plate the receptionist's name was Pam.

"Oh, you must be Pepper McKay. He is expecting you. I'll let him know you're here. Just have a seat. There's hot beverages on the table and bottled water in the little fridge."

The furnishing, décor, and a few clients seated all spoke to the wealth of the firm. Dressed in her black jeans, red striped sweater, and work boots, she felt a bit uncomfortable, but settled into a tan and brown upholstered chair and picked up a magazine. A young man stopped at the receptionist desk, then smiled over at Pepper putting her at ease as he walked toward her.

"Ms. McKay, it's a pleasure to meet you." He extended his hand. "Ms. Denton told me all about you and your rehabilitation work in Salem."

Clasping his offered hand, she gave it a firm shake. She didn't care for a wishy-washy handshake, and his was quite strong, confident. "It's nice to meet you, Mr. Fairbanks. And it's Pepper."

"Please call me Brandon." He turned and led her down the hallway, past a secretarial area. He smiled at the woman sitting behind a desk and ushered Pepper into a spacious office. Pepper noticed he had three single photos a different child in each. Next to them was a portrait of him, a woman Pepper assumed was his wife, and the three cute kids.

"Did Colleen go to live with family? She didn't mention it to me last time we talked, but that was quite a while ago."

"Yes, I believe she is living in a cottage on her brother, Tim's property. The McKay place required too much upkeep for one person, and she felt it was time to turn the property over to you. Ms. Denton said you'd have big plans for the property, which now seems strange, if you hadn't talked to her for a while." A perplexed look crossed his face. "Shall we have a seat?" He motioned to one of the leather chairs across from his Cherrywood desk.

Pepper hesitated for a few moments, then eased into the chair. "I don't know what she meant, but I'm grateful for a place to live. Once I get settled, I'll give her a call."

The amicable smile returned to his face. "Your aunt put all this in motion when she passed away." He handed her a sealed envelope with Pepper McKay scrawled across the front in green ink. "I was instructed to give you this letter when Colleen ended the life estate."

Pepper took the envelope and turned it over in her hands. "Do I open it now?"

"It's not necessary. We have plenty to go over. Once you've seen the property or have any questions, we'll set another appointment. That being said, do you want me to take you to the property?"

"No, it's been five years, but I can set my GPS and find it. It's south of Lobster Cove. Right?"

Brandon nodded.

"Will I be able to spend the night at the cabin, or do I need to make arrangements for utilities and things?"

"I've taken the liberty of hiring Lathen Quartz, a handyman who comes highly recommended and lives in Lobster Cove. He stocked the kitchen for you with mainstays, made sure the utilities and telephone were turned on. I believe Ms. Denton left some furniture for you and most the appliances were recently updated." He scooted several pictures of the cabin and property across the desk to her. "I believe the barn and other buildings will need repairs."

Pepper gasped and put her hand over her mouth as she looked at the pictures. "Oh, this is wonderful."

"There are a few more things we need to go over before you leave. The matter of substantial bank accounts and trusts, most are located in Lobster Cove. Except the estate account, which is in Bar Harbor. I have used the account for estate expenses and maintenance on the property." He slid a spreadsheet toward her. "If there are any questions, please don't hesitate to ask. I kept a thorough accounting of all monies spent, according to the trust."

Pepper's eyes widened when she picked up the spreadsheet. She blew out a breath and leaned back against the chair. "Mr. Fairbanks, is this all mine? What about Colleen, what is she doing for living expenses?"

"Yes, all the funds belong to you. Ms. Denton has an income of her own," Brandon said with a laugh. "Do you have a financial advisor?"

"Nooo…never had enough money to…well…do you have a recommendation?"

"Yes, I can handle that for you. I know a good financial planner. Your aunt set up several investments where she could live quite comfortably off the interest. When she passed, she instructed that all interest be added to principle, unless her partner, Ms. Denton needed it. She didn't. So we can simply reinstate that procedure. I will transfer the accounts into your name, but it would be wise to check on the tax ramifications."

Still perusing the photos, Pepper suddenly looked up at Brandon and said, "I have a question. Suppose I can get the necessary permits to start a wildlife rehabilitation center on the property. Can you help me set up a nonprofit?"

"Certainly. Oh, speaking of wildlife. There was a large mangy dog hanging around the cabin, last time I was there. I contacted the humane society, but the dog is crafty and last I heard they hadn't caught it, yet."

"I'll handle that. I don't want them chasing the poor dog until I get a chance to take a look at him or her. Do you have that phone number handy?"

"Yes, I'll have my secretary call them and relay your message." Brandon looked through the file, located the number, and jotted it down on a piece of paper. He handed the note to Pepper, plus Lathen Quartz's business card from the file. "You have my business card. Correct?"

"Yes, thanks. My head is spinning with all this

information. I'd like to look over the property in the daylight, get settled, and mull over all you've told me. Can we finish up later?"

"Of course. Before you leave today, you need to sign these documents, so you have access to the funds." He handed her several pieces of paper with sticky arrows indicating where her signature was required and a pen. "Meanwhile, I'll draft a proposal regarding a nonprofit, and suggestions as to the trusts and accounts. After you have familiarized yourself with the holdings, we can get together and discuss how you want to proceed. In fact, I'd be happy to meet you at the property. It's nice to get out of the office once in a while."

Pepper looked over the documents that added her name as an owner to several accounts and signed each one, then she pushed up from the chair. "I appreciate all you've done and meeting with me on short notice. I'll be in touch."

Brandon stood. "Not a problem. I'm just glad we found you. I look forwarding to working with you."

"Likewise." She stopped at the little fridge in the lobby, got a bottle of water, then waved to Brandon before exiting through the glass doors. She expected Kaylee to be screaming but was pleased to find her quietly snoozing in her crate. Pepper opened the door and stepped into the truck. "Only a little longer and we'll be home. I'll feed you and see where we can set you up for the night."

As Pepper lifted Kaylee's cage cover on one side, she whistled softly and peered out the window. "Not long now." Pepper checked the directions Brandon had given her, entered them into the navigation system, and put the truck in gear. The parking lot had several more vehicles in it than when she'd arrived. It took some doing, but she carefully threaded the truck and trailer through the lot and turned onto Main Street. She pulled to the side of the road and checked the signs for Highway 3. The route indicated the cabin was a little more than a mile southwest of Lobster Cove. The cheerful voice of the GPS reciting directions reassured her of arrival in less than twenty minutes, with traffic. Now, if she could only be sure this was the right decision, as if she had a choice.

Chapter Two
Lobster Cove, Ready or Not, Here We Come

Cruising down Highway 3, she suddenly remembered that she hadn't called her parents. Did they know Colleen had given up the life estate? Surely, if they'd known anything her mom would have called. *I'll just give 'em a call when I arrive at the cabin. After I figure out where to put Kaylee.* Deep in thought, Pepper missed her turn and got her first look at the little town of Lobster Cove.

She needed dog food anyway. Winding her way through the unfamiliar streets, she turned on First Street from Maple and there it was, the Lobster Cove Grocery Mart. *Yea.* "I'll be right back, Kaylee." Pepper sprinted through the drizzle into the store.

After a few minutes, she darted back to the truck with a thirty-pound bag of premium dog food slung over her shoulder. She dropped it on the front floor board, slammed the truck door. "All set, we'll be home in a few minutes." She put the truck in gear and took off following the signs to the highway. The bird whistled softly. "I know it's been a long day cooped up in the crate, but we're going to love the new place. I can feel it."

The road leading to the cabin was steep and heavily forested on both sides by aspen and pine trees. As if by magic, the landscape opened up into a clearing. The driveway forked off and meandered around to the front of the large log cabin, facing away from the main road with a spectacular view of the ocean. A huge pine tree stood on the left side of the cabin. A couple hundred yards down the slope and further left was a huge ramshackle barn. To the right of the cabin down the slope were two smaller buildings. She sighed. *Just the way I remember it.*

She parked her truck behind a weathered pickup, pushed open the door, and stretched her legs until her toes touched the ground. She hopped out of the truck and took a deep breath. The ocean breeze brought a mixed scent of brine, sand, sun, and kelp. Seabirds whistled and screeched through the air, diving into the white crested waves, proudly emerging with dinner. Turning her attention to the land, she noticed beyond the barn the pond was still there, even a bit bigger than she remembered. Caught up in the smells, sights, and sounds, she didn't hear someone approach.

"Ms. McKay?"

"Sssshit," she yelped and whirled around to see a muscular man, well over six feet, with surfer blond hair nearly to his shoulders, tousled by the ocean breeze. Rounding the corner of the cabin, he waved at her as he approached walking with a slight limp. Deeply tanned, he appeared to spend a lot of time outdoors.

"I'm Lathen Quartz. Glad you made it before dark. The road up here can be treacherous at night if you don't know where you're going. I finished up the enclosed aviary and was getting ready to leave. But now that you're here, I'd be happy to show you around. Help you get settled."

"Pepper McKay, call me Pepper." Extending her

hand toward him, she met his gaze. His large aquamarine eyes were mesmerizing, set above the high cheekbones, full lips, and a butterscotch five o'clock shadow. She gave her head a shake. "Wait. You built an aviary?"

He shook her hand and smiled, shoving his hands in the pockets of his jeans and rocking back on his heels. "Yes, ma'am, Ms. Denton insisted that you'd need one when you arrived. Had me start on it a few weeks back. She was specific. It had to be attached to the end of the cabin where it was sheltered from the wind. Also, she insisted on a heated floor, large sturdy perches, and an entrance directly into the house. I added a secure outside area too, figuring the birds would appreciate it in the summer. How many birds do you have?"

"Huh...one—osprey, she was injured as a chick—but how would Colleen—I never mentioned..."

"I don't know, but the aviary's footprint with the outside area is nearly as large as the cabin itself. We can go into the cabin through the aviary, so you can take a look around. See if it meets your needs. I can tweak it if necessary. But first let's take a look at the barn and the other buildings. They do need a little repair to be usable."

A bit awestruck, she followed him around the property, inspecting the huge barn and the other two smaller buildings. They were larger than she remembered. The land was a bit rocky, but not as bad as she first thought. Following the path down to the beach was less than a third of a mile she guessed. The possibility of a small marine facility was doable; from what she saw. Depending on the scale and requirements, Lathen agreed with her.

Behind the barn, he pointed across the clearing. "You have a freshwater stream running through your property to the spring-fed pond over there. It's pretty good size, maybe twelve to fourteen feet at the deepest point, two feet at the shallowest. One hundred yards across, probably. It attracts a lot of wildlife."

Squinting her eyes against the sun, Pepper asked, "Is that a bench over there?"

"Sure is. Ms. Denton used to pack a lunch, come down here, and sit for hours observing all the birds and creatures that enjoyed the pond. She never had many visitors, not sure she had talents like Ms. McKay. Just my opinion, but I think she found solace in the place after Ms. McKay passed."

"Talents?"

"Oh, you know. Legend has it the McKays…uh…well, they had a way with medicinal herbs and things." He cleared his throat. "There's a raised herb garden in the front of the house and one in the back. I noticed some green sprouts poking through the soil the other day. The other ground level gardens front and back are flowers."

Finally, they returned to the cabin. He led her around the house, through the aviary, which had a sink, refrigerator, cabinets, and counter tops on the wall shared with the cabin. A large window let the sun in over a small holding tank that was set up beside the refrigerator. The entrance from the aviary to the cabin included a screen door and a security door.

Lathen held the interior one open for her and followed behind, closing the door. When he flipped the lights on, there was a warm golden glow as the lights bounced off the wooden beams and polished oak floor. It was just as she remembered. Once inside the cabin, she felt an overwhelming feeling of belonging, almost like the house was welcoming her. She shook her head, chalked it up to wishful thinking, hunger, and exhaustion. *The last few weeks must be catching up with me. My overactive imagination is running wild.*

"Want me to start the fire? Obviously, there is central heat, but a fire lends a homey ambience." He led her into the kitchen and opened the fridge. "Mr. Fairbanks wanted me to stock the fridge and pantry. I stopped by Helen's grocery mart but couldn't resist getting meat pies and sweets from Bea's place, best you'll taste around here. Moving is hard enough without figuring out where your next meal will come from. Speaking of moving, can I help you with your things?"

"Oh, I don't want to bother you."

"It's no bother. I'm happy to help, even if I wasn't on the clock."

"Oh yeah, Brandon mentioned working out a deal with you for maintenance around here and suggested I talk to you about the barn and other buildings. The estate pays you, right?

"That's correct."

"One thing I really need is Internet access, high-speed if available, and as soon as possible." She wanted to be able to contact Gwen, send pictures, tell her about this place and her ideas for a wildlife rescue and rehab facility.

"Currently there isn't Internet here, but I'll see how long it'll take to get service arranged. High-speed, I don't know about but will look into that also."

A loud whistle reminded Pepper that someone was getting impatient. "I need to get Kaylee out of the truck and feed her. I'll take you up on your offer to help me bring things in from the truck. I only need a few things for tonight. Tomorrow will be soon enough to unpack the trailer. I could use your help."

"Not a problem. Usually, I can make it by nine or ten in the morning depending on any emergency repairs that get called in."

"Great, I'd appreciate that." Pepper opened the back door to the truck and hauled out Kaylee's crate. "Okay girl, I'll get you fed as soon as possible. Wait till you see your accommodations, you'll love 'em," she crooned to the bird.

"Wow, that's a big bird. Guess I never saw one up close. Want help with her?"

"No, she might nip since she doesn't know you. But if you could grab the cooler on the floor and bring it along, that'd be great. It has her iced fish in it."

He reached in and grabbed the cooler. "Hey, you want this—wooden thing too?"

"Yes, that's the perch I made special for her, she kinda has a bum leg."

"Oh, what happened to her?"

"Not sure. Probably tangled with an eagle when she was learning to fly, tore up her wing and foot pretty bad. Someone found her on the beach and brought her to the clinic. She was my first rescue. We had a great vet that took care of her, saved her life. Kaylee has never been out on her own, but she can fly and get around pretty well. She enjoyed being the ambassador for the public visits and school programs to bring awareness for what we did."

While Pepper got Kaylee situated, Lathen brought in the items from the truck and trailer Pepper had indicated she would need for the night.

Her stomach rumbled as she returned to the kitchen. "I'm hungry. Want to join me for dinner?"

"Sure, if it's not too much trouble."

"How about we try a couple of those meat pies you bought?" Pepper warmed up the oven, pulled the food out of the fridge, and grabbed plates, glasses, and silverware from a box marked "kitchen stuff" Lathen brought inside.

"I was hoping you'd suggest that," Lathen said as a big grin spread across his face.

They sat down in the kitchen at the oak table with matching carved chairs Colleen had left behind. Pepper forked up a big bite of the meat pie and slid it into her mouth.

"Oh, boy, this is delicious," she said after swallowing and forking up another bite.

"Told you. Best in Lobster Cove." Lathen gobbled up the pie and leaned back against his chair. "I gotta get going, got an early morning. Thanks for the meal."

Pepper got to her feet and accompanied him out to his truck. "Thanks for all your help, I really appreciate it. I'm going into town tomorrow morning and wander around. After I get a sense of what I want done around here, I'll give you a call."

"Sounds good. I'll deal with the Internet service first thing tomorrow. Otherwise, I have a full couple of days with repairs, but I'm happy to work you in when you're ready."

"I'll be in touch." She watched him climb into the truck and fanned herself just a little. *He was one yummy man.* When the engine roared to life, he switched on the high beams and disappeared down the driveway around the house. As Pepper sauntered toward the house, she heard a low growl and saw movement through the trees.

Chapter Three
Pinch Me, I've Got to Be Dreaming

She had forgotten to ask Lathen about the large stray dog Brandon mentioned. Sure the dog wasn't the only wild creature in the area, she walked backward slowly, then climbed the three steps to the back porch. Turning her palm up, she conjured a ball of light and tossed it into the air, illuminating the open area. From the tree line, two eerie eyes glowed out of the darkness, the guttural growl came again from that direction. This time it was quiet, less threatening, more of an unsure sound.

"I'm not going to bother you," Pepper said in a soothing voice, then stepped off the porch. While her pulse quickened, she didn't sense any danger, so she moved carefully to the middle of the clearing to get a better look. At the edge of the clearing, she spotted a huge furry canine stalking toward her. It fit the description Brandon had given her. She blew out a breath, stopped forward movement, and raised her arms slowly above her head.

After the dog stopped and cocked its head to the left, it raised its nose in the air, sniffed, still not taking its eyes off her. Not sure how long she stood rooted to the spot, but the dog eventually lost interest and ran off into the woods. Quickly she walked backward to the cabin, extinguished the ball of light, and opened the back door. She stepped inside, closed the door and leaned her back against it. *Wow, that dog was ginormous.*

The dry dog food she'd purchased was still on the front floor of her truck. Tomorrow, she'd get the food and fill one of the metal bowls she'd purchased and set it at the edge of the clearing, introduce him to her scent. Time to see if she could bring the dog in closer. If the dog had meant her harm, he would have attacked rather than run off. As it was, he appeared to be warning her off what he perceived to be his territory, and he was wrong. Sure she was dealing with a scared creature; she would shift her encounters accordingly.

At the kitchen table, she pulled out the financial papers Brandon had given her and studied them. The sums of money overwhelmed her. She put the papers down and wiped her sweaty palms on her jeans. Having no idea where to start, she decided to check the law firm's references the lawyer had provided. If they checked out, she'd leave the money management in his hands or the hands of those Brandon trusted. A monthly report sent to her would be required. She might be inexperienced in monetary matters in those sums, but she was no fool.

She scrounged around for a paper and pen to jot down a to-do list for tomorrow and a long-term list for the first few months. From what she'd seen of the barn, it could be renovated into several roomy enclosures for recovering birds, with an inside aviary and clinic. The larger of the other buildings could be remodeled with several comfortable kennels and connecting outside run for each. The smaller one could be her office and a lab for onsite testing. The aquatic life rehab would require more thought and planning, but she could adapt something close to the shore. According to the plot map Brandon provided, her property spread all the way to the ocean.

Next she made a list of things she needed to discuss with Lathen. The dog was at the top of the list. Glancing at her watch, she decided it wasn't too late to give Gwen a call.

Gwen picked up on the first ring. "Is everything all right?"

"Yes, everything is fine, well, really better than fine. You should see this place. As soon as I get Internet service, I'll send pictures. The cabin is perfect. There is an aviary attached for Kaylee. That's a long story. But there is a huge barn, needs some work, as do a couple of the smaller buildings, but…Gwen, if I can get the permits, I think this place would be perfect for a rehab center. Which is the reason I'm calling."

"Whoa, there girl. One thing at a time. Kaylee made the trip okay?"

"Yes, of course," Pepper said impatiently. "She's been fed and is sleeping in the indoor aviary."

"Indoor? Heated?"

"Yep."

"I'm coming up there. No, wait, can't, Jodi is on vacation this week. But when she gets back, I'm there."

"Great. Until then, tell me where to go and what I need to do to get this off the ground. I already have my attorney looking into the nonprofit status. He's cute, but married with three adorable kids."

"Just my luck. Anyway, the town council is your first stop, tell them what you want to do, show them your credentials. Get their support. I'll look up the state requirements on the Internet and call you tomorrow with the results. How long before you have Internet service?"

"Soon, I hope. Ooohh—I forgot to tell you about this rugged handyman, I met. He comes highly recommended and will be helping me with the repairs and renovations if my plan gets approved. I don't know if he is available, but I sure am going to check it out. He is so understanding, knowledgeable, and what a hunk. He's offered to help me move in."

"Oh, honey…your judgement in men…Be careful, he sounds too good to be available or more baggage than…Aw hell, reel him in if you can. What about money? You know it takes…Need to start fundraising as soon as the permits are in place."

Pepper sighed, wondering just how much she should tell Gwen, right now. *Aw to hell with it. If I can't trust her, who can I trust.* "There's more than enough money for what I have planned and the property is free and clear of debts. But I'll still do fundraising. Send me your suggestions."

"That's wonderful, you deserve this," Gwen said cheerfully.

As Pepper continued to discuss her plans with Gwen, an idea formed. On the to-do list she'd created, Pepper scribbled the wildlife refuge in Salem and beside it wrote "discuss ongoing contributions with Brandon." She was sure that her aunt and Colleen had favorite charities they supported, so now there would be one more.

"Well, I've gotta go, make final rounds, and head home. I'm bone tired…I know you will be as soon as the adrenaline wears off." Gwen chuckled.

"Yeah, I still have to bring my parents up to speed. Everything happened so fast. I didn't have a chance to call them."

"Oh girl, you are in so much trouble. They don't even know about the magic—or you were forced to—that you were moving?"

"Don't you ever finish a sentence?" Pepper laughed. "What could I tell them? I didn't know where I would go and didn't want to worry them. Now, I'll tell them the whole story."

"Better get to it. I'll talk with you tomorrow. And plan to see me week after next."

"I'll send directions. Night." Pepper disconnected the call and looked at her watch. It was kinda late, but if she didn't call, there'd be hell to pay…She hit speed dial three for her parents.

Her mom, Klaren, picked up before it rang. "Pepper, what on earth is going on with you? I've had so many mixed feelings for several days."

"Mom, it's great…now. The magic around Salem on the anniversary of…well, it was out of control. I used my gifts to protect the rehab clinic and sanctuary. There was…Oh, I don't want to talk about that."

"Slow down, Pep," her mother said.

"Something wonderful happened. You won't believe it." Pepper proceeded to fill her mom in on everything that had happened. She told her about the property and her plans for it. It seemed odd to Pepper that her mother didn't know Colleen had given up the property and even seemed a bit reserved when Pepper told her the reason for Colleen's decision. But Pepper chalked it up to being tired and her overactive imagination.

"Mom, you and Dad need to come for a visit—when I get things settled."

"Just let us know when. If you need help, call. We'll be on the first plane out there."

"Thanks, Mom. I'm exhausted, so I'll talk to you later."

"Okay, baby, take care. Talk to you soon. And be careful. Okay? Love you."

There it was again, reservation and almost worry in her mom's voice. "Sure, Mom, love you too." Pepper disconnected the call and shook her head. *You're losing it, get a grip.* She padded toward the bedroom.

Before turning the lights out, she checked on her bird. The hinges squeaked when Pepper opened the aviary door and tiptoed inside. The room was toasty warm. Kaylee opened an eye sleepily, ruffled her feathers, watched for a second, then closed her eye again. Pepper backed out and closed the damn squeaky door.

Halfway up the stairs, she remembered her suitcase was at the bottom. She huffed out a breath, went back, and lugged the case up to the loft. After her shower, she dressed in sweat pants and a thermal shirt and crawled into bed, immediately falling into a fitful sleep.

By four in the morning, Pepper gave up on sleeping. Too many things bounced around in her head vying for attention. Money was no longer a problem, and she didn't know how she felt about that. Sure, you always dream about being rich, but seemed to her, you just exchanged one set of problems for another.

While she pulled on a pair of worn jeans and wiggled into her favorite oversized purple sweater with a black t-shirt underneath, she worked out the details of a wildlife center in her head. Did she want to rescue and rehab the creatures or did she want to add a permanent placement for aquatic birds? Maybe an area for—no. After working with Gwen, she had a good network of sanctuaries that specialized in caring for animals unable to function in the wild. Working under pressure and on the spur of the moment to save creatures' lives had always been her strength. Not wanting to spread herself too thin, she decided to stick to the rescue and rehab, leave permanent care to those already prepared to handle that situation.

Feeling more settled, she ran a brush through her long light red hair, pulled it back in a ponytail, and stepped out the front door into the swirling mist. She jogged down the path to the beach and ran along the shore to the end of her property, then wound her way past the pond and to the outside aviary. When Pepper swung open the door to the inside aviary, she found Kaylee sitting on the counter next to the fish holding tank.

"Is this your way of telling me you're hungry?" Pepper chuckled, taking out a large fish, and tossing it into the air. Kaylee watched the fish fly toward the ceiling, then she hopped lazily and flapped a couple times catching the food as it dropped toward the floor. She returned to her perch, taking small bites of the fish, all the while staring at Pepper.

"I wasn't gone that long, just needed physical exercise to unwind, get ready for my day. You're not starved."

Kaylee blinked at her several times, then turned her attention to ripping the fish apart.

Pepper ambled into the cabin, leaving the inside

aviary door open. After she fixed a mug of tea, she stood at the kitchen window, holding the steaming mug with both hands, staring out at her property. A loud rumbling in her stomach reminded her it was time for breakfast. Thanks to Brandon, her fridge was stocked. She pulled out eggs, butter, and bacon. She rummaged through the box labeled kitchen stuff, found a frying pan and toaster. Searched the cabinets and found a loaf of whole wheat bread. Plugged in the toaster, popped two pieces of bread in the slots, and pushed the lever.

A short time later, she sat at the kitchen table and scarfed down a breakfast of scrambled eggs, bacon, and toast. Finishing off her second mug of tea, she ran water in the sink, added a squirt of dish soap, and dropped the mug in the water, watching it bob, then sink. What would her first day in the cabin bring?

Chapter Four
Just When You Think Things Are Under Control...
Whap! Fate Slaps You Upside the Head

Lathen pushed open the door to Maggie's Diner, waved to the girl behind the counter, and plopped into a blue vinyl booth next to the window. The blue-checked cafe curtains swayed as he scooted to the middle of the seat and relaxed against the back. So far it had been a successful morning. The intermittent leak at the Sea Crest Inn had only taken a couple hours to track down and repair. Patching the drywall after the repair was a pain, but it looked good when he finished. Matt, the maintenance super was pleased. Overflow work from the inn kept Lathen busy during the tourist season.

Kate sidled up to the cream and chrome table. "What can I get you this morning?" She leaned over, her white polo unbuttoned to show a good bit of cleavage, set a cup and saucer on the table, and poured steaming coffee to the rim of the cup. Kate, born and raised in Lobster Cove, was now just north of thirty years old, single, and still lived life on the wild side.

"I'd like the blueberry pie, with a scoop of vanilla ice cream." He took a sip of coffee, turned his attention to the pedestrian traffic out the window, and hoped Kate would be on her way. She'd been overly friendly the last few weeks, and he'd considered taking her out, but...Friday night before last had changed all that.

"Haven't seen you around for a while. Where you been keeping yourself?" She nudged his shoulder with her hip.

So much for moving on. "Ms. Denton wanted a lot of work done up at the McKay place before she left and the new owner took possession."

"Yeah, I heard there was another McKay witch moving in. Have you met her yet?"

"Ms. McKay's niece inherited the property after Ms. Denton decided to move into the cottage on her brother's property." He shrugged and took another sip of coffee. "Guess the McKay place took too much time and energy to keep up, so she thought it best to turn it over to a new generation."

"That's a nice way of putting it," Kate said as the bell on the door jangled, indicating the arrival of another customer. "I'll be back with your pie." She winked at him and sashayed off to the new customer, coffee pot in hand.

In the kitchen, standing behind the pass through, Joe smiled and waved, his eyebrows raised almost to his hairline as he looked from Lathen to Kate and back.

Lathen blew out a breath and sipped his coffee. This situation couldn't continue, he needed to talk with Kate before the whole town had him in bed with her. She was back with his pie.

"Can I get you anything else? Maybe you'd like to stop by my…"

"No, I'm good." He scooped up a bite of pie with a bit of ice cream and slid it into his mouth. She hovered over his table for several minutes as he ate the pie.

Joe hollered from the pass through. "Order up, now."

Kate's lips set in a thin line. Eyes narrowed, she whirled around to face Joe. Lathen chuckled to himself. *This is the last time I stop in here until I can set Kate straight.*

Forking up the last piece of pie, he glanced out the window and saw a tall, willowy woman with miles of wavy red hair cascading down her back. When she glanced in the window, her smile radiated in sparkling emerald green eyes as she sauntered across the street. Wiping his mouth, he pushed up from the table, tossed a five-dollar bill down, struggled into his jacket, and rushed out the door.

He called out to Pepper and caught up with her a block from the diner on Main Street. "Hey, you finding your way around town?"

"Yes. I've met a few people and introduced myself. Everyone seems quite friendly. I was going to call you later." She stopped in front of the town square and studied the gazebo. "Bet this is nice when it's all decorated at Christmas time."

"It is and for Halloween too." He paused for a beat and zipped up his coat. "You ready to move the rest of your stuff in?"

"Yep. There's not much." She waved a hand in dismissal. "Whenever you're available."

"Be there late afternoon. I have to stop by the high school. They have an electrical problem. So I'll be over right after that."

"Thanks, I appreciate it. Halloween is my favorite holiday. No pressure, just lots of fun, decorations, and celebration. Any idea who I should talk to regarding the permits or zoning for the wildlife rescue and rehab? I want to get started as soon as I can get the okay from the town council. The barn is going to need a lot of work. I want to turn it into an aviary, with holding cages for injured birds, indoor free flight, clinic area, and maybe someday an outdoor flight."

He nodded. "Got big plans for the property."

"Yep. The larger of the two buildings, I'd like to divide it into kennels, and then add outside runs on each with opaque dividers half way up the fencing. Is that possible?"

"Anything is possible. What about the smaller building?"

"I'd like to convert that into an onsite laboratory, maybe an office, storage."

"How about when I stop by later this afternoon, we sketch out what you want, I'll work out a quote, and we can go from there?"

"Sounds good."

"Hey, I'll bring dinner, that way you can spend more time checking out the town."

"I didn't realize we were discussing dinner," she said with a smirk.

"I didn't want you to go hungry if we get all involved in planning your rehab." His smile was short lived as he felt an arm snake around his waist from behind.

"Surprise," Kate said eying Pepper over his shoulder. "You didn't even say goodbye when you rushed out of the diner," she cooed.

Lathen sucked in a breath and let it out slowly. "Kate, this is Pepper McKay. She moved into the McKay property last night. Pepper, Kate, she works over at Maggie's." He wrenched her arm from around his waist and glared at her. This wasn't the time, but...*I need to...*"

"Nice to meet you, Kate. I'll have to stop at the diner in the near future. I'm kinda familiarizing myself with the town today." She glanced at her watch. Where had the time gone? "I gotta get back. If you're too busy this afternoon, Lathen, I can wait."

"Not at all, I'm free after stopping by the high school. You like pizza?"

"I do," Kate volunteered.

Pepper looked from Kate to Lathen, her forehead crinkled. "Pizza is my favorite food group." As she stood in the threesome, clouds obscured the sun, and a fine mist began to fall.

Pointedly ignoring Kate, he said, "Great, I'll pick up a large meat pizza and a couple liters of pop on my way over. We'll get you moved in and spend the rest of the evening working on the plans. Sound good?"

"Yep. See you later. It was nice meeting you, Kate," Pepper called out as she turned and sprinted down the street toward her truck.

The mist increased to a drizzle. Seething, Lathen watched Pepper until she stopped, climbed into her truck, slowly pulled out, and cruised down Main turning left on Maple. He whirled on Kate. While a little voice in his head told him not to make a scene, he ignored it. "Kate, you're a beautiful woman, but I'm not what you're looking for."

"You didn't act that way a few weeks ago," Kate said stiffly.

"I'm sorry if I gave you mixed signals, didn't mean to." In public was the last place he wanted to do this, he'd planned on letting her down easy, but she forced his hand. "I've got to get to the high school."

"You're interested in the McKay witch, aren't you?" she asked, her voice cool.

"That is none of your business. Now you better get back to the diner. Maggie is standing at the door."

"You're going to regret this," Kate retorted, turned on her heel, and flounced down the street.

He waited until she pushed past Maggie and closed the door before returning to his truck, parked in the lot behind Maggie's. Truck door open, he climbed inside and leaned back against the headrest, rubbing his eyes with thumb and forefinger. Wasn't the way he wanted it to go down, but at least he'd made his lack of interest crystal clear. *Better stay away from Maggie's for a while.*

Troubleshooting the high school electrical system took longer than estimated. He called Pepper to let her know, stopped to pick up a couple large bottles of pop, and then drove over to the Pizza Place at Lobster Lanes Bowling Alley. When he walked through the pickup door, all talking ceased, and everyone looked in his direction. Stan stood behind the counter shifting from one foot to the other.

"How's it going? I'm here to pick up a meat pizza. I called it in earlier," Lathen said brightly.

"It's not quite ready yet, only be another moment or two. I'll go check on it." Stan disappeared through the kitchen door.

A waitress breezed through and stopped at the counter, glanced at Lathen. "Heard you and Kate had a spat. Taking her pizza to make up?"

He sighed. "Where'd you hear that?"

"Around," she said, popping her gum and leaning on the counter.

"Well, let me set the record straight. Kate and I were never together, never dated, and never saw each other outside the diner."

She shrugged. "That's what I thought, but… Everyone knows she likes the guys at the Red Club. Didn't think you had kink."

He shook his head and smiled, turned to see Stan, red-faced, standing on the other side of the counter holding a pizza box. Lathen took the box, flipped the top to check it, handed Stan a twenty, and walked out into the cool damp air. This was what happened when you were a single male in a small town with a thriving BDSM club. He grinned at his reflection in the truck window. *Do I have kink? Maybe.* Whistling, he climbed into the truck, started the engine. The radio blared rock and roll. Lathen tapped his thumbs on the steering wheel to the beat and headed for Pepper's place.

****

The dish of dry dog food Pepper had set at the edge of the clearing was empty when she returned from town. She carried the bowl into the house, washed it, and refilled it. On her next trip out to the trailer, she put the bowl back in the same spot and went back into the house. It was time to feed Kaylee. Pepper stopped in the bathroom and braided her long red hair to keep it out of her face and from falling into the fish holding tank when she leaned over. It had happened more often in Salem than she wanted to admit. It took several days to get the fishy smell out.

Whistling for the osprey, Pepper padded into the aviary, pulled on the fridge door, and opened the sealed container of fish. Kaylee landed on the counter beside Pepper waiting for her to toss the fish into the air. A game that they'd played since the bird was a chick. Originally, it was meant to strengthen her wing muscles so she could fly again. But the game continued because Pepper enjoyed the interaction with Kaylee, who also appeared to benefit from it.

The day began to catch up with Pepper when she trudged out to the trailer and peeked in. *Way too much stuff.* She sighed. Unfortunately, she needed some of that stuff. Turning around, she scanned the surrounding area and lifted her arms, swinging them toward the house. Several boxes and a suitcase floated out of the trailer, through the cabin's front door, and settled on the polished wooden floor. That was all it took. Her head pounded, eyes blurred, and her hands shook from exertion and use of magic. There was always a price to pay when using magic for self-gain. She sank to the top step on the porch. T*he rest could wait for Lathen.*

After regaining strength, she unpacked the boxes, put everything away, and went to check on Kaylee, who whistled as Pepper approached the outside enclosure. Watching Kaylee circle the enclosure, negotiate through the door to the indoor aviary, and back out with barely a wobble, Pepper felt a sense of pride from the bird that no one thought would fly again. The move and change in living arrangements seemed to agree with the osprey.

Out of the corner of her eye, Pepper saw movement a few feet from the clearing on the side of the house. A huge black furry dog crouched sniffing the air. Pepper stood still. The dog crossed the edge of the clearing and scooped up a mouthful of food and darted back into the woods.

An unfamiliar copper-colored truck skidded around

the driveway and stopped in front of the cabin. Lathen stepped out, a couple of two-liter bottles of pop tucked under one arm and a pizza box held in his large hands. From the aviary, Pepper rushed to open the front door and take the bottles from him.

"I didn't recognize the truck. That isn't what you were driving yesterday."

"Nope, I use the older truck for work, don't have to worry about the upholstery or beating up the bed with materials for a job." He jerked his thumb toward the copper truck. "That's what I drive when I'm off the clock. Let's eat, I'm starved. After we're done, we'll get the rest of your stuff moved in." He put the box down next to a pan of freshly baked brownies. "Been busy, huh?"

Pepper's stomach rumbled as she carried the bottles into the kitchen and placed them on the table beside the plates, forks, and glasses set out earlier. The pizza smelled so good.

Seated at the kitchen table, Lathen scarfed down two pieces of pizza to Pepper's one.

"Have you had any interactions with the black dog hanging around here?" she asked, finishing her second and last piece.

"Not much. He seems to crave human companionship but is afraid. Not sure what happened to him." Lathen took another bite looking thoughtful. "No collar or tags, I'm pretty sure."

"So, he's a male?"

"Not sure, can't get anywhere near that close. But I don't think he or she is aggressive."

"The dog was here the other night after you left, growling, and he stalked toward me, but the minute I stood my ground, he ran off into the woods."

"That's been my experience as well. You going to try to bring him in?"

"Yes. Though his or her fur is badly matted from what I can see, it appears to be a young dog. Part chow from what I've seen, and he or she deserves a chance at a better life. I'd feel more secure with a dog in the house, especially as big as it is. Appearance alone would scare off intruders. Speaking of that, any chance you could install a security system? I know this is a small town and all, but I don't know anyone."

"Sure can. I saw an empty bowl at the edge of the clearing when I drove up. Thought that might be what you were trying to do. Be careful, it's a big dog." Lathen shoved up from the table. "Let's get your trailer unloaded, so you can take it back to the rental place tomorrow. I know they charge an arm and leg for those things."

"True, gotta take the trailer to Bar Harbor. So, I'd like to go over my plans for the wildlife rescue and rehab too. When I drop off the trailer, I'll stop by Fairbanks law firm and drop off the plans to Brandon. He'll need them for putting together the nonprofit. Guess I need a name too."

"How about Lobster Cove Wildlife Rescue and Rehabilitation Center? It gives the location and what you do all in the name." He pushed the chair in under the table and strolled toward the front door. "Unless you want to make it more personal—McKay's Wildlife Rescue and Rehabilitation? There's been a McKay on this land for as long as anyone in town can remember."

"I like the first one, simple yet functional. I'll suggest that to Brandon and see what he thinks."

"You figure out where you want things, then I'll bring them in, that way don't have to move anything twice," he said, opening the door.

"You can't handle the big things by yourself."

"That's why I brought a moving dolly and ramp." Bounding out the door and down the stairs, Lathen jerked open the trailer and peered inside. "Looks like you got a lot done last night." He looked up. "Hey, your furry friend is checking out the empty bowl. Want to try an approach, while I'm here?"

"Sure." With another bowl of kibble, she joined him at the trailer.

Quietly, with eyes down, she walked half the distance from the cabin to where the dog stood, stopped, placed the bowl on the ground, and backed away. Once she returned to the trailer, the dog took a couple steps forward, then a couple more, shifting its gaze from the bowl to Pepper. The dog finally arrived at the bowl, gobbled up the food, and ran back to the woods.

"Well, doubled the progress from yesterday and no growls. Tonight, I'll put a full bowl a few yards from the back porch." She walked out, pick up both bowls, and carried them into the house.

In no time, Lathen had the trailer emptied, and Pepper put most of the items away.

Standing in the middle of the empty living room floor, she said. "It would be nice to have a couch, rocker/recliner, and TV. My apartment was pretty sparse, as you can tell."

"There's a nice furniture warehouse, Everything for the House, in Bar Harbor. They offer free delivery to Lobster Cove." He pulled his phone out of his pocket. "I'll text you the phone number and address. What's your number?"

She gave him the number. "Any progress with Internet service and Wi-Fi?"

"Yes, I need to do the wiring early tomorrow. The provider will be out tomorrow afternoon."

Pepper chewed on her bottom lip, a habit she'd had since childhood when she was trying to work out a problem. "I wanted to take the trailer back tomorrow morning and stop by the lawyer while I'm there." She grabbed her little backpack and took the cabin key he'd returned to her from a zipper compartment, extended it toward him. "Could you let yourself in the morning? Lock up when you leave. I should be back by noon or so. I want to check out the furniture store too."

"Sure. But the Internet provider has a service window from noon to four. I'd stay, but I have an appointment at ten to repair a couple of wooden steps at the inn. Safety hazard. I had to set out caution signs before I came over tonight. Otherwise, I'd move the appointment."

"No problem. I'll make sure to be back by noon. Appreciate all your help. What about TV cable service?"

"It's all in one, TV's satellite dish. I'll call tomorrow and tell them to bring that equipment too. You didn't have a TV before?"

"No, it quit working, and I never had time to replace it. That's why I'm doing it now. It seems a good time to add a few luxuries. Once, hopefully, I get the wildlife center going…"

Laughing, Lathen said, "Most people don't consider TV and cable service luxuries." He stifled another round of laughter and narrowed his eyes. "You plan to run it by yourself?" He frowned. His brows knitted together.

"What, the TV or wildlife center?" she joked. *He.* "At first—later I'll look for help when needed."

"I don't know much about wildlife rehab, but when a woman here in town started a pet rescue, she nearly did herself in trying to do it all. Don't want to see that happen to you."

"Don't worry, I'll be fine."

"I'll make you a deal. If things start getting dicey for you, call me." He rubbed his chin with his thumb and a few fingers. "I believe I'd enjoy helping you out around here. Fair enough?"

"But you're so busy with your business. I couldn't impose. I don't think your lady friend would appreciate it, either."

He grimaced. "I'll adjust my schedule. If there one thing I've learned through my military career, it's live life to the fullest, there are no guarantees. And I want to help. As far as Kate is concerned, we are only acquaintances. She apparently wanted more, but I'm not interested, not my type. That matter was settled after you left. I'm sorry you wound up in the middle of that."

"Don't be, it wasn't your fault. Wrong place, wrong time, story of my life. Regarding the wildlife center, it's a deal," she said, pleased to be seeing more of him. She'd vowed no more men after…that piece of shit in Salem. But Lathen seemed different. She could feel it, even if she didn't want to.

Pepper pulled out the wildlife center drawings she'd been working on and spread them on the table.

"The barn would make a good rehab facility for birds. With kennels installed in the larger of the other two buildings and outside runs like we talked about, it'll work for other wildlife. The smaller building, we could remodel into a decent laboratory, office, maybe some storage. Is there electrical or heat in any of the buildings?"

Lathen shook his head. "I don't think so."

"Okay, we need both," she said firmly.

"That's doable." He leaned over her shoulder listening to her plans and making suggestions of what might work and how to build the marine habitat by the ocean front. His warm breath on her neck made it hard to concentrate and gave her butterflies in the pit of her stomach.

He pointed to a lightly penciled in room on the left side of the cabin. "What's that?"

"I'm thinking about adding an exercise room onto the cabin. Had a gym membership in Salem to relieve the stress. But that isn't feasible here."

"There's plenty of land, might have to alter the driveway a bit. But that's no big deal."

She twirled the pencil between her fingers while looking at the plans. "Better get the rescue worked out first, then see about any personal things."

"It would be best to order all the building materials together, get a discount, you know. If we get stalled on one of the other buildings, I can always have a crew start on your room. We'll keep the plans independent and charge time separately. I just hate to see you get all the rescue construction finished and cleaned up, just to start in on this project."

"When you put it like that, it makes sense to do it

all at one time. I'll sketch out what I have in mind and see what you think."

"Sounds like a plan." Lathen stretched one arm above his head and arched his back stifling a yawn.

Pepper glanced at the clock. "Wow, where the heck did time go?"

"I've gotta get going, early morning tomorrow. See you about seven. I had a good time this evening."

She walked him to the door, stepped out on the porch, and hugged him. "Thanks for everything."

"You're very much welcome." He sauntered to the truck, climbed in, rolled down the window, and waved before he drove off.

She went back inside, scooped kibble into a clean bowl, and set it outside a few yards from the back porch. There was no sign of the dog after she sat on the steps for a few minutes. Yawning, she walked inside, checked on Kaylee, showered, and fell into bed.

It seemed like her head had just hit the pillow when the alarm went off. She remembered pushing the snooze button only once. But the next time it went off, the LED numerals on the clock read 6:45 a.m. *Oh God, Lathen will be here in fifteen minutes.* A much later start than she had intended this morning.

Chapter Five
A Stranger by Any Other Name
Still Spells Trouble

Pepper flipped the radio on and sang to the songs as she drove down Highway 3. By day's end, she'd have Internet service and maybe tomorrow decent furniture to sit on. The rental place should be on the right-hand side. She scanned the road and spied the rental sign. Making a right hand turn into the lot, she stopped, unhooked the trailer, and walked inside. The office was dusty, but the man at the counter was friendly, and had her on her way quickly.

One item ticked off her to-do list. Next, the furniture store. She checked the map Lathen had given her and drove right to it. After forty-five minutes of wandering around the store, she found a reclining couch and glider/recliner love seat in a rich brown. No need for a single recliner with that pair, so she went to the electronics area.

A sixty-inch curved screen was on sale for a very reasonable price, and a decent brand. That would deplete her rainy day fund. She looked at other televisions but kept coming back to that one. She shook her head. Thanks to her Aunt Ashling, money wasn't a problem. Still, she'd pinched pennies all her life. Spending money frivolously wasn't how she did things. But just this once, she was going to splurge and get that sixty-inch curved screen TV including the surround sound system. Debit card in hand, she approached the counter and paid for the TV and furniture. Made arrangements for delivery and was thrilled to discover the items could be delivered tomorrow afternoon.

Giddy with excitement, she ticked off one more item on her list and headed to Fairbanks Law Firm, and it was only ten o'clock. The law firm's parking lot was full, and she'd forgotten to call Brandon for an appointment. That was all right. She'd simply drop off the drawings and see if she could set an appointment for him to come out to the property. That way he could see what she wanted first hand. Pam, the receptionist, smiled when Pepper walked through the door.

"Nice to see you again, Ms. McKay. Is Mr. Fairbanks expecting you?"

"No, I forgot to call him. But can I leave these drawings and set an appointment for him to come out to my property?" She laid the rolled up plans and file with information on the counter.

"Let me bring up his calendar." She tapped couple buttons on the keyboard, and his calendar began to scroll on the screen. Brandon walked up behind the receptionist and smiled.

"Morning, Ms. McKay. How are you this fine morning?"

"Great. I wanted to drop these off." She pointed to her drawings and documents on the counter. "And make an out-of-office appointment for you to stop by my property. It gives you a chance to review the drawings, then we can discuss what I have in mind for the nonprofit."

"Excellent idea. Will next Monday late afternoon

be soon enough? I've got a full schedule this week."

"Perfect." She shook his hand, said goodbye to Pam, and started toward the door.

A large well-dressed man approached her. "Did I hear you say, McKay?"

"I'm Ms. McKay," she said cautiously glancing back to the reception desk.

"You don't happen to know Colleen Denton, do you?"

Pepper narrowed her eyes. "And you are?" She didn't like the vibes she was getting from him. The hair on the back of her neck was standing on end.

"Oh, sorry. My name is Tom Green. I own the market down the street. Ms. Denton and I had mutual interests, and we'd enjoyed a couple outings together. However, I understand she's left town. Could you put me in touch with her?"

"Mr. Green. Mr. Fairbanks Sr., will see you now," Pam said.

He scowled at the receptionist and said, "Just a minute."

Pepper took several steps toward the door while Mr. Green was distracted, then said, "I'm late for an appointment, so I'll tell Colleen to get in touch." She disappeared, and the door swished shut behind her, Relief flooded through her as she climbed into the truck, locked the doors, and checked her watch. *Plenty of time to make it home by noon and call Colleen.*

****

The black dog jumped off the back porch and bolted into the trees when Pepper turned the truck up the driveway. She smiled to herself, pleased with the dog's progress. Inside the house, she walked into the room that would be her office, put the receipts in a filing cabinet, pulled out the estate records she'd filed last night, and dialed Colleen's cell number. Waiting for the phone to ring, she found a piece of paper and pen stashed in the front of the cabinet.

She picked up on the second ring. "Pepper, I hoped to hear from you. Is everything all right at the cabin?"

"Better than all right. It's fantastic. I'm sorry, I didn't keep in touch with you over the years as I should have. Seems my life was split in a dozen different directions most of the time."

"Honey, there's very little that goes on with the McKay's that old cabin doesn't know. You need to tap in. It's a wealth of information and protection."

"That's how you knew to build an aviary? I was so tired when we arrived; it was so nice to have a place for Kaylee. She settled right in."

"Of course she did, knew it was for her. Pepper, I hope you don't mind my saying, but you've spent most of your life hiding what you are rather than embracing your magic. It's time to change. The cabin and property can help you, as Kaylee can. She is your familiar. The townspeople will assume that you are a McKay witch. Don't hide, live it. There's been a McKay in Lobster Cove for centuries."

"You must be mistaken, Kaylee arrived at the clinic nearly dead. The vet saved her life."

"No. The spirits knew what you needed and provided it in the form of an osprey chick at death's door. Ashling set you on life's path, but her time was short to mentor you. Gwen took over, not a witch but a talented healer. Under her tutelage, you honed abilities as a healer, and your confidence grew. It was the final test in Salem when I knew you were ready for the cabin. You did well."

Her arm went up in the air in frustration. "Sure I did. Lost everything, nearly caused Gwen to lose the sanctuary. Just great," she said sarcastically.

"Wrong again. You saved the sanctuary with your magic, no small feat. Gwen couldn't do that. Without you, she'd have lost the sanctuary and the lives of the creatures there. It was time for you to move on to Lobster Cove, start your own wildlife rescue and rehab, be proud of your heritage. Ashling is very proud of you."

"Is…Ashling is? How do you know, she's…" Pepper chewed on her bottom lip.

"Her spirit never left the property. She felt it necessary to watch over me and now you."

"But how?" Pepper rolled the pen from finger to finger and back again.

"You'll see. Open your mind, accept magic as part of you. Now, there was a reason you called?"

"Uh…mmm. Do you know Tom Green, owns a market in Bar Harbor?"

"Thought so. Yes, he is a difficult man. I believe dark magic follows him, but he doesn't know it. He's also drawn to McKay magic. Stay clear of him."

"He indicated the two of you were friendly. It was a lie, but…he wanted to get in touch with you. I felt the dark magic signature, but it doesn't belong to him."

"Oh, I bet he does. Spurned his advances for the last couple of years. Not my type." She gave a half laugh. "What he wanted was Ashling's magic that surrounded me after she passed. He couldn't figure it out, knew I wasn't a McKay witch, but…still drawn to the magic."

"He's not going to leave me alone, is he?"

"Probably not. Brandon Fairbanks started coming out to the property to work out details, because I refused to come to the office anymore, due to Mr. Green. Unfortunately, Tom was a client of Fairbanks Sr., Brandon's dad, for years before Ashling discovered Brandon. She trusted him completely. He was the only one that could handle her affairs."

Pepper heard a vehicle, then footsteps on the porch and a knock on the door. "Colleen, I have to go. The people are here to hook up the Internet and SAT TV. Talk to you soon."

"Of course. If you need anything, call. Bye, dear. Be careful."

"Bye." Pepper disconnected the call as the hairs on the back of her neck stood. She flung open the door and there stood Mr. Green. "What are you doing here?"

"Stopped by to finish our conversation."

"It was finished. Colleen isn't able to stay in touch," Pepper said firmly.

His brow furrowed and eyes narrowed, he asked, "Is she ill?"

"No, busy. Now if you'll excuse me…" She tried to close the door, but he shoved his foot in the way.

"Ms. McKay, I just want to be neighborly. Maybe we can get together for a cup of coffee or a bite to eat sometime."

She shook her head. "I'm sorry, too much to do." She stared down at his foot. "Please remove your foot," she said in a firm tone, narrowing her eyes as she brought her gaze up to meet his.

A wave of dark magic blindsided her. The searing

pain in her head and nausea made it difficult to stay on her feet. Beneath it all, she could feel his frustration and anger that had something to do with the McKay magic. Knuckles white from gripping the door, she heard the beat of wings, and Kaylee's shrill whistle echoed through the room as the bird swooped in, talons forward, claws extended. Pepper let the door sag open. On Kaylee's first pass, her claws ripped open Mr. Green's face, just below his eyes and across his nose, tearing a gash in his upper lip. He screamed and stumbled backward.

She circled the room tried to dive straight for his neck, swerving just as Pepper slammed the door and pressed her back against it. The pain in her head subsided as she slumped to the floor, blinking rapidly. Receding footfalls and the subsequent roar of an engine told Pepper Mr. Green was gone. Next to her, Kaylee landed softly, tilting her head from side to side, never taking her eyes off Pepper.

Pepper reached out and touched the bird's wing. "Nice flying. I'm fine. Give me a minute."

Gravel crunched in the driveway as another vehicle stopped in front of the cabin. A door slammed, and heavy footsteps pounded up the porch steps. Getting to her feet, her heart thundered inside her chest as she crept to the window and peered out. A van with SAT TV and INTERNET emblazoned in dark blue across the side panel parked in the driveway, and she blew out a breath.

Pepper combed her fingers through her hair and hoped she looked presentable. This time she opened her mind's third eye and saw a stocky man standing on the porch with the van's matching logo on his shirt, studying a clipboard held in his hands. She cracked the door and asked for ID. The soft beat of wings and Kaylee's whistle told Pepper the bird had returned to the aviary.

The man handed her his ID and offered his hand. "Welcome to Lobster Cove, Ms. McKay. I'm Doug Henderson. Talked to Lathen about your needs. I believe they are all listed on the work order. If there is anything else, let me know." He looked around the room. "TV?"

Stationed near the door, she pointed where the TV and sound system would be situated as she looked over his paperwork and the additional connections requested by Lathen for the security system and monitors. It took Doug three hours to install the required wiring and connections and test the Wi-Fi and Internet service. Pepper signed off on the paperwork and stood in the doorway as Doug climbed in his van and left her driveway. Once the vehicle was out of sight, she closed the door.

The laptop was still on and connected to the Internet from Doug's tests. She did a search on Thomas Green of Bar Harbor. It appeared he had done well in the family's grocery business, inherited quite a bit of money from an uncle, and had no connections whatsoever to the magic community. He'd won a local golf tourney with Benjamin Bonchard, of Lobster Cove, for four years in a row. Mr. Green and his wife had grown up in the area and were quite active in social circles until his wife's death two years ago. In the background information she assembled, there was no explanation for his behavior. Baffled, she wondered if dark magic had followed her from Salem. *Highly unlikely*. Had everything from the past month caught up with her and caused a meltdown?

****

Pepper's cell phone chirped. She checked the ID and touched the screen. "Hi, Lathen."

"Did Doug get there and set up the Internet and TV?"

"Yes, Doug was here about three hours. Then checked to make sure the Internet and wi-fi were working. He showed me how to hook up the TV that should be delivered tomorrow along with my new furniture." She sighed.

"Everything all right? Your voice came across a bit shaky."

"It's been a day, but I'm fine."

"Tell you what. I'm almost done here. I'll pick up a couple meals to go and be there within the hour."

"That sounds good. See you then."

She plopped down on a folding chair brought from Salem and opened a cardboard box marked "special things." She pulled out a huge fan lovingly created out of colorful molted wing and tail feathers from birds she'd rescued, rehabbed, and released, or which became a permanent resident of Gwen's sanctuary. The fan was warm in her hand, gave her a sense of security as she spread it out and hung it on the living room wall. The fan covered almost a three-foot-square area of the wall and centered over her new couch. It would be nice to have a comfortable place to relax.

A couple raps on the door, and Lathen pushed it open holding a big bag and a bottle of wine. "You should keep this door locked. You don't know who might come wandering in." His warm, soothing laugh filled the room.

"I locked it after Doug left. I'm positive."

The skin around Lathen's eyes crinkled when he laughed. "Okay, then the door unlocked itself to let me in. Your knight without shining armor and minus the white horse." Nodding his head toward the wine, he said, "You sounded like a good bottle of wine was in order."

Pepper followed him to the kitchen and watched as he put a bag and a Styrofoam container on the table and the wine on the counter. She got out plates, glass tumblers, and wine glasses.

He took out bread bowls from the bag, put them on the plates, cut the tops off, and poured soup into the bowls. "Give up already on the dog outside? Noticed the food bowl is empty, and he was slinking around the back of the house when I drove in. Didn't even run for the hills."

"Oh God, I forgot. Poor thing." She grabbed two clean bowls, filled one with kibble, the other with fresh water, and sprinted out the back door. When she returned dirty bowls in hand, she dumped them into the sink with a couple squirts of dish soap and ran hot water. "I put the kibble and water on the back porch. Maybe he's willing to come closer tonight."

"Could be," Lathen said easily, sliding the remaining food from the containers to the plates. "Must have been one hell of a day, for you to forget about your furry friend." Lathen's eyes softened as he peered at her.

"It was." She spooned up clam chowder from her bread bowl and nibbled at the top cut from the bowl. In between bites the events of her day tumbled out.

Surprised, she had to blink back tears at one point. That confirmed she was running on empty. Nothing a good night's sleep wouldn't fix. In the telling, she left out the dark magic and just let Lathen assume Kaylee flew out because Green refused to leave.

He ate and listened without comment though his eyebrow winged up a couple of times. When she finished explaining, her eyes met his, and he shook his head. "Why did you open the door without first checking to see who was on the other side?"

"I assumed it was the Internet installer." Her cheeks warmed.

"Both of you could have been seriously hurt."

Pepper tried to ignore his scrutinizing stare as Colleen's words floated through her mind. Don't hide, live it. She wanted to but wasn't quite ready to allow him that kind of trust. With trust came the power to hurt her, and she didn't want to go through that again. Feeling pressure on her shoulder, she turned, but no one was there.

"There's something you're not telling me." He reached across the table and covered her delicate hand with his work-roughened one.

She liked the sense of security, well-being, and warmth he radiated, not to mention the tingly feeling she got at his touch. "Kate was right. I am a McKay witch."

He blinked once and stared at her. "Yeah, so tell me something I don't know." The corner of his mouth kicked up in an irresistible boyish grin.

"It's Green. There's something dark about him. I can't put my finger on it. He doesn't wield magic, but he seems to be a conduit for dark magic, or I am.

Sounds crazy, huh?"

"No, not at all. But I'm no expert. Have you talked to Colleen?"

"Yes, the minute I got home. She said he's evil and attracted to the McKay magic. He's the reason Brandon Fairbanks started making house calls out here. If she went to see Brandon, Green would always appear at the law firm. Since he is a client there, there wasn't a lot she could do until Brandon offered to come to her."

"Smart man."

"According to Colleen, Aunt Ashling trusted Brandon without reservation."

"Let's revisit you and the property. I'd like to install a security system inside and around the perimeter of your property. Your third eye as a witch should keep you safe, but as a backup and reminder, the system would warn you when someone approaches from any direction. It makes good business sense for the wildlife rehab center as well. Insurance will probably require it. Not everyone working with you will have magical abilities."

"But you do, I can feel it. As long as we are baring souls here. Want to explain your ability?"

Lathen cleared his throat as a chuckle rumbled from his chest. "I'm a wolf shifter, or was. After a mission with my SEAL team went way south, there were only three survivors. My physical injuries negated my ability to shift, even after they healed. Still retain the preternatural senses, though."

"I see. Uhhh…are you sure it's not emotional and psychological as well? Those types of injuries take much longer to heal than physical, at least in my experience with the rehab of creatures."

The smile faded from his lips. "I don't need to be psychoanalyzed, been through plenty of that."

"Bet you didn't tell them of your abilities. That would make a difference."

"Yeah, they'd put me in a padded room and throw away the key. Now drop it."

She raised her hands, palms up in surrender, leaving the touchy subject alone...for now. "Can we make the security system as invisible as possible?"

"Can do." He gave her two thumbs up. "Oh, by the way. I talked to a couple of the town council members today. There's a meeting a week from Friday. I put you on the schedule. All the necessary paperwork to bring the matter before the council is in my truck." He pushed up from the table. "I'll go get it. Those I talked to seemed quite taken with the idea of a wildlife rescue and rehab on your property."

"That's great news. Brandon is looking over the drawings and working on the nonprofit paperwork and state and federal permits. We meet here Monday between four and five. Can you join us?"

"I'll be here. Let's take the wine and sit in front of the fireplace. Can't be any harder than these chairs." He picked up the wine glasses and the bottle and carried them into the living room.

Pepper disappeared down the hall. She returned with four huge floor pillows in red, bright green, turquoise, orange. "I kept these from Salem, used them when I was up all night with a sick creature. Nice snuggleability. Always washed them after each use and packed them in bags with dried lavender so they'd be ready next time."

Lathen arranged the pillows on the floor and

reached for Pepper's hand. When he pulled, she lost her footing and fell into his lap.

"Well, isn't this convenient," he said as a deep rich laugh floated from his throat and his mesmerizing aquamarine eyes gazed at her.

She squirmed, but he gently held her in place, his arms wrapping around her like velvet chains. A wonderfully warm, cozy feeling enveloped her, cradled in his arms. This intimate awareness seemed foreign to her, but before she could analyze it further, he lowered his head and brushed his lips over hers in an almost questioning manner. The touch of his lips was a delicious sensation. When she deepened the kiss, his tongue traced the soft fullness of her lips and slipped inside touching, caressing, and tasting her flavor. He captured her sigh and gentled the kiss. When his head lifted, she ran the tip of her tongue around her lips still warm and moist from his kiss. She felt as if he'd transported her to another plane of existence and relaxed into him.

The butterflies in her stomach were back accompanied by a titillating desire that swirled through her. *Acting on it was not an option—right now. Too soon.*

As his cheek rested against her forehead, the only sound in the room was the crackle and occasional pop of the fire racing around the pine logs. She glanced over at their glasses. The red wine sparkled in the firelight with unusual bubbles rising to the surface. A giggle escaped her lips, and she said, "Maybe you set the glasses too close to the fire. I believe they are simmering."

Reluctantly releasing his hold, she slid out of his

lap, and he lazily reached for the glasses grasping them by the stem. "Wooo, these are warm, bordering on hot." He moved the glasses to the side away from the fire. "Guess we better get a couple new glasses. Glad I moved the bottle over there." He grinned. "That's never happened before. You distracted me."

"You're actually blaming me?" she teased. "You pulled me into your lap. How's that my fault?"

"You fell into my lap, after getting tangled in the pillows." He got to his feet. "You stay put. I'll get new glasses."

She watched him walk into the kitchen, glance at the cupboards, and pick the one with the door ajar. Lined on the second shelf sat the wine glasses. He took two and returned to the living room and settled on the pillows, next to her.

Glasses refilled, Lathen touched the rim of his glass to hers making a tinkling sound. "To your new endeavor and to—us." He took a sip as she stared at him.

"Us?"

"Yes, us. I've never known a woman like you. I want to see where this leads. Don't you?"

"My luck with men…There's so much to do…I don't think it's wise to become involved."

"Don't overthink it. Let's see where this goes."

She paused for a couple of beats. "What if it doesn't work out…Assuming the wildlife center comes to fruition, working together would be awkward if we could do it at all. I'd lose the best handyman in Lobster Cove. Then what would I do?"

He swirled the wine in his glass and took another sip. "What if it does? You can't rule out that possibility.

Tell you what. I believe in this project, so I'll guarantee I won't abandon the center regardless of the outcome of our relationship. Does that put your mind at ease?"

"You've never broken your word?"

Lathen looked her straight in the eye, never wavering. "No, ma'am. I'm a man of my word," he said seriously.

She sighed. "Okay—we'll see how it goes. I'm not good at doing that—but I'll try." Pepper picked up her wine and took a couple of sips.

"Good." He glanced at his watch. "I can't figure out how time goes so damn fast out here. Tomorrow is going to be a nightmare. My day starts at 5:00 a.m. Got a problem at the old McClintock place. Promised to be there before first light. What's the rest of your week look like?" Lathen finished the wine and set the glass on the floor.

"My furniture is supposed to be delivered tomorrow. Said they'd call in the morning with a window of arrival time. So I guess I'll finish unpacking and familiarize myself with the property. Friday is supposed to be a nice day, thought I'd bike into town and spend the day exploring. Last time I tried, it rained."

"Mind if I check in with you around noon on Friday? Maybe we could catch a bite at Mariner's Fish Fry."

"I'd like that."

She walked him to the door. He leaned down and brushed a kiss over her lips, lingering a moment, then sauntered down the path to his truck, whistling. He started the engine and waved to her before guiding his vehicle out the driveway.

Stepping out the door, she followed the wraparound porch to the back of the house. In the middle of the clearing stood the black dog staring at her. The bowl of kibble she'd put on the bottom porch step was empty. Taking her time, she picked up the bowl, took it in the house, exchanged it for a clean one filled with kibble, and returned to the back porch. The dog ventured closer and now was only a few yards from the porch.

Pepper chewed on her bottom lip while deciding whether to put the bowl on the step and go inside, or stay on the porch but give the dog some space. Finally, she left the bowl on the bottom step and backed away, settling in a chair at the far corner of the porch. The big furball took two steps forward and stopped, watched her intently, then took a few more steps. She remained still. Eventually, the dog came to the step, ate the food, and sat down eying her for several minutes before loping toward the trees. *We are making progress.*

"Goodnight, Ember. See you in the morning," she said quietly. The dog turned at the edge of the trees and looked at her before disappearing. *Wow.* She hugged herself and spun around on one foot. The thrill of earning an animal's trust—there was nothing like it in the world, especially when it needed her care. Rather than feeling only fear and hunger from the dog, now there was curiosity. She raced into the cabin, found her phone, and scrolled to Gwen's number

Chapter Six
Furniture, New People, an Attorney, Oh My

No one knew the excitement of a breakthrough like another rehabber. So when it took several rings before Pepper heard Gwen's sleepy voice, it didn't dampen her spirits.

At the sound of her voice, Pepper's words tumbled out. "Just had a break through with that feral black dog outside the cabin. I talked to him, and he looked at me. Even came within ten feet of me to get food out of a bowl, all while I sat there."

"Whoa, whoa, Pepper?"

"Of course."

"Okay…slow down, let me get woke up." She yawned into the phone. "Now, what about the dog?"

"Remember when you called with the Internet sites for state and federal permits?"

"Oh, yeah…that fuzzy black dog."

"Yep, that's the one. He has a blue tongue." Pepper filled her in on the progress to date. A little about Lathen and the town. "Hey, any chance you can be here by next Friday? We appear before the town council, to see if I can get their blessing. Lathen got the paperwork and put me on the schedule."

"Sounds like Lathen has a thing for you." Gwen laughed. "Jodi should be back by then. I'll do my best."

"Thanks. I'll let you get back to bed. Sorry, I didn't

realize how late it was."

"Sure. Spending time with the hunk, huh? 'Til well after midnight?"

Pepper couldn't keep the smile out of her voice. "Guilty as charged."

"Oh, that's it. I'm going back to sleep. See you soon."

"Bye." Pepper ended the call and checked on Kaylee in the cabin's attached aviary. She yawned wide, then stopped to stretch her legs before trudging up the stairs to her bedroom. Not used to climbing stairs, her legs had cramped up the last couple nights after crawling into the bed.

The warm water felt so good as it ran in rivulets down her body rinsing away the soap and grime of the day. As she let the water cascade down her back, she thought of Lathen, his arms wrapped around her, and the way-too-short make-out session this evening. He caused tingles in all the right places. Was she falling for him? Stepping out of the shower, she shook her head, flinging water all over. *It was too soon to even consider that. Still...* She made sure the windows were locked before falling into bed. *Would Kaylee enjoy getting out and seeing the property tomorrow?*

****

The rain pattered against the window as Pepper wiped the sleep from her eyes. The phone vibrated across her night stand. She picked it up and checked the caller ID, the furniture store.

"Hello."

"Calling to let you know our truck will be there within thirty minutes. You're first on the schedule."

"Okay. Thanks." Shock set in after she glanced at

the clock. *Good God, it was quarter past ten.* She jumped out of bed, yanked on jeans and a sweatshirt, ran a brush through her hair, then raced down the stairs to the aviary and tossed Kaylee her morning fish. Kaylee eyed Pepper irritably and let the first fish fall to the ground.

"Come on, Kaylee, don't be difficult. I've a surprise for you later today." Kaylee spread her wings and took flight, just as Pepper tossed a fish into the air. The bird swooped, caught it midair, and returned to the perch, fish in one talon while ripping it apart with her beak.

"I'll be right back," Pepper said sprinting back to the living room.

The pillows were scattered all over the floor from last night. She poured a bowl of cereal and shoveled a spoonful into her mouth, then picked up the pillows and returned them to their bags, stuffing them in the coat closet. In between mouthfuls of cereal, she vacuumed the room. As she put the vacuum away, the furniture truck pulled up in front of the cabin. *Timing is everything.* Pepper smiled and opened the door.

By the time the furniture was arranged and the TV set up and tested, the sky was blue, and the sun shone brightly. She donned a heavy sweater over her sweatshirt and padded into the aviary. With a stroke of her hand, the leather gauntlet covered her arm and hand. Kaylee ruffled her feathers, stretched her wings, and with several flaps of her wings lapped the enclosure three times before landing on Pepper's arm.

"You ready to check out this place?" she asked strolling out the door. Kaylee lifted off and circled the area as Pepper walked the property. When Pepper disappeared inside the barn, the osprey whistled loudly and carefully negotiated the double barn door, following her inside. After documenting the size, condition, and location of all the buildings on the property, Pepper walked to the pond and settled on the bench. A few minutes later, Kaylee landed on the back of the bench, a fresh fish in her talons.

"Been to the beach, I see. You eat that on the ground. I don't want fish guts on my bench." Behind her, the breeze in the trees sounded like someone laughing quietly. She turned, but there was no one there.

The bird cocked her head and glided to the edge of the pond where she devoured her meal. A light touch on Pepper's shoulder told her there was indeed someone there. She sat up straight, turned slightly, and out of the corner of her eye, she saw Ashling leaning against the nearest tree, the same smug smile on her face as the last time Pepper saw her. As she started to get up and open her mouth to speak, Ashling put a finger to her lips and disappeared.

"There you are." Lathen walked up behind her, eased an arm around her shoulder, and leaned in brushing a kiss over her lips as tender and light as the spring breeze. "Had a break between jobs. Thought I'd come over and see if everything went as planned this morning."

She shivered at the tenderness of his kiss. "Yes, the furniture was delivered and looks great. They even connected the TV to the satellite dish and made sure it worked before leaving."

Lathen nodded. "I see Kaylee is enjoying her outing."

"She is. I decided to bring her outside and start working on her stamina. In Salem, the big birds had to take turns flying in the outdoor enclosure. Free flight outside the enclosure wasn't safe. Here, I think she will gain a lot of strength. And being my familiar, she never strays far from my side. But…" Pepper eyed the back of her bench and Kaylee munching on her catch. "It would be nice for Kaylee to have a sturdy tree branch perch next to the water's edge to enjoy her meals here with me.

"I can do that—familiar?" He sat on the bench beside her, dropping a carrier with a sack and two drinks between them.

Pepper sniffed and peeked in the bag. "Something smells really good."

He handed her a cup of hot chocolate and unwrapped two pieces of vanilla cake with raspberry filling on small plates. "Sweet tooth acting up." Shrugging, he passed her a fork.

She took a sip of the steaming chocolaty liquid and continued. "According to Colleen, a familiar serves a witch, providing protection, as the witch comes into her powers, or in my case, learn to use powers I've kept hidden for years. Our relationship is unusual as I was her protector first, then as she reached adulthood I hid my talents, and she lived at the center. When I resigned and got ready to leave town, she raised hell at the center, until Gwen called and requested I take Kaylee with me. Almost as if she knew what was happening. So here we are."

"Nice arrangement. That explains why she attacked Green the other night." After finishing off his cake and drink, Lathen stood. "I gotta get back to work. It'll be a late night. I have a job at the police station after the regular employees go home. Gotta route power to new computer stations. Are we still on for lunch tomorrow?"

"Sure. Give me a call when you're ready. I plan to spend the day exploring Lobster Cove's shops. Get a feeling for the place before the town council meeting next Friday."

"It's in the bag. But state and federal might be a different story."

"We'll know soon enough; Brandon will be by on Monday. If there were a snag, he'd call, and I haven't heard from him, so no news is good news. Right?"

"Yep. See ya tomorrow." He started toward the driveway.

"Hey, don't you want to see the new stuff?"

"Of course. Looking forward to trying it out. Just not today…Well, maybe a quick peek."

Pepper pushed up from the bench and called to Kaylee. When she caught up to Lathen, he reached for her hand, intertwined their fingers and swung their arms back and forth as they climbed the path to the house. The osprey soared overhead landing on the cabin roof above the door.

As they reached the corner of the cabin, Pepper caught sight of the black dog sneaking around the back of the house. This time the tail was curled over its back, rather than hanging down. *Time for a closer approach.*

After Lathen tried out the double reclining sofa and the glider rocker sofa, he picked up the remote and clicked on the TV. Letting out a low whistle, he flipped through a few channels. "Wow, that's a nice picture."

When he leaned up, the recliner returned to a sitting position, then he opened the chest coffee table and sifted through all the movies Pepper had acquired.

"That is quite a collection of movies for a woman with no TV until today." Closing up the table and getting to his feet, he wrapped an arm around Pepper pulling her close, his lips feather light as they touched hers with tantalizing persuasion. "If I don't leave now...I may not go at all," he murmured against her lips.

Standing on tiptoe, she returned his kiss, shivers of desire zinged through her. When he lifted his head, she whispered, "Is that a bad thing?"

"From my point of view, absolutely not, but I don't think my customers would be pleased. Being it's the police department, I better get going. Wouldn't want to be responsible for a crime spree because their new computer system wasn't up and running." He snorted, then burst out laughing. "As if."

She walked him out to his truck, touched her lips to his once more, and watched him climb into the truck and drive out of sight. Walking up the path, she knelt beside the raised flower garden examining the plants next to the name stakes. Several of her favorites had buds, purple, white, and yellow violets, and red trillium. Tiger lilies lined the outside edge front and back. On the side orange ditch lilies were just coming up beside the lupine.

A grouping of her Aunt Ashling's favorite, lily of the valley, spread next to the house in front of the porch. Pepper leaned over and caressed the tender leaves. She wrinkled her nose and glanced around catching the scent of lily of the valley on the breeze, a cologne her aunt always wore. Out of the corner of her eye, she saw the black dog crouching on the side of the house. He was between the row of lupines that by midsummer would be tall spires of pink, white, and purple flowers and the meadow behind the house. Climbing the steps of the porch, she settled in a chair a couple of feet from the bowl filled with kibble. A fresh bowl of water sat next to the kibble. She watched as the dog crept closer, one paw on the first stair, nose in the air catching her scent.

Chapter Seven
If You Live In Lobster Cove,
the World May Be Your Oyster,
but Your Life Is an Open Shell

Negotiating the rough road from her cabin into town on a bicycle was not as easy as Pepper assumed it would be. Loose gravel, tree branches, and boulders—okay, large rocks—strewn across the road, from God only know where, during the downpour last night made it difficult to stay upright on two wheels. And the potholes filled with water could swallow her and the bike whole, not to mention drench her in mud.

Still she pressed on. The sun felt warm on her back and the fresh air made it all worthwhile, not to mention the calories she had to be burning. Once on the main road, she made it to town in no time. At the gazebo in the town square, she chained her bike to a street lamp and strolled down Main Street, stopping to look in the shop windows, and hurrying by Maggie's Diner. She wanted to avoid a chance encounter with Kate. At Julie's Coffee and Sweet Shop, she stopped and grabbed a snack, then visited with Julie before heading to the bank. In Salem, she had a long banking relationship with State Bank, but her nonprofit would require a working relationship with Morgan Bank, which held several of the estate accounts.

Newly planted flowers lined the flower beds in

front of the bank. Pepper yanked open the glass door and stepped inside. The blue and tan decor gave it a homey feel. A teller at the third window smiled at her, so Pepper walked up and introduced herself.

"We heard Colleen was leaving and a relative of Ashling McKay would be moving in. Nice to meet you. I'm Tammy, what can I help you with?" She flashed a bright smile from behind the counter.

Pepper returned the smile. "I need to transfer my accounts from State Bank in Salem, Massachusetts, to here. Can you do that, or do I need to initiate the transfer from Salem?" Pepper rifled through her backpack and came up with a piece of paper. "Before leaving, I requested the bank fill out a transfer form, but since I didn't know the name of the financial institution I would be contacting, they didn't complete the form. Mr. Fairbanks is my attorney, and he added me to the estate accounts here."

Tammy thought for a moment. "A McKay from Salem, that's interesting."

"Not as interesting as you'd think."

Red patches bloomed on Tammy's cheeks. "Oh, I didn't mean to imply…We did receive the change of ownership papers from Mr. Fairbanks. And of course, we can handle the transfer. Do you have the account numbers and identification?"

"I do." Pepper handed Tammy a driver's license and the account transfer form.

The woman reviewed the documents. "Oh, this will be easy. I'll give your bank a call and get the ball rolling." Tammy walked to the back counter, conferred with another woman, then made a phone call. The other woman glanced in Pepper's direction and returned to the first teller window.

Tammy came back to the counter. "All set. The bank will wire the money tomorrow morning. Your funds will be available by tomorrow afternoon."

"Great. Thanks." Pepper turned to leave.

"Are you going to turn the McKay property into a wildlife refuge?"

Pepper's eyebrows shot up to almost her hairline. She whirled around and stared at Tammy. "Where'd you hear that?"

"It's on the council's agenda next Friday," she said wincing. "The whole town is talking about it. Most like the idea, but some…don't like change."

"The main focus is a wildlife rescue and rehab. But there are always a few animals, due to their injuries, that can't be released back into the wild. For them, I have a network of sanctuaries to contact for permanent placement. Under special conditions, I will have accommodations for those who have special needs and can't be handled elsewhere. So they'll live out their lives with me at the center, but that's a small percentage."

"Well, I think it's a wonderful idea. Good luck."

"Thanks." She shook her head. *Boy, news does travel fast around here.* As she pulled out her cell phone, it chimed in her hand.

"Hi, Lathen."

"Hi, yourself. Ready for lunch? I can pick you and the bike up at town square in ten minutes. That way you don't have to bike across town to Mariner's."

"How'd you know where my bike is?"

Lathen chucked over the phone. "You can't do anything in this town, without someone noticing.

Especially, if you're new."

"So I've noticed. The teller at Morgan's asked me about the wildlife center. I guess if it's on the agenda, the whole town knows."

"Yep. That's about it. But it's a good little town."

"Meet you at the town square." She shoved the phone in her pocket, waved to Tammy, and pushed out the door. Sprinting across Pine Avenue and up Main Street, Pepper nearly collided with Kate on the corner of Maple, next to Maggie's. Kate sent her a scathing look as Pepper hot-footed it across the street. At the gazebo, she turned to see that Kate was still standing on the corner, sucked in a breath, and unlocked the bike lock, in time to see Lathen's truck stop on Main. Pepper hopped on the bike and coasted to the truck. Lathen tossed the bike in the bed and helped Pepper into the truck, then ambled to his side of the truck, climbed in, and headed to Mariner's.

"Is Kate going to be a problem?"

"No, she won't," he said firmly.

Upon their arrival, Lathen waved to Roark, one of the owners of Mariner's, and pointed to the back deck with the picnic tables. "Okay if we just head out there? Like the view."

"Sure. Might be a bit breezy," Roark said picking up two menus and following Lathen. "Rain's supposed to move in later this evening."

"Those clouds been hanging on the horizon all morning. It's actually warming up nicely…for now." Lathen grinned and inclined his head toward Pepper. "Roark, I'd like you to meet Pepper. She inherited the McKay place from Ashling. Pepper, Roark Sullivan owns this place with his wife, Dawn. Their daughter

Malinda works here too."

"Roark, it's a pleasure," Pepper said extending her hand.

He clasped her hand and said, "Nice to meet you too, Pepper. You're the marine biologist turned wildlife rehab specialist. Right?"

"Yes, but…"

Roark waved his hand. "Oh, Ashling used to talk about you quite a bit, before she passed, then Colleen kept us up to date on your adventures. They were very proud of your accomplishments." He started to hand the menus to Lathen. "Malinda will be by to take your orders when you decide."

Lathen held up his hand and waved the menus aside. "We don't need menus." He glanced at Pepper and winked. "Tell Malinda, we'll have two lobster dinners, iced teas, and a couple slices of your famous blueberry pie with ice cream for dessert. Mind if we wander over to the lighthouse for a few?"

"Not at all. But don't be long."

After they checked out the lighthouse and the ocean view from the second story deck, Pepper picked out a picnic table in the center of the Mariner's outside area next to the railing. The sun reflected off the waves as the light breeze carried with it a heavy scent of brine. Pepper watched the harbor seals frolic in the water, then crawl out of the ocean to sun themselves on boulders. Closer to the deck, seagulls squawked at each other and shoved one another off the tall, jagged rocks protruding from the sea.

A waitress stopped by the table with two tall glasses of iced tea with slices of lemons on the rim. "Lunch will out in a few minutes."

"Thanks," he said emptying a couple of sugar packets into the tea, squeezed the lemon over the glass, stirred, and tasted the refreshing liquid. "Mmmm…that's good."

Pepper picked up her glass and took a sip. "After you left yesterday afternoon, Ember wandered onto the porch and ate. I was sitting not more than two feet from the bowl the whole time. She's making good progress."

"You've named her. Sure it's a female?"

"Pretty much. She's going to fit right in, I can tell."

Lathen raised a brow. "If you say so." He slid the half-full iced tea glass to the center of the table as he saw Malinda heading in their direction with a tray full of food.

On the table, she slipped the plates with steaming lobster, small dishes of melted butter, and a basket of rolls in front of Pepper and Lathen. "I'll be back to refill your glasses. Need anything else?"

"Nope, we're good," he said forking up a piece of lobster, dipped in the butter, and popped it in his mouth. "Mmmmm, hits the spot."

Pepper slid a bite dripping with butter into her mouth. "Oh yeah, this is heaven. I worked up an appetite wandering around town. I'll need to bike back home to work off the calories."

"Calorie-free today only," he teased.

Malinda brought two large pieces of pie and ice cream to the table. "Figured since your meal was calorie free, I'd upsize the pieces of pie." She grinned and picked up the empty dinner plates.

Peppers eyes rounded as she stared at the dessert. "I can't eat all this."

"That's okay, I'll take what's left home with me."

He reached for her plate.

"Like hell you will." She slapped his hand. "I'll have the pie put in a small box and stuff it in my backpack."

"Spoilsport."

After they had finished eating, Lathen stood and extended a hand to help Pepper to her feet. "I gotta get back to work, but tomorrow, I've planned a surprise for you. If you're free. Pick you up in the morning around eight o'clock?"

She nodded slowly. "Sure, but I'm not really fond of surprises."

"Oh, you'll love this one. Trust me."

"Will we be gone long? I need to plan for Kaylee's food. I'm not comfortable leaving her out all day, yet."

"Yep, we'll be gone all day. Is that a problem?"

"No, just need to prepare for it. Make sure Ember's bowl is full before we leave. Things like that."

Lathen took the bike out of the back of his truck. "You sure you don't want me to drive you home? That hill is a lot easier coasting down than peddling up."

"No, I'll be fine. After that lunch, I need the exercise."

His gaze meandered over every inch of her body. "You look fine to me. In fact, more than fine, downright delectable," he said nibbling at the base of her throat.

"Stop that. You'll have the whole town talking about us." She pushed him away but not before planting a smacking kiss on his lips.

"Oh, don't worry about that. They already are."

She slapped at him before mounting her bike. "See you tomorrow morning."

"Yep."

In the lowest gear of her mountain bike pumping hard up the steep incline to her cabin, her legs ached, sweat dripped off her chin, as she gulped in air. *Hell, I'm not even sure I'm going to make it all the way. Why didn't I listen to Lathen?* After a few more minutes, Pepper jumped off the bike and stumbled over to a boulder beside the road, nearly toppling over. That was it. She plopped down to rest. She wiped her face and neck with the bottom of her shirt and waited for her breathing to return to normal, then pushed the bike up the road. The cabin was a welcome sight as she trudged up the driveway.

Once inside, she opened the door to the aviary, then padded back to the living room and collapsed on the sofa. With a whistle and the beat of wings, Kaylee entered the room, landed on her perch next to the couch, and tilted her head at Pepper, as if to say, what's the matter with you?

Pepper relayed her day's adventures to the bird. After she had finished, Kaylee whistled and flew back to the aviary. Within a few minutes, Kaylee returned, this time her whistle shrill and impatient. "Okay, okay, I get it. You're hungry." Pepper hobbled to the aviary, pulled out fresh fish from the fridge, and tossed a large one in the air. Kaylee swooped, caught it, and landed on a branch to pick at the fish.

"Soon, you'll be able to hunt for yourself. Won't that be fun?" Pepper sat on the chair inside the aviary to watch Kaylee tear at the fish and gobble the meat. Thinking back years ago when she had to hand feed the young osprey to keep it alive.

Exhausted, Pepper returned to the living room,

stretched out on the couch, and flipped on the TV, tuning into a detective program she liked.

****

Outside a dog's menacing growls, followed by a man's cursing and screaming, then a squeal and thud had Pepper on her feet running for the door. As she skidded to a stop with her hand on the door handle, she remembered what happened the last time she opened the door without looking first. She flipped on the security lights and pulled the edge of the curtain aside. The barking, snarling dog had someone pinned to the ground with its front paws, teeth bared, its muzzle only inches from the man's face. She swiped a log from the woodpile and stepped out onto the porch. Right away, she recognized Mr. Green as he squirmed from under the dog who had a deep gash above its right eye. A thick iron rod lay on the ground a few feet above Mr. Green's head.

"What the hell are you doing here, and what have you done to my dog?" Pepper shouted flinging the log to the ground and yanking her cell phone out of her pocket. She tapped in 9-1-1, the operator answered on the first ring. "This is Pepper McKay." That was all she had time to say, so she left the line open. When she circled her arm above her head, the wind picked up. As she spread her fingers wide, the rain came down in sheets, lightning streaked through the night sky, and thunder shook the ground. The dog glanced up at Pepper, blood clouding its eye, barked once, and barreled into the woods. Mr. Green started to get up off the ground, and Pepper shoved her foot on top his chest. "Don't move. Or I'll…"

"You'll what?" Mr. Green rolled to the side and

grabbed Pepper's leg. Slick due to the rain, he couldn't hold on and Pepper kicked his side and jumped out of reach.

She sliced her arm through the air. Unseen forces slammed Mr. Green to the ground. His eyes glowed an eerie green. Pain erupted in Pepper's head. He was drawing on her magic. Suddenly, a rainbow shower of knife-sharp feathers zoomed out of the cabin door, across the air, and sliced through the man's clothes, pinning him to the ground. Red and blue flashing lights reflected against the cabin's wet exterior. The sirens' wail echoed all around her, and Kaylee's scream broke through the chaos, then everything went black.

Chapter Eight
Seeing Is Believing—But Not Always

Lathen slammed on the brakes as he turned into the driveway behind the police vehicle. A rainbow of slivers rose from the ground and streaked into the cabin. He rubbed his eyes, shook his head, and jumped to the ground searching for Pepper. The 9-1-1 call came in at the police station as he'd finished the wiring and was testing the computers. When he arrived, she was lying on the ground, and Kaylee circled above her screeching. As he knelt over her, she bolted upright.

"She's hurt, Ember's hurt. She tried to protect me. We gotta find her." Pepper struggled to her feet, pushing Lathen aside. He grabbed her arm, and she wobbled righting herself against his massive chest.

"You're not going anywhere," he said firmly.

She twisted out of his arms. "Yes, I am, and you're going to help me. Don't you understand, she tried to protect me. Green swung at her with that metal pry bar, connecting above her eye. She was bleeding profusely and may have a head injury. She'll die without our help," Pepper wailed. Still woozy, she staggered forward, then fell against Lathen's shoulder, looking toward the trees.

Officer Harris frowned and shot Lathen a look. "Everything all right over here?"

Lathen nodded. "Yes, we're good. Apparently, Mr.

Green hurt her dog."

Nate Harris hauled Mr. Green to his feet and propped him against the huge tree in the front yard. "What is going on here?"

Mr. Green mumbled something about being attacked by a huge black monster and a flying demon from hell. Once the paramedics cleaned him up and determined his injuries were not life-threatening, he refused treatment, and Office Harris placed him in the back of the squad car.

Lathen took hold of Pepper's shoulders. "Okay. Okay. Calm down. Do you know where she ran off too?" Leaning toward her, he whispered, "You know she won't let anyone near her."

"She will. Things changed the instant she tried to protect me and he hit her with the bar. I felt it, heard her whimper, yet she still kept him pinned to the ground. Ember only ran away when the police got here, Kaylee showed up, and the feathers—oh, never mind."

Lathen blew out a breath and slid an arm around her waist. "Oh, there's going to be a lot of explaining about those feathers. They look like the ones hanging on your wall. I hope I'm the only one that saw them returning to the cabin. What the hell, Pepper?"

Officer Harris strode back to where they stood interrupting the conversation. "Can I get a statement, Ms. McKay?"

She hurriedly relayed what happened, leaving out a few hard to explain details as a paramedic joined them.

"I need to get you checked out."

Frustrated, she blew out a breath. "I'm fine. But my dog is going to die if I don't get her some help." She glanced pleadingly at Lathen and shifted her eyes to the paramedic. "Please, I'm fine. A little wobbly on my feet." She acknowledged, not telling them out the pounding headache. "Let me find my dog, then you can check me out."

"No, ma'am, it doesn't work like that." He flicked a tiny flashlight across her eyes, checked her vitals. "Your pulse is racing."

"No shit. Just had an altercation with a mad man. And my dog…"

"I understand. You seem to be all right, but if you…"

"I won't. Now pplleassse." She begged.

"Okay, sign this release indicating you declined medical treatment, and you're free to go." The paramedic shook his head.

She took a deep breath, signed the damned release, handed it back to the paramedic, and turned her attention to Lathen. "I'm not sure what's going on myself. But right now"—Pepper tugged him toward the edge of the forest—"we gotta find Ember. She's this way."

They stumbled across the clearing lit by the crescent moon and flashlight beams sweeping in front of the cabin. Lathen's preternatural vision located Ember lying in the tall grass, a few yards inside the forested area.

Pepper knelt down beside her. "Can you walk?"

The dog struggled to its feet only to collapse on the ground with a howl. Its pleading eyes turned on Pepper, then Lathen, as its head slumped to the ground.

She looked across the field to where the emergency vehicles were still parked. "I'll stay here with Ember. There is a sling harness with leashes attached at either side and a canvas body carrier in a cardboard box in the spare room at the end of the hall. The box is labeled rehab and emergency supplies. It's on top of several containers stacked in the corner. Would you get it?"

"Sure." Lathen hurried across the clearing and into the cabin, emerging a short time later with the box. "Couldn't tell what you wanted, so I brought it all."

"Thanks. She's drifting in and out of consciousness, so we'll use the carry sling." Pepper unfolded a large piece of canvas with cloth handles, rolled the dog onto the material.

Lathen grabbed both sides of the sling and hefted Ember from the ground. "Pepper, you hold on to my waist, and we'll all make it back to the cabin safely."

By the time they reached the cabin, only Chief Johnson remained. "I've called the vet. Dylan Foster was on call. She should be here soon."

"Call her back, don't want to bother her. I can handle it," Pepper said, her hand tingling as she caressed the dog, soothing it into a relaxed state.

"No. After what you've been through tonight, you can't," Lathen growled. He'd seen the toll magic took on a practitioner and knew Pepper wasn't up to it.

The chief glanced from Lathen to Pepper, cell phone still to his ear. "Already done. She's on her way. Lathen, you got things here?"

"Yes. Thanks."

"In the morning, I'll need you both at the station for additional statements to help clear up this mess. Mr. Green will spend the night in jail."

"We'll be there."

By the time Pepper spread a blanket over the coffee table and Lathen eased the dog on it, Dr. Foster strode through the open door. After a thorough exam, she determined that it was a glancing blow that split the skin above the Ember's eye. It took fourteen stitches to close the wound.

"Since you've worked for a rehab clinic before, you know that head wounds bleed profusely. Your dog's lost quite a bit of blood, but with a few days' rest and confinement, she should be fine. If you can ice the area to keep the swelling down, all the better." Dr. Foster closed her medical bag and handed Pepper a prescription bottle. "Antibiotics, one twice a day for a week. Don't want infection to complicate her recovery."

"Thank you, Dr. Foster, Pepper said.

"Oh, call me Dylan." Picking up her bag, she glanced at Pepper. "Welcome to Lobster Cove, Miss McKay."

"How'd you know...and it's Pepper."

"This is a small town. Word travels fast. If you need a vet for your planned facilities, count me in."

"I appreciate that. I'll be in touch," Pepper said stifling a yawn.

"I'd like to see Ember in a week."

"I'll bring her in."

"Lathen, when you get a chance, stop by the clinic. There're a couple projects that need your attention." A tired smile curved her lips when she stepped through the door. "Good night."

"Thanks again," Pepper called before closing the door. She turned to check on the dog. Ember's eyes blinked open with a wild-eyed look, and a low growl rumbled from her throat.

Lathen moved closer to Pepper. "I have the entire

day off tomorrow, but I'm not sure you are going to feeling like taking part in my surprise. I can reschedule it. For next weekend if you want."

She comforted the dog, and Ember went back to sleep. "Next Saturday would be best. I need to stay here and keep an eye on her, finish up the proposal and drawing for Brandon. Meeting is on Monday." Pepper's eyes drooped, and she stifled another yawn.

"I know, have it on my calendar. We also need to prepare for the city council meeting next Friday."

Pepper plopped on the couch and rested her head on the back. Lathen settled next to her. "You need to get some sleep. I can spend the night on the new couch and take the first shift on Ember."

"I don't want to bother you. But I could use your help getting a crate unpacked and moving her in. When she wakes up in a strange place, she could injure herself trying to escape. Can't sedate her, due to a possible head injury."

Lathen raised an eyebrow and looked skeptical.

"I know the vet said she didn't think there was serious head trauma, but she also didn't prescribe a sedative. Best to err on the side of caution."

"I wasn't questioning you. Just thought with your ability to sooth her, sedatives aren't necessary. That's all. Where's the crate?"

"In the spare room. I'll get it."

"No, your color is just starting to return to normal. Stay here, I think I saw it when I brought out the medical supply box."

"Should be leaning against the wall, next to where the box was."

"Brought most your rehab supplies, did you?" he

asked grinning.

She bristled and snarked. "Never know when you'll need 'em. So yes of course I brought…"

He grimaced and swallowed hard, biting back a retort. "Wasn't being critical, only observant." He pushed up from the sofa and padded toward the room. "I'll get the crate."

When the crate was set up and the patient transferred, Lathen paused, then headed for the door. "Do you want any help with the meeting prep this weekend?"

"Huh, oh…yeah, I could use the help. Hey listen, I'm sorry about biting your head off. Didn't mean to, just tired."

"I know. My offer still stands. I'll sleep on the couch. You are no good to anyone exhausted."

"Okay, I'll sleep for a couple of hours, but if she wakes up and becomes agitated. Wake me."

"Will do. When you wake, I'll go home, get a shower, change, and bring breakfast. Then we can get started on the paperwork and updated drawings."

She mumbled something he couldn't make out as she trudged down the hallway, stopped at the door to the spare bedroom, and turned. "Thanks."

"You're welcome." After a few minutes, he went in to check on her. Pepper curled up in the center of a king-size bed, her breathing was even and shallow. He took the blanket folded at the bottom of the bed and tucked it around her.

Back in the living room, he toed off his shoes, stretched out on the sofa, and fell into a fitful sleep. His dreams were interwoven between his last covert mission and something dark and evil chasing Pepper.

Yanked out of sleep before dawn by the unthinkable, he sat up, sweat pouring off him, checked on Ember, and walked to the kitchen to put on coffee. All his preternatural senses screamed danger, but he couldn't figure out why. Pepper stirred in the other room.

He slipped his shoes on. The hinges creaked as he opened the door. Ember shifted but didn't wake. Outside on the porch, he stretched his back and legs out. The back and hip injury he'd sustained in the blast during his last op continued to give him problems. Straightening, he shifted his weight to the good leg and started down the steps. Eventually, he was able to maintain a slow jog following the trail to the beach, around the barn, and stopped at the bench near the pond and stood still. Once warmed up his muscles were much more cooperative.

The moon cast silvery shadows across the landscape. His rapid breathing and the waves crashing on the shore were the only sounds. Perched on his good leg, he rested his other foot on the bench, leaned his arm on his knee, and looked around. Strange silence enveloped the area, no insects, no birds, nothing. It was as if the whole world waited for the sun's orange glow to spread across the eastern horizon. A slight pressure on his shoulder raised the hair on the back of his neck. Whipping around, he glimpsed the figure of a woman materializing behind the bench.

"You're up early," she said in a whispery voice.

"Couldn't sleep." He rubbed his eyes and stared. "Aren't you Ashling McKay? Deceased?" There were pictures of her in the cabin when he'd met with Colleen over the aviary. "Can't find the light?"

The women floated across the uneven ground

leaving phosphorescence smudges on the earth. She settled back against the tree a few feet from the bench, foot propped against the trunk and arms crossed. "Think you're amusing?"

As he looked at Ashling, the tree branches bent forming a protective canopy above and around her. The water on the pond, earlier smooth as glass, now had white capped waves over the water.

"Nope, just wondering what the hell is going on around here." He sat on the edge of the bench and twisted to face her. "Are the legends true, now that a McKay witch has returned to the property?"

"Something like that. But there's a challenge to the McKay magic. A malevolent spirit is looking to feed off the McKay magic, make it his own. Mr. Green is a conduit for this spirit. Whether he's acting of his own volition, I can't be sure."

"So why are you telling me all this?"

"Because you care for my niece. Difficult times are ahead."

"Shouldn't you have this conversation with Pepper? My magical abilities are...well...damaged."

"Not as bad you think. That's a discussion for another time. Pepper's been through a lot before coming here, and it's made her stronger. But what lies ahead...she'll have trouble going it alone. If you're not up to the task, you need to leave—now. Maybe Gwen..."

"Up to what task? I've been damn supportive so far." Lack of sleep and his quick temper were not a good mix. Knowing this, he turned and walked toward the cabin. "You need to talk to Pepper."

With a wave of her arm, the wind howled through

the trees and spun a water spout across the pond. "I fully intend to…Sit down and listen to me." Raising her other arm, her magic propelled him toward the bench and unceremoniously dropped him on the seat.

Immediately, he pushed to his feet and stood defiantly, though pain stabbed through his leg into his back. "This is not the way to gain my allegiance. For Pepper's sake, I'll stick around—for now. But you leave me the hell alone. Got that?"

Her image wavered back and forth, then shot straight up into the tree and disappeared, leaving a trail of mist in her wake.

Pepper was moving around the bedroom when he returned. Rather than stay to discuss recent events with Pepper in his thunderous mood, he left her note, explaining he'd gone home to shower and change and would return later. As he climbed into his truck, he glanced backward and saw her peeking out the bedroom window.

Chapter Nine
Too Much Activity and Stress…
Drives the Magic Haywire and You See Ghosts

Pepper heard his truck start up and wondered why he was leaving without a word. It wasn't like him. But there were chores to do, so she walked into the aviary, tossed a fish to Kaylee, who promptly caught it and landed on her favorite perch.

Ember's whimpers and barks brought Pepper running into the living room. The dog was clearly unhappy with the current situation.

"Okay. I'll take you outside, but on a leash only, and after you've done your business, we're coming back in. Give me any static, and it's back in the kennel for you. Understand?"

The dog cocked her head, ears flat against her head, and gave Pepper a long hard stare.

"Suit yourself." Pepper walked to the door and opened it, stepping out onto the porch. She took a deep breath of the fresh morning air and turned to the dog. "Well?"

Resigned to her fate, Ember stood, stretched, and let her tail curl over her back.

"That's what I thought." Pepper strode back to the crate, opened the door, and hooked a leash to the harness she'd put on Ember the night before.

After a brisk walk around the property, Pepper

settled into a chair in the kitchen and spread the plans across the table. She looked down at the dog resting at her feet. "A brushing and bath is in your immediate future, girl." Ember slanted one ear and cocked her head to look up, then settled her head on her paws, closed her eyes.

Tires crunching on the gravel of the driveway brought Pepper to her feet. She padded over to the window and peered out. Clouds obscured the sun as Lathen thrust the truck door open.

At the knock on the door, Pepper said, "Come on in."

Lathen pushed through the door. "Pepper, don't leave the door unlocked, especially after what happened…"

"I didn't. It was locked until I heard your truck." She flicked her wrist. "I unlocked it for you, and now—it's secure again."

He crossed the hardwood floor to where she sat, leaned down, cupped her chin in his hand, and kissed her lips lingering for a moment, then straightened. "What ya working on?"

She looked up at him and ran the tip of her tongue around her lips. "Revising the barn drawing and incorporating your sketches for the marine rehab building down at the beach. Do you have access to the materials necessary to make it happen?"

Leaning over, he put his hands on her shoulders and examined the drawings. "Yep, it may take me a while to get everything here. But once you give me the go ahead, I'll get it coming."

****

Monday afternoon, Pepper was working in her

flower gardens when Brandon Fairbanks' vehicle made its way up the driveway. Getting to her feet, she brushed the dirt from her knees and was surprised to find him dressed in jeans and a polo shirt.

"Nice to see you again. Thanks for coming."

"It's the highlight of my week. "He grinned and extended his hand. "I worked from home this morning, so casual attire was the theme of the day. Hope you don't mind."

"Not at all. I wanted to show you the changes that have already been made and what is in the plans."

"Great. And I have good news. With your work history, education, recommendations, and certifications it was a slam dunk getting the state and federal licenses approved. As far as the nonprofit status of 501(C)3, the IRS had no problem approving Lobster Cove Wildlife Rescue & Rehabilitation. Dylan Foster's vet sponsorship info you provided and her willingness to consult for injured wildlife was a great help."

"That's wonderful news." She reached her hand out to shake his, and instead swung her arms around him in a bear hug. "Thank you so much," she said, sure the smile on her face would be there forever.

Brandon grinned, a bit taken aback at her exuberance, and it showed. He cleared his throat and continued. "Now, I wasn't sure whether you wanted a Migratory Bird Permit, but I went ahead and completed the process with the US Fish and Wildlife service. I figured you wouldn't turn any injured creature away. So best to have the proper paperwork."

"You're exactly right." She beamed.

"That permit should be approved and sent directly to you soon." He handed her a manila folder with the other licenses and permits obtained. "Keep this in a safe place. Make copies of your licenses and permits and display them in a prominent place. Which brings me to the subject of an office."

"I thought I'd use part of my home."

"I wouldn't advise it. Keep your private residence and life completely separate. There seems to be room for a small office in the corner of one of the other buildings or even the barn without encroaching on the aviary."

She looked at her watch. Lathen was supposed be here by now. "Mr. Quartz was going to meet you here to go over the new plans. But…"

Footsteps on the porch followed by a loud knock on the door, and Lathen walked in the door. "Sorry I'm late. A job ran longer than expected." He reached out to shake Brandon's hand. "Good to see you again."

"Likewise." Brandon clasped Lathen's hand. "Pepper, we need to talk about my services and that of Mr. Quartz. Do you want to continue my services on retainer?"

She motioned to the kitchen table and took a seat. The men did the same. "At this point, I think that would be best. At least until I get the wildlife center up and running. Then we can visit this subject again. I also want you to remain the attorney for my business dealings."

"I'm willing to do that. As for Mr. Quartz…"

"I'd like him to be an employee of the nonprofit?"

"Excellent idea. We need to open bank accounts for the wildlife center. I've set an appointment for you next week with the financial adviser, so we can get the estate settled. He can advise you on any changes in investments or tax shelters."

"I don't want to change any of the charities Aunt Ashling supported, and include the Salem wildlife refuge. After reviewing the rest of her portfolio, I'll leave things as they are." Pepper checked off that item from her to-do list.

"If you are looking for federal funding, I can do some research on that as well. Once you get the Migratory Permit, federal funds could be an option, especially if you are part of a catastrophic rescue effort."

"True, that can be pricey." Pepper pulled her bottom lip through her teeth as she considered.

"It's always a good idea to have several financial avenues available."

"Agreed. Let me know what you find out."

Lathen spread out the revised plans on the table and glanced at Brandon. "Do you want to walk the property, then look at the plans, or vice versa? The mist is rolling in. Might be a damp walk."

"That's all right. I could use a bit of fresh air. Best do it first before it thickens into fog." He glanced out the window and looked over at Pepper. "Are you ready for the town meeting?"

"I think so. Still putting the finishing touches on the presentation." She opened the door and watched the mist crawl along the ground, then reached for her jacket hanging on the hook next to the coat closet. "I'd like to go over it with you and Lathen when we return."

****

Early Tuesday morning, after a rough night, Pepper stepped out of the aviary into the bright sunshine, allowing Kaylee to fly overhead. Following the rocky path with Ember at her heels, she arrived at the beach, while the osprey banked and swooped across the water. Pepper breathed in the briny air, closed her eyes, and her mind's third eye opened. Suddenly, she was soaring through Kaylee's eyes over the white-capped waves that sprayed over the rocks and came crashing onto the shore. A shadow danced in the water. Her wings folded back and talons forward, she dove. Her timing a little late, the fish slipped through her claws. She emerged from the water with wings spread and gained altitude riding the air currents until she spotted another meal and streaked toward the water, claws extending. This time her talons tightened around the wriggling scaled body, and she surfaced with a large fish. The osprey's exhilaration and pride flowed between bird and witch.

With the beat of wings overhead, Pepper blew out a breath and opened her eyes. *Whew! What a rush.* She whistled for Kaylee to follow and climbed up the rocky path to the pond. The bird called loudly, then circled, landing gracefully on a large branch, still clutching her prey. Kaylee ripped pieces of flesh with her beak and gobbled them down.

Pepper settled on the bench, the hairs on the back of her neck prickled. At the water's edge, Ember's ears perked up. She barked once and trotted back to Pepper's side. She heard whispers and turned to see Ashling's wispy form leaning against the huge pine tree. "Ashling, is that you?"

The form solidified. "Of course it is, girl. Who were you expecting? Lathen?" Her familiar throaty laugh floated through the air. Pepper leaned back and crossed one leg over the other.

"No, he'll be here tomorrow," she said flippantly.

"I'm so glad to see you. Colleen alluded to the fact you were still on the property. There are so many things I want to—"

Ashling waved her hand impatiently interrupting. "Had to watch over Colleen, but it became too dangerous. I didn't realize…oh never mind…it's my fault." She kicked at the dirt with her foot, her wispy form having no effect, and changed the subject. "That's one fine man you got there. But he's damaged goods. Unless you can bring him around, he's of no use to you."

"Excuse me." Pepper paused to rein in her rising temper. Ashling had always been outspoken, but…meddling in her personal affairs was off limits. "What business is it of yours? He's a war hero and a great person. He treats me—let's just say we get along." This was not the conversation she'd hoped to have with her dead aunt. There was so much she wanted to know. "He can design and build anything which makes him invaluable in planning the wildlife center I'm creating on the property. If you're interested?" she added as a jab.

"Be that as it may, he's still damaged, unwilling to come to terms and move on. As I told him, it's all in his mind. Physically he's able to phase, but mentally—" Ashling shrugged and rolled her eyes. "Survivor's guilt holds him back. He can't help you in that condition. As a shifter, he'd be a great asset."

"An asset? What the hell are you talking about? Wait, you communicated with him? When?"

"The night Tom Green was skulking about and got more than he bargained for from your feral dog. The man and his demons pose a serious problem."

"Oh, I don't think he'll be back," she said breezily. "Lathen and I stopped by the police department and gave statements. A restraining order was issued against him, in addition to the charges filed. Legal ramifications of his behavior will keep him busy for a while."

"You couldn't be more wrong. The spirit controlling him is after the McKay magic and will stop at nothing to get it." The aura around Ashling shimmered bright red, then faded in on her. "A mere restraining order means nothing to magical creatures."

"I'm glad to see death hasn't reduced your penchant for the dramatic," Pepper deadpanned, hoping that was all it was. Battling with malevolent spirits in her new home wasn't something she wanted to deal with. "By the way what is your fault?"

"This is serious business, child."

Her heart sank as she nodded in understanding. "What are we dealing with? What did you do?"

A wan smile strained the ghost's features. "I'm not completely sure. But it has something do with my death and leaving the property without a McKay witch in residence to protect the magic. I had no idea that the stories told by the old ones were true." She shook her head. "I should have paid more attention."

Pepper's forehead creased in confusion. "I thought the McKay magic protected the witch, not the other way around?"

"It may be a type of symbiotic relationship. But you need to research the family history. Find out who has a vendetta against the McKay's."

"Where do I start?" Pepper asked getting to her feet. The ocean breeze fanned long strands of hair around her face.

After a few moments of silence, Ashling snapped her fingers. "When your father and I were very young, I remember an old relative bragging at family get-togethers about how his grandfather married a powerful witch. Then he stole her magic and cast her aside for—I don't remember the rest. Seems to me they had a child—but I can't be sure. Check with your father. See what he remembers. That could be a good place to start." She moved closer and touched Pepper's shoulder. "I'm sorry. I never meant for this to happen. I was just trying to provide for Colleen."

Feeling a cold patch on her shoulder, she looked into Ashling's face. "I know. Would they have lived in Lobster Cove?" Panic gripped Pepper's throat as the ramifications of the situation hit her full force. "For God sakes," she squeaked. "I go before the town council on Friday to ask for approval on the wildlife center application."

"Then I suggest you get moving." Ashling's body shimmered around the edges, faded to mist disappearing into the tree.

"Wait, Aunt Ashling, I need more..." Pepper huffed out a breath and plopped down on the bench. *How do I wind up in these frigging situations?* After several minutes, she pushed to her feet and motioned for the dog to follow. "Time to give you a good brushing and a bath." She whistled for Kaylee and sauntered up the path toward the cabin.

Chapter Ten
Reining in Magic—Easier Said than Done

Wednesday morning Lathen stopped by Pepper's after his morning appointments. He pushed the unlocked door open. Pepper sat barefoot at the kitchen table in black sweatpants and a worn faded tie-dyed t-shirt.

"Wow—what happened? You look like…" He paused and sucked in a breath.

As he spoke her eyes turned toward him. There were dark circles under them. Her long red hair was pulled back in a ponytail and, without warning, frizzed straight out from her skull like she'd stuck her finger in a light socket, then smoothed and hung down her back. Suddenly, she flipped her hands toward the ceiling and ran for the empty sink, elbowing the faucet out of the way. Her fingertips turned orange and emitted a rainbow array of sparks, settling into a bright orange, then sputtered out. Over the sink, she extended her hands in front her, shoulders slumped, when multi-colored stars sparkled forming an arc across the ceiling, then winked out.

Lathen's eyes rounded as he stared at her with an eyebrow arched. "That's quite a display."

"Yeah, yeah, I know." She shook her hands and flexed them. "It's been a really rough twenty-four hours. Don't know what to do about it. To top it all off, the town meeting is day after tomorrow. Gwen is due here in a couple hours, and I'm a mess. Ummm, oh hell. This has never happened before." She paused, peered around the room, then shrugged. "But I never faced the loss of McKay magic either." Tears welled in Pepper's eyes, and though she tried to blink them away, one trickled down her cheek, and she swiped at it with the back of her hand.

He gathered her against him and asked, "What can I do to help? When did it start?"

"After you left Monday night, I fine-tuned the presentation for the town meeting, fed Kaylee, and went to bed." She shook her head. "My dreams were filled with demons trying to use my magic against me, destruction of the town, and the creatures spoke in languages I couldn't understand. I'm sure it stemmed from the encounter with Mr. Green. But Aunt Ashling was in them too."

"Sounds like a bad nightmare."

She straightened and pushed away from him. "As it turns out, it's a lot more than that. A discussion with my aunt yesterday clarified a few things." Pepper whirled around, hands on hips and asked, "And why didn't you tell me about your conversation with my aunt?"

Surprised at her sudden mood change, he took a step back and said calmly, "Still coming to terms with that discussion. I intended to talk to you about it this morning. But when I arrived..." He spread his arms wide toward her, quickly dropping them to his side.

"Ok, so talk."

"Your aunt voiced insights that I didn't agree with, alluded to something bad coming, then issued an ultimatum regarding…whatever is happening between us. I didn't know what to think or how to react. So I returned to the cabin, heard you moving around, checked on Ember, and left. It's not every day you're goaded into a heated conversation with a ghost. I was pissed and left to walk off my anger before starting my jobs for the day."

She chewed on her bottom lip and leaned one hand on the back of a chair, as her ponytail continued to shift from frizzed out to normal and her fingertips turned a light orange. "Ashling didn't explain what she meant?"

"Something about a challenge to the McKay magic and an evil spirit controlling Tom Green and trying to feed off the magic or making it his own. I don't remember exactly."

Pepper closed her eyes for a beat and shivered. Easing into the chair, she related to him all the information her aunt had given her. Lathen listened intently as he grabbed a chair, flipped it around, and straddled it. He rested his arms on the chair back and chin on his arms, flicking his gaze from her pale face to her fading orange fingertips.

After a few minutes of silence, he hopped up from the chair and flipped it around, shoving it under the kitchen table. "I think you need a walk."

With a raised brow, he carefully grabbed her hands and turned them over examining them closely. "You're finished with the fireworks for the time being?"

A corner of her mouth turned up in a rueful smile, she shrugged and attempted to pull her hands from his. "No clue."

"A quick jaunt around the property will drain some of that nervous energy and…" He couldn't help but grin when he looked at her, red hair sticking straight out in a huge, wavy fan around her face, after breaking the band that held it in a ponytail.

"You think this is funny?" she growled.

He bit the side of his cheek to keep from laughing. "No...no...not at all." He paused watching her, knowing there was no good answer. "Okay, well, maybe a little." The laughter he'd tried to hold at bay came rushing out.

She pressed her lips together and narrowed her eyes at him while trying to wrestle her tresses into a tight braid over her shoulder.

"Oh, come on, you know..." He started to say she looked funny, but figured he'd dug a big enough hole with her as it was. After she finished braiding her hair, he yanked her out of the chair and tugged her to the door, calling for Kaylee and Ember to follow. "I'm aware the situation is serious, but we can't do anything about it until you are under control. With Gwen due here soon, this is the best thing I can think of. If you have a better idea, speak up."

"I don't," she said grudgingly.

"Then shake it out and move." After pausing to stretch for a few minutes, he set the pace as fast as he could manage. The black dog trotted ahead of them. Kaylee glided above whistling, he thought as if to encourage Pepper along. On the beach, they chased the waves, enjoying the ocean's spray, and watched the osprey catch dinner. Ember barked and charged into the water in pursuit of the gulls but never catching one.

"You know—" Lathen started but stopped. Pepper's strong, steady gait up the path to the pond made him think she may be spoiling for a fight if

Ashling materialized. But she didn't. The pond was clear and calm; a light breeze rustled the leaves as they trooped toward the barn. Inside he paused to discuss the improvements with Pepper and the time frame for completion.

"I'm still waiting for the lumber and fencing, but figure to start Monday morning. The equipment and supplies for the marine building shipped late yesterday, probably be a couple of weeks before they arrive. I'm pleased everything is close to the schedule we set," Lathen said.

She blew out a breath, leaned backward, then bent at the waist propping her hands on her knees. "You were right. I feel much better." Pepper righted herself and led the way out of the barn and up the path toward the cabin.

Halfway up the path, he slipped an arm around her waist and gently pulled her to him. "Glad to hear it. Appears the frizzing hair and sparking fingers have subsided over the last half hour or so."

Lathen brushed a long curled lock of fiery hair from her face and cupped her chin. Leaning into her, he breathed in her scent of vanilla and lavender with a slight citrusy tang, then touched his lips to hers. His tongue teased her luscious lips apart and traced their full softness. He captured her gasp as his mouth moved over hers. His breathing increased as her body curved into him, breasts firm against his chest. He went hard. Desire spun through him as his wolf awakened and demanded to be sated.

Breaking through the sexual haze, he reluctantly loosened his arm. "Unless you want me to take you right here, we better start walking." Lathen gazed into her eyes and caught movement out of the corner of his eye. The corner of his mouth curved slightly. "Smile," he whispered against her ear, "we got company. Is that Gwen standing on the porch, hand shading her eyes, probably searching for us…uh…you?"

Pepper jerked away and peered toward the cabin, a blush rising from her neck all the way to her cheeks. "Shit. You knew Gwen was there." Pepper swiped at his shoulder.

He sidestepped her and raised his hands, palms up in a gesture of surrender. "I just caught sight of her."

Pepper rushed up the rocky slope, cleared the steps, landed lightly on the porch, and threw her arms around Gwen. "You can't believe how glad I am to see you."

Gwen stifled a laugh with the back of her hand, glancing in Lathen's direction. "Sure you are." Lowering her hand, a wide grin formed on her lips, she said innocently, "I didn't interrupt anything, did I?"

Lathen sauntered up on the porch checking his cell phone. "Nothing that can't be handled later." He winked at Pepper and offered his hand to Gwen. "Lathen Quartz."

Pepper shot him a dark look. "He's the handyman I was telling you about. Lathen, this is Gwen, my best friend and former employer at the wildlife refuge in Salem."

Gwen shook his hand gently. "Please to meet you. I've heard a lot about you." Her thin, dark eyebrows curved up.

"Right back at you." He motioned with his phone. "Have an emergency call at the inn, gotta go. Nice meeting you, Gwen. See you both day after tomorrow." He moseyed down the stairs and climbed into his truck, waving as he headed down the rocky road.

After he had left, Gwen fanned herself with an imaginary fan. "You didn't tell me he was drop dead gorgeous, and those eyes." She turned to watch his pickup bump out of sight. "He can work on my…."

Pepper smiled and bumped hips with her friend, knocking her off balance. "He's off limits."

Gwen raised an eyebrow in question and shook her head. "Too bad. The good ones always are. Now show me around this place. It looks wonderful." She hugged Pepper again. "I'm so happy for you."

****

Pepper, Lathen, and Gwen walked toward the Lobster Cove council chambers of the courthouse armed with revised blueprints, state and federal permits, and licenses. When they pushed through the door, Pepper noticed Kate sitting in an aisle seat close to the center of the room. Lathen put an arm out and stopped Pepper in her tracks. He nodded to the back row, where Tom Green sat reading the paper.

"He shouldn't be here. There is a restraining order against him. Tom can't be within one hundred and fifty feet of you. Let's go back out and catch one of the sheriff's deputies on duty." Lathen nudged Gwen ahead of them and back out the doors.

The foreboding feeling Pepper woke up with this morning was back. The knot in the pit of her stomach tightened, even though the three of them had worked nonstop yesterday on the presentation. Nothing should go wrong, but she was still haunted by her aunt's revelations and that damn waitress from Maggie's. There were no further confrontations, but Kate gave her the stink eye, every time their paths crossed.

Officer Harris strode across the floor toward the door to council chambers. "I need you three to wait out here. Got a little problem with a restraining order violation inside." He yanked open the door and walked inside. A few minutes later he exited with Mr. Green in tow. The officer nodded in their direction. "Go on in now."

As Mr. Green was being escorted out of the building, he glared at Pepper. "I have the right to be in a public place. I was here first."

Pepper's head pounded, and she felt lightheaded. "Go on ahead, I need a drink of water."

Lathen took one look at her and said, "No, you need to go in with us. There's water inside."

She closed her eyes and drew in a long breath. "Okay, let's go." No *way am I going to let some conduit for evil keep me from pursuing my lifelong dream. Especially now that I have the means to make it happen.* She jerked open the door and strode through followed by Gwen and Lathen.

There were only two issues on the council's agenda, and Pepper was up first. The proceeding was short. Gwen told the council members about Pepper's qualifications and experience. They looked over the local paperwork, revised blueprints, building permits, and state and federal documents and unanimously voted to allow Lobster Cove Wildlife and Rehabilitation to go forward. The only hiccup came when Kate stood and opposed the petition. The council members, most of whom had known her since she was a child, saw her for what she was, a woman scorned, and issued her a warning to stay away from the McKay property.

"This isn't done," Kate warned giving Pepper a

scathing look, before leaving in a huff, closing the council room doors harder than necessary.

Pepper thanked the council and indicated a grand opening would be planned for early fall. Everyone would be invited. After the trio left the chambers, Pepper let out a sigh of relief.

"A celebration is in order," Lathen announced. "And I know just the place." He took Pepper's hand and put his other hand on Gwen's shoulder and ushered them out of the room. "You aren't leaving until tomorrow morning?" he said to Gwen.

"Well, I had planned to leave right after the hearing, but I'll call Jodi and tell her I won't be back until Sunday." She turned to Pepper. "I'm so glad you got approval. Your property will make a wonderful and much-needed rescue and rehab facility."

They piled into Lathen's truck. After a short drive, he turned the truck into the graveled parking lot of a building with a green awning over the front. "Here we are."

Walking through the door, both women paused. The tables were covered with white linen tablecloths and crystal stemware winked in the candle light. They were seated by a maitre d' who handed them an extensive wine list and menus with the promise a waiter would be right with them. Gwen picked up her cloth napkin and fingered a fork, turning it over in her hand. "This is real silver. Never been to a place like this."

"Me either," Pepper said quietly. "At least not since I've been on my own."

A waiter dressed in black evening attire approached the table. "Good evening, Mr. Quartz, would you like something from the bar to begin?"

"Yes, bring us a nice champagne with a creamy bubbly finesse. We are celebrating tonight." He nodded to the two women.

"Of course, sir."

Pepper giggled. "You made it appear like this is a threesome. We'll be the talk of the town."

Lathen raised a brow. "That wasn't my intention. But…taking two beautiful women to dinner isn't on my usual agenda. Have you decided what you want?"

"Steak and lobster for me," Pepper said. "Mom used to say there was no better place for surf and turf than The Cliffside.

"With that endorsement, I'll have the same." Gwen closed her menu and laid it on the table on top of the others.

The waiter returned with a bottle of champagne, showed the label to Lathen. When he nodded approval, the waiter poured the rich amber liquid into the crystal wine glasses and set the bottle on the table. "Enjoy. May I inquire what are you celebrating this evening?"

"Pepper McKay's application to the town council for Lobster Cove's Wildlife Rescue and Rehab Center was approved this afternoon." Lathen beamed and motioned to Pepper sitting next to him, covering her hand with his.

She felt her cheeks warm and grinned. "It was an exciting day."

"So I heard." The waiter leaned over and said quietly, "Most the town was pulling for you. Look forward to your grand opening." He straightened. "Are you ready to order?"

"Yes. We'll all have the steak and lobster," Lathen said.

"Excellent choice."

The dinner was delicious. They talked about Pepper's early days with Gwen, about the days before Pepper, and everything in between. But Pepper still couldn't shrug off the uneasy feeling that followed her since her conversation with Ashling. Maybe it was time to drop all this in her father's lap.

Chapter Eleven
Ever Wonder What Boat Tours
and History Lessons Have in Common?
Not a Thing—as It Turns Out

Saturday morning, dressed in black jeans, gray sweater, and boots, Lathen stood back as Gwen and Pepper said their goodbyes. Gwen promised to try to return for Lobster Cove's Fourth of July Celebration as she checked him out from head to toe. Gave his male ego a boost, though he would never admit it.

Astounded at Kaylee's progress, Gwen asked that Pepper document her rehab techniques for the bird. Giving her one final hug, Gwen descended the porch steps and got into her SUV. With tears in her eyes and Lathen's arm around her waist, Pepper waved to Gwen as she drove out of sight. Ember stood at the edge of the porch, and Kaylee soared overhead.

Pepper finally turned from the porch railing and nudged Ember inside, whistling for Kaylee to come in also. The osprey flew through the open door, across the living room, and banked a sharp turn down the hall into the aviary and settled on her favorite branch, blinking slowly as Pepper followed her in.

Pepper tossed a fish for Kaylee, grinning as the bird swooped and dived with precision for the meal. Lathen watched her for a few minutes, then returned to the kitchen and filled the dog's food and water bowl.

Turning as she stepped behind, she leaned against him and wound her arms around his neck. "So what is this surprise you have for me?"

"You just have to wait and see. Grab a coat and your slicker. Rain isn't predicted, but…" Lathen said holding the door, waiting for her to grab her stuff.

The fog was beginning to lift as he pulled into the parking lot for Claws and Effect Boat Tours. "I thought you'd enjoy a boat tour along with a history lesson of these parts. And it looks like the perfect day for it. Robert Mathison, he owns the place, is knowledgeable about Lobster Cove's colorful history. Might be a great place to start your investigation and research into who's after the McKay's magic." He rubbed the back of his neck. A feeling of uncertainty washed over him again.

"Do you know if anyone involved in the Salem Witch Trials in 1692 and '93 settled here? Maybe their descendants still live here," Pepper asked.

"Nope. I'm fairly new to the town, but if there is, we can probably start at the town hall, take a look at the birth and death records. But you might want to keep your reasoning to yourself until you find something. Don't want to go around…well, you know."

She quirked a brow and smirked. "I thought you said they all know."

"There's a difference between enjoying colorful folklore about your town and knowing it's true." He shrugged. "Ashling said things could get dicey."

"Did you know that Maine was part of Massachusetts until 1820? So it kinda stands to reason that maybe the rumors are true. The witch could've fled from Massachusetts into the arms of a McKay who exploited her and took her powers on the promise to return them. When he never did, a disgruntled descendant or maybe the witch herself is looking for retribution? Far-fetched, I know, but…"

"This area wasn't even settled until early 1780. Call your father. See what he has to say about Ashling's recollection. That's where I'd start." Lathen opened the door to Claws and Effect, where several people milled around waiting for the first tour of the day.

"Good morning, everyone. If all of you will follow me, we'll get this tour started." Robert led the little group past a lobster boat, to a large forty-foot fishing boat moored at Pier 1. Getting under way, he pointed out the large trawlers on the opposite side explaining the different types and how they were used. Mr. Mathison was a wealth of information on the fishing industry and Lobster Cove's part in it. Also on boats and equipment used today and as far back as the 1800s. When the tour boat passed within sight of her property high on the cliff, Pepper asked about the town's history and the McKay property in particular. He was evasive and joked that every town had a colorful group of characters and Lobster Cove was no different.

In his jovial booming voice, he changed the subject. "Pepper, I hear that your petition for the wildlife refuge and rehab was approved. Excellent use of your land," Robert said then lowered his voice. "Maybe put the longtime rumors to rest." Resuming his announcing voice, he pointed toward her land. "Can we expect Lobster Cove Wildlife Rehab and Rescue to have a grand opening early fall?"

Pepper nodded. "Provided we're done with the construction and everything is up and running. Barring no large-scale emergencies."

"Well, you've got the best man for the job. Lathen will have it finished ahead of schedule, mark my words." Mathison turned the boat around and headed back to port, pointing out the geographical features and wildlife of interest along the way.

The group disembarked, Pepper and Lathen thanked Robert for a wonderful tour and said they'd keep him informed of the grand opening. On the way to the parking lot, Lathen noticed Pepper seemed to be in a much better mood and more relaxed than she'd been since Ashling's appearance.

"How about a late lunch? I'm starved."

"Fine with me," Pepper said.

"We can stop by Ned's Lobster Shack, grab a bite. Then on the way to your place, pick up dessert and a couple meat pies for later at Sweet Bea's. At the cabin, we can brew up some coffee and relax a bit."

"Sounds good. I'd like to get home before it gets too late, so I can call my parents. I haven't talked to them since I called my mother on the first day here. The conversation was a little odd," she said climbing into the truck.

"How so?" Lathen started the engine and drove a couple of blocks to Ned's.

"I can't put my finger on it. My parents have always been supportive, but it was like she wasn't telling me something." She grimaced. "But I was so tired, I could have imagined it." She pushed on the truck door as he came around and opened it for her.

"Where do your parents live?" He grabbed her hand and twined his fingers through hers as they strolled to Ned's.

"Colorado."

"Wow, that's a long way from here, as well as in culture and lifestyle." He pulled open the door, and the enticing aroma of lobster and homemade biscuits wafted out as they walked in and sat at a table.

After reviewing the menu, they placed an order and Pepper continued. "Yeah, Mom said Dad was tired of the sea, and the Rocky Mountains seemed to have a draw for him. I grew up on the western slope. Learned to ski almost before I walked. Loved river rafting, camping, hiking, all the Colorado-type things until I was sixteen and spent a summer with Aunt Ashling. After that, it was all about the animals, marine biology, and the ocean. Mom and Dad weren't happy, but...never objected when I wanted to spend every summer with Ashling. Dad would roll his eyes and Mom would make other suggestions while giving Dad a strange look. But in the end they supported my choice."

"Bet they're proud of you," Lathen said as the waitress brought their order.

"Yeah, I think so. They came to Salem to visit a few times, but Dad always seemed antsy after a few days to get back. Mom loved the history and wanted to see and revel in all the famous places. Mom and I took a little side trip to Boston a couple of times. She was a history professor, retired now." Pepper took a bite of her lobster roll. "These are really good."

"Good thing you like lobster." He took a drink of coffee and waved the cup toward her. "What did your dad do?"

"He was a biology professor specializing in zoology."

"So you took after your dad."

"Guess so, never thought about it." Finishing her

last bite, she pushed the plate away. "Ready?"

"Yep. Can't wait for vanilla cake with raspberry filling, huh?"

"You got it." She smiled at him as they walked to the truck.

The stop at Bea's was short. Lathen purchased four meat pies, two for later tonight, two for the freezer, and two pieces of vanilla cake. By the time they arrived at Pepper's place, it was closing in on six o'clock. Ember was on the back of the couch watching out the window. She jumped down and met them at the door. Pepper paused to scratch the dog's ear and watched her race outside. Lathen kept an eye on the dog as Pepper checked on Kaylee. He heard Pepper open the holding tank and toss the bird a large fish. When Pepper returned to the living room, he was relaxed in the rocker recliner with a piece of cake. Pepper's piece sat on the coffee table beside the reclining sofa. Ember lay next to the sofa eying the plate of cake on the table.

"Did you want me to start a fire?" Lathen asked around the bite of cake he'd just popped in his mouth.

****

"That would be great, if you don't mind." Pepper sat down on the sofa with her piece of vanilla cake, forked up a piece, and slid it into her mouth.

"Don't mind a bit." He pushed up from the rocker and stoked the fireplace with wood and took off in search of newspaper to get it started.

With a snap of her fingers, Pepper had a roaring fire in the hearth when he returned. "Figured you were as tired as I am." She smiled at him, closed her eyes, and reached for the phone.

"Appreciate it." He reclined the section of sofa

completely and took another bite of cake.

After tapping in her parents' number, she held the phone to her ear. Her dad answered on the first ring.

"Hi there, Pep, everything all right?" His voice was calm but with a slight edge to it that Pepper detected immediately.

"Of course, why wouldn't it be?" she said soothingly.

"Oh, no reason."

"Pops, I got a few questions for you. Would now be a good time?"

"If you mean is your mother here, she is not."

"Good. She told you I inherited the McKay property in Lobster Cove. Right?" Pepper chewed on her bottom lip while considering how to broach the subject of Aunt Ashling's ghost. She was sure other magic families had ghostly relatives that popped up from time to time, but not hers.

"She did. Congratulations on your plans for the wildlife center. Your aunt would be proud."

"As a matter of fact, she is." Pepper paused for a couple beats, then charged ahead. "A few unsettling things have happened around here. I was sitting on the bench by the pond, you know the one, and Ashling materialized leaning against the big pine. When Mom visited Colleen after Ashling's death, did she ever mention seeing her?"

"Nooo." There was a long drawn-out pause, then he sighed. "I wondered if Ashling would stick around, especially with Colleen alone on the property. What else is going on?"

Pepper told him about Tom Green, omitting the last encounter, her telephone call to Colleen, and the conversation with Ashling. "Do you remember anything like that going on at the family reunions?"

"Yes, vaguely, I was pretty young at the time. But over the years, Ashling brought it up once in a while, especially when the last McKay on the property died, and it required either her or me to take up residence. By that time, I'd married your mother, and she was leery of the McKay magic. Not that the Abbott magic is any less, but she always said it was more dignified. Whatever that means." He chuckled. "Partially my fault for dragging her to the family reunions where tales such as Ashling told you abound. Our large Irish family tended to embellish stories of long-gone relatives, good and bad."

"Gee, I seem to remember tales you spun while I was growing up. I believed wholeheartedly…"

Her dad snorted. "Me—never."

"Until Mom set me straight."

"She always was a killjoy. Not that it mattered. Your mom always said there was too much power, especially on the family property. Besides, it was Ashling's choice since she was the eldest. As far as I know, she never had any problems after moving onto the property."

"I wondered why the land went to me rather than you. From her cryptic remarks, the trouble started after she died and allowed Colleen to live there for as long as she wanted. Ashling said it was her fault for leaving the property without a McKay witch. Does that make sense to you?"

"If you believe any of the tales handed down generation to generation, yes. Separating fact from fiction could be a daunting task."

Pepper groaned. "Wrong answer. I'm up to my eyeballs with the wildlife center construction. I got the final approval necessary on Friday from the town council. Now, my goal is to get it up and running before cold weather sets in. And magic snafus are not part of the plan," she said firmly.

"May I suggest we bring your mom, the historian, in on this to research the McKay family and any caveats regarding who lives on the property? With my help, of course."

"Think she would? It could validate her opinions of the McKay magic. Tough on you." Pepper teased, kicking back in the recliner, taking another bite of cake.

"Or it could put to rest her misgivings. Either way, being involved may alleviate her anxiety over you living on the property alone. The Tom Green incidents are just going to increase her desire to pop out there and protect you."

"Couldn't we just leave that part out for a while? Concentrate on confirming Ashling's suspicions. Protecting the magic? Everything else should fall in line."

"Don't think that's a prudent plan. If your Mr. Green is after the McKay magic, he could be dangerous. Your safety is my number one priority. If something happened to you, I would never forgive myself and your mother—I shudder to think…"

"Pops, Lathen has installed a state of the art security system. The magic is also working to protect me and…"

"Who's Lathen?"

"He's the handyman that the estate hired to maintain the property after Colleen left and before they found me. I've secured his services for the wildlife center's construction." She scraped the last remains of extra frosting and cake crumbs from her plate with her fork and slipped it into her mouth.

"Hold that thought. We'll get back to Lathen in a minute. Are you telling me there was no one with a connection to the McKay's on the property for a period of time?"

"Yes, but only a couple weeks…"

"There's your part of your problem. If Tom Green was aware the magic was without a McKay witch…You need to research Tom Green."

"I have, there's nothing to indicate he has any magical connections. By all accounts, he's a well-to-do widower who runs a grocery store, a good golfer, and this whole situation is way out of his behavior pattern."

"Then someone or something is controlling him. Check out acquaintances and friends." Her father paused.

Pepper could hear him tapping a pencil on the desk or table top. A habit he'd had ever since she could remember when he was thinking about something. She smiled at the memory. "I don't really…"

"Better yet, send the research to your mom. She'll get to the bottom of it. I bet you're planning a big celebration on Halloween in Lobster Cove, huh? The town has always gone overboard at Halloween, so you'll fit right in." He chuckled. "You know, you may be able to use that to your advantage, if what Ashling suspects is true."

Her dad's quick change of subject caught her off guard. She'd forgotten how often he used to do that, especially when he was mulling something over unrelated to the conversation at hand. He'd always taken multi-tasking to a new level. Quickly she caught up with his thinking and asked, "How so?"

Duncan's voice turned conspiratorial. "Your mom just drove up. Let me bring her up to speed—and deal with her misgivings, then get back to you."

"Sure. Hey Dad, why don't you and Mom plan on coming to the grand opening around the end of September and stay for Halloween? You wouldn't have to stay at the cabin. The Sea Crest Inn has wonderful rooms and a fantastic view, as you know. Or there could be cottages available."

"Sounds like a plan. I'll be in touch. If you need any help with the center, we are available for that too. It's been quite a while since I've been on my old stomping ground."

"Oh, I have someone helping me. He's got things under control so far."

"He? Oh yes, Lathen. What do you know about…"

"Enough." She giggled. "Talk to you later." Pepper ended the phone call. *Wish I hadn't let that slip about Lathen, yet.* Since leaving for college, she'd not shared a lot of her personal life with her parents. Usually, because there was nothing to share but work.

"Informative talk with your dad?" Lathen asked.

"Yes. Hey, I've meant to ask. Do you know a Benjamin Bonchard?"

"Sure, Ben works in the clerk and recorder's office at the courthouse. Been there forever, so I've been told. Why?"

"I did a little research on Mr. Green." She shook her head. "Everything is contrary to his recent behavior. He's golfing buddies with Ben Bonchard. I thought maybe Ben could shed some light on Tom."

Lathen frowned. "Ben's a weird duck. Nice enough. You'll probably run into him if you are going to check out the birth and death records."

"Gonna put that off for a bit. Dad's going to talk Mom into doing research on the McKay family for me. That way I can devote all my energy to the wildlife center."

"Provided there are no more encounters with Mr. Green," Lathen grumbled. "I don't like you staying out here by yourself, especially since the last encounter with Tom and the fact that he showed up at the council meeting. Complete disregard for the restraining order."

"That is troublesome, but you're almost done with the security system. Right?"

"Finish it up tomorrow. But tonight…" He pushed up from the couch and gathered up the cake plates and forks, then strode toward the kitchen.

Pepper followed him and put a pot of coffee on, fixing a cup of tea for herself. "I'll be fine."

"I've got a bad feeling about this whole situation." Lathen tossed the paper plates and plastic forks in the trash with more energy that necessary.

"Well then—" She came up behind him and wrapped her arms around his waist, leaning her cheek against his muscular upper back, molding her body to his. "I guess you just have to stay here tonight."

Motionless for a moment, he turned in her arms, cupping her chin. He tilted her face up to his, eyes searching hers. A tingle of excitement raced through her as his fingers trailed sinuously up her arm. She felt his heartbeat increase as he lowered his mouth to hers. He caressed her lips, trailing soft kisses across her cheek, slowly along her jawline to the pulsing hollow at the base of her throat. She brought his mouth back to hers, parting her lips. His tongue slipped between them touching, stroking, and exploring. Her emotions whirled and skidded. Was she ready for where he was leading her? As if he heard her thoughts, he lifted his head and murmured, his breath warm against her ear, "I accept your invitation, but I'd better sleep on the couch—unless..."

Chapter Twelve
If You Build It, They Will Come
—Feathered, Furred, Scaled, and Finned

The curtain flapped gently in the breeze. Floral scents from the flower bed below the window mixed with a light ocean brine wafted through the room. Lathen blinked and looked down to see Pepper still asleep, nestled against his chest. Her long copper lashes tickled as they brushed against his skin when she opened her eyes. The memories of last night floated through his mind as she licked her full lips and a slight smile curved the corners of her mouth.

He pulled her closer and touched his lips gently to hers. "Good morning."

"Morning…Ummm…You're up early."

"Watching you sleep. How about a shower? Then we'll get on with our day."

"Together?"

"A lot more fun that way."

"Oookay." She started to push the sheets away, then pulled them up to her chin.

He raised a brow and flashed her a sexy grin. "Now that's a moot point." Whisking her out from under the covers and into his arms, he said, "I like you naked." He padded toward the shower, nibbling his way down her neck. His tongue licked the swell of her breast and teased her nipples until they were hard little berries.

"So that's the way you want to play." She shifted in his arms, wrapping her legs around his waist arching her warm, wet center against his erection.

He stepped into the shower and leaned his back against the wall cupping his hands under her ass. "Whoa there, girl, not so fast." Seating himself at her entrance, he teased with a couple tiny thrusts. He lowered her to her feet and trailed kisses from her neck to her belly button, then knelt between her legs, gently spreading them.

She squealed and tried to escape his tightening grip on her thighs, only to brush herself against his chin. Trying to balance on one foot to turn away, she whispered, "Now who's going too fast?"

Grinning up at her, he grasped her flailing leg, slung it over his shoulder, and slid a finger into her warm channel. She gasped, her soft body thrust toward him, spreading wider, giving him more access. She ran her hands through his sun-kissed hair and curled her fingers in the strands, pulling his mouth against her. She moaned.

Unable to control the pulsing pleasure, she threw her head back and screamed, holding him in place until the last shudders left her body. "Ooooh—the things you can do with your tongue." She breathed, leaning back against the shower wall, legs still spread giving him all the access he wanted.

A slow smile spread across his lips as he squatted balanced on the balls of his feet, his fingers continuing feather light caresses.

She pulled him up to her and wrapped her fingers around his thick length, caressing the tip with her thumb.

He jerked in her hand and groaned as she tightened her grip. "You're going to be the death of me." Closing his eyes, he loved the feel of her soft hand around him.

"Oh, I hope not, looks like you still have plenty of pleasure to give." Her gaze wandered over his naked body. An open foil package glinted in the subdued light on the corner shelf. She continued to caress him as she reached for and smoothed protection over him. He thrust toward her with a hiss, as surges of lust ripped through him. Reaching down with both hands, he scooped her up in his arms. "Enough."

She giggled and wrapped her legs around his waist, this time guiding him to her entrance with a gentle hand, letting him slide through her grip before he slipped inside. He felt her stretch as he thrust more urgently. *Control was never a problem—until now—with her. What was it about this witch?* The heat of his body coursed down the entire length of hers as he cupped her ass cheeks, spreading her wider, seating himself deeper and pressed her back against the shower wall.

She squealed. "It's cold. You did that on purpose."

He gave her a sly wink, his breathing increasing. "Oh, I'll warm you up." And he thrust into her, filling her completely over and over until passion raged and shuddering ecstasy surged through them. Spent, he guided her slide down the wall until her feet touched the floor, wrapped his arms around her, and held her against his warm chest and away from the wall.

When she was able to speak again, she said, "You sure know how to please a woman."

He grinned. "You're not so bad, yourself."

She wiggled against him, curving her body into his.

"You don't want to start anything we don't have time finish." He smirked, tamping down his excitement before he had a raging hard-on again, and flipped the shower on. The cold blast of water had the desired effect as he shielded her from the stream. "We have a security system to complete," he bit out adjusting the water to the desired temperature. "Then I'll take you to bed again, and show you pleasure."

"Oh, pretty cocky aren't you," she shot back.

A wide grin spread across his face and he shrugged. "Well, if you say so."

****

Pepper dried her hair, dressed in jeans and a powder blue sweater that hugged her curves, then followed the enticing aroma of coffee into the kitchen. Lathen stood barefooted in jeans, with the top button unbuttoned, a worn work shirt unbuttoned down the front, his hair glistening from the shower.

He turned in a circle, holding the shirt open, revealing his bare chest. "You like the look?" His gaze met hers and traveled down. "Nice sweater." Reaching out, he fondled her breast over the sweater.

She slapped at his hand. "You've had your quota for this morning."

He pouted. "Better be nice to me, or I won't give you the alarm code."

After a breakfast of bacon, eggs, toast, hash browns, and juice, Lathen got to work on the security system. He determined installation would take at least a couple days given his other business obligations. Leaving her unprotected was not an option. It was agreed he'd stay at the cabin until the entire system was operational. They discussed the location and installation of night-vision cameras outside in the woods and surrounding property. The video cams were strategically installed to eliminate blind spots around the exterior of the cabin. On the interior, the entire first floor was under video surveillance, backed with motion detectors and alarms on the upstairs windows. Leaving Pepper's privacy intact but secure. The entire surveillance system was accessible by smartphone with the best encryption available.

By the end of the second day, all systems had been tested and were up and running. Lathen set up a computer monitoring system in Pepper's bedroom with a set of screens in the living area.

"I think you are secure from non-magical beings." He walked over to the bank of monitors in the living room. "Let me show you how it all works."

Pepper stood, hands on the chair back, as he demonstrated the system downstairs. They moved to the bedroom. He had her operate the system checking out the video zones and making sure she could operate the entire system alone. While she sat in the chair staring at the computer screens, he leaned over and brushed his lips across her neck, inhaling her scent.

"Are you sniffing me?" she asked turning in the chair bringing his lips to hers. She lingered over the kiss, enjoying its dreamy intimacy.

"Guilty as charged," he murmured against her lips and buried his nose in the space between her neck and shoulder. "I love the way you smell, citrus mingled with a touch of mint. Smells so fresh. I'm going to miss being with you twenty-four-seven. Need to make more time for us, when I'm not staying here."

"Could be a while. Between your business and this

project, there aren't enough hours in the day."

His eyes sparkled with mischief as he pulled back. "Oh, that's going to change. Tomorrow is my last scheduled service call until we're done here. Farmed out the other calls. July Fourth is coming up, and we are going to take the entire day off. The town pulls out all the stops on the celebration, and we are going to attend all the events. It'll be fun."

She turned back to the monitors with a sigh, surprised how well the system covered the property and the cabin. She liked the secure feeling it gave her.

On the way downstairs, he cupped her ass, then released it as she slapped at him. "That's about it. One project completed." He blew out a breath. "Hope the property and cabin can keep you safe from the magic creatures looking to invade." He kissed her on the cheek. "By the way, have you heard from your parents since you talked to your father?"

"No, but Dad or Mom will call when they have something. Mom is thorough, so it could be a while. I'm considering a visit to the library and clerk and recorder's office shortly. See what I can find out on this end."

Lathen shook his head. "I'd rather you not go alone."

"I'll go in broad daylight, early morning, and be back long before dark. You don't have time to chaperone me with all the building supplies and workers scheduled for the center. You said yourself that everything is on schedule. Let's keep it that way."

"You're right," he said with a frown. "But check in throughout the day and when you change location. Humor me."

"You got it. I'll schedule that midweek next week, if I don't hear from Mom or Dad by then."

"Any communication from Ashling?"

"No, too many workers and delivery people coming and going. And by end of day I'm exhausted and head straight to bed, as you know."

"True. Should slow down in the next few weeks." He waggled his eyebrows. "Then we can take care of needs of a different nature." His gaze wandered over her body.

Sending him a saucy smile, she purred, "I'm counting on it."

"If you don't stop teasing me, I'm going to take you upstairs and the schedule be damned." He lunged for her.

She sidestepped him and put the desk between them. "Okay, I didn't mean to tease you."

"Like hell you didn't." He drew in a breath and let it out slowly shoving away from the desk. "Speaking of schedules, are you going to be around in the morning to sign for equipment being delivered? I need to take care of an emergency service call to the inn first thing in the morning, then stop by the hardware store to pick up miscellaneous odds and ends needed here."

"Sure. I have a lot of medical, lab, and specialty supplies coming and want to check them off as they arrive, before I release the delivery driver." She settled down at the desk with stacks of paperwork piled high. Then blew him a kiss as he started toward the door.

He reached up in the air and pretended to catch the kiss, then held that fist to his heart, giving her a devilish grin. "Until tonight." The door closed behind him.

****

The past week had zoomed by without paranormal interference of any kind. Since she hadn't heard from her parents, she cleared her calendar for the whole day and headed into town to do a little research on her own. She had kissed Lathen goodbye and promised to check in at regular intervals. First stop on her list, the library. A records search dating back to the late 1600s turned up nothing relevant to the McKay's but the witch trials and information she already knew or discovered online. She thanked the lady that helped her and headed to the clerk and recorder's office. When she walked in the door, a shiver shot up her spine as an older man came to the counter.

"May I help you?" he asked in a bored tone of voice.

"Yes, I'd like to review any records you have dating back to the early 1700s of births, deaths, and marriages. That kind of thing."

"Your name, miss?"

"McKay, Pepper McKay."

The man's entire demeanor changed. He straightened and hung on her every word. "I'm afraid those will be rather limited because Maine was part of Massachusetts during that time. You'd have better luck with the Massachusetts records. I can get you a name of someone that may be able to help you at the state level."

"That's okay, my mother is doing research also. She has more experience at that sort of thing. Just thought I'd see if I could help her along. Now I know why it's taking her so long," Pepper said with a soft laugh.

He smiled, but it didn't reach his eyes. "You set up

a wildlife center on the McKay property."

"It's not done yet. Grand opening is scheduled for September. You should stop by."

He nodded in acknowledgment. "Your mother doesn't happen to be Klaren McKay?"

An involuntary shiver slid up her spine again, only this time she felt a disguised magic signature. "Yes, she is. Are you Benjamin Bonchard?"

"The very same. Did your mother tell you about me?" A wide smile spread across his face.

Forehead wrinkled in confusion, she asked, "No, why would she? I saw you and your partner won the golf tourney for the fourth consecutive year. Is that right?"

Ben shrugged. "Yes, we play well together." Then staring at her intently, he asked, "Will your mother be attending the grand opening?"

"That's quite a record." She glanced at her watch and backed toward the door. "I've got to be going, lots to do. It was nice meeting you."

He came around the corner of the counter and grasped her arm. Dark magic zinged up her arm. Shocked, she twisted free and glared at him.

"Say hello to your mother for me." He turned his back and shuffled off.

What the hell was that all about? She shook her arm, hurried out of the office and down the hall of the courthouse to the elevators. Changing her mind, she moved to the door marked stairs, yanked it open, and sprinted up the steps to the first floor, flung open the courthouse doors. Once on the sidewalk, she stopped to catch her breath and grabbed her cell phone out of her pocket, punched in speed dial two for Lathen.

"Hi hon, checking in?"

"Headed home. Tell you about my day when I get there."

"Everything all right? You sound winded."

"Yeah. Strange things. Tell you about it when I get home." She climbed into her truck, locked the doors, and eased out of the parking lot, hoping not to draw attention to herself. *Am I overreacting?* Relaxing back in the seat, she replayed the events in her mind as she drove home.

Pepper climbed out of the truck into the arms of Lathen, who was waiting for her in the driveway, Ember standing beside him.

"You okay? What happened?"

She clung to him, loving the scent and feel of his muscular chest pressed against her and strong arms around her. Laughing, she touched her tippy toes to the ground, as the heat rose in her cheeks. "I overreacted to something that happened at the clerk and recorder's office."

After studying her for a moment, he shook his head, still holding her hands. "I'm not buying that. What happened?"

As she relayed the events of the afternoon, his eyes rounded, and he blew out a low whistle. "You need to call your mom. Find out what she knows about Mr. Bonchard. You said your mom and dad went to high school together. So if he went to school with your mom, wouldn't he have also known your dad?"

"It would stand to reason since they all attended Lobster Cove High School. Afterward Mom and Dad went off to college together. Apparently, Ben stayed here." Pepper bent down and scratched Ember behind the ears. "Come on, girl, let's make a phone call." The dog trotted after her into the house, Lathen behind them both.

The phone rang several times before her dad picked up. "Hi, Pep. To what do I owe the honor of your call?" he joked.

"Hi, Pops. Is Mom home?" Pepper settled into the rocker recliner and leaned back.

"Oh, so that's how it is. Discarded like an old rug."

"You know better. How's the research going?"

"Slow. If there is something to the story of Aidan McKay stealing Sarah Dustin's magic, we haven't found it. All the records indicate a happy marriage, six children, and they were married over sixty years when Sarah, she went by the name Dusty, died of natural causes. Otherwise, a few family feuds and squabbles, but nothing out of the ordinary was recorded." Her father paused for a couple of beats. "I guess those confrontations could have led to disgruntled relatives that festered over time. But overall, the McKay clan seems to be a close-knit group. Your mom's out in the garden. I'll go get her."

"No, wait. Do you know a Benjamin Bonchard? I guess he went…"

"Yes, Ben was an old flame of your mother's until she came to her senses senior year, and I made my move." He chuckled. "Why?"

"I had a strange encounter with him this afternoon." Pepper brought her dad up to speed with recent events. "It seemed almost like he's still got a thing for her."

Duncan roared with laughter. "After nearly forty years, that's ridiculous." He sobered and said, "The use

134

of dark magic is troublesome...Are you sure about that?"

"Positive."

Duncan paused. "He was never a very talented warlock but seemed harmless back then." A door banged on her dad's end of the line.

"Is that Mom?"

"Yep." He filled Klaren in on the details of the conversation so far and handed over the phone.

"Hi, Pep, how are you?" her mother asked warmly.

"Good. I heard Pops fill you in. Was your breakup with Ben amicable?"

"It was so long ago. But as I remember, he wasn't happy—furious in fact, blamed your father. Why?"

"He's best buds with Tom Green. Dad gave me a synopsis of your research to date. No skeletons in the McKay closet. Plenty of ghosts, though." Pepper giggled and continued. "Seems to me, he is the common denominator. I'm going to dig a little deeper, see if he ever left town, was married, any kids. Psycho tendencies. Stuff like that."

Lathen eased onto the sofa beside her, shaking his head. "No. I don't want you digging around anymore." He reached for the phone. She pulled away and waggled a finger in warning, tapping the speaker icon on the phone. "Mom, you're on speaker, so Lathen can hear your thoughts."

"Lathen, nice to almost meet you. Our little girl hasn't told us a thing about you. However, Gwen has filled in some blanks."

"What—Gwen...I'm going have a talk with her." Pepper huffed.

"Pep, we gotta find out what you are up to

135

somehow. Anyway, I agree with Lathen. I'd rather you didn't do any digging. Let me. Your encounter may have put him on alert. With all you have to do for the rescue and rehab, you don't want him causing mayhem. If he's teamed up with a relative looking for revenge, I'd like to know who, before we get blindsided."

"Unless he's in cahoots with Tom Green. Then it is an ongoing situation. I keep waiting for the other shoe to fall."

"But it's been quiet for a while, right?" her mother countered.

"Yes, but…" Pepper heard her mom cover the mouthpiece on her end of the phone. There were muffled voices, but she couldn't make out what they were saying. "Hey, I'm still here."

"We know you are, dear. Trying to hammer out a few details on an idea. Tell you what. We'll get it all figured out and call you back. Meanwhile, spread around that I will be at the grand opening. But don't get near Ben again. Please."

"Okay. Pops is coming too. Right?"

"Of course, he wouldn't miss it for the world. But let's keep it quiet."

"Oh, I see where you going with this. You think he's capable of…" She picked at the hem of her shirt. "What would be his point after all these years?"

"I don't know what to think. Lathen, keep an eye on our girl. Make sure she's safe."

"I'm doing my best, but your daughter is a bit headstrong and well—stubborn." Lathen held up his hand to fend off a swipe from Pepper as she leaned across the sofa, the rocker bucking her backward as he stifled a laugh.

"Oooh, don't we know it. I blame it on the McKay Irish genes. Take care and be careful. We'll be in touch."

Pepper ended the call and shoved up from the rocking reclining couch. "Guess we better get back at it."

"Yep. Want to see how the marine clinic is coming along? Got most the equipment installed, and it's looking good." He caught her hand and entwined their fingers while they strolled down the path to the marine area.

****

The days and nights blurred together as Lathen, Pepper, contractors, and volunteers worked feverishly on the clinics and habitats for the center. The barn was renovated into an indoor aviary with holding cages for injured and rehabbing birds. Lathen designed and supervised the building of the marine clinic and rehab center on the McKay beach from the ground up. It was no easy feat, but he was pleased at how the clinic integrated with the habitat, along with the ocean pool and water system. Pepper's background in marine biology was invaluable. They spent long nights until the sun came up poring over the plans, inventing solutions to specific problems for filtration. He crossed his arms over his chest and surveyed his creation with pride.

To the plans, Lathen added an outdoor aviary at one end of the barn, for the nice weather. Pepper disagreed they needed it, but he maintained better to build it now than wish they had. His position was the same at the mammal habitat. He built a few permanent quarters separated from the temporary ones for injured and rehabbing animals. Better to build now and not need them, than to need them in the dead of winter and be unable to build them. Besides he knew Pepper's heart. There would always be a disabled creature she couldn't bear to send to a sanctuary, even Gwen's.

On the marine facility they agreed. Extra wash tubs with sprayers, stainless steel counters, examining tables, and rehab pool supplied by ocean water with optional filtration system in the event the ocean's water at their beach was compromised or contaminated. She wanted a locked cabinet for medicines in the aviary, mammal, and marine habitats. Gallons of the dish soap necessary to clean oil from feathers and skin with dispensing ports at all the tubs and counters.

Against Brandon's suggestion, Pepper maintained a private office in the cabin. But the files and day to day business would be in the main office Lathen designed as an addition to the mammal habitat. By the first of July, they were ahead of schedule and set the grand opening date for September to coincide with the autumn equinox. One of only two days of the year that the day and night are exactly equal, in balance. Coming to Lobster Cove had balanced her life, so she thought the timing fit. At least it sounded good as they worked on a draft for the fliers. When Pepper went into town, she made sure to mention that her mother would be attending the grand opening.

Around noon on Friday, July 3rd, Lathen hobbled through the barn converted to a finished aviary and glanced out the door at the other projects scattered on the land. All were well ahead of schedule. And the addition to Pepper's cabin was finished. Working on it in between projects had been a piece of cake and kept him from sending workers home when any of the projects stalled. But the fourteen-hour days and strenuous work had taken a toll on his back. The damaged nerve in his leg was screaming for relief. He leaned against the wall and reached for his phone to let Pepper know what he was thinking. She agreed.

Fifteen minutes later, he had all the volunteers and contractors gathered in front of the mammal habitat as Pepper walked out the door and stood beside him. "Everyone, could I have your attention? Pepper and I want to thank you for all your hard work and keeping us ahead of schedule. So we are knocking off early today, and I don't want to see anyone here until Wednesday morning. Enjoy a few days off."

A cheer when up from all the workers.

"See you all at the Lobster Cove Fourth of July celebration, tomorrow. Now get out of here." Lathen smiled as the employees beat feet to their cars.

Pepper slung her arm around Lathen's waist and hugged him.

Lathen groaned. "Not so hard."

"Hurting? Want to use the newly installed whirlpool in the mammal habitat?"

"No, I want a hot tub installed in the cabin," Lathen grumped.

Pepper pursed her lips and a brow winged up. "Not a bad idea. Want me to…"

"I was only kidding." He leaned over and kissed the corner of her mouth.

"I'm not. We can seal off part of the exercise room for a hot tub, use it year around. It would be great to soak in, relax aching muscles, and with all the large double-insulated windows you installed in the front, enjoy the scenery. And I can think of lots of alternate uses for it, some therapeutic. Others—" She slid her hand over the bulge beneath his zipper and laughed seductively. "—not so much."

"Add it to the list. Right now, I need to lie down and stretch out, before my back locks up," he said, limping toward the house. He never figured out why the wolf genes hadn't completely healed his injuries. If he ever returned to the pack, maybe the family doctor could…Well, that wasn't going to happen—unless things with Pepper worked out, then an introduction would be required. *Wouldn't that just beat all?*

"I'll join you," Pepper said.

Chapter Thirteen
Fourth of July Celebration
—Not for the Faint of Heart

By midmorning on the fourth of July, the fog and clouds had burned off, and the sun shone brightly in a clear blue sky. Main Street was lined with spectators waving flags of all sizes, waiting for the parade to begin. Several including Pepper and Lathen brought chairs and sat in front of the throngs of people standing behind them on the corner of Main Street and Oak Avenue. Looked like the whole town had turned out. Small children played along the street waiting for the festivities to begin, their faces painted in a red, white, and blue motif.

Pepper was decked out in a red and blue tank top with white glittery stars scattered over it, blue jeans, and red shoes. She had a light sweater tied around her waist. Lathen was dressed in the red striped shirt Pepper had laid out with his blue jeans and boots. After the stimulating massage she'd given him yesterday and a few painkillers, he was mobile and feeling better. Over the past couple of weeks, Pepper encouraged him to bring over some of his clothes and personal items for the nights he stayed with her, which was quite often these days.

The thought of how to get the hot tub and have it installed without Lathen's knowledge bounced around her mind. She never used magic frivolously or for personal gain, but this wasn't only for her. It would ease his pain, and he'd done so much for her. And if their relationship worked out the way she hoped, he'd be a permanent fixture in her life. But getting the tub and installation without his knowledge, now that was the quandary.

"Hey, babe. What you thinking about?" Lathen asked.

Yanked out of her thoughts, she smiled over at him and said, "Nothing, just vegging."

He quirked an eyebrow. "Hear the high school band tuning up? They must be ready to start the parade."

She listened but shook her head. "I don't hear anything."

"You will." He pointed down Main Street, and a few minutes later the band turned the corner from Pine Avenue onto Main Street. Next appeared a vintage car club, floats from various businesses in Lobster Cove, and finally the equestrian club atop their noble Andalusian steeds.

Pepper twisted in her chair and said, "Did you know the Andalusian was known for its prowess as a war horse? The horse came from the Iberian Peninsula, where its ancestors have lived for thousands of years. Nobility prized the breed and used it as a tool of diplomacy by the Spanish government. Kings across Europe rode and owned Spanish horses."

"Liked the horses, huh?" Lathen asked, his eyes twinkling.

"Of course."

After the last one had passed by with red, white,

and blue streamers braided in its mane, Pepper and Lathen folded up their chairs and strolled toward the town square. People gathered around the few food vendors or spread their picnic lunches out on the grass and enjoyed the social atmosphere. Frisbees zoomed across the grassy area, volleyball nets popped up, teams chosen, and games played over the course of the afternoon.

Without warning, a ripple of alarm skittered up her spine. Pepper whirled around just in time to see Benjamin Bonchard saunter through the crowd, headed right for her. She grabbed Lathen's arm, inadvertently jerking him away from his conversation with Mike and Jean, a couple of volunteers that helped at the center. Lathen eyed her with mild irritation as his brows knitted together.

"Excuse us for a minute," she said pleasantly. Taking a few steps from the couple, Pepper jerked her chin in Ben's direction and whispered, "That's him, and he's headed this…" Before she could get the words out, Ben was at her side, grabbed her free hand, and a disturbing awareness zinged up her arm and across her shoulder. By the time it reached her temple, she felt lightheaded and yanked her hand free as Lathen stepped in front of her, forcing them both to take a step backward.

"I don't believe we've met," Lathen said, eyes narrowed, tense and watchful. "I'm Lathen Quartz. And you are?"

Caught off guard, Ben flicked a steely gaze to Lathen. "Ben Bonchard, clerk and recorder's office," he said sharply. In a sudden switch of demeanor, his eyes softened and his voice became cordial. "I didn't know you were with Pepper. We met a few days ago. She left without the information she was seeking." He thrust a piece of paper at Pepper. "This is the gentleman's name and phone number, who can assist in your records search."

"Thank you," she said coolly, taking the paper from his grasp with her thumb and index finger.

He stared at her hand momentarily, then returned his gaze to her face. "I hear Klaren will be attending the wildlife center grand opening. You must be excited. Shame your father won't be accompanying her."

"That hasn't been decided, yet. Mom will be here to help me wrap up a few things before the opening," she said airily.

The corners of his mouth turned up in a solicitous smile. "While she's here I'd like to get together and catch up. Tell her I'll be in touch." He nodded to Lathen, wandered through the crowd, and disappeared.

"What was that all about?" Lathen asked.

"Hell if I know. This sounds ludicrous, but it felt like a warning. Trying to scare me?" She shivered at the memory of his touch. "He'll learn I don't scare easily. Too bad you didn't shake his hand. Maybe I could figure out if he controls the dark magic or it controls him."

"Thought about it. But he would have learned more about me than we want him to know. He's got an agenda. The less he knows about us, the better." Lathen wrapped his hand around hers and gave it a squeeze. "Want an iced mocha?" he pointed to a booth behind the gazebo. "Then we mingle and visit before the boat decorating contest."

At dusk, the mist rolled in, but it didn't dampen the

revelers' enthusiasm. Pepper and Lathen followed the crowd over to the harbor where several boats were lined up and decorated with different kinds of patriotic colored lights. A variety of bulbs burned steady, while others flashed, chased, and twinkled. One pleasure craft had a flag draped over the bow made up of red, white, and blue lights that blinked in time to "The Star Spangled Banner" playing in the background.

After casting votes for the best display, they returned to Lathen's pickup and drove the short distance to the Sea Crest Inn, where everyone gathered for an ice cream social to benefit local charities. Local bands presented the entertainment for the evening. Music ranged from country to rock and roll, and even a group that did a respectable job on the *1812 Overture* as the spectacular fireworks display exploded in the night sky.

They found the best view of the fireworks and Lathen stood, his arms wrapped around Pepper's waist, as she leaned into him. During a lull in the fireworks, someone tapped on his shoulder. He craned his neck to see Matt Redmond, the maintenance supervisor for the Sea Crest standing beside him.

"Sorry to bother you," Matt said sheepishly. "But the ice cream machine is froze up. We've tried all the usual fixes, nothing works. Any chance you could take a quick look at it? We still have people in line that bought tickets. It's for charity, you know."

Glancing around, Lathen sighed and whispered against Pepper's ear, "I'll be right back, don't move." He tightened his arms around her for a moment, then released. "Sure, Matt. Lead the way."

Matt looked apologetically at Pepper. "I won't

keep him long. Promise." Then he strode through the crowd with Lathen close behind him.

The ice cream machine was about ten yards from her. Pepper watched him lean toward it, then step behind the machine. She turned her attention back to the shower of colorful lights bursting in midair.

A cold shiver ran up her spine as goose bumps crept up her arms. Pepper reached down to untie her sweater from her waist, and someone grabbed her around the middle and covered her mouth with a hand. Excruciating pain exploded through her temples. Instinctively, she sank her front teeth into the palm of the hand covering her mouth. He cursed and shook his hand free. She screamed, stomped backward grinding her heel onto his foot, then whirled around, elbows out, and connected with the bridge of his nose. A split second later, she shoved her knee up hard into his groin. Blood spurting from his nostrils, hands cupping the family jewels, he yelled a stream of curses as he hit the ground and curled into a fetal possession. A big burly man pounced on the attacker, yanked his arms behind his back, and pressed a knee to his ass as the attacker writhed in pain.

The burly man glanced up at Pepper. "You all right?"

Bent over at the waist, forearms resting on her thighs, palms together, she gulped in air and said haltingly, "I'm okay. Thanks." As she battled to keep the magic furor at bay, her hands tingled. She shook them out and clasped them tight together. *Can't release magic among mortals.*

Pepper's scream brought Lathen bounding through the crowd, just as Pepper landed the final blow and

Sven, the big burly man, subdued Tom Green.

"What the fuck are you doing here? Restraining order mean nothing to you?" Lathen snarled, jabbing the toe of his boot in Tom's ribs. Leaning over, his arms enveloped Pepper calming her angry energy. "You okay?"

She nodded. A faint orange glow emanated from her palms slowly spreading to her fingers. A tiny spark snapped at the tip of her pinky. His large hands eased over hers to stop the progression of sparks. A vibration of feet pounding the ground had them both glancing up as a uniformed police officer sprinted toward them.

The officer flashed Sven a tight smile and leaned over to clasp the cuffs on Green. "I'll take it from here." Green fought against the handcuffs, and the officer yanked him to his feet by the arm. "You again? What happened?" the cop asked Tom, noticing that his eyes suddenly glazed over and he stilled. The officer shook Green, who slumped to the ground unconscious.

Brows knitted together, the officer bent down and put two fingers on Tom's neck. He pushed the button on his radio, just as sirens wailed, red and blue lights swept across the area, and an ambulance screeched to a stop. "I want everyone to stick around," he shouted. "Chief and another officer will be here shortly to take statements."

The officer stepped out of the way while the EMTs prepared Tom Green for transport and loaded him into the ambulance.

****

Lathen listened while Pepper gave her statement. He added what he saw and they were released. On the drive to the cabin, Pepper rested her head on his shoulder, his arm wrapped around her. Nostrils flared as he inhaled her citrus and wildflower scent mixed with the adrenaline that fueled her flight or fight response, now diminishing as she relaxed against him.

For the first time since that terrible day his SEAL team's mission had gone horribly wrong, the sensation of phasing had thrummed through his body as he shoved his way through the crowd to get to Pepper. He actually had to restrain the response. *Could I have phased? Was the overwhelming desire to protect Pepper so ingrained, his wolf's physical ability to shift kicked in?* He didn't have the answers tonight, but... Restless in the seat, he flexed his torso and leg muscles. A coiled ready-to-spring sensation felt familiar. A slight smile crossed his lips.

Pepper tilted her head up to peer at him. "Uncomfortable?" She tried to slide over giving him more room, but his arm tightened around her pulling her closer.

"Never felt better in my life," he said confidently. The predator awareness was back, and he reveled in it.

Her eyebrow arched in question as he felt her eyes linger on him and shot her a quick glance.

"So has trouble always followed you around?" he wanted to know.

"...Nooo, well, not exactly. At least not to this level. You're aware of the final incident in Salem, but the ten years prior was calm, except for deadbeat boyfriends."

"Which, I am guessing, is why you learned to defend yourself so well. Magic didn't do it for you?"

"Magic is hard to use in the presence of mortals. Besides, it's forbidden. You know that."

Lathen raised an eyebrow. "Someone forgot to tell Mr. Green or Mr. Bonchard. And what about those flying feathers the night Tom showed up at your place?"

She shook her head. "I still have no idea what happened that night. Must have been the cabin or land, some kind of protection enchantment that triggered it. Glad no one else saw. Need to talk to Ashling. Seemed the feathers took on a life of their own."

"Oh—Green saw, all right. He was babbling about all kinds of things as they took him away."

She shrugged. "Strange, if he's any type of magical creature, he'd know better than to say such things." Pepper looked up at him, her forehead creased. "Things just don't add up."

The truck slowed to a stop in front of the cabin. "We'll remember this Fourth of July for years to come," Lathen commented with a frown.

"It was a wonderful day, right up until the last few minutes. Even then, it could have been much worse."

"True." Lathen climbed out of the truck and walked around to Pepper's side, opening the door and holding his hand out. Ember trotted off the porch, tail wagging furiously as she greeted them.

Pepper leaned over and scratched the dog's ears. "Geesh, I can hear Kaylee's whistles from here."

Lathen ambled up the porch steps and settled into one of the chairs. Ember nudged his hand, and Lathen patted her head and rubbed down her back. "Feels good, huh, girl?"

****

"I'm going to let Kaylee out, so she can join us. Want to just sit here for a while, enjoy the peace and quiet while we can?"

"That's what I had in mind." He grabbed her hand as she passed and pulled her down for a long, intimate kiss, before releasing her.

The kiss sent her stomach into a wild spiral as her pulse raced. She cupped his chin in her hand and tilted up, her eyes met his. "You know—I could be in…"

Before he could say anything, she turned and hurried into the house and released Kaylee. Pepper watched her fly through the house and out the door, whistling loudly as she soared above the house, then settled on the porch railing. Pepper leaned against the kitchen door frame, hand to her heart. *What possessed me to almost say I loved him?* She knew it was true, but opening herself up like that, a recipe for disaster.

On top of that, tonight in the truck something had changed with Lathen. She sensed it first when he'd hovered over her, the calm he exuded while clasping her hands to keep them from sparking. Then while she was nestled into his shoulder, his warm, woodsy scent was different, infused with a light spicy tang and something else, something wild. Too tired to figure it out tonight, she padded into the kitchen and reached for a favorite bottle of wine. "Want something to drink?" she yelled, forgetting temporarily that, with his preternatural abilities, raising her voice wasn't necessary.

"Beer would be great. Thanks."

Pepper grabbed an ice cold beer from the fridge and poured herself a large glass of wine. Walking out onto the porch, she handed the bottle to him and eased down in the chair, took a sip of wine, and closed her eyes.

"Sore, huh? I bet that elbow aches like a bitch." He reached for her arm. "We got something special, you know that."

She nodded and leaned back in her chair while he rolled the cold beer bottle gently over her elbow between swigs. "Cold will keep the swelling down. Should ice it before going to bed."

"Thanks, I'll do that." She paused. "Want to spend the night?"

The corner of his mouth kicked up in a sexy as sin grin. "I thought you'd never ask."

Chapter Fourteen
Circle the Wagons Before All Hell Breaks Loose
—A Lesson in Self-Preservation

It was still dark when Pepper barely heard her cell phone ring. Sleepily, she felt on the night stand, nearly knocking her glass of water off, then rolled over to see a light flashing from her open backpack on the floor beside the bed. She swung the pack on the bed by the strap, dumping the contents all over the bed. She grabbed the phone, tapped the screen.

"Hello?"

Her dad's voice boomed through the phone. "Are you and Lathen all right?"

She wiped the sleep from one eye with her finger and blinked. "Yes. What's wrong?"

"Your mother insisted that something was terribly wrong last night. We tried your cell several times, but you didn't answer. She's on the phone now arranging for airline tickets. Klaren, don't confirm those, Pepper's on the line."

"There was a minor altercation at the Fourth of July celebration in town, but nothing serious," Pepper said.

Awake now, Lathen's brows shot nearly to his hairline. He reached for her phone whispering, "You tell them or I will."

She yanked the phone out of his reach and vaulted

out of bed before he could grab her. "Well, it's a bit more than that."

"I'm putting you on speaker so your mom can hear everything."

As she watched Lathen getting dressed, Pepper recounted the events of the evening, trying to brush over the ending. Nearly losing track of what she was saying a couple times as Lathen's movements around the room would have put an experienced pole dancer to shame. Finally, he zipped up his jeans and pulled his shirt on slowly.

"You encountered both Ben and Tom Green?" her mother asked pointedly. "And didn't think that was a big deal?"

"Have you talked to Ashling about this?" her father, Duncan, asked.

"No, you woke us—uhh—me up. Got in late last night and haven't had a chance to even process what happened, much less recount it for everyone," Pepper said irritably. "But after breakfast, that's next on the agenda. Okay?"

"No, it's not okay, you could have been killed," Klaren said. "We're coming out there."

"Mom, now wait a minute. You've already reserved a cabin for mid-August. That's only a few weeks away. I'll be fine until then. Green's in police custody, and I doubt he'll be getting out anytime soon."

"That's what you said last time. And Ben is still...well, I think we need to be there."

"Pops—Talk some..."

"No, Pep, I'm afraid I have to side with your mother this time. Besides, we'd like to be there to help you finish the wildlife center and visit with old friends.

Truth is—"

Klaren interrupted. "There are always a thousand little things for the grand opening itself. Like invitations, caterers, decorations, rental of tables and chairs—oh, all kinds of things. We could help with those. You know this is a big social event for a little town like Lobster Cove. That would leave you and Lathen free to take care of the day-to-day issues of making sure the facility is ready."

"Why do I get the feeling there's something you two aren't telling me?" Pepper asked pacing around the room.

"Well, we agree that Benjamin Bonchard is the common denominator and may have an ulterior motive, but beyond that, we're still investigating. Be careful." A light tapping could be heard over the phone. "I'm going to talk to the owner and see if we can get the cabin earlier."

"Dad, that really isn't…"

"We'll be in touch with our arrival date. And say good morning to Lathen for us. Love you." He chuckled, disconnecting the call.

Pepper sat down on the side of the bed. "Guess I better have a chat with Ashling."

Lathen eyed her appreciatively. "While I love what you're wearing, I'd prefer that you get dressed before hunting up ghosts." He snickered. "And I don't want to explain to the workers why the boss lady is wandering around naked."

She stuck her tongue out at him and seductively undulated out of reach. "You gave the workers several days off."

He lunged and pull her to him, running his hand up

and down her naked body, and groaned. "Tease. Now get dressed before I strip and take you to bed."

"What are you waiting for?" She nibbled along his jaw, teased the corner of his mouth with her tongue.

"I promised Matt I'd be over this morning to check on the ice cream machine. If I'd come early, he offered to buy us breakfast. Then we'll come back and visit Ashling. Or not…" He lifted her off the ground, and she wound her legs around his waist.

Her phone rang at the same time his buzzed on his hip. She waggled her finger. "Not meant to be—"

"Rain check." He growled, lowering her to the ground and taking his phone out of its clip. "Hello." He paused. "Yeah, we're on our way." Listening to Matt, Lathen motioned to Pepper, pointing to the truck and mouthed "Coming?" eyebrows raised.

She nodded, ending her discussion on the phone with the store manager regarding the flyers for the grand opening. Pepper wanted to get those in the works before her mom showed up and tried to take over. She meant well, but Pepper had her own way of doing things and sometimes mother and daughter didn't see eye to eye.

"The special paper I ordered for the flyers is in. The copy shop is going to run a proof to make sure the ink on the sculptured paper is the effect I want. Can we stop by there after breakfast and take a look?"

"Sure thing."

The ice cream machine was humming along when Lathen stopped to check on it. After reviewing the manual, he made a list of parts necessary to keep the machine running glitch free. On their way to breakfast, Lathen suggested strongly that Matt order the parts right away. "You know there is no way of telling how long the repair I rigged up will last. Give me a call when the parts arrive. I'll be happy to run over and install them if you don't trust your staff."

Matt grimaced. "It's not that, it's just with it being our busy season, I'm afraid he'd rush through it and…well…you know. I'll call when the parts arrive." He glanced at Pepper. "How you doing?"

"Great. Elbow's a bit sore, that's all."

"Your display in self-defense was the talk of the town. By the time it was chewed over by everyone, sounded like you were invincible. The weird part, Mr. Green didn't remember a thing when he came to at the hospital."

Pepper felt the heat rise in her cheeks. "Really? That is strange. I was just lucky." She shrugged.

After brunch, it was off to the copy shop. The flyer's textured surface made the muted ocean, blue sky, and mist settling over a spit of land pop. The artist's rendering of an osprey and other seabirds in the sky was perfect. A dark seal sunned on a rock, while slick gray bottlenose dolphins frolicked in the ocean alongside other marine mammals. Exactly what she had in mind. In the bottom left was a picture of Ember, the center's first rescue. Arched across the top in soft turquoise letters was Lobster Cove Wildlife Rescue and Rehabilitation Center. A small red lobster was depicted crawling up the curves of the capital C's. Printed below the title, large silver letters read "Grand Opening—Everyone Welcome!" Pleased with the flyer, she signed off on one thousand copies, paid for the paper, graciously accepted the free print offer, and left the shop.

Lathen and Pepper strolled hand in hand through the streets visiting with the shopkeepers, talking with friends, and stopping for a late afternoon snack at Bea's.

The sun was sinking low in the west by the time Lathen pulled into the driveway and got out of the truck. Nearly sprinting around the vehicle, he grabbed her hand and tugged her toward the pond. "Let's take a walk."

"Wait, I want to let Ember and Kaylee out." She slipped her hand from his grasp and held up her index finger. "I'll be right back." The minute she pushed the door open, Ember wiggled her way out, waited for an ear rub from Pepper, and rushed to Lathen, who knelt down and pushed the dog over, giving her a good belly rub.

A few seconds later, Kaylee flew out the door, banked, and headed straight for the beach. Pepper walked back to Lathen and looked down at the dog. "Traitor." Ember wiggled her tail and raised a paw. "Oh, too late for sucking up." She laughed and ruffled the dog's fur.

He entwined his fingers with hers and strode toward the pond. The closer they got, the more she felt a subtle hum of magic. Glancing toward the pond, her eyes widened and she sucked in a breath. "Oh wow." Sitting at an angle to the old bench was a new one, created out of gnarled wood sanded smooth, woven together to form a unique high back, curved arms, and smooth seat, supported by four stout but twisted legs. In old-fashioned lettering, the name McKay was meticulously carved on the arching back.

"Well, what do you think?" he asked nearly

dancing from one foot to the other like an overly excited kid.

Running her hand along the sleek wood, she said, "It's beautiful."

"I gathered pieces of wood scattered on the ground, sanded it so the branches fit together tongue-in-groove style. They were almost—cooperative," he said in a low hesitant voice.

"Of course, they're enchanted." Pepper settled into the bench caressing its arms. A sense of well-being enveloped her when she twisted and used her finger to trace the carved letters across the back. Beside her, she patted the seat inviting Lathen to join her. "This is beyond wonderful. Where did you find the time?"

"Funny thing, after I started gathering certain pieces, my pile grew overnight, and once I sanded each piece, it practically assembled itself. There's kind of a vibration to it. Sounds crazy, huh?"

"Not at all. I'm surprised you can feel it." She leaned her head against the back and sighed.

"I didn't at first, but it became stronger over time."

"Or you became more in tune with it." Narrowing her eyes at him, she asked, "What's going on with you?"

"Not sure, I'm working through some things. Let you know when I get it figured out."

A loud snort came from behind them. Ashling stepped out of the curling mist near the tree. "I'll tell you. The man is—let me rephrase that—The beast roams within, making him whole again."

Lathen scowled at her. "Must you be so dramatic? The beast never left me, just my ability…"

"Oh, hogwash. You couldn't get through the guilt."

As she spoke the fog crept along the ground as if trying to escape the broad sweep of the wind that grew stronger and shoved ominous dark clouds across the sky. "But now...hold that thought. I gotta go. Been doing a little research of my own, and I may have the answer to what's going on around here. Ever heard of the *minion curse*? Nasty bugger and a hundred times stronger than a normal spell."

"Ashling, we need to talk to you. Does Benjamin Bonchard meaning anything to you?"

"The nasty piece of work Klaren was dating when Duncan stole her heart? Let me get back to you." Leaving a curling mist in her wake, Ashling disappeared.

Pepper jumped to her feet. "Ashling, you come back here. What do you mean a nasty piece of work? Ashling!" Pepper threw her arms in the air and let them drop to her sides. "Now what am I supposed to do?" With a heavy sigh, she narrowed her eyes squinting at the last tendrils of mist winding around the tree. Kaylee stared at Pepper from her perch low on a branch.

Storm clouds dissipated in a shimmering silvery moonlight that bathed everything in an eerie white glow. Dark shadows danced from the trees through the swirling mist across the pond as the waves lapped at the shore. A bullfrog serenade was silenced momentarily by the beat of wings and screech of an owl on its nightly rounds searching for food. A light ocean breeze brought a chill to the evening. Ember came trotting back from the edge of the pond, circled twice, and settled on the ground beside Pepper.

Lathen patted the seat she'd vacated. "How about we relax and enjoy the full moon?"

She peered up at the moon and back to him. "Doesn't that stir something primal in you?"

With a half laugh, half snort, he wrapped his arm around her as she settled in beside him. "That's a myth. Werewolves phase whenever the mood strikes. Not because the lunar configuration dictates. Do witches in their pointy hats fly on their broomsticks across the night sky during the full moon?"

She harrumphed. "Of course not."

He shrugged. "Same thing. So when can we expect your parents?"

"They haven't called back, so just showing up is probably what they have planned." She frowned.

"Anything I should know before they get here?"

"Nope. Dad's easy going, Mom—well, she's a take-charge kind of person, but…"

"So should I plan on spending the nights at my place while they're here?"

"Nope, I like things the way they are. How about you?" she asked.

He leaned over and brushed his lips over hers. "Uh huh."

They slipped into a comfortable silence, her head cuddled on his shoulder and his cheek resting on top her head.

The blaring sound of his phone shattered the quiet. He yanked the phone from his belt and glared at the screen. "Not tonight, Matt." He turned the phone off.

Chapter Fifteen
Look What the Full Moon Dragged In

The next morning after feeding Ember, Lathen grabbed a piece of toast and orange juice. He turned on his phone, as he followed Pepper and Kaylee to the beach where the osprey hunted her own breakfast. Ember cut him off as he ambled down the path looking at the phone's screen. There were three more messages. He joined Pepper sitting on the retaining wall to the marine enclosure and played the first one. "Hey, Lathen, it's Matt. Nothing's broken, so don't worry. But there is a stranger asking for you around town. He didn't leave a name, only said he'd go back to your place and wait. I didn't want to send him out to Pepper's before talking to you first. Since my first encounter, Roark and Rob called me. He'd been to their places asking questions also. Call me when you get this message." Lathen listened to the other messages, which said the same thing, no name but a description of a big guy.

"What do you make of that?" Pepper asked casually, sliding her pack off her shoulders and dabbing at the extra butter on her toast with a paper towel. She took a swig of the orange juice she'd brought along, bit into the toast, and looked expectantly at him as she chewed.

Lathen scratched his head, popped the last bite of

toast in his mouth, and finished the orange juice in his glass. "I don't know. Not expecting anyone. I was rough on a couple of suppliers when the material didn't show up on time, but…they're too far away to make it personal."

He shrugged. "Guess I'll go back to my place and see if he's there."

Pepper picked up her backpack, slung it over her shoulder, and whistled for Kaylee. "I'm coming with you."

"No, you're not. I have no idea who this person is, and I'd rather find out without putting anyone in danger."

"You haven't told me much about yourself, your time in the special forces, or why you took up residence here, with no friends or family. If there are skeletons in your closet, it's time to call them out."

"Don't be ridiculous. It's probably nothing, and I'll be right back."

"I'm going." She flounced up the path. Stopped to close the aviary door after Kaylee flew in. Ember raced ahead and scrambled over the front to the back seat of the truck when Pepper opened the door.

Lathen shook his head at the wet paw prints and got into the truck. *Who the hell is looking for me?* On the way to his cottage, he ran through all the possibilities in his head. The man wasn't a local, or Matt and Roark would have known him. A tourist would have no reason to look him up. He'd spoken with Jim and Les, the other survivors of his SEAL team, a couple weeks ago. It wouldn't be either of them, though they were both big guys.

When he left the service, he made it abundantly

clear his hacking days for the government were over. Turning onto his street, he slowed, drove around the main house to his cottage, and saw a large black SUV, clearly a rental, parked in front with one occupant. Appeared to be male. He drove past and returned to the main road, pulled off to the side, and stopped. Tapping his fingers on the steering wheel, he glanced over to Pepper.

"What wrong?"

"Nothing, just thinking. You and Ember stay here. I gotta check out that car." He leaned over and pulled something from under his seat, tucked it in his waistband, and opened the door.

"We're going with you." Pepper reached for the door handle.

Lathen jumped out of the door, slid over the hood and slammed her door shut. "I'm a goddamned Navy SEAL. I've got this. Stay put."

Pepper's eyes rounded as she sucked in a breath and sat back in the seat, arms crossed over her chest. "Oookay."

Lathen walked across the road and followed the driveway around the main house until he had a clear view of the vehicle. A newspaper the man was reading obscured his face. Lathen relaxed a little. Hand behind his back on his weapon, he crept to the car and yanked open the door. The man dropped the paper, jerked toward him, then smiled.

"Kolby. What the hell are you doing here?" Lathen stood dropped his hand from his back and extended it. "Where's Hayley?"

"She's at the SeaCrest Inn. When I couldn't locate you, we decided to check in a couple hours ago. She wanted to stay and enjoy the view, take a walk while I looked for you again. The people in this town are sure tight-lipped."

"We protect our own. Is something wrong?"

"Nope. Time for you to come home."

"We discussed this. I'm not going back to Alaska. I've made a home here. I've met someone and found my peace with the world." *I hope.*

"Okay…then you should understand. Dad has found someone too, and after all these years, he's going to get married again. You need to be there. It's time you both set aside your differences. He was only doing what he thought best—after your injuries and you wouldn't even try to…Life is just too damn short. You, of all people, should know that."

The muscle in Lathen's jaw pulsed. His lips pressed together in a slight grimace. He paced to the front of the vehicle, changed direction midstride, and returned to his brother. "I'm glad he found someone. He deserves to have a life mate—and be happy. But I'm not going back to the pack lands. I can't."

"Why the hell not?"

"I'm committed to something here."

Kolby slammed the SUV's door. "You could fly up there, attend the wedding, and fly back over the course of a few days. Surely, you can find that kind of time for your family. Can't you?"

"Dad doesn't know you're here. Does he?" Lathen shot back.

"I told him I was going to find my brother and have a discussion with him."

"And I bet he told you good luck."

Kolby laughed. "Not in so many words, but close.

Are we going to stand out here and air our dirty laundry for all to hear, or are you going to invite me in?" He nodded to the curtain in the main house's window that was still moving, as if someone had been looking out and slipped to the side. "By the way, where's your truck?"

"His truck is parked out on the road," Pepper said coming around the corner of the house, Ember close at her side. "Where he left us."

"I thought..." Lathen's hands clenched and unclenched as he shoved them in his pockets.

"I got concerned when you didn't come right back. So Ember and I decided to check things out. When it didn't look confrontational, thought it was safe to surface." She grinned at Lathen and stepped toward the man, hand extended. "Pepper McKay, and this is Ember."

With a shit-eating grin spread across his face, Kolby grasped her hand and looked from his brother to her. "Pleased to meet you, Pepper. I'm Kolby Quartz, Lathen's brother."

Lathen took hold of Pepper's hand. "Could I have a word?"

"Sure, but only one."

He turned to his brother. "Excuse us for a minute."

Lathen grasped her elbow and walked around to the front of the main house. "What are you doing?" he hissed through his teeth. "This is family business."

"And...Oh—I'm not family. I get it." She wrenched her arm free. "Ember and I are going back to the truck." She held her hand out. "Keys, please. Your brother can drive you back to my place to get your truck and the rest of your stuff will be outside."

"Now hold on, Pepper. That's not what I meant."

"Keys." She continued to hold her hand out and tapped her foot impatiently.

Lathen shot an irritated glance at his brother, then returned his gaze to Pepper. Yanking his hand out of his pocket with the keys, he dangled them above her hand.

"Now just listen to me. I want to get things settled with my brother. Then I would like to bring him over to your place along with his wife this evening, we can go out to dinner at The Cliffside, and you can get to know them. You know how I feel about you. So please give me a bit of breathing room where my brother and family issues are concerned. I don't mind discussing the issues in front of you, but Kolby may not appreciate it."

She swiped at his hand and snatched the keys. "I'll think about it." Pepper paused, then called over her shoulder. "Nice to meet you, Kolby." With that she sashayed away toward the truck. Pepper called Ember who was still sitting at Lathen's feet. "Us girls gotta stick together." The dog gave him a longing look but trotted obediently after Pepper with one more look back.

"Wow, got a spirited one there. Is it serious?" Kolby asked raising one eyebrow.

"It's none of your business." Lathen looked at the genuine concern and interest in his brother's eyes. "But yes, she's the one."

"Have you told her?"

"That is really none of your business."

Kolby stared down at the ground, kicked the dirt with the toe of his boot. "I lost the brother I knew. Even though you came home a hero, you were never the same."

"Some hero. Eight good men died that day."

"I get it, survivor's guilt. Your injuries were more than physical, but man, you should have let us help. Not shut us out. When you became sullen, angry, and those violent outbursts…" Kolby shook his head. "Being deliberately hurtful to those who loved you, the behavior…Dad as pack leader had to take action. He didn't want to, but you wouldn't… Well, that's all in the past."

"Is it?" Lathen turned on his heel and marched toward his cottage. "Coming?" He unlocked the door and pushed it open. It smelled musty and unlived in. When he turned on the light, dust motes floated in the air, and he realized just how much Pepper's cabin had become home.

Kolby followed him in, looked around, and sniffed. "Don't spend much time here, huh? You really are serious about her." He shook his head again.

"If you don't quit shaking your head, it's going to fall off your shoulders. Then where will you be?" Lathen punched his brother in the arm and moved to open a couple windows.

Staring wide-eyed, mouth agape at first, then Kolby suddenly roared with laughter. "You haven't said that to me since we were kids."

"Yeah, I know. Been a struggle, but I've finally found my place, and we'll see about the rest. Now tell me about this woman Dad is going to marry." Lathen plopped down on a well-worn sofa. "I'd offer you a beer, but…all I have is water."

His brother settled into a chair across from Lathen. "That'll work. Dad was taking several people on a guided tour of Denali. She was among them. She's from a pack in Montana, near the Canadian border. Anyway, they hit it off and exchanged information when it was time for her to leave. They emailed and chatted over the Internet for a few months and Dad decided a long-distance relationship wouldn't work. Pushed her away, like he always did when a woman got too close as we were growing up. I told him what a dumbass he was being, he exploded, and stomped out."

"I bet you were on his shit list for a while." Lathen snickered, shoved up from the sofa, and ambled into the kitchen. He took a couple of glasses from the cupboard, pushed the ice dispenser on the fridge, and did a tiny fist pump when cubes hit the first glass. When he returned to the living room, he handed his brother a glass of ice water.

Kolby reached for the glass and snorted. "The funny thing is the next day, Amy—that's her name—showed up on his doorstep unannounced and took him to task. She doesn't take any of his shit." He took a long drink from the glass.

"I'd like to have seen that." Lathen took a sip from his glass and wondered what Pepper was doing right then. Probably had a tall glass of iced tea with lemon…his brother's voice grew louder as it always did when he knew Lathen wasn't paying attention.

"Me too," Kolby said continuing the story. "I heard what happened from Hayley, who met Amy at the nail salon later that week. Dad hadn't said a word to us. Anyway, Amy never went home, and the rest is history."

"So you decided it was time for me to patch up things with the old man," Lathen said narrowing his eyes.

"It's time to be a family again. I miss you. Dad misses you."

"I doubt that."

"You've changed. I could tell that the minute you yanked open the car door and didn't point the gun at me. Yeah, I saw the gun at your back."

Lathen shrugged. "I didn't have any idea who was looking for me. I had Pepper and Ember with me, didn't want to take any chances. You could have called first."

"If you'd given me your number. We had a heck of a time finding you. Actually, Hayley found you. She has a friend who does skip tracing for a PI in Anchorage. It didn't take her long to find you. And here we are." Kolby raised his arms shoulder high and spread them apart, then dropped them into his lap.

"How long are you going to stay?"

"Don't know. I've got six weeks leave I need to take or lose. Hayley just quit her job. And we've never been to Maine."

Raising a brow, Lathen stared at Kolby. "Why'd she quit her job? You guys aren't leaving Alaska?"

Skirting the subject, he said, "Now tell me about Pepper."

"Nope, what's going on, bro? Spill it."

Kolby below out a breath. "I'm not allowed... Aww, shit...Hayley's pregnant. You're going to be an uncle. But if you let on that I told you..."

"Congratulations. Didn't know you had it in you," Lathen said.

He grinned. "Well, really it was..."

"Oh, dude, don't go there. So that's the real reason you're here. Family man brings the stray back to the pack. You taking over from Dad?"

"It's not like that, and you know it," Kolby shot back.

Lathen took a deep breath and blew it out slowly. "Pepper is a certified wildlife rehabilitation specialist. She is building the Lobster Cove Wildlife Rescue and Rehab Center with my help. That's where I spend the majority of my time."

"You're kidding. Right? The tough Navy SEAL, hacker extraordinaire is…what?"

"Until I met Pepper, I was the town handyman. Made a damn good living too."

Kolby's eyebrows shot up to his hairline. "I don't believe it."

"Believe it. My time is my own, don't answer to anyone. I took the jobs that interested me, set my hours, rates, and met a lot of nice nonjudgmental people that I call friends now."

"I take it Kate at the diner isn't one of them?" Kolby smirked.

Lathen gave a half laugh. "Nope, she's not among them. What'd you do, canvas the whole town?"

"Just about." Kolby looked at his watch. "I should get back to the inn. Hayley is probably wondering what happened to me."

"Could you drop me off at Pepper's place first? Then go get Hayley and meet me back at the rescue in a couple hours. We'll go out to dinner. I'm buying."

"Hey, not going to turn that down. But aren't you in trouble with Pepper?"

"Yeah, but it'll be all right."

"She knows the family secret?"

"Yes."

Kolby drove up the driveway to Pepper's cabin and

parked behind Lathen's truck. As Lathen climbed out of the SUV, Kolby opened his door, stepped out, and looked around. "Nice place she has here. Great view. Hayley would love it. Looks like the construction is about finished. Still got a lot of work to do interior wise?"

Lathen closed his door and walked around to stand beside his brother, looking out toward the ocean. "We're getting there. Had back orders on equipment slow us down, but that's to be expected. Grand opening is planned for late September. We'll be ready."

Kolby shaded his eyes with his hand watching a few gulls swoop and dive over the water. "Dad's wedding is planned for the third Saturday in August. That's plenty of time to work around your schedule here and be back long before the grand opening." He glanced sideways at his brother.

"I don't think it's a good idea." Lathen ran his fingers through his hair and rubbed the back of his neck. So many thoughts and feelings bounced around in his head. His relationship with Pepper, his father, the pack, his brother, going home again, and phasing. He had to try and soon. Feeling a little overwhelmed, he sighed.

As if his brother knew what was going on in Lathen's head, Kolby grasped his brother by the shoulder and shook him a little. "Dad would love to meet Pepper. You know if you plan to make her your mate, you're going to have to introduce her to the pack. I take it she's not a Were? So why not do it all at once?"

"I don't have to do anything. No, she is not a Were. But I'll consider it and discuss the situation with

Pepper." He paced to the front of the truck. "I'd better go in and talk to her. See ya in a couple hours? Oh, nice casual dress is required at The Cliffside."

"Count on it." Kolby stepped back in the truck and waved as he circled the cabin and turned onto the road.

Walking up the log steps slowly, Lathen's hand was poised to knock on the door and changed his mind. Dropping his arm, he sidestepped to the red Adirondack chair and settled in. He had to figure it all out. His father getting married after all these years. She had to be pretty special, so he didn't have an issue in the remarriage. His mother died giving birth to him. His father raised the two of them by himself and ran the pack too. A daunting job for a mated werewolf let alone a widower with two young pups.

Looking back, he saw what a son of a bitch he'd been. It was no wonder his father told him to get it together or hit the road. He'd chosen to disappear, angry at the world and spoiling for a fight. That lifestyle wore on a man. Drifting around, eventually he found a place in Lobster Cove at high tourist season. His skills as a handyman were in strong demand. As fall set in, he kept getting calls for repairs and set up his business. Now, things were—Pepper made all the difference. If he hadn't messed things up beyond repair, she'd meet his pack. What to do about the wedding? He found that he actually wanted to go. But what if he was still considered the outcast? Too many what-ifs.

He pushed up from his chair, noticed Ember lying between the two chairs and Pepper sitting in the other one staring out across her property.

She didn't glance in his direction but said, "Had some thinking to do. Huh? Been out here quite a while."

He eased back into the chair, leaned over and scratched the dog's ear. "Yeah, it's been a day. And it's not done yet. I invited Kolby and his wife, Hayley, to meet us over here in a couple of hours."

Peppers eyebrows shot up as she spluttered, "You what?"

"Now just hold on," he said in a calm voice, feeling anything but. "Said we'd meet here, and I'd take everyone to dinner at The Cliffside. A nice place for you to get to know my brother and his wife. Maybe tomorrow we could show them around the place. Kolby was very interested. He works for the US Fish and Wildlife Service out of the Anchorage office. And his wife will love a tour."

"What made you think any of you would be welcome? Not to mention it's not ready for visitors."

Ignoring the last statement, he said, "Because you and I have something special. I'm not going to walk away from you or the center. I've made a lot of mistakes in my life, but I've learned from them." The breeze rippled his hair as he got up and walked to her. He bent down, hands resting on the chair arms at either side of her, and brushed his lips over hers lightly at first, then deepened the kiss as she returned the kiss hesitantly. Straightening, he ran the back of his hand over her cheek and down to her chin. All the while their gazes locked.

When he returned to the chair, he laid it all out for her, about his dad, the wedding, the circumstances under which he left, and why. He couldn't bring himself to mention the physical change he felt on the Fourth of July, not until he was sure, one way or the other.

She leaned back and blew out a breath. "You have had quite a day. So are we going to make time to attend the wedding?"

"I'm not sure. But you'll be the first to know. Fair enough?"

"But the grand opening and…gotta have time to work it all out."

"I know, but I got to sort things out. Trust me."

Tires crunching as a vehicle turned into the driveway caused Pepper and Lathen to turn in that direction.

"Too late to tell 'em they're not welcome," Lathen said, hoping he'd smoothed things over enough with Pepper, she'd be cordial.

"You're all welcome." She took Lathen's offered hand and stood. With his arm around her waist, they walked down the steps together and greeted their guests.

Hayley jumped out of the SUV and ran toward Lathen, wrapping her arms around his neck, nearly knocking him down. He released Pepper to steady himself and Hayley. "Hey there, girl, shouldn't you be a little more careful?" The minute the words left his lips, he froze and glanced at his brother.

A laugh bubbled up from Hayley's throat. "I knew he couldn't keep a secret, especially when I let him go off by himself looking for you." She took him by the shoulders and shoved him an arm's length away. "You are looking good. The sea air agrees with you. Or…" Hayley shifted her gaze to Pepper. "Your life has taken a huge turn for the better."

Lathen drew Pepper back to his side, arm around

her waist. "This is my girlfriend, Pepper McKay. She owns this property, and we are turning it into a wildlife rescue and rehab center."

"Nice to meet you." Then a spark of recognition flickered in Hayley's eyes. "Ooohhh...One of the maids at the inn said this property is steeped in legend. A McKay witch has lived here since the early 1800s. Aidan Duncan McKay and his wife, Dusty, were the first."

"Hayley," Kolby sputtered his eyes rounded in surprise. "What a thing to say. Sorry for my wife, pregnancy seems to have affected her good manners."

"What...what did I say? I was just talking with the staff about Lathen. He's really well liked around here. The maid said he was living with the McKay witch; she seems to be well respected too."

"Hayley!" Kolby said.

Lathen, looking uncomfortable, ignored his sister-in-law's comments and said, "Pepper, this is my brother, Kolby and his wife, Hayley." It didn't matter to him if they knew she was a witch, but he wasn't sure how Pepper wanted to handle it.

She exchanged a knowing look with Lathen, a twinkle of mischief lit her eyes as she turned a wide-eyed gaze in Hayley's direction. "What? A witch? Really? Is that what the townspeople think?" Unable to hold onto her composure any longer, she dissolved into a fit of giggles at Hayley and Kolby's horrified expressions.

Lathen smirked and kissed Pepper on the cheek as Ember trotted down the steps to see what all the commotion was about. Kaylee whistled loudly to be let out of the house, hanging by her talons from the screen door.

Pepper shrugged. "I guess they'd be right. But…I haven't turned anyone into a toad in"—she paused and put her index finger to her chin, tipping her head slightly—"at least a couple of weeks." She leaned over and gave Kolby and Hayley a hug. "Nice to meet you both." Taking a step back, she put her arm behind her and flicked her hand. The door to the cabin flew open with Kaylee soaring out and into the sky, making a large circle over the cabin before heading for the beach.

Lathen peered at Pepper. "You know she ripped the screen again."

Pepper grimaced, nodding.

"If you are going to continue to leave the door open between the cabin and aviary, I'm going to put stainless steel screen on all the doors and windows. Otherwise, we'll be replacing them constantly."

"You have a bird that big living in your house?" Hayley asked.

"She is an osprey and was my first rescue, years ago at a Salem wildlife sanctuary where I worked. We're inseparable." Pepper tilted her head in Ember's direction. "And Ember's my first rescue here at the Lobster Cove Wildlife Rescue and Rehabilitation Center."

"Is anyone hungry? 'Cause I'm starving," Lathen declared. "If you give us a minute to change, we can all head to The Cliffside.

"We need to wait for Kaylee to get dinner, anyway." Pepper let her thoughts flow to the bird. "She'll bring her catch back and eat it in the aviary. I don't want her alone outside at night."

"Come on in and have a seat. We'll only be a

minute." Pepper motioned them up the steps and into the cabin.

Chapter Sixteen
Departures, Arrivals, and Weddings
—Life Happens While You Try to Make Plans

Over the course of the next six weeks, Lathen and his brother reconnected. Kolby and Hayley helped out at Pepper's when they weren't exploring the great state of Maine and surrounding areas on their own. The center was on track, Pepper and Lathen were able to show Kolby and Hayley around, and all enjoyed a long weekend in Boston seeing the sights and enjoying the food. When Pepper's parents called, she told them that Lathen's brother and wife were visiting for an extended stay and that it would be much more convenient for all if they'd stay with the original schedule. As it turned out, Duncan and Klaren were unable to get into the cottage until the third week of August. Which was perfect, especially if Lathen decided they would attend his dad's wedding. She intended to nudge him in that direction every chance she got. Having never traveled to Alaska, she was excited at the prospect, but more than that, Lathen needed his family connection to finally put everything behind him. Maybe then they could build a life together.

Pepper spent quite a bit of time with Hayley, showing her the property, the plans for the center, talking wildlife and babies. Hayley told stories about Lathen's youth, touched on pack dynamics, his decision to join the military and become a Navy SEAL. The changes and difficulties he encountered when he returned home. It was nothing that Lathen hadn't already told her, but told from Hayley's prospective, Pepper gained insight into Lathen's psyche. Always watchful, she was thankful Ashling didn't make an appearance, and Tom Green seemed to have taken a vacation from harassing her. But she had a feeling things would change drastically once her parents arrived.

The night before Kolby and Hayley caught a plane to Alaska, Pepper fixed a dinner of meat ravioli, cheesy garlic bread, and homemade vanilla ice cream with chocolate chips. On a tray, Pepper brought out bowls of ice cream and spoons and set them down on a small table on the porch. Lathen followed with a pot of coffee for refills and Pepper's huge mug of tea.

Kolby scooped up a big spoon of ice cream and slid it into his mouth. After a few seconds he said, "This is great. It's been a long time since we've had homemade ice cream. Thanks." His brows furrowed together. "Lathen, how about the wedding? Can you and Pepper try to make it?"

In the ensuing silence, Hayley blew out a breath. "We've had a wonderful time with you and Pepper. We could have so much fun in Alaska showing Pepper the sights—together. Kolby could take a couple days off, and we could go visit Denali. Pepper, you'll love it."

"Nice sell, Hayley," Lathen grumbled. "I can't promise anything—but we'll give it our best shot."

Pepper jumped out of her seat and hugged Lathen, then Hayley and Kolby. "Everything will be fine, you'll see," she said confidently to Lathen. "Mom and Dad will be here to take care of Ember and Kaylee, not to mention…well, it will all work out." She spooned up some ice cream, popped it into her mouth, and savored its flavor. She'd made sure there were plenty of chocolate chips in her portion of ice cream.

"Then it's settled. Let us know your flight info and we'll pick you up at the airport."

"Okay." Lathen looked over at her. "Pepper, can you handle the reservations and contact Hayley with the info? You've got the schedule in your mind."

"Sure. I'll take care of it."

"Kolby, I have one stipulation. No one but the two of you will know we are coming. Fair enough?"

"I can live with that." His brow creased in confusion. "Can I ask why? Dad will be unhappy if you arrive the day before the wedding and he leaves on his honeymoon without getting to spend time with you. That's not right either. The pack will welcome you with open arms. You know that."

"You can ask, but I don't have an answer. Just a gut feeling that's the way it needs to be. I left behind some hard feelings and situations."

"If you're talking about Sofie, she is engaged to Walter now. A winter wedding is planned. Your history is water under the bridge, trust me," Kolby said wincing. "Well, maybe not exactly."

"Who's Sofie?" Pepper wanted to know.

Lathen stiffened and shot Kolby a dark look. "Way to go, bro." He huffed out a breath. "She was my girlfriend a long time ago. We split under less than ideal conditions when I left."

"You have a way with women, don't you?" Pepper chided, watching Lathen glower at his brother. If looks could kill, Hayley would be a widow on the spot.

"Except you. I know when it's right," Lathen said, his posture easing a bit. "We'll try to arrive a week before the wedding, but will have to return the day after. Isn't that about right, Pep?"

"Yes, that's the approximate time frame we can wiggle out of here without much problem." Pepper couldn't keep the smile from her face despite Sofie. Things were going so well, she hoped that trend continued when her parents arrived.

Well after midnight, Hayley yawned wide and leaned over against Kolby. "I think we better get going. Got an early flight to catch tomorrow, then it's back to the rat race for him." She poked her husband in the ribs.

He jumped and narrowed his eyes at her. "Yeah, you're right. It's been great. We look forward to seeing you in a couple of weeks." He pushed up from the porch swing and helped Hayley up.

"Night, drive careful," Pepper said as she hugged first Hayley then Kolby.

Lathen hugged his sister-in-law and reached out to grasp Kolby's hand and ended up grabbing his shoulder and giving him a bear hug. "I'm glad you came. Thanks."

Watching the headlights on the SUV disappear down the road, Pepper felt a tear slide down her cheek. She was going to miss them. Having dedicated most of her adult life to her profession, she'd never socialized much. The time spent with Hayley and Kolby showed her what she'd missed. An arm snaked around her waist as Lathen pulled her close. He wiped the tear away with his thumb and kissed her cheek, his scruffy butterscotch beard rough against her skin.

"We'll see them in a couple weeks. How about we go inside, take a look at the schedule, and make flight reservations? That way when we see them off tomorrow morning, you can hand them a copy of the itinerary. I'm sure Hayley will have every waking moment planned out for us."

"It will kinda be nice to have someone else in charge for a while. Don't you think?"

Lathen shook his head. "I'm not sure about that. But it will be fun to have some time away from here before it gets crazy with the grand opening and whatever tasks follow in the life of a rehab specialist."

Pepper went inside and turned the computer on. *Best to get the reservations confirmed before Lathen changes his mind.* She pulled up a site that was known for cheap rates and punched in Bar Harbor to Anchorage, AK. Several options flooded the screen, all between twelve- and seventeen-hour flights. *This would definitely require first class tickets.* She stretched her legs and wiggled in her chair at the thought. "Hey, Lathen, come in here. I need your input."

He ambled into the home office. "For what?"

She pointed to the screen. "See the flight times and the layovers? No matter which way, we are going to have a bad case of tired butt by the time we arrive at the hotel in Anchorage."

Looking over her shoulder, Lathen pointed to a flight. "This one is actually a bit longer, but it gives us a six-hour layover in Seattle. We could have dinner at the space needle, enjoy the view, and get back on the plane for a three-and-a-half-hour flight to Anchorage. That one also originates in Bar Harbor, through Boston, but goes to Seattle rather than Minneapolis and the last leg

182

of the trip is shorter. Both options arrive around one o'clock in the morning."

"Seattle it is. What about the hotel?"

"Let's just book one close to the airport. We'll be dead on our feet by the time we get the rental car and get out of the airport with our luggage." He pointed to a well-known upscale hotel on the screen. "See what's available there."

She clicked on the link, checked out the virtual tour of rooms, amenities, and available Wi-Fi. "We'll be there two nights?"

"Yep, then we gotta go on to Half Moon Valley, northeast of Talkeetna."

Pepper pulled up a map of Alaska and zoomed in. "I don't see any Half Moon Valley," she said, chewing on her bottom lip.

"You won't find it on any map." He chuckled and pointed to an area between Talkeetna and Cantwell. "Our pack lands are remote, and we discourage visitors. Just take my word on the location. I can find it."

"Okay, is it close to Denali then? I'd love to tour Denali National Park, spend a couple nights. Think that could be arranged?"

"I wouldn't be surprised. But we'll have to wait until we get there." Lathen straightened and yawned. "It's an early morning if you want to see my brother and sister off. I suggest we call it a night."

****

An orange ribbon formed in the eastern sky as Lathen pulled into the inn's parking lot. He got out, joined Pepper on her side of the truck, and silently closed the truck doors. Kolby and Hayley were stuffing their bags in the back of the SUV when Lathen clamped a hand on Kolby's shoulder.

Kolby yelped.

Lathen let loose a hearty laugh. "Surprise." Then slapped a hand over his mouth as Pepper shushed him.

Kolby swung around and punched him in the shoulder. "Don't you know better than to sneak up on people, especially at this god-awful time of the morning?"

"Hey, sneaking up on people used to be my mission, regardless of the time. Wanted to make sure I wasn't out of practice." He snickered quietly.

Pepper handed Hayley a copy of the airline reservations. "We managed to eke out ten days for the trip."

"Wonderful, I'll get reservations at Denali National Park. Good thing Dad took a couple weeks off before the wedding, or we'd have a heck of a time keeping your secret. He's a guide at Denali."

Kolby shook his head. "Better wait until they arrive. No way a reservation under the name Quartz won't attract attention."

"Maybe use my maiden name?" Hayley mused.

"Maybe, but…"

Pepper's eyes rounded. "Wow, no one mentioned what he did for a living."

"Yeah, you are going to fit right in with this family," Hayley said smugly.

"Let's not get ahead of ourselves. We're still taking it one day at a time," Pepper said.

"The man is smitten with you. And you…well hiding your feelings is not your strong suit." Hayley winked and gave her a hug. "Mark my words. See you soon." Hayley climbed into the SUV. Pepper closed the door and stepped back. Lathen joined her after saying his goodbyes. The SUV's engine roared to life, and Kolby rolled his window down and waved as he drove out of the parking lot.

"Guess we better get back home. Mom and Dad are due here day after tomorrow," Pepper said with a sigh. "I hope Mom's got the situation with Green and Bonchard figured out."

"Strange we've not seen either of them since the Fourth, and I'm glad. Would have hated to explain that to my brother on top of everything else." He opened the truck door for Pepper, lifting her up by the waist and settling her into the seat.

"You know I am perfectly able to get into the truck by myself."

He fastened the seat belt around her. "I know, but then I wouldn't have an excuse to do this." He took her chin in his hand and tipped it up. His lips pressed against hers, then gently covered her mouth.

His moist, firm mouth demanded a response, and she slid into the kiss with a moan, wrapping her arms around his neck, fingers sliding into his hair. Heat swirled in the pit of her stomach.

Raising his mouth from hers, he gazed into her eyes and murmured, "This is not getting our work done." He chuckled when her eyes went wide.

"You're such a tease." She huffed out and reclaimed his lips until…someone cleared his throat behind them.

"We do still have a few rooms available. Your brother just checked out of a nice suite," Matt said a wide grin spreading across his face.

Slowly, Lathen straightened and turned to meet

Matt's gaze. Pepper stifled a giggle at Lathen's predatory stance.

"Out here to harass us, or was there something you needed?"

"When I saw your truck, I originally wanted to catch you before you left, to see if we could get on your schedule. But finding you in such a…well, this was just too much fun to pass up."

"And my schedule could be filled for the next eight months."

"Okay, okay. Seriously, we need another computer terminal wired as soon as you could get to it. I know we should get used to calling someone else, but when you're finished with the job, it always works. The other guys…not so much." Matt shrugged.

"I've got a lot on my plate right now. Pepper's par…uh…mom is arriving the end of the week, and we'll be out of town for a couple of weeks immediately after that." Lathen blew out a breath and braced his hand on Pepper's knee.

"We have all the materials. Just need you to install them," Matt pleaded.

"If you want to drive me home and make sure everyone is where you want them. This afternoon would be the best opportunity, given the schedule we worked out last night," Pepper said helpfully.

Lathen scrubbed his hand over his face. "Okay. This time, but it's going to cost you. And Matt, you gotta give the others a chance—experience will make them more efficient. They're good guys."

"Thanks. I really appreciate it. I'll even comp you a room."

"Hey, watch it, or we might just take you up on

that offer sometime." Lathen smirked, as he climbed into the truck.

The minute Lathen parked the truck, Pepper rushed to let Ember and Kayley out to enjoy the partly cloudy, misty day. Ember followed her out to the center's office/lab as she set up files and ordered last minute supplies. The thought of meeting his pack, not to mention his father, had her stomach in knots, but she wasn't about to let him know. *What if they don't like me or don't want him involved with a witch?* The sound of the file drawer shutting with such force caught her off guard. Anger peaked without any cause but her internalizing imagined scenarios. She blew out a breath and straightened as the door swung open.

Whistling, he stepped inside and hesitated for a beat. "Everything is set up for today, and we're in good shape for the rest of the week. I'm headed back to the inn. Need anything on my way back? Shouldn't take more than three or four hours, including testing."

She shook her head, chewing her lip. "Nope. Any preference for dinner?"

He crossed the room, cupped his hand under her chin, and tilted her face toward him until their eyes met. "What's wrong? If you need me here, I'll…"

"No—no—nothing like that. You go ahead. I'm fine."

He knelt down. "You're not fine, and I'm not leaving until you tell me what's going on."

"Nothing. Might be a bit overwhelmed with everything, but as soon as it's organized, I'll be fine."

"Still waiting for the other shoe to drop, huh? We don't have to go to Alaska."

"Yes, we do. That's the least of my worries." She

lied. "It's been way too quiet around here. Which makes me think he's waiting for Mom to arrive."

"If that's the case, he's not very smart. Think about it. Would you rather battle one witch or take your chances with three or more? We'll be ready for him. So don't worry." He brushed his lips gently over hers. "Until tonight." He released her chin and strolled toward the door, pushed it open then turned. "Better? You know my pack will love you. Now me...that's another story."

The corner of her mouth turned up in a weak smile. "Of course they will. What's not to love," she said with more confidence than she felt.

His brow winged up as he stepped out the door. "I'll pick up meat pies for dinner." The screen door banged closed.

"Sounds good. See ya soon." Pepper rose from her chair and walked to the door, watching him get in the truck. Returning to her desk, she picked up her phone. "Come on, Ember. Let's go sit by the pond." She heard Kaylee's whistles in the distance.

The bench Lathen made was her favorite. After easing into the seat, she pulled out her phone, opened her favorites list, and tapped Mom and Dad. Klaren picked up on the first ring.

"Hi, Pep, your company leave?"

"Yep. All went well, no sign of Green or Ben. Even Ashling made herself scarce. Lathen and I will be flying to Alaska next week. I'll give you a copy of our itinerary when you get here. Also, wanted to check on your arrival time and flight number."

"Eight a.m., Friday, on flight 2840. But your father and I have decided to rent a car, so no need to pick up us. We'll holler when we arrive in Lobster Cove and get settled in the cottage. Now why did you really call?" her mom asked in a cheerful voice.

"How'd you know? Never mind. I'd like you to take care of something for me while we are in Alaska."

After she had finished talking with her mom, Pepper relaxed against the bench, tucking the phone in her pocket and closed her eyes.

"Glad my timing fit into your plans." A voice rustled over the water lapping at the shore.

"Hello, Ashling." Pepper sighed and opened her eyes. "Thanks for…"

"Wouldn't have bothered your guests, had I been here, but as it turns out, I was off doing some research and investigations on my own. It appears that weasel Bonchard has been calling up spirits related to McKay's by blood or marriage. Looking for a maleficent spirit to join forces with, so he could gain control over the McKay magic. Mysteriously, all those efforts ceased when you arrived."

"We have already deduced something like that was happening. Thanks for confirming it."

"Wait, I'm not finished. After that, he made contact with evil spirits and started messing with black magic curses."

Pepper leaned forward. "He's planning to use that to what end? Curse me? He's not going to scare me off this property. We'll beat him at his own game." Pepper stood and paced down to the pond and back.

"That would be difficult. I think it's time you and your parents call in my coven. I know you've never joined a coven, but my sisters would be willing to help you. Ravyn is high priestess now of the coven. Might want to contact her. When are your parents due here?" Ashling asked.

"Friday morning. Lathen and I fly out to Alaska the following Thursday. We'll be gone ten days or so unless it's imperative I stay here."

"No, you need to go with Lathen. He needs to set things right, and you are the catalyst." Her aunt paced with her leaving a trail of mist along the ground. "Call Colleen. Tell her we are going to need a coven of thirteen, which will include her. Time frame unknown at this point."

"And when Mom and Dad arrive?"

"You act normal; we don't want to tip anyone off. It may work to our advantage your leaving for a few days. Duncan and Klaren can connect with the land's power, making a stronger magic force to be reckoned with when the time comes." Ashling circled the tree twice.

Pepper stopped and watched Ashling with a bemused look on her face "I wish I knew what the hell you are talking about."

"I'll spell it all out for you once your parents get here and see if they agree with my conclusions. I mean no disrespect, but in recent years, you've disengaged from your magic until your life or the lives you cared about were in danger. That behavior is unacceptable. You're a powerful witch. Now, act like it." Ashling raised her arm and pointed her finger at Pepper, then disappeared with a pop. Mist scattered through the air, finally settling to the ground.

Kaylee whistled loudly, careened around the tree, her wings back beating in an effort to slow and land on the bench beside Pepper. "Some good you are. She's gone." The bird looked around, ruffled her feathers, and lifted off gracefully to perch in Ashling's tree. As if to say, I knew that.

"Come on, girls. Time to get back, close the office, and head for the cabin. Lathen should be back soon and we need to fill him in over dinner."

****

The rest of the week was uneventful. Contractors finished their tasks, most of the back ordered material arrived, and Lathen was happy as a clam.

Thursday night Pepper fell into bed and was asleep before her head hit the pillow. When she rolled over, a sliver of moonlight shone through the window. His side of the bed was empty. She rubbed the sleep from her eyes, pulled on a plush white terrycloth robe, and slipped her feet into otter slippers her parents had sent to her from their visit to the Monterey Bay Aquarium.

Padding downstairs, she found Ember stretched out across the closed door, no sign of Lathen. When she stepped outside on the porch, he was walking up the path, dressed in only his black silk boxers, breath curling around his head in the crisp night air. She breathed a sigh of relief and tilted her head to the side, her brow raised in question as he approached.

"I couldn't sleep. Clear nights are such a rarity around here, I went for a walk." Hesitating at the base of the stairs, he rolled his shoulders and stretched from side to side one arm over his head then the other. "Feel better now." He bounded up the stairs, encircled an arm around her waist, and pulled her close, planting a smacking kiss on her lips. "Miss me?"

"It would have been nice if you'd told me. All the weird things happening around here—I was concerned."

"Sorry to have worried you. But you were so sound asleep, I didn't want to wake you." He smirked. "I told Ember where I was going."

Hand on hips, Pepper grumbled, "Well…she failed to relay the message." She paused for a second, her forehead creased. "Why didn't you take her with you?"

Silent for a couple beats, he shrugged. "Who would have been here to protect you?"

She huffed out a breath and slipped inside the cabin. "You're incorrigible."

He followed her inside, closed the door with his bare foot, and followed her up the stairs with Ember trotting behind them.

By the time Pepper and Lathen dragged themselves out of bed, the sun had cleared the horizon and workers were going about the daily activities.

Pepper yawned wide and stretched her arms above her head, watching Lathen shuffle into the bathroom. "Dad and Mom should be here before noon."

Lathen stopped just inside the door, turned toward her, and leaned his shoulder against the frame. "Should we plan on taking them out to dinner or fixing something here?"

"Probably something here, barbecue? Steak, potatoes, corn on the cob? I've time to make double fudge chocolate cupcakes with buttercream frosting."

"Ohh—my favorite. Sounds great." He flipped on the shower, raised an eyebrow. "Want to join me?"

"Sure. But no messing around. We don't have time," Pepper said emphatically. Swinging her feet to the floor, she stood, slipped out of her red tank top and matching silk panties. She padded into the bathroom, wound her arms around his neck, and slithered against him.

"Geez, talk about mixed messages." He pulled her hard against him and unceremoniously turned his body so she was under the warm shower spray.

"What are you doing?" She sputtered, twisting out of the spray and pulling him into the water.

"Making sure there is no messing around." A mischievous smile turned up the corners of his lips, as he sidled up behind her. He caressed his soapy hands over her firm breasts while rivulets of water ran down his back and steam filled the air.

She slapped at his hands playfully and spun in his arms. "My turn."

"Okay, but no messing around." He chuckled, nuzzling her neck while her hands lathered his chest and slipped lower. Something primitive and raw stabbed through him as he nearly sank his teeth into her shoulder to mark her as his.

The strange sensation rolled through her, as if they were connected, but started to fade when he gently pulled away laving the inflamed area with his tongue.

"What just happened?"

"Sorry, I got carried away," he murmured apologetically.

She didn't know what to say, or what to do with the elated erotic feelings crashing through her body, unsure whether they belonged to her or him or both.

****

The cell phone vibrated across the desk. She grabbed it, looked at the screen, and held up an index finger to the deliveryman standing in front of her. "I need to take this. I'll only be a minute." She rounded the desk, phone to her ear, and slit the tape on the two boxes sitting on the ground. The delivery man pointed to his watch impatiently. Pepper nodded.

"Hi, Mom. You arrived safely at the cottage?"

"Sure did."

"Great. Let me call you back. I need to check a delivery that just arrived."

"All right. Talk to you soon."

Pepper disconnected the call, ripped open the boxes, and checked them against the manifest and her order list. "Everything is here. Sorry for the delay, but last time I was shorted several items. It turned out a box had been left on the truck by mistake."

The man shoved his clipboard in front of her and pointed to the line marked with a red X. She signed off on the shipment and returned his clipboard. "Thank you and have a nice day."

He grumbled something about running late and shoved the screen door open with his boot, letting it slam shut.

She picked up the phone, hit redial, and waited.

"Hi, Pep. Get the delivery taken care of?"

"Yep, the alternate drivers are so rude, but I had to check the shipment. Enough about me. How was your flight?"

"Wonderful. Got to the rental counter and was able to upgrade the car to an SUV, to fit all our luggage. The drive here was a pleasant surprise. I don't remember ever seeing such a clear sky, but looks like the fog will be rolling in later this afternoon."

"How about you and Dad come over whenever you're ready. We'll show you around the place before the weather moves in, and Lathen will grill up steaks."

"Sound yummy. We'll be there in about thirty minutes."

"Perfect." Pushing up from the desk, she walked outside, glancing around for Lathen. When she caught a glimpse of his light blue denim shirt as he disappeared around the corner of the aviary building, she dashed across to the newly constructed path to meet up with him. It sure was easier to negotiate the path than stumble over the rocky ground, which was the reason that Lathen had suggested a pathway system between the buildings. At first Pepper was afraid that it would look too commercial. Now the walkways were complete, they appeared natural and were much more serviceable. *A nice touch.*

When she reached the side of the building, she spotted Lathen with his back to her, holding a set of plans and talking with a group of workers. She eased up to him and caressed his shoulder lightly, trying not to startle him.

He turned his head lazily toward her. "Good afternoon—beautiful. What can I do for you?" Turning back to the group, he said, "Give me a minute, guys." Lathen took her arm and walked a few yard away. "No use giving them more to chew over than usual."

Sunlight glistened off his windblown hair and the sweat at his brow. She liked the look. "Mom and Dad are coming over shortly. Can you take a break and walk the property with us?"

"Sure thing. I need to finish reviewing the pump installation with the guys, but after that, I'm yours."

She watched him walk back toward the guys, enjoying the way his muscles flexed under his shirt and the way his jeans fit his great ass. The guys shot him knowing looks, then winked at her. Their actions were all in good fun, so she didn't mind the innuendos. Besides, he was sleeping with the boss.

Hands raised up in surrender, he said, "Hey, when you got it, you got it." He grinned. "Let's get back to work."

The rumble of an engine and crunch of tires on gravel meant her parents were early. She sprinted to the cabin in time to see them getting out of the vehicle and looking around. Ember stood at alert on the porch as Kaylee soared overhead.

"Glad you made it," she said wrapping an arm around each of them. "Well, what do you think?"

"I like what you've done with the place." Her father said kissing her cheek. "I don't remember the cabin being this big."

"It wasn't. There's Kaylee's aviary addition on one side and the exercise room on the other, which isn't quite finished." She winked at her mom.

Klaren hugged her daughter, then held her by the shoulders at arm's length. "You look wonderful. This place agrees with you."

"Better you than me." Her father drew in a deep breath as the breeze brought with it the scent of brine. "Though I always loved the ambiance of the sea."

"Where's your young man?" Klaren wanted to know. She shaded her eyes with her hand and pointed with the other. "Is that him walking toward us?"

"Yes."

"Wow, nice physique. No wonder you keep him around."

"Momm," Pepper said drawing out the word in exasperation.

Duncan poked his wife in the ribs as his arm wrapped around her. "Down, woman," he said with a chuckle.

"Just because I'm on a diet doesn't mean I can't look at the menu." She cackled, fanning herself, then schooled her features into a pleasant expression when Lathen approached.

"Mom, Dad, this is Lathen."

He grasped Duncan's extended hand. "Nice to meet you, sir."

"It's Duncan, son. But the pleasure is ours." He glanced at his wife and back to Lathen. "You've put quite a bit of work into this project. Nice job."

"Lathen, my mom, Klaren," Pepper said, her lips twitching to suppress a giggle as her mother wrapped him in a warm hug.

"Pepper's told me a lot about you." He returned the hug.

"Only good things, I hope," Klaren said with a smile. "Nice to finally meet you, Lathen."

"How about a tour of the place. We've spent way too much time sitting," Duncan said, stretching his legs and glanced at his wife who nodded emphatically.

"Certainly. Follow me," Lathen said, entwining his fingers through Pepper's. "How about we start with the facilities and wind up back here at the cabin, where I believe Pepper's got cookies and lemonade prepared."

"Sounds great."

Lathen led the way to the kennels and lab/office buildings, then showed them around the marine habitat/clinic and holding area, past the pond, and finally through the wild bird aviary.

As they exited the aviary, Pepper suggested, "Why

don't you two relax by the pond while Lathen and I get the drinks and cookies."

Her father cleared his throat. "Looking to turn us over to Ashling?" he inquired, a grin playing at the corners of his mouth.

"Nope, just going to get it out of the way if she is inclined. Tonight, we have a great dinner planned of grilled steaks, baked potatoes, corn on the cob, and fresh baked rolls with Mom's favorite fruity red wine. You and Lathen can get acquainted, and we can discuss recent events without interruption, hopefully." Pepper eyed the tree beside the pond and snickered. "And our trip to Alaska. You are planning to stay on the property with Ember and Kaylee while we're gone? The guest room is ready."

"Of course, dear," her mother said. "If you don't mind, I could use some of that wine rather than lemonade if we are expected to deal with Ashling."

"Wonderful idea." Her father nodded.

When Pepper returned with the wine, Ashling hadn't made an appearance. Lathen set up a folding table and placed the plate of cookies, along with cheese and crackers, in the center. Pepper poured the wine into glasses. Her dad picked a glass and swirled the red liquid around and handed his wife a glass. She sniffed, sipped, and smiled.

"Very nice," Klaren said

When Pepper and Lathen reached for their glasses, Duncan raised his glass in a toast. "Sláinte."

Lathen's forehead creased as he raised his glass.

"It's an old Gaelic toast, means health," Pepper whispered to him, then raised her glass. "Sláinte."

A tendril of mist wound its way down the tree.

"Well, if you're done with the wine tasting, can we get down to business?" The amused voice of Ashling intervened.

Chapter Seventeen
North to Alaska—

After an early morning flight from Bar Harbor to Boston, the plane took off again and touched down at Seattle airport just before five o'clock in the evening. Lathen took their carry-on backpacks from the overhead compartments and walked stiffly toward the door.

"Two legs of the journey complete. We'll grab a cab or the shuttle and have them take us to the Space Needle. We can check on reservations for the SkyCity Restaurant on top the needle, then walk around the area for a bit."

"Sounds great." Pepper ambled after him.

The timing was perfect. They caught a shuttle to the Space Needle, but there was a forty-five-minute waiting list at the Space Needle's SkyCity. Lathen made a reservation, then picked up a tourist map of the area to peruse.

Pepper glanced at her watch. "This should work out perfectly. Explore the area, come back and eat, play tourist a bit more, then catch a cab back to the airport."

"Sounds good. But we need to be back at the airport a couple hours before our flight, just to be on the safe side. Let's start at the Space Needle's observation deck. We only have about thirty minutes left before dinner."

"Looks like the line is shorter to the observation deck than it was when we arrived. Let's go." She grabbed his hand and tugged him toward the elevators.

While they were waiting in line, Lathen took the tourist map out of his pocket and circled a few attractions, then handed the paper to Pepper.

She took the map and studied it, leaning against the wall. "After dinner, we'll check out Pike Place Market, then the sculptured gardens, and maybe a walk along the waterfront?"

When Pepper stepped off the elevator onto the observation deck, which towered over 500 feet above the surrounding area, she sucked in a breath. "This is fantastic." She rushed over to the edge. "You can see forever."

"We're lucky, it's a clear day. Often there's drizzle and the area is shrouded in fog or mist. Kinda like Lobster Cove." He looked at his watch, then followed Pepper around the observation deck. She took pictures, handed her camera to an older man and asked him to take their picture, and several times she simply stood mesmerized by the view.

Five minutes before their reservation time, he wrapped his arm around her waist and guided her toward the restaurant.

"This was such a wonderful idea. Thank you," she murmured, leaning back against him.

Once seated, he noticed she had a hard time keeping her eyes open. They'd been up before dawn. He wanted to make sure everything was in place so things ran smoothly in his absence. Pepper explained Kaylee's routine as well as Ember's to her mother and emphasized that neither one was allowed outside after dark. Emergency phone numbers were given to the necessary people including her parents. And now their long day had caught up with them.

It seemed like they had just ordered when the waiter set a plate of wild king salmon in front of Lathen and slid Mary's ranch chicken in front of Pepper. He considered ordering a glass of their favorite wine, but reconsidered. Staying awake was already a problem.

After several bites, Pepper dabbed at her mouth with a napkin. "Mmmm, this chicken melts in your mouth."

"The salmon is excellent," he said around the final bite of salmon. "Better get going, if we want to get to everything before heading back to the airport." He paid the check and touched her lower back guiding her toward the exit. His hand slipped lower as she stood in front of him at the elevators. The ridge beneath his zipper pushed against the cloth as he shifted to release the tight feeling and slipped his hand to her waist. Leaning over, his lips touching to her ear, he said, "You're driving me crazy and you know it. I don't buy that innocent act."

She turned her head back toward him. "I have no idea what you are talking about. I'm dead tired and suspect you are too." But she licked her lips slowly before twisting to face forward again as the elevator doors opened.

He sighed and followed her into the elevator, making sure she stood in front of him.

Watching Pepper's eyes go wide at the sculptured gardens made him grin. Her delighted laugh was contagious when the fishmongers at Pike Place Fish Market threw fish, played games, and performed with customer's purchases. After all that, the trip back to the airport was quiet and uneventful.

He even relaxed a little until they walked into the airport and their flight began boarding. The closer he got to Anchorage, the tighter the knot in his stomach clenched. One bright point of this whole trip was seeing his brother and Hayley again for a couple of days. Until Kolby showed up, Lathen hadn't realized how much he missed his brother.

On that rage-filled night so long ago, he'd left the valley and swore never to return. Yet, here he was and with a woman he hoped would someday become his mate. *What the hell am I doing? Second-guessing events yet to happen?* He shook his head to clear his thoughts as Pepper squeezed his shoulder.

"It's going to be fine, I can feel it." She smiled reassuringly. "They're boarding first class. You ready to sit for another few hours?"

"Hell no, but I don't see any choice. My pacing would make the staff and other passengers nervous. You?"

"Not really, but I am so looking forward to spending time with Hayley. According to her emails, she has every second of our days in Anchorage planned. We do get to sleep until noon tomorrow."

"That was generous of her. Considering we don't even arrive until one o'clock in the morning," he grumped, plodding toward the gate, boarding pass in hand.

On the plane, Lathen settled into his chair, thankful for the larger seats giving him more shoulder and leg room. Leaning back, he looked over at Pepper, who was already asleep. Her luscious lips formed a pout, almost like she was displeased with someone in her dreams. He smiled and glanced at his watch. Only four more hours and they'd arrive in Anchorage, where the whirlwind would begin.

****

The plane touched down, and Lathen stared out the window. The landscape looked familiar, but he was surprised to find the anger he'd carried the last time he boarded a plane here gone, replaced by confidence in who he was and uncertainty of how he was going to handle the upcoming days. Would his father still see the man he was back then? Would he be welcome or still treated like an outsider? Which, if he was honest with himself, was of his own doing. Ignoring his roiling stomach, he took a deep breath and laid his hand on Pepper's arm, gently shaking her awake.

"We're here. Let's gather our things and see how much of our luggage the airline has lost." He grinned as she blinked up at him.

She jerked upright. "Oh no. What if they lost the dress I bought for the wedding? It's the only one I have."

A brow lifted, he turned to her. "Really? Only one?" He shrugged. "Then you and Hayley will have to go shopping and replace it."

She pushed up from the chair and glared at him. "Yes. There isn't much call for dresses when you work wildlife rehab and rescue."

"I see your point. But I like the way those jeans fit your tight ass anyway," he said, fending off her slap at his arm.

Once Lathen had secured their backpacks from under their seats, they walked up the aisle and out the door to find baggage claim. When the couple rounded the corner to the conveyor piled high with suitcases, a red-faced man stood chucking black suitcases onto the floor.

"They lost it. I knew they would. Happens every time," he shouted as a uniformed service rep strode across the floor to his side.

"Oh, look here," Lathen said grabbing three pieces of blue soft-sided luggage and matching garment bag, setting them on the floor. "It's all here."

The man gave Lathen a eat-shit-and-die look as the service rep, talking in a conciliatory voice, tugged the irate man toward a set of offices.

Lathen picked up the luggage, Pepper took the garment bag, and they rushed to the rental counter. One drowsy attendant greeted them. Pepper handed him the paperwork she'd printed off the computer and requested an upgrade to an SUV at no charge, a special deal she'd found while booking their flights. She signed the necessary paperwork and tossed the keys to Lathen.

"We're all set. Beddy-bye, here I come."

The next morning, Lathen's phone vibrated itself off the edge of the night table, making a soft thud as it hit the carpeted floor.

"Aren't you going to answer that?" she asked in a sleepy voice.

"No," came a muffled voice from under the pillow. "It's Hayley and I'm not ready to get up." He lifted one corner of the pillow and peeked at Pepper. "Are you?"

"I am now." She sat up and rubbed her eyes with her fists.

Lathen groaned and sat up swinging his feet to the floor, snatched at the offending device. By that time, it had quit ringing. He checked the caller ID. "Told you."

"Call her back. See if she wants to meet us for breakfast in about—an hour?"

"Better make that lunch, it's nearly noon. I'll just text her." Getting to his feet, he sent a quick text off to Hayley, then padded toward the bathroom. "I'm going to jump in the shower." He waggled his eyebrows. "Want to join me?"

"Is that all you think about?" She chuckled. "Oh, yes, you're male, that is all you think about. I'll join you, but that will screw up our time frame to meet your sister-in-law."

"Literally." He smirked. "So be it." His text alert went off, and he checked the screen. "Kolby and Hayley will meet us for lunch in an hour at a Mexican restaurant on Old Seaward Highway, just down the street from Kolby's work. Guess we only have time for a quickie."

"Or not." She flipped the shower knob and stepped into the spray, splashing water on him.

****

"Boy, I can't believe our luck," Lathen said, holding the door for Pepper as they walked out of the bright sunshine into the restaurant. "Sunny and in the seventies in Washington. We get here and it's sixty-five, not a cloud in the sky."

"Some things are meant to be." She smiled back at him.

Hayley stood and waved from a table near the back. A strong hand gripped Lathen's shoulder from behind.

"I gotta agree with you, girl. Great timing, bro," his brother said as the door closed behind him. "Nice to see you again."

Once seated, they checked out the menu and ordered. When the waiter left the table, Kolby asked, "How long do we have before you head to the valley?"

"We'll leave Sunday afternoon, drive up to Cantwell, and stay at the Old Lodge there. Made a reservation under Pepper McKay, just in case Jimmy still works there."

"He does, but should be off shift by the time you get there. Dad will want you to stay with him and Amy," Kolby said firmly.

"We'll see how the first meeting goes, then decide from there. The Old Lodge isn't far from the valley."

"Depends on whether you're on two or four paws." Kolby laughed.

Hayley jabbed a fist in his ribs. "We discussed this. If Lathen has something to tell us, he will. Otherwise, shut your pie hole," Hayley said, her eyes narrowed.

"Since Pepper only has two, we'll be traveling by vehicle. But big brother, feel free to run whenever you feel wolfy," Lathen shot back, an easy grin forming at the corner of his mouth. His brother's eyebrows shot to nearly to his hairline, then one winged up in question.

"What is that supposed to mean?" Pepper wanted to know as everyone at the table burst into gales of laughter.

"It's an inside joke from their high school days," Hayley said wiping her eyes with her hand. "Male werewolves never grow up. Kolby used to egg Lathen on about…"

Lathen frowned. "I don't think so, Hayley. Somethings are best left alone."

Hayley nodded at Lathen, then shielded her lips

from him as she mouthed to Pepper, "I'll tell you later."

He shot a warning glance at his sister-in-law. "Kolby, control your mate."

"Hey, there is no controlling her—between the hormones and her fiery—well, you know. I'm looking out for number one. The rest of you are on your own." He smirked and caught her hand as she attempted to jab him in the ribs again. "Hayley cleared her schedule to play tour guide this afternoon. If that works for you. When I get off work, we've planned a barbecue at the house." Kolby glanced at his watch.

The waiter returned with a tray of drinks, chips, and salsa. "Your food will be out shortly," he said with a quick smile.

Lathen nodded to the waiter and continued. "Sounds great. We can drop off Hayley's car at the house as soon as we're done here, and I'll play chauffeur."

"That'll work." Kolby glanced at his brother. "After dinner, there're a few things I'd like to discuss with you while the girls plan tomorrow. I've taken the day off. And we'll call it an early night because I know you two are beat. Sound good?"

"I've got the guest room all ready for you unless you would rather stay in the hotel…clear across town," Hayley said, emphasizing the last three words slowly. "That way we get to spend more time with you."

Lathen looked over at Pepper, who nodded. "If it's no bother, that would be great."

Their waiter returned to the table carring a tray stacked with food. He set the plate of steaming chicken enchiladas, rice, and beans in front of Hayley, two tacos and a cheese enchilada plate went to Pepper, and large combo plates with rice and beans for Kolby and Lathen. In the middle of the table, the server slid a plate of fresh tortillas. He glanced at the empty basket of chips. "Do you need more chips and salsa?"

Kolby glanced around the table. "No, we're good."

After they finished the meal and ate sopapillas for dessert, Pepper groaned. "I'm stuffed. Now I need a nap."

"No time for that." Hayley laughed. "We got shopping and sightseeing to do."

Lathen rolled his eyes. "No one said anything about shopping until now. I'll just nap in the car while you two shop."

"Nope. You need to pick out Dad and Amy's wedding gift." Hayley snickered. "Unless you already have." She glanced at Pepper, who shook her head.

"Oh, hell, this is a setup." He looked to Kolby for help.

"You're on your own. I'll rescue you after work. Have a great time. I gotta get back." Kolby took the check from the waiter as he paused at the table, glanced at it, and handed him a credit card. "She can sign for it and collect the receipt." Kolby pointed to Hayley. "See you all tonight." He rushed across the room and shoved open the door.

"Thank you for lunch. Can we at least leave the tip?" Lathen asked rising from the chair and reaching for his wallet.

"Yes, thanks, that was so nice of you." Pepper chimed in.

"Nope, it's taken care of, and you're welcome." Hayley's eyes softened as she glanced from Pepper to Lathen. "We're so glad you're here. It means so much to Kolby, and Elijah will be ecstatic."

"That remains to be seen," Lathen mumbled.

"Follow me," Hayley said.

After dropping the car off, Hayley jumped into the rented SUV and gave directions to a department store where they could find a wedding gift. He picked out a gift card to a sporting goods store for his dad. Pepper found a wooden statue of two whimsical moose, arms entwined, sitting on a log holding a wooden sign that said "Our Home" she thought Amy would love and looked to Hayley who agreed.

Next she suggested a visit to the Potter Marsh Bird Sanctuary, part of Anchorage's coastal wildlife refuge. As they walked across the field, Pepper spotted a moose and baby at the edge of the field. A few minutes later, Lathen tapped her on the shoulder and pointed to a nest with an adult eagle guarding a fledgling teetering on the edge.

"Hayley, didn't you bring a scope?" he whispered.

"Yep, right here." She pulled a small scope out of her backpack and handed it to Pepper.

Looking through the scope, Pepper said, "Wow, look at that little guy. I think he's ready to take off." The words were no sooner out of her mouth than the eaglet spread his wings and took a short, wobbly flight, landing on a lower limb. The adult bird called to the baby and then joined it on the limb.

"It's probably time to go home. Kolby should be there by now," Hayley said. "Tomorrow, how about a hike at Lake Eklutna? The scenery is spectacular. There're a couple extra kayaks in the garage. The lake is a peaceful place to glide across. Lots of wildlife too."

"Great," Pepper said.

"Works for me."

Kolby had the barbecue started when Pepper and Lathen came trooping in behind Hayley, who gave Kolby a sweet kiss as she passed by him.

"Have a nice afternoon?" Kolby asked.

"Once we got the shopping over, we had a great time."

"Saw a moose and her baby, and an eaglet fledge at Potter Marsh. I had a great afternoon," Pepper said, plopping down on a dark brown sofa behind a long glass-topped coffee table. She stared up at the dark beams set across the light wood ceiling and decided it was a nice contrast and went well with the cream colored walls.

Lathen followed Kolby upstairs to the guest room and set down the baggage. "You've updated a few things since I was here last. It looks nice."

"Thanks. We like it. The small bedroom next to ours"—he pointed to the room across the hall from where they were standing—"will be the baby's room. Oh, by the way, you and Pepper are the only ones that know about the baby. Didn't want to overshadow Dad and Amy's big day. So don't mention it."

"Of course. Better let Pepper know," Lathen said grinning as the girls' voices rose and fell between gales of laughter. "They sure seem to get along."

"Like two peas in a pod," Kolby agreed. "You got a good woman there. She's a keeper."

"Yeah, I know." Lathen shifted from one foot to the other. His mind shifted to Lobster Cove. Were Ember and Kaylee behaving themselves? Had Ben made an appearance? Leaving Klaren and Duncan so soon after they arrived may not have been the best idea.

What if something happened? He shook his head and noticed his brother was looking at him expectantly. "What?"

"Are you?"

"Am I what?"

"Going to make it permanent?"

"Make what permanent?" Apparently, while his mind wandered, Kolby had continued talking.

"Pepper. Are you going to make things permanent with her? Soon?" Kolby hesitated for a couple beats. "You're a damn fool if you don't."

"I've been called worse," Lathen said simply. "But to answer your question, I hope so. There's a lot going on back home that has to be settled. But after that, yeah, I plan to make things permanent."

"Oh?"

"It's her family stuff." He shrugged.

"Don't wait too long," Kolby chided.

"Don't worry. It'll work out." *I hope. Right now I want to concentrate on getting through the next few days. Dad. The pack. I don't need anything else right now.* He blew out a breath and headed downstairs. "You coming?"

Still standing in the hallway in front of the guest room, his brother frowned and started down the stairs. He raised an eyebrow as he passed Lathen on the way to the kitchen. "Remember what I said."

"I think you have your hands full." He hissed back. "Don't worry about me."

"Who's worrying about what?" Hayley turned to him, wiping her hands on a towel tucked in her waistband.

"Nothing." Glad to see Pepper, he wrapped his arm

around her waist and pulled her against him, brushing his lips slowly over hers in a tantalizingly seductive kiss. "Miss me?" he growled.

"Of course." She ran her tongue over his lips and twisted away. "Help me set the table." She gave Kolby an intense look and jerked her head toward the sliding glass doors where Hayley was staring at the grill, a large, clean fork in her hand. "I'm not sure she knows what she's doing."

"Haayleyyy. How long ago did you put those on the grill?" Kolby asked opening the sliding glass door and taking the fork from his wife. Her answer was muffled as the door slid closed.

"Yep, setting the table is a good thing," Lathen said taking four plates and a stack of silverware from Pepper's hands.

Kolby intervened in the cooking just in time. The steaks were grilled to a perfect medium rare. The baked potatoes nestled on top of the coals steamed at the foil seams. "Looks like we're ready. Grab your plates and pick a steak and potato."

A frosted-glass salad bowl sat in the center of the table with small bowls at each place setting as the couples settled around the table.

The conversation was light as they consumed the food. Hayley brought out a chocolate silk pie for dessert and suggested they take pie and drinks out on the back porch. Kolby made sure the gas patio heater was on and slid the glass door open.

"Your view is spectacular," Pepper said, standing at the railing before settling into a chair.

"It was one of the selling points of this house," Hayley said.

After pressing the last of pie crust crumbs onto the back of her fork, Pepper yawned. "The dinner was delicious, and that pie was to die for."

"Sure was. But if you don't mind, we're going to call it a day." Lathen pushed up from the chair.

"Of course. Got a full day planned tomorrow," Hayley chirped.

Lathen looked at Kolby, who shrugged. "It'll be fun."

The next morning, breakfast was a quick one. They loaded kayaks in Kolby's truck and headed for the lake. The spare kayaks were wide and glided effortlessly across the lake leaving only little ripples in their wake. Except when Pepper spotted a river otter and splashed her paddles through the water in an effort to get a better look. Which wasn't appreciated by the otter.

On the lakeshore, they beached the kayaks and sat on the beach, eating turkey sandwiches, chips, and bottled water. Pepper stuffed the trash back in the wet bag, and the couples glided their kayaks across the lake, stopping a couple times to watch the wildlife at the water's edge.

By late afternoon, tired and hungry, the group trouped back to the pickup, tied the kayaks in the bed of the truck, and headed home. Kolby called in dinner to a local restaurant and when he stopped to pick it up, Lathen bolted out of the truck and into the building before Kolby could catch him. Lathen paid for the dinners and strode back to the truck a grin on his face. "Too slow in your old age."

"In your dreams, little brother," Kolby shot back.

Once they all sat down around the table and unpacked the meal, everyone was quiet, lost in their own thoughts as they ate. Except Hayley, who kept nodding off. Pepper insisted on cleaning up, then they said their goodnights and headed off to bed.

Rain pattered on the windows as Lathen opened his eyes and looked at the clock on the bedside table. The overcast morning had let him sleep longer than intended. He nuzzled Pepper's neck, inhaling her intoxicating citrusy scent while she slept. "Time to get moving," he whispered in her ear.

Hayley prepared a huge breakfast of scrambled eggs, hash browns, bacon, and orange juice. When they finished eating, Lathen and Pepper packed up to drive to Half Moon Valley.

Hayley gathered cinnamon rolls, a jug of iced tea, and bottles of water into a bag and handed it to Pepper. "For a snack on the way there."

Kolby took Lathen's outstretched hand and grabbed him in a hug. "Everything is going to be fine. Relax." Then he hugged Pepper and kissed her cheek. "Welcome to the family," he whispered. "See you both in a few days."

Tears trickled down Hayley's cheeks as she clung to Pepper. "See ya soon. You keep that big lug in line." She smiled through her tears.

"I promise," Pepper said fiercely. "See ya on Friday?"

"Yeah, late afternoon after Kolby gets off." Hayley scrubbed her hands over her face.

Chapter Eighteen
Sometimes the Best Laid Plans of Men and Wolves
Veer Off Course with Surprising Results

Once in the SUV, Lathen was anxious to get the first meeting with his father concluded. Good or bad, at least the not knowing would be over, and maybe the knot in his stomach would ease a bit for the first time since leaving Maine.

"Hey, Pep, have you heard from your parents?"

"Yeah, a couple times. A storm blew in the day after we left. Mom was afraid to let Kaylee out to feed, so she tried to coax her to eat the frozen fish we keep for such incidents. Kaylee let the fish drop and refused to eat. So Mom picked up the fish and walked away. Later in the day, she thawed out a new fish, tossing it like I showed her, and Kaylee reluctantly caught and nibbled on that. Otherwise, things are running smoothly. Ember's been Mom's shadow since we left."

Laughing, Lathen said, "Gee, Kaylee has become a diva."

"No, she's always wanted her way. I told you about the day I left Salem."

"Yeah, I forgot about that."

By late afternoon, his fingers entwined through Pepper's as he stood on his father's doorstep. Deciding to forgo the lodge in Cantrell for the moment, he would see how things panned out here. The last thing he needed was for Jimmy to see him and blab to his Dad. Lathen blew out a breath and raised his hand to knock. The door flew open, and a stocky man an inch or two shorter than Lathen with dark blond hair graying at the temples stood, eyes wide as his jaw dropped.

"I'll be damned, it is you," his dad said as he wrapped his long arms around Lathen, then grasped his shoulders and pushed him out at arm's length. His father's eyes searched Lathen's face and softened. "You look real good, son." He gripped Lathen's shoulder, then stopped for a beat, peering at Pepper, as if he'd just noticed her. "Who is this gorgeous creature you've brought with you?" Lathen's dad stepped aside and motioned them through the entrance touching Pepper on the arm. For a fleeting moment, surprise flickered through his eyes.

"Elijah, who is it?" A woman's soft melodic voice came from the other room. A tall, dark-haired woman with high cheekbones and huge brown eyes slipped into the room and stopped. "It's not..." Her gaze shifted from Lathen to a family photograph on the fireplace mantel and back to him. Her eyes widened, and she let out a quiet breath. "It is. Welcome, Lathen." She took a few more steps forward.

"Son, this is Amy, she's my..."

"Your soon-to-be wife," Lathen finished for his father. "Nice to meet you, Amy." He reached out and gave her a quick hug.

"How'd you know?" Elijah stammered, then quickly regained his composure and took Amy's hand and brought her beside him.

It wasn't often Lathen caught his father off guard, but it made him feel almost on equal footing. He circled his arm around Pepper's waist and said. "Dad, I'd like you to meet Pepper, she's…we're…my girlfriend." Introductions were getting tedious, he had to define their relationship. It was time to let her know where he hoped the relationship was going and what he wanted from her. A commitment…hard for him to believe, but that's what he wanted and was willing to give her in return.

"Welcome to our home, Pepper," Elijah said, studying her for a couple of beats. "Come on in, sit down." He led the way to a dark brown leather sectional with cream accents in front of the massive fireplace. "If you don't mind my asking, what brought you here?"

Lathen shrugged. "Kolby and Hayley came to Lobster Cove several weeks ago looking for me."

His father raised an eyebrow and rubbed his chin with his thumb and forefinger. "I didn't know they were searching for you."

Lathen nodded his head. "After asking several of the business owners around town that happen to be friends, Kolby finally camped outside my cottage until I made an appearance. Don't spend much time there." He ran his fingers through his hair and rubbed the back of his neck. "Pepper is starting up a wildlife rescue and rehab. I've revamped several buildings for her, and we created a marine habitat and clinic on the beach of her property in Lobster Cove, Maine. I spend most my time there. With her." There, he'd made it plain he was living with her. When he glanced over at Pepper, she beamed at him. He sat up a little straighter.

"The grand opening of the center is toward the end of September," Pepper said. "So after Kolby told us the news, we worked out a schedule that allowed us to take time off to attend your wedding." Her hand flew to her mouth. "Sorry, that's Lathen's tale to tell."

"No, you are doing fine." Lathen took her hand in his and held tight.

Elijah eyed Lathen suspiciously. "Just like that?"

"Well—not exactly. That is the reason Kolby came looking for me, but we had several long talks over the five weeks he and Hayley spent in and around Lobster Cove."

"Was he gone five weeks? I talk to him at least once a week, and I don't remember him saying he was out of town or even leaving Anchorage. Oh, wait…I do remember him mentioning trying to find you. But I never figured…"

"Dad, you must have lost your leash. I mean, touch." Lathen smirked.

"Still a smart ass," Elijah said returning the smirk.

"Yeah, some things never change. Anyway, Kolby said he talked to you several times, but I asked him not to mention anything about me, until—well—there were things I needed to work out."

Glancing around the room, he thought it seemed brighter, cozier than he remembered growing up or the last time he was here. The sectional was new. Pictures hanging on the freshly painted crème-colored walls weren't what he remembered. Missing was the worn dark wooden mantel over the fireplace they'd hung stockings on at Christmas. It had been replaced with a burnished light wood one, still with his father's signature carving of two wolf cubs with an adult prominent on the scalloped edge. He brought his gaze back to his father. "Made some changes. Huh? Looks

219

great."

"Sometimes, it's—time to let go. Amy had ideas when she arrived and I agreed. Not to—the memory of your mother. But…"

"Dad, I didn't know my mother. You did your best to be both Mom and Dad to us while still being the pack alpha. And did a damn fine job." He shifted and loosened the grip on Pepper's hand after noticing her clenched jaw and the ends of her fingers turning color.

"I don't know about that. I could have—didn't know what to do with you after—" His dad relaxed against the sofa, his shoulders slumped. Amy put a hand over his.

"I became a danger to the pack?" He stared at his father, lines around the rugged face, and eyes were prominent. *Older than I remember, but Amy's put a sparkle in his eyes that was never there before.*

"I knew you were hurting, but…couldn't stand by and let you take us all down with you. Something had to give. I'm sorry, but I had no…"

"It's all right. Anyway, it's been a summer of extraordinary events and changes in my life. And as Kolby was so kind to point out during one of our heated discussions, time to pull my head out of my ass and join the world again. Pepper was a catalyst for that even before Kolby came along."

Elijah's lips twitched, then he roared with laughter. "It takes strong women to handle the men of this family. I had a similar experience with Amy here." He patted her thigh and looked lovingly into her eyes. "And we all know Hayley keeps Kolby in line, even before they were married."

The intimate exchange between his dad and Amy

made Lathen a bit uncomfortable.

A buzzer sounded in the other room. Amy got to her feet. "I hate to interrupt, but before you arrived, we were just about to throw salmon steaks on the grill since the rain had stopped. The baked potatoes are done. If you want to join us, I'll grab a couple more steaks out, and, Pepper, you can help me with the salad while the guys grill the steaks."

Pepper stood, started to follow Amy, paused, then glanced at Lathen.

"If it's not too much trouble. We'd like that." He nodded, watching Pepper accompany Amy into the kitchen. When his father stood, Lathen pushed up from the couch and joined him on the deck, where the coals were more than ready. Elijah shook more briquettes out of the bag, tossed them onto the white-hot ones in the grill.

"Son, I'm glad you came back."

"I'm not back. My home is in Lobster Cove with Pepper at the rehab center. I found peace and belonging there."

For a fleeting moment, disappointment clouded his father's eyes before he said, "I'm happy for you. But I didn't see a ring on your woman's finger nor sense a claiming bite. What are you waiting for—or is it her?"

"It's tough to explain. There are problems within her family that need to be straightened out before I can subject her to that kind of claim or commitment. I'm sure you've deduced that she is not a werewolf."

His father nodded slowly.

Lathen paused. "She's a witch, a white witch, but powerful all the same." It was happening again like it used too, rambling when his father gave him that sharp, knowing look.

"I see." Elijah continued to stare at Lathen without saying anything else.

"When the time is right, we'll discuss it," he said firmly. "Until then she needs her space and concentration on her family situation."

There was a long pause before his father spoke.

"Smart man." The corner of his father's mouth kicked up in a crooked grin. "The woman and Lobster Cove have been good for you. I wish you'd come back to the pack lands, but I understand why you can't."

"I appreciate it. Dad, Pepper would like to see Denali, spend a couple of nights inside the park. Can you recommend a good guide and place to stay? It's been so long since…"

His dad's grin widened. "Amy—Amy."

She pushed open the sliding glass door and stepped out. "What are you bellowing about out here, Eli?"

"How'd you like to spend the next couple days in Denali, with Pepper and Lathen?"

Her brows knitted together, then smoothed out. "Oh, are you going to lead a tour, six days before our wedding?" she asked incredulously as Pepper peeked over her shoulder.

"I was thinking about it. A tour of four, spend a couple nights in the backcountry and stay at the Lodge inside Denali if I can work it out. The plans for the wedding are done. Could be back Wednesday evening, or so."

"Sound great. When do we leave?" Amy said, wiping her hands on the towel she held.

Elijah turned to Lathen. "Watch the steaks, don't overcook them. Might want Pepper's done a bit more than ours," he chuckled. "I need to make a couple phone calls. Plan on leaving at first light tomorrow."

Lathen turned the steaks until they were done to perfection. *I don't think I'm the only one that has changed around here.* Pepper stepped around Amy and joined him.

"Are we really going to Denali tomorrow morning?" she squeaked. "Really? Just like that?"

"Just like that." He nodded. "Guess there is no use bringing our stuff in the house. We'll spend the night at Cantrell and meet them here before dawn." Lathen's normal low rumble pitched higher at his excitement. As a boy, the backcountry had always been his favorite place with his dad.

Elijah came into the dining room just as Lathen sat the platter of steaks in the middle of the table. "All set. We'll take my truck, since I don't think your rental company would appreciate you taking their new SUV where we're headed."

After dinner, clean-up was a joint effort, and then they settled on the couch again to enjoy Amy's special chocolate cheesecake with graham cracker crust and cherries on top. Elijah threw more logs on the fire to chase away the chill of the late summer night, so he said, but Lathen thought it was more for ambiance.

He glanced over and saw Pepper try to stifle a yawn. But he was unable to stop the jaw-popping yawn that sneaked up on him. The whirlwind trip had caught up with him. "I guess we need to be going. Made reservations at the Lodge in Cantwell." Standing, he helped Pepper to her feet.

"You'll do no such thing. Call and cancel" Amy said, Elijah nodding beside her.

"We have a newly remodeled guest room waiting for you. Bring your stuff in, spend the night. At dawn, we'll be ready to go. Easier all around," his father declared as there was a knock on the door.

Elijah glanced at this watch. "Shit, who the hell's coming around here this time of night?" He yanked open the door to a tall, lanky man with jet black hair and muscular body. His face was tense and his lips drawn into a thin line.

"Sorry about this, Eli, but Todd got himself into a terrible mess. Caught in a car he stole from Jason on the road into Cantrell. Three sheets to the wind, he's threatening to show the deputies who arrested him just how big and bad he is. I got the call about three minutes ago as I was…uhh…driving by on the way home."

"Dave. Come on, you were sticking your nose where it doesn't belong. Don't think I haven't noticed the increased traffic past my house because there is a strange car parked outside." He gave a bark of laughter and sobered. "Have them release him into your custody. Lock him down in the community center and let him sober up. Get Clara to fix him three meals a day, and we'll deal with him when I get back. Tell her we'll work compensation out later."

"When he gets—well, you know like he does." He shifted from one foot to the other. "Where are you going? Isn't Saturday the big day?"

"Yes, that's why you as my second in charge should be handling this, not bothering me."

Dave winced. "They won't release him to me, only you."

Resigned, Elijah huffed. "Okay. Go on out to the truck. I'll be there in a minute." When he closed the door, he turned to the group. "Gotta handle this—might be gone a while. We still leave at dawn. Only, Lathen, you may need to drive while I get a little shut eye." He blew out a breath. "Todd's gonna wish he'd never been born, when I'm through with him," Elijah fumed as he strode out the door.

Lathen's lips twitched and then turned up in a wicked grin. "Boy, I don't envy Todd. Seen that expression way too many times." Pulling the door open, he peered outside and chuckled. "I'm going to go get our stuff out of the SUV. Dad and Dave are gone, and I don't see any more vehicles in the immediate area."

He gathered their luggage while Pepper called The Lodge in Cantwell and canceled the reservations. When he returned, she was still on the phone.

"He just walked back in. Put Dad on the phone." Pepper covered the phone with her hand. "Dad said there's been some trouble with the back-ordered supplies. Supposedly someone canceled the order?" She shrugged and handed her phone to Lathen.

"Duncan, what's going on?" Lathen listened intently. "Okay, there's been some kind of mix-up. The order form, back order, and shipping status notice are together lying on Pepper's desk in the pending box. Pull 'em out and call the distributor in the morning. Find out who canceled the order, then tell them to get the pipe coming immediately."

He paused a couple beats. "We'll haggle over the freight when I get back. If they give you any static, talk to Desmond, he's my super on the project. Have him order from an alternate source and just get it here."

Lathen listened another minute or two. "Yeah, don't worry about the cost of shipping. I'll handle that later. Oh, we'll be out of touch until Wednesday evening, going into the backcountry in Denali."

He nodded and listened for a moment. "If I have cell service, I'll call. Otherwise, I'd appreciate it if you and Desmond could handle it. Gotta get that pipe."

He handed the phone back to Pepper. "Your mom wants to talk to you." Pacing to the door and back several times, he paused beside Pepper.

After Pepper got off the phone, she glanced at him and caught his arm. Standing on tiptoe, she whispered in his ear, "Don't worry. Dad has a way of making things happen, even if it's not…" She waggled her hand back and forth. "—exactly how—uh—mortals would do it…if you get my drift."

Lathen grinned. "Got it." He kicked off his shoes and picked them up. "Breakfast at five a.m., so we are on the road by dawn about six? Ready to head to bed?"

"Sure. Good night, Amy." Pepper gave her a hug.

"Night, Amy." Lathen wrapped an arm around her and squeezed. "The guest room, top of the stairs to the left? My old room?"

"Yes, so your father told me."

A couple of hours before dawn, after a restless night, Lathen was relieved to hear the rumble of his father's truck as it pulled into the driveway. He considered getting up for a moment, instead rolled over and gathered Pepper to him and fell into a deep sleep.

He opened one eye when Pepper's warm, moist lips pressed against his. When he opened the other eye, Pepper was standing over him fully dressed. The sunlight filtered through the white lace curtains, and the birds chirped to greet the morning. Bolting upright, his nostrils flared at the enticing aroma of freshly brewed coffee along with the sizzle of bacon coming from downstairs.

"We're late." Lathen checked his watch.

"Relax, breakfast is ready. Amy and I decided to let you and your dad sleep while we prepared the food. Neither of you had a very restful night. Besides, she said road construction on Highway 3 will slow things down anyway."

"Okay. Highway 3 is the only road in and out of Denali. Dad won't be happy."

"We'll let Amy handle that. She's getting Elijah up as we speak. She thought we'd all enjoy what he has planned for this evening more if the two of you got a bit more sleep. Tomorrow morning will be good for the dawn tour of wildlife in the park." Pepper stepped away from him as he reached for her, paused in the doorway, smiled, and blew him a kiss. "Get dressed. Food's getting cold."

After breakfast, Elijah tossed the keys to Lathen. "You drive. Still remember the way?"

"Of course. There were times when the memories of our trips to Denali were all that kept me going." He paused for a couple beats. "We're staying in the cabins at Back Country Lodge?"

"Yep. Tonight we'll go on a twilight tour in the truck. Pepper will love it. Tomorrow at dawn we'll hike to an area known for wildlife sightings. Afterward, we'll catch lunch and join a bus tour up Park Road with a good friend. First time I've been a tourist rather than the guide. Kinda looking forward to it." His dad climbed in the back seat of the truck beside Amy and rested his head on her shoulder, his eyes blinked slowly as he scrubbed his hands over his face and sighed.

Arriving about midmorning, Elijah went to pick up the keys to the cedar cabins, while Lathen carried the bags to the cabin doors and waited.

Lathen unlocked the door and dropped the bags, watching Pepper rush through the room out to the deck of their cabin and stared into the pristine Alaskan outdoors. "This is a dream come true," she said in awe.

He stepped behind her and slid his hands slowly along her shoulders, feathering his fingertips at the sides of her breasts, then wrapped his arms around her waist, pressing her against him. His lips brushed the side of her neck and breathed a kiss there. When his lips touched the shell of her ear, he whispered, "Tonight, we'll be alone, and I'll have my way with you."

She shivered in his arms and twisted on tiptoe to nibble at his neck while gently caressing her fingers over his chest. "Promises, promises." She turned around and leaned against him staring out into the Alaskan wilderness.

A light knock broke the spell. "You two ready for lunch and a hike?" Elijah's deep baritone voice resounded on the other side of the wooden door.

"Sure, we'll be right there," Lathen called out and brushed a gentle kiss at her neck, inhaling her luscious scent. "Until tonight." Pepper slipped on a hoodie, and they joined his dad and Amy on the front deck.

Elijah led them along less traveled trails, where wildlife was abundant. A young golden eagle screamed and swooped after a bald eagle who'd crossed into its territory. As they walked along a ridge, down below a grizzly lumbered across the meadow. The bear stopped for a beat, nose in the air. Pepper stood mesmerized, then grabbed her camera, taking a shot before the bear disappeared into the trees.

She blew out a breath. "Such a majestic animal."

"True, but dangerous if confronted," Elijah said quietly leading them further into the backcountry. The occasional rustle of leaves or cracking of a twig were the only sounds. He held out his hand and stopped, pointing at a huge bull moose several yards ahead to his left. Pepper raised her camera and Elijah held up one finger as the animal's head swung around to look in their direction. After a couple minutes, the moose returned to eating. Elijah nodded for Pepper to snap the picture, and they retreated to a trail leading to higher ground.

By late afternoon, the group headed back to the cabins. Returning from the hike, Lathen said, "I think we'll have dinner in our cabin, kick back, and enjoy a little alone time, if that's all right with you two."

A sly smile crossed his father's lips as his hand slid from Amy's waist to her hip. "I was thinking the same thing. How about we postpone the twilight tour drive until tomorrow night?"

"Sounds good. See ya tomorrow morning. At dawn?" Lathen verified.

"Yep." his dad confirmed.

****

As Pepper waited, Lathen pushed the door to their cabin open and swept her up in his arms as they entered the room, pushing the door closed with his foot. He let her down on her feet inside the small kitchenette. He walked to the blinds pulled to one side of the sliding glass doors at the end of the room beside the bed and closed them.

She picked up a room service menu and waved it

toward him. "Do you want order off this menu?"

When he turned around to gaze at Pepper, a slow seductive smile curved the corners of his lips. "Not what I'm hungry for." He took off his flannel shirt, tossed it on the bed, and stalked toward her. Her eyes grew round as she watched his approach. In one smooth action, he wrapped his arms around her waist and pulled her close.

Air whooshed out as she squealed. "What are you doing?"

"Having my way with you, as promised." He picked her up, sat her on the counter, positioned himself between her legs.

She watched the growing ridge beneath the zipper of his jeans. Desire shot to her intimate parts, even as she tried to wiggle away.

He feathered his fingers down her sides, across her belly, settling at the waistband of her jeans, unbuttoned and slid them over her hips as she continued to shift from hip to hip.

Lathen brought his mouth down on hers hungrily. Parted her lips with his tongue, exploring the recesses of her mouth, her tongue joined his touching, tasting, enjoying the sensation. The caress of his lips on her mouth and down her neck sent shivers through her. Pepper leaned her head back as he nudged aside her purple scooped-neck sweater and slid his tongue between her breasts. His hand slid under her sweater and released the clasp of her bra. Fingers curled in the bottom of her sweater, and he tugged it over her head, leaving her firm mounds bare to his gaze. The sweater dropped to the floor while his hands caressed her breasts, his mouth licked, and teeth scraped lightly over her nipples, then sucked the rosy peaks.

When his mouth moved to her belly, she moaned and arched up to him. Hand on his chest, she pushed against him reaching for his zipper, drawing it down and flicking her thumb under the button of his pants, releasing it. In one quick swipe, she pulled his jeans and underwear below his hips. Her foot slipped between his legs and shoved the denim below his knees. The jeans pooled on the floor, and he stepped forward out of them, his erection brushing between her legs where she was already hot, already wet. In her entire life, no man had made her feel like this, enveloped in a sexual haze, willing to allow...anything. Even on the kitchen counter.

His nostrils flared at the scent of her arousal. "Ready for me, are you?" Lathen asked seductively.

In answer, she arched her hips toward him, spreading her legs wider, an invitation. His eyes met hers and held for second. She felt the heat as his gaze wandered over her naked body, pausing between her legs for a beat. He lowered his head and growled, vibration teasing her breast as his tongue flicked over the nipple. The tip of his tongue circled her belly button, then licked further down until he trailed wet kisses along the soft flesh where her hip connected to her thigh. He bent lower and rested his hands on the inside of her upper thighs.

Pepper scooted to the edge of the counter trying to get closer as his thumbs stroked her. She squirmed, moaned, and leaned back on her elbows, pulling her knees out to her sides, feet resting on the counter's edge, then on his broad shoulders.

Pausing, he studied her and brought his gaze back

to hers. "You are absolutely beautiful," he whispered, his warm breath caressing her center.

Never a screamer during sex, she couldn't help the scream that ripped from her lungs when the first climax crashed through her. Wave after wave pulsed as he held on to her hips until she stilled. Her chest heaving, he pulled away with a soft kiss..

"Now that's pleasure," he said with satisfaction. "Ready for round two?"

She shook her head, feeling the heat rise to her cheeks as his gaze blatantly swept over her naked body splayed on the counter before him.

Chuckling, he said, "Sure you are." He got to his feet and took a nipple into his mouth, teasing it with his tongue as he pressed against her opening. Slowly, he slid inside, then pulled out, only to repeat the action deeper each time.

She closed her eyes, enjoying the sensation of him sliding inside her as her muscles clenched around him.

"Like that, don't ya." When he lifted her off the counter and buried himself to the hilt inside her, he shivered.

"Nearly lost it, huh?" she snickered, wrapping her legs around him, leaning back as he carried her to the bed. He pulled out and tossed her in the middle of the bed.

"Not even close." He crawled between her spread legs on the bed, trailed kisses from her hip and thigh across her belly. Finally took her mouth with his, positioning himself at her opening, teasing her entrance.

With a quick thrust of hips, she knocked him off balance, pushed him to his back, and straddled him. Pepper held his gaze, pressing his arms into the bed above his head, and grabbed a condom from the nightstand. She grinned wickedly and hovered her wet center over his erection. "My turn," she chirped, caressing him. His eyes closed, a low rumble came from his throat. He arched up. She slithered along his body, biting lightly on his nipples, soothed them with her tongue, and pressed her breasts against his wide muscular chest. She loved the feel, the scent of him.

Her hand pressed against his arms, she teasingly commanded, "Stay." *Well, I'm surprised that worked.* Sitting up, she tore open the package and slipped the condom over his impressive length. Hands braced on his arms again, she lowered herself until he was pressed to her entrance. She wiggled a bit, took in a little more, squeezed, then rose up and slowly slid down taking his entire length inside her.

He moaned and swore as she moved until he pushed her hands away and grabbed her hips and held her in place. "Don't," he growled.

Too late. She felt him struggling for control and shifted, wiggled, and smiled at his groan of defeat.

He reared back and flipped her, exchanging positions, thrust into her until waves of ecstasy throbbed through her body. With one final thrust, he threw his head back, and howled as pleasure washed over him. Spent, he rested on top of her, the majority of his weight on an elbow. He rolled to his side and cradled her in his arms as she snuggled against his chest feeling the beat of his heart as their legs entwined. Lathen buried his face in her thick hair and nuzzled her neck. "Next time," he murmured.

"Next time what?" she asked sleepily.

"I'll make you mine."

****

A sliver of moon cast very little light before dawn when Lathen and Pepper met Elijah and Amy at the truck. The bright dome light of the truck came on as Amy opened the door and held the seat forward allowing Pepper to clamber in as Lathen did the same on the other side. Amy swung into her seat. The neckline of her sweater shifted to reveal a fresh bite mark between neck and shoulder.

"Couldn't wait until after the wedding," Lathen cajoled.

"That, my son, is none of your business." He paused for a beat. "Well, at least I didn't howl without leaving a mark," his dad shot back with a devilish grin.

"Touché," Lathen said. "Where are we heading this morning?"

"Wait a minute. Someone mind telling me what's going on?" Pepper asked, heat creeping up into her cheeks.

"Have Lathen explain it to you—later," his father said gruffly, narrowing his eyes at Lathen in the rear view mirror. Amy punched Eli in the arm, glaring at him. "Okay, okay, it's a wolf thing," he grumbled and glanced back at Pepper and Lathen. "What part of the six million acres of Denali would you like to see today? After we see the park from my special place."

Driving the Park Road, Eli suddenly steered the truck into a pullout. "We need to walk from here. This morning is absolutely perfect, don't get many of these." They hiked for a bit and he said, "Here. Look east."

An orange ribbon covered the eastern horizon, then spread out in shades of gold, pink, and orange. Pepper put her hand to her mouth and sucked in a breath.

"Wow, it's absolutely—breathtaking." She swung her camera up and focused in on the spectacular sunrise.

"Just give it a few minutes, then look toward Mount McKinley. The clouds aren't going to obscure the mountain today, what luck."

"Isn't McKinley the highest peak in North America at 20,310 feet on the south side?" Pepper asked.

"Yes. What'd you do, check all the fun facts of Alaska before you came?" Eli winked at her. "Look west now."

The sunrise reflections sparkled pink across the majestic snow-covered peak. Pepper switched her camera lens and begin shooting pictures of the mountain.

As they wound their way down the path to the truck, her stomach gurgled loudly. Pepper put a hand over her belly. "Didn't eat much last night.

Eli chuckled, "Figured. Let's find something to eat. Then we'll catch the tour bus and relax while we enjoy the tour."

"Good plan. Bet we're all hungry." Lathen smirked, scraping the mud off his boots on the running board before stepping into the truck.

"It's the werewolf metabolism, as you're well aware." Elijah paused for a beat, glanced up at the sky. "I'd hoped the aurora borealis would make a rare appearance while you were here. But it's a bit early. Viewing season is from September to March." He clicked his tongue. "I checked around. The consensus is that she'll be a no-show."

"That's too bad." Pepper sighed.

"You'll have to come back early spring." Eli shot a sideways glance at Lathen.

"Dad, you're incorrigible."

"September through March, we'll keep that in mind," Pepper said.

Elijah parked in front of the Glacier café. Red and white checked curtains adorned its windows along with a sign proclaiming "All You Can Eat Breakfast."

"This establishment is about to lose money on you three," Pepper joked, climbing out of the truck following the others into the restaurant.

"The food is delicious, and ol' Pete's a shrewd businessman. His prices compensate for the locals' appetites." Eli waved at a thin man with a long gray braid standing at the counter. "Pete, you know Lathen, and this is—Pepper."

Pete's eyebrows shot nearly to his hairline as he glanced at Lathen, then turned his attention to the women. "Never figure out how the Quartz men garner such gorgeous women." He winked a pale blue eye at Amy. "Have a seat anywhere. Need menus?"

"The girls will," Eli said sliding into to a red upholstered booth beside Amy. Lathen waited for Pepper to slip in on the other side, then joined her.

She watched wide-eyed while the others scarfed down copious amounts of breakfast meats, eggs, and pancakes. She was the last to finish one egg, bacon, toast, and juice.

"Ready to head out?" Eli asked, "Can't wait to ride along on a tour and give the guide grief." His eyes sparkled with mischief, lips turned up in a devilish grin.

Shortly after everyone was seated on the bus, Bill bounded up the stairs and stopped, cocked his hat, and stared for a moment. "Well, what luck. You have two guides for the price of one."

Eli shook his head vigorously, holding his hand forward, palm up. "Not today. I'm playing tourist."

The other people on the bus twisted in their seats to look at who the guide was talking about.

"Okay, but…no funny business." He narrowed his eyes at Eli.

"Wouldn't dream of it." A devilish grin spread across his face.

Bill began with what they could expect to see. During the tour, he asked for a few minutes of silence so they could appreciate the tranquility of the area. A bear sow and her cub ambled several yards out during a stop for pictures and viewing. Mt. McKinley, Wonder Lake, and the Alaskan wildlife were a few of the tour highlights.

Pepper felt like a sponge soaking in all the information Bill provided about the six million acres of Denali divided by only one ribbon of road. The guide was good, but in her opinion, Eli was better.

Bill suggested before snapping a photo. "Turn around 360 degrees to observe all that surrounds you, from the semi low-elevation taiga forest, to high alpine tundra, snowy mountains, culminating with the tallest peak in North America, Denali at 20,310 feet. Which, by the way, is the third most topographically isolated summit on Earth after Mount Everest and Aconcagua."

"Wait, wait, just a second," Pepper cajoled. "I thought Mt. McKinley was the highest."

"Well…" Bill eyed Eli suspiciously. "It's the same mountain. You see in 1975 the Alaskan Legislature asked the U.S. Federal Government to officially change the mountain's name from McKinley to Denali. Alaskan people had always called it Denali. It was a gold prospector in 1896 that called it McKinley and started the ruckus. In September 2015, the president of the United States announced the official renaming of McKinley to Denali."

Eli held his hands up in a gesture of innocence. "Pepper's a walking facts of Alaska brochure. I had nothing to do with this." He chuckled.

Bill gave him a dubious smile. "We'll discuss this later."

Thanks to Eli's specially arranged request, the tour took them to the old gold town Kantishna, a place most visitors never got to explore.

For lunch, they stopped at the exclusive Kantishna Roadhouse, which Pepper thought was a good thing. She'd heard Lathen's stomach growl several times on the tour, even though light snacks and drinks were provided.

The Roadhouse offered several interpretive activities. Lathen and Eli drifted toward the gold panning presentation, while she and Amy watched the Alaskan dog sled demonstration.

At the end of the nearly twelve-hour tour, Eli stopped Bill and slipped something into his hand and slapped him on the back. "Great job. Thanks."

"Any time. See you at the wedding." Bill grinned and strode off toward another knot of tourists.

Walking back to the cabins, Pepper suddenly stopped and hugged Eli tight. "This was wonderful. Thank you so much."

Appearing a little uncomfortable with the sudden show of affection, Eli returned the hug and released her. "You're very much welcome. Amy and I needed a break from the wedding crush. Thanks for the idea."

Pepper looked dubious for a beat, then smiled and intertwined her fingers through Lathen's, leaving Eli and Amy at their cabin. "Anytime. Goodnight, Amy, Eli."

Lathen echoed her good nights.

****

After a quick breakfast Wednesday morning, Lathen and Pepper brought the bags out to the truck. Eli already had Amy's stuff packed inside the storage box in the bed of the truck, lid still opened.

"Thank you for an unforgettable experience, Eli," Pepper said giving him a big hug. "The trip was a dream come true."

Lathen nodded as he hefted the bags up into the storage box and closed the lid. "Thanks, Dad, I really appreciate it." He walked around to the passenger side of the truck where Amy held the front seat forward. He clambered into the back seat. Sitting behind Amy gave him more leg room.

Eli held the seat back, while Pepper crawled into the back seat. "Anytime." He climbed into the truck, closed the door, and started the engine.

Pepper leaned back in the seat. In a couple of hours, they'd be back in Half Moon Valley. *How would the pack handle an outsider in their midst, let alone a witch?* She wiped her damp palms on her jeans. The unknown had always been one of her greatest fears.

Chapter Nineteen
Go North, the Wedding's On
—After the Damage Is Repaired

After stopping for dinner, they arrived in Half Moon Valley in early evening. When Lathen got out of the truck, he wrinkled his nose. "Smells like the whole pack stopped by while we were gone." His father's nostrils flared as little lines creased his forehead.

"Had a lot of visitors while you were gone. Well-wishers for your wedding?" Lathen asked.

"Doubt it. Probably people looking for you," Elijah grumbled. "Word's out, you're back. At least we had a few uninterrupted days together. Denali was a great get-away. Now, business as usual." He unlocked the door and pushed it open.

"Sorry. We could lie low out of town, till the wedding," Lathen offered, walking through the door, Pepper close behind him.

Eli tossed his keys on the table by the door. "Don't be ridiculous. Kolby and Hayley will be here Friday for the celebratory dinner the whole pack is preparing. It'll be held at the community center. Don't see what all the fuss is about."

"Tradition," Lathen said. "You were the most eligible male for years, the Alpha to boot. Then you fall for a woman from a pack in the lower forty-eight. Bet that broke some hearts."

"S'pose so." He glanced at his watch. "Speaking of the center, I better go take care of the Todd situation. Get him out of there, since that's where the wedding and reception will be held. The women of the pack probably aren't too thrilled with me as it is." He shrugged. "Nothing to be done about it. There's plenty of time for them to put up the damn decorations."

"Elijah, you promised." Amy cooed, sitting on the sofa and taking her shoes off.

"I know, I know, but I don't have to like it. Never liked people fussing over me or my boys," he said, voice gruff. "Lathen, you want to ride along?"

"Probably not a good idea," Lathen said, shoving a few logs into the fireplace and crumpling several sheets of newspaper. "Where's the matches?" His fingers ran along the smooth surface on top the mantel. Nothing. He turned around and jumped back as flames raced up the pieces of wood. Staring at Pepper, he raised an eyebrow, tilted his head in question.

She shrugged. Pink patches bloomed on her cheeks.

He was as surprised as she appeared to be when she sidled closer to him.

With her lips close to his ear, she whispered, "I didn't intend…thought about it, but…Sorry."

Amy's gaze flicked from Pepper to the fireplace and to Lathen, but she said nothing.

Oblivious to the situation, Eli continued, "Why not? It'll confirm the rumors, set the record straight. You're only visiting. Then maybe people will quit driving by and beating a path to my door." Eli snapped his fingers. "When are you going to introduce Pepper to the pack?"

"Probably at the dinner. But don't give anyone the wrong idea. We're not engaged or anything." Lathen looked over at Pepper, who'd now followed Amy's example, ditched her shoes, and tucked her feet up under her on the sectional facing the fireplace.

"No…but it looks pretty serious to me. And will to the pack too," his dad said. "Your scents are mingled."

"Understood. I'll handle it," Lathen said. "Pepper, you okay with me introducing you to the pack? I don't have to—right now."

"I'm part of your life, and if that requires some kind of introduction, I'm fine with it. Can't be any worse that your intro into my world." She laughed. At Elijah's questioning look, Pepper added waving a hand dismissively, "It's a long, convoluted story that's best left untold."

Eli raised an eyebrow. "Well, let's get this over with." He jerked his chin toward the door. "We'll be back in a few, ladies."

When they arrived at the Community Center, Dave was waiting outside and walked up to the truck. "Did you have a good time?"

"Sure did. How'd things turn out with Todd?" Eli asked, stepping out of the vehicle and walking toward the center.

"Well, as it turns out, Jason refused to press charges. The sheriff was willing to let us handle his intoxication, with the warning, if it happened again, there'd be no intervention on our part." He grimaced. "Before you go in, there's something…"

Eli yanked open the center door and was slammed with a strong bleach smell, barely covering up other less inviting scents. Pieces of sparkly white paper hung torn in the corners along with ripped streamers of maroon and black from the ceiling. Face flushed with anger, his jovial voice of a few minutes ago dropped to a deadly calm. "What the hell happened here?"

"Had a little trouble containing Todd in his drunken rage. Finally, had to stun him when he started to phase. I probably should have shifted to contain him. The damage to the common room would have been less. But it was date night for Lori and—just didn't want to destroy—" He shrugged. "Had to cancel the plans anyway."

"Hazards of the position," Eli said flatly. "Should have phased and knocked him out cold. You will next time."

The splintered door at the far end of the large common area caught Lathen's attention. He walked over and peered in. Traces of food stains covered the walls along with several fist size holes in the walls. Todd was inside with drywall tools and spackle, repairing the damage.

Todd eyed him. "You back, huh?"

"Only for the wedding." Lathen blew out a breath, joined his dad and Dave. "Lot of work to do before the festivities."

"You got that right," came a female voice from the doorway. A stout sable-haired woman stood, hands on hips, with two large bags on the floor beside her. "You're going to make Todd pay for the decorations he destroyed. Right? I just got back from replacing what he tore up. Thank goodness the custom decorations we ordered weren't up yet."

"Hello, Lynne," Eli said.

When Lathen turned around, her eyes shifted to

him. "Well, I'll be damned, it is you." She strode over and wrapped an arm around his neck. "It's about time. Things better with you?"

"Yes, they're great. Thanks for asking."

"I gotta get home. Welcome back, Lathen." She crossed the room and pushed the door open letting it bang shut.

Eli rubbed the back of his neck, lips set in a thin line. "So what's the plan?"

"We've been working to get the placed cleaned up. Todd is repairing the room, and the new door is due to arrive tomorrow morning. We'll finish taking down the torn decorations and paint tomorrow morning, so Lynne and the girls can get the place decorated. We should be ready for Friday night's dinner. He didn't get as far as the kitchen."

"If you need a couple extra hands, Pepper and I will be happy to help. We can be here tomorrow morning," Lathen offered.

"Amy and I are available," Eli said grudgingly.

Dave was quick to answer. "No, Eli, you and Amy don't need to be here." He paused, scrubbing his hand over his face. "But, Lathen, we could use your help and your lady's, if she is so inclined."

"If you refer to Pepper as my lady, she'll probably pop you one. It's Pepper," Lathen said. "See you in the morning."

Eli grunted strode to the door. "The first time I— should have stayed and handled Todd myself." He jerked open the door and climbed into the truck.

"Cut Dave some slack. You can't always be here." Lathen jumped in the passenger's seat.

"I have been up till now." His father shot back,

starting the truck and shoving it into gear.

"You're not going to cancel the honeymoon to watch over him."

"Of course not, Amy would—" Eli guided the truck to the road and turned left.

"Exactly…Are Rod and Cal still your backup?"

"Yes."

"If you don't mind, I have a suggestion," Lathen said as the truck coasted to a stop in front of the house.

"I'm all ears," his dad grumbled, cutting the engine.

"Talk to all three of them in the morning. Make clear that Dave is acting alpha and the others are his backup starting immediately until you return from your honeymoon. That way, you're out of the loop. It's sink or swim time for them. I'll bet they'll step up and be fine. It's time for you to back off, as hard as that may seem."

Eli nodded solemnly, got out of the truck, and walked up to the house. Before he opened the door, he turned and clasped Lathen on the shoulder. "I'm proud of you, son."

"Thanks." He shoved the door open.

"Everything all right?" Amy asked.

"Yeah. A few minor repairs Dave's got Todd working on. Lathen has volunteered to help tomorrow along with Pepper. Everything will be ready on Friday. Including the damn decorations." The corner of Eli's mouth kicked up in a crooked grin.

"Me? Sure, what do you need?" Pepper asked, chewing on her bottom lip.

"You'll see when we get there. Be a piece of cake," Lathen said, caressing his knuckles over her cheek, twining a strand of her soft hair around his finger.

****

By the time Lathen and Pepper arrived the next morning, Todd had patched the walls and applied a fresh coat of paint to the room he'd wrecked. On the top rung of a ladder in the community room, he paused with a long-handled paint roller in hand, light blue paint spattered all over his clothes and wire-rimmed glasses. "Morning, Lathen."

Dave stood in the center of a group of men assigning tasks as he checked them off on a clipboard. When he saw Lathen walk in, he said, "Rod, Cal, and I have a meeting to attend. Can you take over here? Eli said it's kinda your area of expertise." After making a final note, he handed the clipboard to Lathen.

"Happy to. Anything I should be aware of?" Flipping through the pages, he ran his finger down the list.

"Nope, all there. Tasks assigned." Dave looked up and over Lathen's shoulder when the door banged opened. "Uh oh." Dave stiffened.

Lathen twisted around to see what the problem was. Standing in the doorway was a tall, curvy female with dark hair streaked with red and huge chocolate brown eyes. He sucked in a breath and shot a glance at Pepper, who was talking to someone across the room. About the time he turned around to face the woman, she'd already crossed the distance between them and slapped him across the face.

"So it's true, you're back," she said in a low sexy as hell voice.

Fists clenched at his side, Lathen said, "So it would seem, but only for dad's wedding. Good to see you,

Sofie. Not." Her hand came up, but he dodged the blow and grabbed her wrist. "That's enough."

"It certainly is." Pepper appeared at his side, her hand formed in a claw, fingertips turning orange.

Sofie jerked free and coughed, clutching at her throat, choking out the words. "What the hell?"

Lathen put a large callused hand over Pepper's, gave a slight shake of his head, and stepped in front of her. "Sofie, this isn't the time or place. I'm sorry about the way I ended things. But that was a long time ago, and we've both moved on. Congratulations on your upcoming wedding to Walter. He's a lucky guy." He searched her flushed, angry face and in a calm tone said, "Now…if you're not here to help, please go on home."

"Bastard—do you know—"

He cut her off. "I apologized. There nothing more to say." He shoved one fisted hand in his pocket and flexed one at his side should she decide to swing at him again.

"You've got what you came for. Now let's go home." A large man with shaggy black hair, high cheekbones, and piercing gray eyes strode across the floor and took hold of Sofie's arm.

"Walter?" Lathen asked, his lips twitching. The man had certainly grown into his feet. Lathen exchanged a quick look with Dave, who remained tight-lipped.

"Yeah." Walter nodded in Lathen's direction. "Come on, Sofie. We don't want any trouble."

Still rubbing her throat, she allowed Walter to escort her out of the building.

Pepper turned to Lathen. "What did you do to

her?"

"I said a lot of things I didn't feel, trying to—I don't know, make one of us feel better. Then I disappeared."

"Huh, well I guess you deserved that. You know what they say about a woman scorned," Pepper mused. "Good she got it out of her system before the dinner tomorrow night."

"Still remains to be seen." He sighed and glanced at the group that formed around them. "Everyone, back to work. Dave, you better get going."

Dave peered at his watch. "Got that right." Turned on his heel and sprinted out the door, which slammed shut behind him.

Lathen stalked over to the door. "I'm going to fix that damn thing, right now."

Other than the rough start to the day, Lathen was pleased with the way things went. The Community Center had never looked better. Pepper won over the women of the pack as they worked side by side to redecorate the center and make sure the kitchen was in working order. Truth be told, their laughter and chatter helped ease Lathen's nerves. *Now all I have to do is make it through the dinner, the announcement, and wedding. Can't wait to get back to Lobster Cove.*

When Pepper flitted past, he caught her arm. "Ready to head to the house?"

"I am. Just let me say goodbye to the girls." Raising a hand, she waved and called out to the women gathering packaging and papers and stuffing them into bags. "See you tomorrow…afternoon. What time do I need to be here?"

A petite woman with blond hair and green eyes

smiled at Pepper. "Around three should be fine, dinner is at five, the band arrives at seven, and we'll party till dawn, so put on your dancing shoes." Her cheerful voice dissolved into gales of laughter.

"I'll be here, Jan. Bye, everyone." Pepper put her arm through Lathen's.

As they strolled toward the entrance, a chorus of goodbyes and see-you-tomorrows echoed behind them. The door did not bang closed after them but released a whooshing sound as it shut.

Lathen grinned at Pepper as she looked back at the door. "Nice job," she said climbing into the SUV. "What can I expect at the dinner?"

He closed the door behind her, slid over the hood of the SUV, and opened the driver side door. "I'm not sure. I hope anyone else that has a beef with me respects Dad enough to let it go until they've left on the honeymoon."

"But aren't we leaving shortly after the ceremony and reception?"

"That's the idea. But before I leave this time, want to make sure I'm welcome back." He pulled up and parked behind Kolby's truck. "Kolby and Hayley must have left Anchorage early."

Pepper hopped out of the truck. "Hayley's here. I've got so many questions for her after talking with the girls from the pack." Pepper sprinted toward the door.

"You could ask me," Lathen called after her but smiled as she yanked open the door and nearly collided with Hayley. *Two peas in a pod. Feels good to be part of the family again.* He ambled up the steps. Through the doorway still standing wide open, the women's excited chatter wafted out into the evening air.

"Thought you two weren't coming until tomorrow night."

Kolby shrugged. "Worked a double shift last night and today, so we'd have an extra day here. Besides Dad wanted me to bring the computer system and printer he ordered for the Half Moon Community Center, so you could install it while you're here."

Lathen's eyes narrowed giving his dad a hard stare. "And just when am I supposed to get that done?"

"Thought you'd have time tomorrow. A computer expert like you…shouldn't take long." His dad shot him a lopsided grin.

"It won't if we have all the components and correct cabling. If not…" Lathen grumbled.

"Oh, I made sure we got everything because Dad and I were going to try to do it ourselves. You know what tech guys charge to do that?" Kolby asked.

"Yes, I do. In fact, that's part of what I do in Lobster Cove. I'll give you the family discount." Lathen smirked.

Gales of laughter and excited conversation drifted from the kitchen where the women gathered.

"Boys, let's take a run. I've had enough of women's chatter already." Eli winked at Amy through the doorway, then paused for a beat, glancing over at Lathen. "Or a walk—whatever."

"A run is fine with me," Lathen shot back. His dad's eyes narrowed as Kolby's widened in surprise.

"Ladies, we'll be back," Lathen said leading the way out the door.

****

Leaving Kolby and Hayley with his dad and Amy, Lathen and Pepper drove to the Community Center.

Upon their arrival, half the pack was already there. The guys were moving and setting up tables. One across the front, chairs facing the other rows of tables. A large white glittery banner with black and maroon lettering hung on the wall behind the front table said "Elijah and Amy, Wishing You Love, Luck, and Laughter All the Days of Your Life Together."

Most the women were in the kitchen. Jan stuck her head out when Pepper and Lathen arrived. "Pep, see all the vases and flowers on the main table?"

Pepper glanced at the table and nodded.

"Could you put the flowers in the vases and put two on each table. Lathen, could you help Todd set up the buffet tables—I think there's four—and spread the maroon tablecloths over them. Thanks." She ducked back into the kitchen.

"Well, I guess your acceptance wasn't a problem," Lathen said cheerfully.

"Yeah, but they don't know my secret," Pepper said, picking up a vase and adding flowers.

"I wouldn't bet on it. Your little display yesterday didn't go unnoticed. By now, it's possible the whole pack knows, but being of a magical nature ourselves, probably won't make a lot of difference. They like who you are."

"Really?"

"Really. Now you better get those flowers on the tables 'cause I imagine she has more for you to do. She's quite the task master, I've heard." Lathen strode over to where Todd was standing one end of the table in his hands and picked up the other end. In short order, they had all four tables up and covered with the cloths.

Jan stuck her head out of the kitchen again.

"Lathen, I could use you…"

"Todd and I have finished with the tables. Now I have a computer system to set up and cabling to run, so don't delegate anything else for me today."

"Oh, good. The other system died a couple of weeks ago. How long before we'll be able to use new computer system?"

Lathen smiled and shook his head. "If I have everything, everyone leaves me alone, and stays out of my way, three, maybe four hours." He took a knife out of his pocket, slit the boxes open, and set the components on a table. Checking the computer, printer, wiring, and other peripherals, he gave a low whistle. "Nice setup." After dismantling the old system, he had the new system online and tested in less than three hours.

Pepper finished the flowers and put paper plates, plastic ware, cups, and napkins on the first table of the buffet line. Jan popped out of the kitchen and slung an arm around Pepper's shoulder. "I think we're done. Thanks for your help." Jan stood hands on hips surveying the room. "Good job, everyone."

By the time Eli and Amy and the rest of the pack arrived, the warming dishes were steaming with prime rib, mashed potatoes and gravy, homemade dinner rolls, and a veggie medley. There were hot dogs and hamburgers for the kids. The dessert table had two huge chocolate sheet cakes with "It's About Time" written on one and "Elijah and Amy" on the other in white icing. Eli's signature logo, an adult wolf with two pups, had been altered by adding an additional adult wolf with a pink bow between her ears across the top of the cakes.

Eli and Amy, Lathen and Pepper, Kolby and Hayley were escorted to the head of the buffet line, then ushered to the front table facing the rest of the tables. The remainder of the pack waited patiently in line to get their food.

Once everyone was seated, Kolby shoved to his feet, champagne flute in hand, and cleared his throat. "It's said in a happy marriage, the husband expects the wife to cook, clean, do the laundry, walk the dog, and care for the children. Then still look stunning when the husband gets home from work."

The men in the room guffawed and shook their heads, while the women snorted, and gave him hard stares. One yelled out, "What planet are you from?"

Kolby held his index finger up. "But wait…The husband's job is to thank his lucky stars that the wife keeps him around. Congratulations, Dad and Amy—I wish you both many years of happiness." Kolby lifted his glass of champagne toward his father and Amy, took a large gulp, and sat in his chair, leaning over to whisper in Hayley's ear, "Boy, am I glad that's over."

Hayley covered her mouth to stifle a giggle when snickers and murmurers of approval swept through the room. "You're lucky you weren't booed out of the area with that kind of ridiculous toast."

"It was supposed to be funny," Kolby said, red creeping up his neck.

Lathen took a deep breath and stood, all eyes upon him as his gaze swept the room, his deep, rich voice a bit shaky. "First, I want to thank you for welcoming me back into the pack without reservation and accepting Pepper. You have no idea how much it means to me." He cleared his throat and paused for a moment wiping his sweaty palms on his pants, straightened his shoulders, and shifted his gaze to his dad.

"After all the times my dad has been there to share my big life moments, some good, some terrible, it's an honor for me to be here today to share his. No matter how tough I made it, he was always there, as dad, mentor, and confidant." Lathen paused running his fingers through his hair. "Now once again, he'll be a husband and loving companion to Amy, a woman who put that sparkle back in his eyes. Words can't convey how happy I am for him. But I have to say, Amy, you're a brave woman to take on this man. I wish you both love and laughter all the rest of your days." He picked up his flute, nearly knocking it over in the process, and raised it to his father. "Sláinte, as Pepper's family would say." Lathen took a long swig and eased into his seat.

Elijah got to his feet. "Thank you all for sharing in one of the happiest days of my life and welcoming Amy into our pack with open arms. A special thanks to my sons and their mates for making Amy feel like a part of our family." He settled in his seat, leaned over, and took Amy's mouth with his in a searing kiss.

Hoots and wolf whistles echoed through the room.

"Shut up and eat, you bunch of heathens," Elijah said with a hearty laugh.

"Hey, Dad, I think you need to alter the famous family logo to match the cake." Lathen jerked his chin toward the dessert table.

"Top of my to-do list, after we return," Eli said with a grin, his gaze slid lovingly to his mate and soon-to-be wife.

After the dinner, everyone pitched in to help clean

up. Lathen made sure the tables were wiped down and put away. Pepper gathered the vases, added water to the flowers and set them on one table for use tomorrow. Eli and Amy were tasked with seeing that the band, who were talented members of the pack, were set up in the right area. The celebration lasted well into the early morning hours.

As Amy and Eli got ready to leave, a couple of women tried to get Amy to spend the night at one of their houses, in keeping with the tradition of the groom not seeing the bride before the wedding. Amy thanked them graciously but said she was staying with Eli and that she'd blindfold him. Eli snorted and gave a bark of laughter as the women clicked their tongues and wagged their fingers at them.

When most the pack departed, Lathen, Kolby, Pepper, and Hayley stayed behind to help set up for the wedding ceremony. The decorations from the dinner were left in place. Folding chairs were set in rows, a platform and arch decorated with white and maroon roses was moved to the front of the room, flanked by silver candle holders of varying heights including maroon candlesticks.

Red fading to yellow fingers of sunlight spread across the horizon as the couples headed home. "It's going to be a long day," Lathen said getting out of the SUV, parked in front of Kolby's truck. Kolby, Hayley, and Pepper nodded in agreement as they padded quietly into the house and fell into bed.

It was mid-afternoon when Lathen woke up to the aroma of freshly brewed coffee wafting into the bedroom. He rolled over and drew Pepper to him, nibbling on her neck. The desire to claim her was getting stronger by the day. He didn't know how much longer he'd be able to control the beast within. They needed to talk but not until they got back to Lobster Cove and saw what was brewing.

Pepper turned her face up to him and brushed her lips across his. "Good morning," she said sleepily.

"Good afternoon." He returned her kiss lingering longer than he should have. "Something tells me we better get moving."

"Suppose so, but all we have to do is get Eli and Amy to the center on time. Jan said she'd get her husband and brother to help move the seven-layer marble cake into the community center kitchen. Did you know she baked and decorated it herself?" Pepper yawned and sat up, and swung her feet to the floor. "We set out the plates, plastic ware, napkins, punch bowls, and cups on a table at the far end of the room near the kitchen before we left. The punch is already prepared and bottled in the fridge."

"Just waiting for someone to spike it." Lathen laughed getting to his feet. "And they will."

"That's why there's canned soft drinks in the fridge as well." She giggled. "I'll share the shower with you if you promise no hanky-panky."

"None?" He gave her crestfallen look.

She shook her head adamantly. "None."

"Okay," he said reluctantly, crossing his fingers behind his back. A seductive smile turned up the corners of his mouth.

****

Standing in the family's warm, cozy kitchen, Lathen said, "It's time, Dad. You got the truck packed for your trip to the airport, right?"

"Yes, son. We're packed. Let's get this show on the road." He reached for Amy and snatched her to him. "Ready to be Mrs. Quartz?"

"I am," Amy cooed, smoothing her light pink dress with embroidered multi-colored rosebuds on it. She twirled on her white pearl pumps. "Lucy from the pack made it for me. Eli and I were okay with new jeans and matching maroon shirts. But the pack wasn't having any of that. So we'll wear those on our honeymoon."

"You two aren't the least bit nervous?" Hayley asked.

"Too old for that. Besides, what is there to be nervous about? We've been mated since our trip to Denali with Lathen and Pepper. This ceremony is merely a formality and a reason for the pack to have another party," Eli said with a smirk. "I'd much rather get to the physical…"

"Elijah Quartz, don't you dare go there," Amy scolded.

"And to comply with the legal requirements in the State of Alaska," Kolby added snickering.

Lathen led the way out to the SUV. Kolby and Hayley piled in the back, and Pepper hopped in the passenger seat. Lathen checked the back of the vehicle, then got in and started the engine. "I see you got the tin cans. Dad's gonna kill us when he discovers them tied to his bumper."

"Too bad," Kolby snorted. "Jan's sister's kids are going to tie them to the bumper during the reception." Lathen pulled out onto the road behind his father's truck. The entire pack, less Sofie and Walter, were crowded into the Community Center when he pulled up and parked the SUV.

The ceremony was short. Pepper took the wedding pictures promising to email them to everyone when she returned home. Lathen had two pieces of Jan's cake, which was excellent, and not a crumb was left by the end of the reception. He and Kolby laughed their asses off when Amy and Eli got in the truck and started down the road, the tin cans rattling.

Eli stopped the truck, got out, and yanked off the tin cans, threw them in the back of the truck, but didn't bother with the "Just Married" lettering scrawled across the back window. Only shook his fist at the group gathered to see them off, then laughed and waved as he climbed back into the truck and peeled out, sending gravel and rocks in all directions.

Lathen and Pepper spent the night in Anchorage with Hayley and Kolby. With Pepper's help, Hayley fixed a big breakfast of ham and cheese omelets, hash browns, bacon, and orange juice. In between omelet bites, Pepper suggested they come to the Cove for Thanksgiving. Lathen nodded in agreement, chewing on a piece of bacon.

Hayley squealed, and Kolby looked thoughtful for a few seconds, then said, "That's three months away. I'll see what arrangements can be made at work for time off. No promises, but we'll do our best."

After breakfast, Lathen smiled, watching Hayley stuff blueberry muffins and cinnamon rolls in their carry-on luggage. Her way of making sure he and Pepper wouldn't starve while winging their way to Lobster Cove. *Yep, family was nice.*

Chapter Twenty
Back to the Lower Forty-Eight
—Surprises Abound

Tired but excited to be nearly home, Pepper and Lathen departed a misty Bar Harbor airport shortly after one a.m. Knowing their return flight would be in the wee hours of the morning, he'd left his work truck in the airport's long-term parking lot when they embarked on the Alaska trip.

When Lathen turned into the driveway, he turned the headlights off and coasted around to the front of the house and cut the engine. Her parents' car was parked in front. Pepper slipped out of the truck and quietly shut the door as he got two suitcases from the bed of the truck. Pepper lugged their two carry-ons and her backpack to the door and fished the keys out of her backpack. Quickly unlocking the door, she sat the bags on the floor and was nearly knocked over by a wiggling, barking, black ball of fur.

"So much for a quiet entrance." She giggled, holding the door for Lathen, who was trying to negotiate the entrance and avoid mowing over the dog.

Pepper moved out of the way, bent down, and scratched Ember's ears, while Lathen stowed the suitcases against the wall.

"We'll deal with them later," Lathen whispered, his foot on the first stair to the loft.

A soft whistling grew louder by the minute. "I'd better greet Kaylee before she wakes Mom and Dad. Go on up to bed. I'll be there in a minute."

"Too late. We heard Ember bark and knew it was you." Her mom's sleepy voice carried down the hallway. "She's been really restless for a couple days. Almost like she knew you were on your way home." Klaren shuffled to the aviary door and hugged her daughter. "Did you have a good time?"

"Yes. Lathen's dad is a hoot, and his new wife is really nice. They welcomed Lathen and me with open arms. Tell you all about it in the morning."

"It is morning." Her mother laughed. "Glad to hear it. You should know, Kaylee never relaxed, seemed on edge the whole time you were gone." Klaren padded back to the guest room. "See you when you get up."

The door to the aviary creaked when Pepper pushed it open, and a sliver of light shone across the floor. Kaylee whistled a greeting, then promptly turned her back, holding her feathers tight against her. "Oh, I know you're glad to see me. Just get over yourself." She stroked the bird's wing, crooning softly. "See you later this morning. We'll go down to the beach."

Kaylee ruffled her feathers, shook them out, then blinked slowly and settled on her perch.

This time when Pepper pulled the door closed, it made a long drawn-out crreeaak. Pepper grimaced. The sound shot up her spine like fingernails on a chalkboard. *Lathen needs to look at that.* She walked to the stairs, reached for the banister, and paused, glancing around. *It was sure good to be home.* She coaxed her tired legs up the stairs. Ember tilted her head, watching Pepper for a second, then trotted up the stairs and barked once inside the bedroom.

****

A light rain pattered on the window as Pepper tried sleepily to roll over. She didn't remember climbing into bed last night. Lathen's muscular arm was wrapped around her like a velvet chain and had her trapped. Still snoring softly, he made a snuffling sound when she tried to crawl out from under his grasp and drew her closer. His eyes blinked open. "Good morn—Probably afternoon by now." He glanced out the window at the gray sky. "Still raining, huh?"

"Would seem so." The curtain rippled as a cool breeze wafted through the room. Goose bumps ran up her one arm outside the covers, and she shivered. "Did you open the window last night and leave it open?"

"I remember opening it to breathe in the salty air, but I distinctly remember closing it because it made a thud and Ember barked. But I was exhausted, so…" He shrugged. "Are you cold?" Lathen curled his body around her.

The heat radiating from him warmed her arm when she yanked it inside the covers. "You know you could get up and close the window," she suggested.

"I could, but then we'd both be cold," he grumbled but got up and closed the window. His nostrils flared and he inhaled deeply. "Freshly brewed coffee. Ready to get up or…do I need to heat you up more?" he said, a suggestive tone in his voice and a come-hither look in his eyes.

Her stomach rumbled in response. "We better get up. I'm ravenous, and we need to see how things went while we were gone."

"Always the killjoy," he said with a laugh and

lunged for her.

She neatly stepped out of his path, causing him to nearly fall on the floor. "Always the sex-starved male."

"Once again, thanks for noticing." He scrounged inside the drawer designated for his stuff and pulled out the last pair of briefs. "This is it, or would you rather me go commando?" He caught her gaze and waggled his eyebrows.

"There's more in the bags downstairs. Just have to wash 'em."

He pulled on the briefs and walked to the closet. "Gee, don't sound so enthused." Inside the closet, he pulled out a worn pair of blue jeans and old rust-colored sweatshirt and yanked them on. "Seriously, we need to discuss a permanent plan of cohabitation, make it official."

"Oh, I thought it already was. You haven't slept in your cottage for a while," she said tying her hair back with a blue ribbon that matched the soft blue sweater she'd pulled from a drawer. Wearing only a black bra and matching panties, she sashayed into the closet.

"You do realize, if you don't get dressed quickly, you won't be leaving this room anytime soon."

A laugh bubbled up from her throat as her stomach rumbled again. "I know," she said airily. After slipping into her jeans, she pulled the sweater over her head and adjusted the ribbon tied around her ponytail.

Lathen opened the door, and freshly brewed coffee aroma flooded into the room. "Guess everyone is up but us."

Pepper breathed deeply. "Yep, I smell mom's famous bacon, egg, and cheese casserole. My favorite." She licked her lips and sprinted down the stairs, Lathen right behind her.

When they entered the kitchen, her dad was flipping blueberry pancakes on a griddle and her mom had just taken the steaming casserole out of the oven. Pepper kissed both her parents on the cheek. Klaren sat the dish on a hot-air-balloon-shaped trivet in the middle of the large oak table and stuck a serving spoon in it. She turned, picked up two mugs, handing a mug of coffee to Lathen and herbal tea to Pepper.

"Figured the food aromas would bring you two down here. Pull up a chair and enjoy," Klaren said cheerfully. "The tea I made from your garden herbs, quite tasty. Tell us all about your trip."

Lathen pulled out Pepper's seat. "Thanks, but you didn't need to do this. I'm sure you want to get back to your cabin and meet with friends around town."

"To be honest, we've had a really good time here. Duncan has been playing in your lab and down at the beach, taking water samples and heaven knows what else." Klaren laughed and flung her arms in the air and let them drop. "Not to mention getting in the workers' way out there."

"I have not," Duncan protested. "Lathen gave me assignments, and I completed them all as requested."

"Oh, so you got the pipe situation taken care of?" Lathen asked.

"I, or rather, we did. Funny thing, the supplier insisted that someone called and canceled the order, but the name and phone number of the calling party didn't match anyone we have here. Chalked it up to a mix-up, and they sent the shipment rush, no charge. Said you'd done a lot of business with them, and they appreciated it."

"Huh, that is strange. Oh, well, as long as everything got here, we're set." Lathen locked his fingers behind his head, leaned his chair back on two legs, and blew out a breath. "Thanks for helping out."

"I enjoyed it. Retirement is great, don't get me wrong, but I liked getting up and having something to do." Duncan winked at Lathen. "Klaren has had a good time too. She loves the computer system here. Got a lot of research done after walking to the beach with Kaylee on her daily flights."

"Yep, had good talks with Ashling too. Ember and Kaylee were always on guard the whole time you were gone." She paused. "Lathen, chairs are meant to have four legs on the floor." Klaren joined the others at the table, poured orange juice into the glasses, and sat down.

"Yes, ma'am." Lathen brought the chair down on four legs, then buttered and poured blueberry syrup over half the pancake, took a bite. "Mmmm, this is great," he mumbled around a mouthful of pancake, then reached for the maple syrup and poured that on the other half.

Pepper popped a fork full of casserole in her mouth and rolled her eyes. "Wonderful. I've missed this. It's been years."

"If you'd invited us up to Salem more than a couple times over the last several years—" Klaren started, but Duncan shook his head. "No matter, we're glad you've found your place. Oh, we set off the alarm system a couple of times. Forgot it was on," she said sheepishly.

"I know, got an email from the alarm company. Knew it was you from your disarm code." Pepper took a sip of tea, held the mug up. "This is really good. Dried the plants on the porch?"

"Not exactly. Kinda used scrap lumber and some plexiglass your dad got to build a greenhouse," Klaren said. "Connected it to the Kaylee's aviary."

Pepper's eyes went wide. "I didn't see a greenhouse last night." She put the last piece of bacon in her mouth and chewed. "Did you get the other project we discussed finished?"

"Sure did. Easy as pie and turned out perfect," her dad said. "We'll take a tour after breakfast." He sipped at his coffee. "Also brought an extra coffee bean grinder we had sitting around." Duncan pointed to the counter next to the toaster.

"No wonder this tasted different. What'd you use?"

"Columbian and a little Hawaiian we brought with us. Gotta order it over the Internet unless you are on the islands," Duncan said. "Left you a bag in the cupboard. Brought two with us, since we didn't know how long we'd stay."

"Speaking of staying," Pepper said shifting in her chair to glance at Lathen. "His brother and Hayley are going to try to make it out here for Thanksgiving. Lathen is going to bring it up to his dad and Amy when they get back from the honeymoon. If you two could stay through Thanksgiving, it would be fun for us to be together for the holiday. You'll love his family." She went on to describe Kolby and Hayley, Half Moon Valley, the people, their visit to Denali, and the wedding. She left out the problems Lathen feared when showing up at his father's house and things of that nature.

Her parents exchanged looks and her dad said,

"Sounds like you two had a wonderful time. Denali is on our someday list. We don't have any plans for Thanksgiving and the cottage is ours until December first, if we want it."

"Then it's settled," Pepper said enthusiastically. The holidays were just another day when she was in Salem. The rescues had to be fed, cleaned, and cared for. Seemed to be a busy season for their little center. But this year, she was excited at the prospect of family for the holidays. *I wonder if Gwen could get someone to cover for her for a few days?*

"I'll go ahead and email Dad. That way they won't make other plans for Thanksgiving. Now let's see this greenhouse." Lathen pushed up from the table.

Lathen and Duncan gathered up the dishes. Pepper and her mom rinsed and put them in the dishwasher, turning it on.

"Right this way," her mom said striding down the hallway. She opened the door to the aviary and walked through the room to a new door beside the big window looking toward the meadow. She pushed the door and held it open. Inside there were several drying lines extending the full length of the building, a low wooden bench stretched along one wall with a corner table, and a tough plastic plant center on wheels sat beside the table. Potting soil, pots, starter pots, and small hand tools had been moved from the storage shed into the greenhouse. The framework was two by fours, the walls and ceiling of quarter-inch plexiglass. A top vent in the roof finished it off. The outside door opened into the herb garden and had a security lock.

"It's kinda overkill for the security lock on the outside door since the greenhouse is plexi. But made sure the door from the greenhouse into the aviary is a security door and lock. I noticed all the security you have around here, and the foreman said it would be required for the interior door."

Lathen walked around and checked the framing, bench, and corner table. "Where'd you find the plant center?"

"The hardware store had it out front for their sidewalk sale. It was the end of the day, and the mist was turning into rain. Your dad haggled with the owner and got an even better price," Klaren said proudly.

"I don't think he wanted to drag the thing back inside and dry it off," Duncan said, the corner of his mouth kicked up in a grin.

Pepper tugged on the drying lines, ran her fingers over the plant center, and smiled. "Nice. Thank you two very much."

Her dad led the way back through the house and into the empty exercise area. Half of it had been walled off, with a large window between the two rooms, next to a door.

A smile spread across Lathen's face as he stared in the window and saw a large hot tub, tendrils of steam rising in the air. Benches lined the back wall of the room, and hooks were installed on the short wall. Windows to the outside faced the ocean and had automatic insulated blinds installed. There were two skylights installed in the roof.

Pepper opened the door and said, "Surprise." She pointed to the ceiling. "The skylights and windows are set up with electronic openers. They are on a sensor system and can be programmed to open automatically in case it gets too moist in here."

"How did you get—was Desmond in on this?" Lathen wanted to know.

Pepper made a motion of locking her lips and throwing away the key. "I'll never tell. But the trip was timed perfectly. Mom and Dad executed the rest of the plan for me."

"I think we'll put this to good use this evening," Lathen said, waggling his eyebrows.

"Well, we better gather our stuff and see what's been happening at the cottage," Duncan said, walking toward the living room. "But if you don't mind, I'd like to continue to help out, if you need me."

"Before you leave, let's go check with Desmond. I'm sure there are still lots of finishing touches you can help with." Lathen and Duncan went outside to find the foreman.

Pepper walked back into the kitchen and fixed two mugs of orange spice tea, took a sip from one mug, and handed the other to her mom. "Gotta go get groceries and supplies tomorrow. Want to come along?"

"I'd like that. I'm sure your dad will want to be here early tomorrow morning to help out. After shopping, we could have lunch at Maggie's. I love the food there."

Pepper frowned. "Well…" She considered a possible encounter with Kate. Pepper straightened and pushed the thought aside. "That would be fine." She wasn't about to let Kate control where she went. If a problem arose, she'd deal with it.

"Is there something wrong, dear?" her mom asked.

"No, not at all. Just thinking what all I need to get in town. Seems like I've been away a lot longer than ten days." She tucked a wayward piece of hair behind her ear and sat down on the couch.

Duncan burst through the door. "Klaren, you ready to go?"

"Yes. I guess so." Klaren raised her mug. "I'll bring this back tomorrow. Duncan, you need to carry the suitcases out to the car."

He grabbed two suitcases, and Lathen picked up an overnight case and garment bag. "See you tomorrow bright and early," Duncan said, taking the bags from Lathen, putting them in the trunk of the car. "I'll stop by the hardware store and pick up the items we discussed."

"See ya tomorrow," Pepper called as the car started down the driveway. She watched until their vehicle was out of sight and turned to Lathen standing behind her, his arm wrapped around her waist, and sighed. "Alone at last."

"My sentiments exactly. Family is nice, but I'm ready for a little you and me time this evening."

"I'll just whip up spaghetti and garlic bread. There's a nice wine in the fridge. We can eat dinner in front of the fireplace and enjoy the quiet."

"Sounds like a plan. Gotta get back to work." He leaned down and gave Pepper a smacking kiss, then grinned as several workers passing by the back porch gave a low wolf whistle.

Pepper stepped off the porch and ambled down the path to the office and lab, Ember at her heels, Kaylee circling overhead. "Now don't you go too far. Looks like we have a storm brewing," she hollered at the bird. Eying the dark skies and mist moving in, Pepper watched the osprey land in a nearby tree and begin preening. "Good girl."

Once inside the office, she looked through the mail her mom had opened, date stamped and arranged in descending order of date received. Pepper clicked on the email icon and groaned at the one hundred and two unread messages. Wading through them, she smiled at the one from Hayley indicating Kolby had arranged time off at Thanksgiving, so they'd be in Lobster Cove for the holiday.

An email from Brandon verified that all the funds had been transferred, and he was ready to close the estate. Her head drooped a couple times, so she closed the email and shoved up from the desk. Urgent emails handled, she needed to get moving, take in fresh air.

When she opened the door, the wind-driven rain slapped at her face, and she took a step backward. About that time Kaylee swooped in, the tip of her wing slicing close to Pepper's cheek as she rounded the room, settling on the back of Pepper's chair. She quickly closed the door, got paper towels, and knelt down to wipe up the rain spattered floor. *How had I missed that the storm had blown in?*

She'd almost gotten to her feet when Lathen shoved the door open. Her hands went up to deflect the door, and she avoided the main blow to her head. But shoving her hands up rocked her off balance, and her butt hit the floor.

"Lathen," she squealed.

"What the hell are you doing behind the door?" Lathen asked as he helped Pepper to her feet. "Are you all right?"

"Wiping up the wet floor. I'm fine. But you're dripping water all over the floor—again."

He locked the door, took the roll of paper towels

from her, and mopped up the floor. His lips twitched as amusement sparked in his eyes.

"You think this is funny?" Pepper demanded.

"Afraid so. It's like in the movies, but I've never seen it happen in real life. And we both look like drowned rats." Unable to hold back any longer, he roared with laughter. Ember eyed him suspiciously from the opposite corner of the room.

"Yeah, I guess." Pepper tried unsuccessfully to keep the laughter from her voice.

Lathen peered out the window. "Looks like the storm is letting up. But I think we are in for an all-nighter. Let's make a run for the house while we have a chance."

Kaylee was still soaked, not to mention a bit peeved, so Pepper pulled on the leather sheath from her desk, wrapped a towel around the bird, and asked her to step up. Holding the osprey close to her body, Pepper moved toward the door. Lathen called Ember to his side and opened the door. He slammed the office door behind him, then ran to the cabin.

Inside the house, Kaylee indignantly flew to her perch and fluffed her feathers out. Ember shook water all over, and Pepper grabbed towels from the bathroom. When she returned, Lathen had logs stacked in the fireplace.

"Do you want to do the honors, or do I have to hunt up newspaper and kindling?"

Pepper grinned and shook out her hands. "I'd be happy to." With a flick of her fingers, flames raced up the logs. Her grin faded for a moment. "I really didn't mean to start the fire at your dad's house. I just thought about it and poof." She shook her head. "Never happened before." She took the homemade spaghetti sauce out of the freezer and put six cubes in each bowl and popped them into the microwave.

"You'd better keep a lid on that poof when mortals are around. Were you stressed, like when you had the sparking fingers or frizzed hair?"

"No, I don't think so. You were more stressed over the visit than I was. Speaking of the visit—" Pepper walked into the kitchen and put water on to boil for spaghetti and noticed a loaf of fresh French bread her mom had baked. "It didn't go anything like you expected. Did it?"

"No. I left under pretty bad circumstances."

"Hayley told me. You were hurting in so many ways."

The muscle in his jaw tightened as he sliced the bread and handed the pieces to Pepper. "Hayley should mind her own business."

Spreading the garlic and butter mixture over the bread, Pepper put it on a pan and slipped the garlic bread into the oven. She wiped her hands on the towel and hung it over the oven handle. "You were her and Kolby's business, and the pack's too, so I am told."

"I don't want to rehash all of this. I've straightened my life out and thanks to you found peace and meaning. Now drop it. Please."

"Okay, one more thing. Are you still happy taking it one day at a time?"

"Yes, for now. I—well—am half in love with you or—maybe all the…But no pressure. Your family situation is weighing on you. I understand that. At least mine is settled. I think everyone likes you better than me."

Huffing out a laugh, she wanted so badly to ask him if he could phase, but decided against asking. He'd tell her in his own time. Something had changed inside him, she could feel it. If Ashling badgered him about it again, Pepper was going to...well, guess she couldn't kill a ghost. She giggled at herself and shook her head. But she sure could...do something.

"Pepper, where'd you go?" He touched her arm gently. "What's so funny?"

"Oh, nothing."

He raised one brow and started at her. "You're a terrible liar, you know that?"

"I know. It was just something Ashling said, and I thought I'd throttle her if she brought it up again."

His brow winged up higher, and his lips twitched. "But she's already dead."

"That's what was so funny," she explained, dumping the spaghetti into the boiling water and stirring it.

"I think you need sleep," he said with a smirk. Taking her chin in his hand, he tipped it up and kissed her affectionately. Holding her tight against him, his cheek rested on top of her head. *How did I get so lucky?* Sizzling came from the stove as the pot of spaghetti boiled over, burning on the smooth cooktop.

"Arrg. Now look what you've done." She swatted him away from the stove and took the pan off the burner. Snapped her fingers, the stove top was clean, and she put the pot back on the burner. "Not a word, not one word."

"Didn't see a thing." He took a large wooden fork and stirred the spaghetti, pressed it against the side of the pan, and pronounced it ready.

The timer went off for the garlic bread. She grabbed the pot holders and took the pan out of the oven, set it on the counter. "I'll let you get the wine while I put the bread in a basket. Want to eat in the living room, in front of the fireplace?" She took out two plates and forks, sat them next to the stove.

"Yep. I do." He took two wine glasses from the rack under the cupboard and plucked the wine from the fridge.

Kaylee whistled and circled the room, landing back on her perch. She shifted from foot to foot, then shook out her feathers watching every move Pepper made.

"I better go feed the spoiled bird." Pepper pulled the curtain back and watched the torrents of rain flood across the driveway and down the path. At least it wasn't coming down sideways anymore. "Not going back outside with the storm still raging." Pepper sauntered into the aviary and tossed a fish from the holding tank up in the air for Kaylee, who flew in right behind Pepper. The bird dove after it, caught it in one talon with ease, landed on her feeding perch, and begin to rip into the fish. "Night, Kayl." Pepper closed the door and left the light on automatic timer.

When Pepper returned to the family room, Lathen had the spaghetti served in the bowls, forks and napkins by each. The grated Parmesan cheese was in a smaller bowl with spoon and the basket of garlic bread on the coffee table in front of the recliner sofa facing the crackling fire. Ember lay crosswise in front of the door.

"Looks great and smells delectable," Pepper said, plopping down on the sofa beside Lathen. "It feels like we have been caught up in a whirlwind." Her shoulders slumped, and she leaned her head against his powerful chest. "Now my whole body is turning to jelly and my eyes won't stay open."

"Know the feeling. But for me it's good. The tension I've carried for so long is gone." He stretched his arms above his head, then lowered them caressing her cheek with his fingers, then her neck, and finally wound one arm around her shoulder pulling her close. He breathed in and sighed. "I love your scent, all citrusy and fresh."

She wrinkled her nose and turned to face him. "You're sniffing me."

"Only a little. It's a wolf thing." His tummy rumbled. "And the wolf is starved. Better eat before it gets cold, or we fall asleep and Ember will have it all."

"And we'll be cleaning up after her," Pepper said with a laugh. Untangling herself from Lathen's arm, she reached for her bowl and plucked a piece of garlic bread from the basket taking a big bite. "Yummy."

Lathen grabbed his bowl of spaghetti and twirled his fork in it, slipping a bite into his mouth. "Mmmm. This sauce is delicious." After that, they ate in silence with only the crackle-pop of the fire and patter of rain on the windows.

"Labor Day weekend is in a couple days. Think we could kick back and relax all three days? Maybe join Mom and Dad at The Cliffside for dinner one evening," Pepper said, gathering up the dishes.

"Sounds great. I'm going to give the workers Friday off too." He rinsed the dishes, she put them in the dishwasher, and turned it on.

"I'm beat, let's head to bed," she said, flipping off the light.

"I'll be right up, want to bank the fire," he said.

****

A bright beam of sunlight greeted Pepper as she blinked her eyes open and looked at the clock. She jerked upright kicking at the covers. "Shit, it's nearly seven. Mom and Dad will be here soon."

Lathen opened one eye and tugged her back down on the bed. "So…they know their way around the kitchen and still have a key."

"That's not the point. We should be working by now," she insisted, trying to escape his hold.

"The crew won't be here until eight o'clock. Just a few odds and ends left to finish up. Fill the salt water storage and holding tanks on the mobile unit, test a few systems, and we're ready for the grand opening."

"Great, but I want to be up and dressed when my parents arrive."

"Okay, okay," Lathen said lazily. "I'll go down and get the coffee started. Going to try that bean grinder. Loved the coffee yesterday." He slipped out of bed, yanked on work jeans, a black t-shirt, and blue checked flannel shirt.

Pepper watched him out of the corner of her eye. His muscles were more defined these days, and he carried himself differently…or maybe it was just the tight t-shirt. She shook her head and grabbed her favorite pair of light blue jeans and pink and white striped sweater.

Sitting across the table from Lathen, she said, "What do you think of getting a few zip-up hoodies with our logo on them for us to wear at the grand opening?"

"Might be a good idea, especially for those attending the soiree who are not from Lobster Cove."

"'I'll check it out while Mom and I are shopping this morning. We're going to have lunch at Maggie's."

"Bring me back a lobster burger. Probably one for your dad too."

"I hope Kate doesn't…"

"The women in my pack were putty in your hands. Kate is a mere mortal. You'll be fine." He pushed up from the table and winked at her.

Gravel crunching on the driveway caught Pepper's attention at the same time Lathen paused at the window. "Your mom and dad are here," Lathen said cheerfully.

A short time later, Pepper and her mom were on their way to the Moose Stop in Bar Harbor. She'd called the shop inquiring about purchasing hoodies and have them embroidered with Lobster Cove Wildlife Rescue and Rehab's logo on them. Turned out Pepper's mom and dad wanted one, and she decided to order one each for Elijah, Amy, Kolby, and Hayley as gifts. After discussing a cost break with the owner of the shop, Pepper ordered fifty. If they sold well, she'd order more. If not, she still got the ones originally decided on for less.

Pepper pulled into the parking lot outside Lobster Cove Grocery Mart. After stocking up with all the essentials and a few not so necessary, they stopped by Cliff Notes Bookstore. Kaylee had destroyed a book her mom had been reading when Klaren refused to let her out during the storm. Pepper replaced the book.

Passing by the window of Jewels of the Sea, Klaren saw a pair of black pearl earrings she couldn't live without. They strolled by several other local businesses on their way to the Lobster Cove Anchor to verify the dates the grand opening ad would run in the newspaper.

"Well, shall we go get the truck and drive to Maggie's, or just walk down the block, eat lunch, and walk off the calories?" Pepper asked.

"Weather's good, so let's plan on walking back to the truck after lunch," her mom suggested.

Walking by Maggie's, Pepper peered in the window, straightened her shoulders, and shoved the door open. Kate zipped past as Pepper and her mom looked for a place to sit. The place was hopping, but they finally slipped into one of the blue vinyl booths vacated by a young couple. Sandy stopped by the table with menus, turned over and filled the coffee cups. Kate stared daggers at Pepper every chance she got.

"What in the world is that waitress's problem?" Klaren asked.

Pepper sighed. "It's a long story."

"Uh oh, an old girlfriend of Lathen's? Why didn't you say something? We could have gone somewhere else?"

"No, more like an acquaintance that wanted to be more. She blames me for that not happening. And I'm not about to let her control where I go." Pepper shrugged.

Sandy sidled up to the table. "What'll you have?"

Pepper ordered four lobster burgers, two to go, and four pieces of blueberry pie. She paused. "I think we'll take all of it to go." Sandy nodded. Suddenly, the hair on the back of Pepper's neck stood on end, and she glanced around the room for the source. "Speaking of old flames, look who just walked in the door."

Klaren swiveled her head in time to catch Ben's attention. "Aw shit, this could be interesting."

Ben smiled, made a beeline for their table, and slid in next to Klaren. "Remember me? You haven't changed a bit." He touched her hair and stared into her eyes, then leaned back against the booth.

She blanched. "Oh, I wouldn't say that. How are you, Ben?" Klaren asked cordially with a cool edge to her voice.

"So you do recognize me. You and Duncan passed me in front of the hardware store last week, never said a word."

"Didn't see you. We were running an errand for the construction foreman at Pepper's place." She scooted against him. "We are on our way out. Nice to see you again."

Ben didn't move. "We need to get together and catch up."

"I'll let Duncan know and see if we can work something out."

"Oh, I meant you and me. Duncan and I were never friends. He bewitched you and…"

"No, Ben, I broke up with you because you were smothering me. Had nothing to do with Duncan."

"He had all that power, the McKay land, and you couldn't see beyond that," Ben said sweetly. "I understand. But you're back."

"Only to attend Pepper's grand opening," she said carefully.

"Mom, we really need to go. Nice to see you again, Ben." Pepper slid out of the booth and stood, waving to get Sandy's attention.

Ben narrowed his eyes and sneered at Pepper. Suddenly she felt like all the walls were closing in. She shook her head and discreetly pointed her fingers under the table at Ben's feet. She used her backpack as cover, sparks flew from her fingertips. Ben yelped. Patrons in the diner stared at him when he jumped up and took a menacing step toward Pepper, his dark eyes glittering with fury. The closed-in feeling dissipated. Pepper sucked in a breath and sidestepped Ben to grab her mother's arm, pulling her out of the booth. "Time to go. See ya around."

Ben shook himself, face contorted, tight lips curled back baring white crooked teeth. "Be certain of it." He snarled in a low voice. Glancing around, he straightened and strode out the door.

She blew out the breath she was holding and directed her gaze at Sandy.

"Order will be up in a minute," she called out, pushing a smiling Kate out of the way and reaching for a bag the cook had just put on the pass through.

Pepper paid for the order including a good tip for Sandy and wished the truck was parked closer.

Chapter Twenty-One
If Things Are Running Smoothly,
a Kink In the Works Is Inevitable

Saturday morning, Pepper woke up to loud pounding on her door. She slipped into a robe and sprinted downstairs, tying her belt at the waist as her phone rang. Lathen moved from the kitchen doorway, set the beans and coffee pot on the counter, wiped his hands on a paper towel, and hurried toward the door.

She picked up the phone, touched the screen. "Hello?" Pepper tried to listen to what was going on at the door as well as the phone conversation.

Lathen opened the door to find Roark Sullivan standing on the porch. "I think we have a serious problem. Several seal pups washed up on the shore this morning, some dead, some badly injured, and others disoriented. Gulls are just sitting on the shore, rubbing themselves on the sand. Really strange."

Lathen held the door open, and Roark stepped inside.

He sucked in a breath and continued. "I called Dr. Weaver. He's headed to my place, and Dr. Foster is headed over here but suggested I bring this little fellow directly to you." He held out a tiny bleating seal pup wrapped in a blanket, and carefully uncovered its side and right flipper. "See—looks like he has burns on his skin. He's weak. Poor guy. Doc said you could rinse him down in a tub, make him more comfortable 'til she gets here."

"Yeah, we can do that," Lathen said, glancing over at Pepper.

She stuffed the phone in her pocket, sidled between the Roark and Lathen, then peeked at the pup. "Poor babe, we'll get you fixed up," she cooed and turned her attention to Lathen. "Take the pup to the marine building, fill the decontamination tub with water, and rinse the pup until doc gets here." She tipped the little face, and the pup rubbed its muzzle and eyes on her hand, then jerked away. "Looks like a chemical burn, maybe its eyes too. Rather have Dylan take a look before we do anything but rinse. Try to make this pup comfortable in a tub of clean salt water, rinse her off good, pat her dry, and fill the tub with clean water. Let her sit in it if she will. Dylan should be here by then."

"Got it. Who was on the phone?" Lathen asked.

"Lizzy. She said the beach behind her house was littered with seabirds of all kinds scooting across the beach, rolling in the sand. Some just sitting there. Kinda like you described, Roark."

"Speaking of my place, I need to get back there. But I'll spread the word we have a wildlife emergency. It's been a long time since we've dealt with this type of situation, but you can bet most the town will be here within the hour. This will be your command post. Right?"

"Hadn't thought that far, but yes. We can send the volunteers to where they are needed once we get a handle on what happened. Since Dylan is headed here, I'm going to go out to Lizzy's house and see what we got over there."

"Better put some clothes on first," Lathen suggested before taking the crying seal pup and rushing out the door. Pausing in the middle of the beach path, he called over his shoulder, "Leave a note on the door for Dylan to come on down to the marine center."

As Pepper yanked on jeans and a sweatshirt, she considered a couple of birds treated at the clinic and the dead seal that had washed up on the beach two days ago. Looked like there'd been a spill of some kind up the coast. She tapped her finger to her lips and remembered reading about a cruise ship that had an accidental release of waste at Bar Harbor beginning of the week. The boat's captain claimed it was gray water and only a small amount. *Looks liked he lied.* Seems she read that same ship had run aground and may have been leaking fuel before the incident. She grabbed her waders and rain slicker and called Dylan's cell phone. It went to voice mail.

Sprinting out the door, she jumped in the newly stocked emergency responder van and turned the ignition key. The engine roared to life just as Lathen yanked the door open, baby seal still in his arms.

"The clean saltwater recirculating pump failed in the marine clinic. Backup isn't online yet. I can't get any water into the tubs. Gonna have to try to repair it, which will void the warranty. But I don't see another alternative."

"Shit." She jumped out of the van and raced down the path behind Lathen.

Once inside the building she glanced at all the empty stainless steel tubs, set in the counters, lining the walls. The baby seal still keened in Lathen's arms. Her gaze shifted to the stacks of five-gallon buckets stacked on the cement floor next to the huge pump Lathen pointed out. He snapped his fingers. "I think I can rig a bypass, but that's going to take time."

Pepper drew in a breath and blew it out. "I can buy you some time." She skirted the center island and put her hands on the huge pump. Closing her eyes, a barely visible spark bounced from her hands to the pump, it whirred to life, and water flowed from the tap into the first tub.

Backing away, Pepper put her hands on her hips. "Fill all the tubs and all the spare five-gallon buckets we have. Let's start the filtration system at the beach. I suspect waste and fuel spilled into the water from that crippled cruise ship docked in Bar Harbor. Test the filtered water before you fill the spare tanks. Our clean saltwater isn't going to last long, if that's the case." She took the young seal from him and gingerly dipped it into the filling tub. Using her hand, she poured water over its face and finally sat it in the tub and with one hand reached for a clean towel.

"Switched the filter system on. It's a good thing I filled the holding tanks on the van last night to check for leaks. Figured we'd use them for storage in a pinch and wanted to see how the fittings stood up to saltwater. Strange how things work out."

A quick grin crossed her worried lined face. "Good thinking." After the water in the tub reached several inches deep, she turned it off and rinsed the seal thoroughly with the sprayer, then opened the drain.

The door banged open, and Dylan rushed directly to the baby seal. At the moment, the seal was quiet, its big eyes watching everyone. "Okay, where are we?"

Pepper filled her in on what had been done and the

status of the situation at the present time. Finally, she blew out a breath and switched her attention to Lathen.

"The filtration is working perfectly." Lathen gave her two thumbs up. "I've called in a few extra workers to get the backup pump online while I rig a bypass. I hope the hell that one works. We got the installation parts yesterday. They were back ordered." He gritted his teeth. "When I get a hold of the pump supplier..."

"Good job." She lowered her voice and tugged Lathen toward the door, out of the vet's earshot. "I can't stay here to maintain the magic, need to check the birds on the beach." She chewed on her bottom lip, reaching for Lathen's cell phone. "I'll call Mom and Pops, see if they are available." Tapping in the number, she put the phone to her ear and heard an echo of the ring tone as the door to the building flung open. Klaren and Duncan stood in the doorway.

"Got a strong feeling our help was needed. What can we do?" her dad said glancing around the room.

Quietly, Pepper said, "Pump failed. I'm forcing it to circulate and pump the water by magic. Mom, can you sustain the alternate power source?"

"You betcha."

"Dad, would you go to the beach and draw water samples? You can test them in the lab. Know your way around there. Right?"

"I'm familiar with your setup. Played around taking water samples while you were gone. Most came back normal, but the one I took the night you got back tested strange. Thought I'd made an error, but never got around to taking another. The samples are still in the lab."

"Great, we may need those. Lathen has the keys.

He'll unlock the lab for you. I'll bring more samples from further up the beach where we have injured birds. Thanks." She stepped to the door. Lathen caught her around the waist and pulled her in for a lingering kiss before releasing her.

"So much for a relaxing weekend," he said.

Duncan and Klaren moved out of the doorway as Pepper scooted through, first kissing her mom on the cheek and then her dad. "Dylan, if you need anything, just ask. I'm headed up the beach to Lizzy's where she's reporting more birds down."

"Probably need to set up cleaning stations in those areas. Bring the worst cases here or to my clinic, depending on the severity of the injuries. Stay in touch," Dylan said. "After I get this tiny seal settled, I'll call the rehab centers up and down the coast and see if anyone else is experiencing this situation. Maybe get some more mobile units down here to help."

"Nothing like trial by fire, or in this case, water and creatures," Pepper said bounding out the door. "Call Bar Harbor first. I vaguely remember something in the paper last week about a fuel or waste spill from a cruise ship that ran aground and wound up there."

"Hey—wait up." Lathen grabbed a stack of five-gallon buckets. "These belong in the van. Sawyer and Sons donated several yesterday. I sanitized them and thought they'd be useful in the van. I'll keep the rest here."

She grabbed the buckets and sprinted to the vehicle through the mist and drizzle.

****

Lathen tossed Duncan the lab keys. "You know where you're going?"

He raised a hand and snatched the keys out of the air. "Yep. Got it. On my way."

Flipping his attention to Klaren, Lathen said, "All set?"

She nodded, watching the water flow into the tubs. "Do you want me to turn the water off?"

"Not necessary, they have an automatic shut-off at five inches." He paused, considering the morning so far. "On second thought, I'd appreciate you keeping an eye on the level. If it overfills, just turn the manual knob on top until the water stops."

"Will do."

"If you need anything, I'll be in the workshop for a few. Gotta see if I can scare up parts to circumvent the pump until we get the second one online. If I have to get parts at Sawyer's Hardware in the Cove, I'll let you know. There're a couple guys coming by to put the backup pump online. They'll know what to do, but if they have questions, send 'em on up to the workshop." Lathen strode up the path to the mammal building where he'd built an addition for parts storage and a workshop.

Within fifteen minutes, he returned carrying a bucket full of parts and a tool belt slung around his waist. "Got it. How's the little one doing?"

"Better. Burns are definitely chemical. She's resting now in one of the cubes in a couple inches of water." Dylan examined the interior of a cube. "Nice invention those cubes. Your creation?"

"Yeah. If you can use a smooth surface, a bit of clean water, and wave sounds, the marine animals are going to do better than in wire cages and pans of water amid the chaos."

"Exactly. We need to talk about these later." Dylan ran her fingers over the smooth surface of the cube.

"Of course. I'm headed to the aviary, figure there'll be a few birds that can't be left on their own to heal."

Duncan burst through the door with several water samples in plastic stacked tubs. "Got a toxic cocktail of fuel and some kind of waste and cleaning chemicals. If I had to guess, the crew of that cruise ship mixed up the chemicals. Whatever they're using is not biodegradable. But the levels shouldn't cause this type of damage to wildlife."

"Probably what we are seeing came from Bar Harbor," Dylan said.

When Lathen started up the path, he noticed several cars parked and people piling out. Still more trudged up the driveway in the dreary weather. He reached for his cell phone, touched Pepper's name. She picked up on the second ring.

"What's up?" she said breathlessly. "Got my hands full here."

"Appears most the town has turned out to volunteer. Where do you want me to send them?"

"Up here. Got washing stations set up, and we'll move down the beach until help comes from up north. Several rescues up there are going to take in the animals once they're vet cleared. We're only getting a few of the contaminated animals as opposed to Bar Harbor."

"Dylan agrees with you. The birds and mammals probably are coming from there. Duncan says the water is contaminated but not to the point it would cause this kind of damage to wildlife," Lathen said.

"At least that's good news," Pepper said.

Over the next several days, Lathen noticed the

number of injured birds and animals found on the beach lessened. Pepper was finally able to return to the facility and care for the creatures that were too ill to be treated and relocated. Most of the weary townspeople that rushed to help returned home. A few remained to take shifts caring for the injured birds housed at the center. He and Duncan helped the larger rescue centers transport the animals and birds to be relocated and released at a later date.

Kaylee set up vigil over the seal pup, helping to heal with her own brand of magic until the pup was ready to be released to a rehab with other seals. She wasn't allowed to free feed from the ocean. Pepper fed fish from the holding tank and when that ran out, it was frozen fish or land rodents Kaylee caught herself.

Finally, two weeks after the initial onslaught, things gradually returned to normal. A week prior to the grand opening, Lathen, Pepper, Duncan, and Klaren were gathered around the kitchen table.

"Well, can't really call it a grand opening, though we'll have to use what's left of the printed fliers. Most of the town has seen firsthand how everything works," Lathen said. "And were very impressed with the facility and you, Pepper. Congrats."

Pepper's cheeks pinked. "It was everyone pulling together that got the job done. How about we dub it a celebration of a successful rescue? Drop the tours and set all the food up in the barn—I mean aviary. It's empty and clean now. Just have a party."

"Good idea. Anyone that hasn't seen the facility, we can show them around individually." Leaning his chair on its back two legs, Lathen garnered the stink eye from Klaren until he dropped back to four and grinned.

"Gwen called the other night. Word of our little rescue had reached her. She's still coming up to spend a few days with us." Pepper grinned. "Even though it's not a grand opening."

"Look forward to seeing her," Klaren said.

"I hate to bring it up. But no run-ins with Tom or Ben that I'm unaware of?" Pepper asked hesitantly.

"Well, not exactly run-ins but a total of fifty-two voice mails and text messages. If I ever find out how he got my cell number, someone is going to spend the rest of his or her life as a toad," Klaren said vehemently. "I've caught glimpses of him here and there. Once he stopped me in the market and apologized for his behavior at Maggie's. But that's it."

"When did it jump from ten to over fifty? And the market?" Duncan asked, his lips pressed into a thin line. "You didn't mention that. I don't like this."

Klaren shrugged. "Sorry. It was only a few minutes, a couple days after the incident. He seemed sincere. Then we got busy and…I just…Oh, I don't know."

"It's a matter of figuring out if he is behind the attacks and what motive he has, then disarming him," Pepper said. "If it's a curse we're dealing with, as Ashling believes, a counter curse and some type of punishment is in order. By the way, did either of you talk to her coven?"

"Yes, I've been in touch, and they are more than willing to help. Name the date and place they'll be there," Duncan said. "Ben's reputed to have dabbled in black magic for several years now, according to Ravyn. He was booted from their coven shortly after Ashling's death five years ago."

Klaren's eyes rounded. "When did you talk to members of the coven? You didn't tell me."

"When you were out shopping with friends yesterday. Ravyn returned my call. I was going to tell everyone at once."

"Oh, well, if I'd known that…"

Pepper chewed on her lip and rubbed her chin. "Okay, lesson learned, spread the information when you get it. No holding back."

Everyone murmured in agreement.

"If you believe in Ashling's theory, and I do, maybe we can use Ben's disturbing infatuation with Mom to our benefit. He might confide in her if he thought…never mind, it's too creepy," Pepper said.

"No, it's not. I agree with Pepper. Ashling's theory is the only thing that makes any sense after all my research into the McKay's. Ben's of the opinion that I married your father only because of his power and the McKay property," Klaren said pressing her hand to the table.

"Little did he know about my dazzling personality and prowess in bed not to mention…"

"Oh, Dad, stop—that's way too much information." Pepper groaned sticking her fingers in her ears and squishing her face up.

Though she tried to hide it, concern on Pepper's face worried Lathen. Not to mention, an unstable witch using dark magic endangered everything they'd built and Pepper's family. This situation had gone far enough.

Chapter Twenty-Two
Lobster Cove Wildlife Rescue and Rehabilitation
Center Grand Opening Turns into Celebration
of Successful Rescue

The day of the celebration arrived. Dressed in jeans, a white blouse, and her new hoodie with the center's logo splashed across the back and her name embroidered on the left chest, Pepper stepped out into the dreary morning. The drizzle from the night before continued. She dashed back into the house and donned her purple rain slicker, pulling the hood over her head. The mist swirled around her like a lost spirit as she followed the path toward the seabird aviary, Ember at her side. Kaylee had been released earlier to feed and now circled high overhead, anticipating Pepper's destination. The bird landed in a tree outside the aviary and waited.

When Pepper heaved the heavy wooden door open, she glanced up to where Kaylee sat. "Oh, come on in." And moved to the side. The osprey soared by her landing on one of several perches set up inside. The wind blew the door closed behind Pepper. Several tables were set up end-to-end, running the entire length of the building. The blue and purple logo with white lettering was centered in the middle of each tablecloth. Thankfully, Lathen had turned the heat on to chase the chill away of the September day. She paused and admired the entire arrangement. He stood at the end of the building talking on the phone. Pepper ambled closer then heard snippets of conversation.

"Glad you and Amy will be able to spend Thanksgiving with us." There was a short pause. "Yeah, Kolby and Hayley will be here too, along with Pepper's parents. She will be thrilled at the news. What's that?" Another pause.

"I'm going to be what? Well, that makes you Grandpa, doesn't it?"

As she got closer, she couldn't make out what he was saying but heard Eli's gravelly voice as Lathen held the phone away from his ear.

"Yeah, Kolby told me about it when he and Hayley visited the Cove. He wanted to wait until after the wedding to tell you, so it wouldn't take away from your day." Lathen paused and smiled at Pepper. "Hey, he's your son, just my brother. How's Amy feel about all this?"

He held his index finger up.

"That's a good thing. Dad, I'd love to talk longer, but today is the grand opening—uh—really a celebration of our first successful rescue. But I'll tell you all about it, later. Okay? I really need to finish getting things ready. Pepper is standing here prepared to crack the whip." A hearty laugh rumbled up from Lathen's chest. "That could be fun, but inconvenient at the moment. Yeah, me too. Talk to you soon." He ended the call and glanced at Pepper.

"Hello, beautiful." He reached out, and his hands circled around her waist, lifting her off her feet.

She squealed, feet dangling a foot above the floor. "Put me down."

He gazed up at her. "It'll cost you," he said seductively, then lowered her until his lips pressed against hers, then gently covered her mouth.

She quivered at the sweet tenderness of his kiss.

His mouth moved to her ear whispering, "Dad and Amy will be here for Thanksgiving."

"That's wonderful," she said dreamily turning her head so her lips touched his and deepened the kiss.

"Ummm…Am I interrupting something?" Gwen asked.

Lathen let Pepper slide down his body until her feet touched the floor. "Why, as a matter of fact, you are. But since you've driven all this way for our celebration, you're forgiven, this time." He chuckled and released Pepper.

"Oh, I didn't know if you were going to make it after the message you left last night. Things worked out?" Pepper asked.

"Yeah, we took possession of the poached birds. Their condition wasn't as dire as first thought. Jodi stayed the night. The vet is supposed to be there this morning. So I left at three a.m. to get here in time, but I can only stay a couple of days rather than the week I'd planned."

Pepper hugged Gwen. "I'm just glad you made it."

"Can I get a quick tour before everyone starts arriving?" Gwen asked.

"Of course. Lathen, you got this handled?"

"Yep. Go ahead and show Gwen around," he said.

Reaching into a red bag, Gwen pulled out several DVDs and said, "I almost forgot. Made one of these and got a couple more from other rescues. They're interactive DVDs for kids, teaches about the environment and why rescue and rehab are important to the survival of our wildlife. Thought maybe you would have a place we could set up for kids to view the videos. I could handle that for you." She shook the bag. "Got lots of handouts, badges, and small plush creatures too."

"What a great idea. There'll be lots of kids here, and I was wondering how to entertain them. There's plenty of room in the mammal habitat. We can set up there. In fact, we'll go there next on your tour." Pepper pointed to one of two buildings across the way.

After she had given Gwen the grand tour, they were headed up the path to the cabin when several vehicles pulled up behind the caterer's van.

"Looks like the party is on. I need to run down to the barn, make sure Lathen is ready, and see what Kaylee wants to do."

"I'll just go back and set up the children's entertainment. Does the computer we brought from your office need a password?"

"Yes. The same one I used in Salem to access your computer. I'm not very creative and only have so much memory to keep all the passwords straight." Pepper pointed to her temple and laughed.

"Know what you mean." Gwen followed the path to the mammal habitat, disappearing inside the door before Pepper cut back and sprinted to the seabird aviary.

"Hey, handsome, need any help?" she called yanking open the wooden door. "Kaylee."

The bird came swooping down from the rafters. Pepper sheathed her arm in leather and held it out waiting for the bird to land. "Are you going to stay here and watch over things, or would you rather return to your aviary? Remember no fishing at the beach."

The bird cocked her head to the side and blinked.

"Okay, but I'd prefer you to stay in the rafters at the far end while we've visitors."

"Talking to that bird again?" Lathen grinned and jogged to the end of the tables. "I'm going to stay here and see that everyone gets fed. Lock the cabin and set the alarm. Don't want anyone wandering inside."

"I'll do that now. Gwen is in the mammal building. She brought things for the kids to do. I'll relieve her later, so she can grab a bite. Mom and Dad are on their way down here. If you have a group that wants a tour, maybe they can stick around while you're gone. Your hoodie looks great. Black suits you," Pepper said, pulling at the hoodie's drawstring.

He struck a pose, then turned, raised his arms half way up, curling them at the elbow showing off his biceps. "This is all yours." Turning in a circle, he struck another pose, then roared with laughter.

Over the next several hours, the drizzle stopped and the sun peeked out making things warmer but muggy. By Pepper's estimation, most of the town showed up, enjoyed the food and chewing over the events of the past couple of weeks. Dylan Foster stopped in for food and had a few updates on the rescue birds and animals. All doing very well. The baby seal had adjusted to his new family group and become a bit of a ham. Colleen, her brother, and his family stopped by later in the afternoon to see the changes. She spent time down by the lake while the rest of her family checked out the interactive programs set up in the mammal habitat.

Gwen had her hands full. Not only did the children find the interactive programs interesting, but they were popular with the adults too. Duncan and Klaren came up to relieve Gwen for a bite to eat. Brandon Fairbanks and his family stopped by along with a couple other lawyers from the firm and their families. Pepper waved at them in passing. There were so many people. She was only able to get a quick chat with Colleen before hurrying off to check on other guests.

It was early evening by the time Lathen and Pepper waved good-bye to the last visitors.

"We're going to head to the cottage. Call you tomorrow and work out a time to get together and work on the family project," Duncan said as Klaren nodded behind him.

Pepper unlocked the cabin and deactivated the alarm for Gwen, so she could get a warm bath and climb into bed. She was asleep on her feet. Lathen helped Pepper clean up the mammal habitat, gather all the DVDs, and return the computer to its rightful place in her office. As they trudged up to the cabin, Ember trotted out of the woods.

"Been guarding the property, huh, girl?" He reached down and scratched behind her ear.

Kaylee whistled from the tree branch above her aviary.

"I know you're hungry. I'll be there to feed you shortly," Pepper said plodding up the path to the cabin.

"You go on in and feed her. I've got a surprise for you. Meet me at the hot tub when you're done." Lathen winked at her as he held the door open. She scooted inside and hurried toward the aviary.

****

Lathen picked up a bag he'd stowed beside the couch and walked toward the other end of the cabin. The hot tub bubbled and the moist air billowed out when Pepper yanked open the door. Several candles lined the room. Their flames cast shadows that danced on the walls.

A soft sigh escaped her lips as she stepped inside, the door closing behind her. "This is so romantic." She sniffed. "Smells like lavender in here."

Lathen lounged in the corner of the hot tub. His heavy-lidded gaze traveled over her. A seductive smile curved the corner of his lips. "Welcome, my lady," he said in a deep rich baritone. "Your wish is my command. Clothes are optional, but I took the liberty of bringing your bikini." He pointed to the bench on the far wall, where a turquoise string bikini hung from the corner.

"Lathen, Gwen is staying with us. I don't think…"

"Gwen is dead to the world in the guest room. The sun will be high in the sky before she stirs. But if it will make you feel better, we can lock the door. I've already lowered all the blinds over the windows except the ones looking out to the sea and where the full moon rises." He made a deep purring sound in his throat.

She giggled. "I don't see what use putting on the bikini would serve, since you want me naked anyway."

When he didn't make a move, she stood still her green eyes sparkling with mischief. When she started to unbutton her blouse slowly, one button at a time, he settled back against the tub, steepled his wet fingers together, and pressed them to his lips watching her every move.

"Strip for me," he said in a husky voice.

Her eyes flew open at his commanding tone. She paused for a second, then pushed the blouse off her shoulders, slowly letting it fall to the floor. Next, she unclasped her red lace bra and leaned over, breasts spilling out as her bra joined the blouse on the floor. She straightened, her gaze hot and proprietary.

Ignoring the wolf prowling inside him demanding that he take her, Lathen watched and licked his lips, his erection straining to get out of the swimsuit. "Bring those beautiful breasts over here," he rasped.

Her hips swayed seductively as she stalked toward the tub, sliding her hand down her belly to her waist, unbuttoning her pants and slowly lowering the zipper.

He rested his head back on the ledge of the tub. She leaned over him, brushing her lips, then her breasts over his mouth. Reaching around her back with his hands, he held her in place, sucking on each nipple until they turned raspberry. When he released her, she undulated away, the jeans slipped to her hips. Facing away from him, she stopped, wiggled out of the jeans and red lace panties, spread her legs, and bent over peering at him from between her long limbs.

He sucked in a breath. After watching her wriggle into those panties and matching bra this morning, he'd imagined all day exactly how he was going to remove them. Watching her take them off was better. He felt like he was going to explode and wanted nothing more at that moment than to bury himself to the hilt inside her, yet he continued to just watch.

Snatching the bikini from the bench, she raised her leg and stepped up on the seat. Balanced on one foot, she slipped the bottoms on first one leg and then the other. She leaned over, wiggled her breasts into the top, tied the string behind her back, and slid into the bubbling fragrant water.

Anticipation made his heart pound as she slithered around him and nibbled at his neck. She breathed a kiss at the hollow of his throat, trailed her lips along his jawline, and touched her tongue to the corner of his mouth.

Turning his head, he took her tongue into his mouth, tongue twined with hers in a sinuous dance as her flavor spun into him.

When he reached for her leg, running his hand up her thigh, she moved to straddle him.

Slowly pulling away, he whispered, "Now, I get to take it off you." When he tugged at the string behind her back, her firm breasts spilled into his awaiting hands. The nipples hardened against the rough pad of his thumb. He teased the peak with the tip of his tongue, laving circles around the hard little berry, sucking one, then the other into his mouth. A little moan escaped her throat as she arched against him. He cupped her ass, holding her center tight against him.

Leaning back, she caressed her fingertips over the sinewy muscles of his chest, twining her fingers in the hair at his taut lower stomach. Her eyes held his as she traced her lips with the tip of her tongue and slipped her fingers under the waistband of his low-slung swimsuit. He groaned. "Are you trying to kill me?"

"Not exactly." She shifted and wrapped her long slender fingers around him. Unable to speak, he moaned at the contact and jerked his hips toward her. The touch drove all thoughts out of his mind except his unquenchable desire to be inside her. This quick reaction and insatiable appetite were something he thought would diminish, but it only grew stronger. Everything within him screamed with the need to claim her. Clinging to control by the thinnest thread, he pulled her hand away from him. "Not yet," he murmured. Trailing kisses down her neck, he reached down and tugged at the string on one side of the bikini bottom.

The scent of her arousal reached his nostrils. He pulled her bikini bottom aside and teased a finger inside her, then two, curled them toward the sweet spot, and pumped a couple of times. Her eyes closed, and she whimpered, spreading her legs wider, arching against his hand. With a mischievous grin, he asked, "Ever done it in a hot tub?"

"Noooo," she said, opening her eyes to stare at him. "We don't have…"

"The bubbles make it fun. Let me show you." He untied the other strings on her bikini bottom and let it float away. Then he reached for her waist, never taking his eyes off her, loving the red patches that bloomed on her cheeks. Lifting her up, he watched the water lap between her spread legs and lowered her over a stream of bubbles. She squirmed as they caressed her, then he thrust two fingers back inside. Her frantic moans told him exactly how close she was to orgasm. He worked his fingers faster until she crashed over the edge to a shuddering climax, her fingers digging into his shoulders. When she finally slumped against him, he swept her up in his arms, stepped out of the hot tub, and carried her to the door, unlocked it.

Her eyes flew open in horror. "You're not going to carry me out of here, us both buck naked, with Gwen in the guest room?"

"Honey, the danger of getting caught is half the

fun," he whispered sprinting across the room and up the stairs, shoving the bedroom door closed with his foot. "See? Safe and sound," he panted against her ear, his breaths coming in gasps and not just from sprinting.

"But what about all of our clothes?" she asked breathlessly.

He shrugged pulling her against him. "She'll know rather than guess what we did tonight." He quieted Pepper with his lips slanting over hers. She thrust her tongue into his mouth eagerly, demanding a response his body was more than ready to give.

Settling her on the bed, he ripped open the foil package and sheathed his erection.

"Hurry," she said anxious to have him inside her.

He eased between her legs and spread them wide with his knees. Lathen teased her slick entrance as she bowed up under him. Her scent intoxicated him. The feel of her was amazing, and he thrust inside. She moaned and pulled her knees up on either side of him, spreading wider allowing him deeper, stretching her.

Together they found the rhythm that bound their bodies in exquisite harmony, soaring higher to the peak of ecstasy. At that moment, his desire to mark her as his own was undeniable. When her gaze met his, she tilted her head to the side, giving him the access needed. He sank his canine fangs into her shoulder, marking her as his for eternity. He licked at the wound until it began to heal. A multi-colored rainbow of streamers burst out of thin air above the bed and winked out quickly, leaving no trace.

"What the hell was that?" Lathen asked, pushing up on one elbow, leaning to shield her with his body.

"I'm not sure. Never happened before, but I

suspect it has something to do with our...umm...you know—pleasure." She grinned shyly at him, touching the new bite mark with her fingertips.

"Oh, is that all." His body relaxed. "There's something I need to explain..." he said, his gaze drifting over the mark, his forehead creased.

She put her finger to his lips. "Tomorrow," she murmured and closed her eyes.

He tucked her head under his chin as her body molded to his, and they slipped into a blissful sleep of sated lovers.

Next morning the whirr of the coffee grinder woke them. Lathen buried his head under his pillow. "Are your parents here already?"

"No, I don't think so. Gwen's a coffee addict, and she loves fresh ground coffee, even though she doesn't have a grinder and rarely has time to enjoy it. Bet she saw the grinder yesterday and found the coffee this morning." Pepper grinned. "Well, guess we better get down there before she—"

"Getting up," Lathen said, his voice rough and just a bit irritated. He yanked on a clean pair of jeans and a blue sweatshirt.

"You can't still—want to—?" She rummaged around in her dresser drawers and pulled out a lilac pair of silk panties and matching bra.

He paused to watch her slip into the underwear. *She's going to kill me.* "Shit, woman. I'm male, that's all I think about, and a werewolf is a carnal creature. I wanted to explain about last night—the bite..." Lathen ran his fingers through his hair and rubbed the back of his neck.

"Plenty of time for that. Besides, Amy, Hayley,

and the women of the pack kind of filled me in, so I understand and allowed it. Besides from what they said, protection comes with the bite. At present, I can use all the protection I can get." She pulled on a green sweater over a mint-colored blouse and slid into a pair of black jeans. Picked up her hoodie with the logo and tossed it up on her shoulder.

"But there's more to it. A lot more. Serious commitment, for eternity." He grabbed her arm.

She stared at him. "Do you regret the action?"

He shook his head vehemently. "No. Absolutely not…But you may, some day."

Quiet for a couple beats, Pepper chewed on her bottom lip and shrugged. "Doubt it." She picked up a sack and pulled out a pink hoodie with the rehab's logo. "I forgot to give this to Gwen yesterday. She'll love it."

"Pepper, you're taking this way too lightly." He huffed out a breath and threw up his arms, letting them drop to his sides.

"Lathen…I'm not. Only we have bigger things to deal with at the moment. When I was feeding Kaylee last night, Dad called. On their way home, they saw Ben's car parked by the side of the road just before our driveway splits off."

"Shit. Why didn't you tell me?"

"We were—uh—otherwise occupied." She grinned. "Besides, that was much more enjoyable than discussing Ben."

"I didn't see him skulking around anywhere and Ember patrolled the forest without incident," Lathen said with a frown.

"Mom believes the magic kept him off the property and Dad agrees with her. It's gained a lot of strength with both Dad and me here. You can feel it surge at times. Dad said it used to do that when he was a kid and all the McKay's gathered on the property."

"Crap, that's going to piss him off."

"Possibly. Mom and Dad will be over this morning. Thought we should walk the property. They wanted to see Gwen anyway."

"Gwen knows about..." Lathen asked.

"Yes, she knows I'm a witch. We never really talked about it, but she knew I used powerful magic to save the rescue in Salem. That's what set everything in motion."

"I remember you telling me."

"Shall we go down and face the music? If Gwen saw our clothes scattered all over, she'll never let me forget it," Pepper said with a grimace.

"I doubt she saw anything. Your clothes are strewn over the hot tub room."

"True."

"I'll go open the shades and clean up while you visit with Gwen." He paused, walking to the large bedroom windows overlooking the driveway. "Your parents are here."

"Figures. So the day begins." She walked over to him and leaned in giving him a long tender kiss. "I loved last night. All of it."

"Me too," he murmured against her lips. "Just wish..." Lathen squeezed her tight, then let go.

****

Pepper found Gwen sitting in the living room holding a mug of coffee and staring out the window across the meadow. Kaylee quietly preened on her portable perch until she caught sight of Pepper and whistled.

"Morning, Kaylee, Gwen. How'd you sleep?"

"Like the dead. Figured you'd have a late night too. Saw the grinder yesterday and helped myself to a mixture of coffee beans. It's heavenly." She inhaled deeply over her coffee cup. "Feels different than the last time I was here. Kinda like Salem before you left."

Kaylee let out a loud whistle. Pepper said, "Okay, okay. I'll let you outside, but fish only at the pond. The beach is off limits for food."

"I envy your ability to converse with the creatures." Gwen sighed. "I miss you."

"It's a blessing and a curse, depending on the day." Pepper laughed. "So that's why you kept me around so long."

Narrowing her eyes, Gwen said, "You know that's not true. I didn't even know about your gifts until…well…you saved the rehab and decided to leave."

"Morning, everyone," Duncan said breezing into the room with a large bag from Bea's, followed by Klaren with five cups of steaming liquid in a holder. Lathen, who'd let them in the front door, brought up the rear.

Klaren set the drinks on the kitchen table and walked over to hug Gwen. "We brought breakfast," Klaren sang out, looping an arm around Lathen and kissing Pepper on the cheek. "Figured you'd still be feeling the effects of yesterday. Great turnout, by the way. Seems the whole town supports your project." She glanced from her daughter to Lathen. "But you both look great."

"Had a good night," Pepper said waving her

mother off, pulling plates out of the cupboard, stacking them on the table.

Over breakfast Gwen related the latest happenings at the Salem rescue. Klaren and Duncan touched on the subject of Ben but otherwise kept the conversation lighthearted.

"How about we take a stroll around the property to walk off all the calories I brought from Bea's?" Klaren joked.

"I'm in," Lathen said. "The sun's still out, but the clouds are rolling in, supposed to be socked in by late afternoon."

"If I had a physique like that, I'd never worry about calories," Gwen said poking him lightly in the stomach. "Adds new meaning to washboard."

Hiking through the forest on the far corner of the land, Gwen found a triad of dark crystals. She pointed to the ground. "What are these? Do you have them here for a reason?"

The others gathered around. "Didn't put them there," Pepper said glancing at her father.

"I ran this entire area day before yesterday, they weren't here then," Lathen said.

Pepper raised an eyebrow.

"It was during my morning run. I do it almost every day," he said easily. "A great stress reliever, not that I have any stress around here."

Duncan took a cloth bag out of his pocket, ran his hand over it a couple times, and turned it inside out over his hand and picked up the crystals. He drew the bag around them and tied the leather drawstring. He tucked the pouch in his pocket. "Don't think they belong here," he said firmly. Silently to his wife and daughter, his words floated through their minds. *It's his attempt to access the property through dark magic. Didn't work.*

"Okkaay, then…" Gwen kicked at the scorched earth where the crystals had been and glanced at Pepper. "Someone tried to start a fire using the magnifying properties of those crystals. Probably kids." She shrugged. "Never understand the consequences of their actions until it too late."

The rest of the property was clear. They set up a croquet course in the meadow and played until the afternoon storm chased them inside.

****

Two days later as Gwen packed her car to leave, a vehicle came tearing up the driveway. Two teenagers jumped out, racing around to the back, jerking up the hatchback.

Pepper sprinted around the car followed by Gwen and saw a crate completely covered except the front. A large brown bird with golden highlights on its head and neck struggled to one foot. A wing hung useless. The bird's weak cry worried Pepper. "She's in shock."

Breathlessly the girl introduced herself as Judy and explained that they were driving up Hwy 3 and saw the bird struggling on the ground. It was wound in some type of fishing line. They cut the line and threw the thick blanket, now covering the crate, over the bird.

"At first I tried to hold the bird on my lap, wrapped in the blanket. But it was so strong, Rick"—she pointed to the other teen—"worried that we were doing more harm than good. So we stopped and released it into the crate Rick uses for transporting his dog and headed straight here."

Pepper nodded.

Judy drew in a long breath and continued. "We were here for your celebration and watched the videos she"—Judy pointed at Gwen—"showed. We didn't have anything to stabilize the wing and that beak…"

"You did fine." Pepper turned and hurried toward Gwen's car, conjured a pair of long leather gloves and returned. Opening the crate door, she closed her eyes, focused on the bird and her ability to calm it. She reached in and picked up the bird. "It's all right, you'll be fine," she cooed quietly to the bird. Then turned her attention to the others. "Let's get her to the aviary." Holding the bird tight to her chest, Pepper sprinted to the building.

Gwen, who ran ahead, had the extra-large padded crate out and open next to the examining table.

Pepper eased the bird onto the table. "It's a juvenile female golden eagle. You can tell by the dark-banded white tail and white patches on the primaries." She handed her phone to Judy. "Scroll down to the name Dylan, when she answers, tell her what's happened and I don't think transporting the eagle to the vet office is a viable option at this time."

The girl stood wide-eyed staring at the phone in her hand. Rick shook her shoulder. "You can do this."

As Pepper stood at the table, she saw Gwen look up from examining the bird and smile. Lathen's strong hands reached around Pepper and held the bird gently. "I saw you take the bird and run. Grabbed your emergency bag by the door. Thought it might be faster than looking for everything here. We need a rolling cabinet stocked with emergency supplies right by the table."

"Great." Pepper ducked under Lathen's arm and held the bird's wing in place. Gwen took vet wrap and secured the wing to the bird, leaving the good wing free.

"Excuse me," Judy said. "Dr. Foster will be here within the hour. Do you need to talk to her?"

Pepper took the phone, explained what they'd done and the condition of the bird, and listened to Dylan's suggestions.

Gwen snipped the remaining line from the bird's foot, checked the lacerations. "No serious damage here. Antibiotic salve should do the trick."

Pepper nodded in agreement.

The eagle treated and resting, the group walked back to Gwen's car. "You guys did a great job today," Pepper said to the teens. "The only thing I would suggest is that next time you call us when you discover an injured creature. That way we can be prepared and tell you how best to act. Or if it's better you stay and observe until one of us gets there. Today, you two saved this young eagle's life. Good job."

Judy's face blushed red, and Rick stood next to their car digging the toe of his shoe in the dirt. "Thanks," they said in unison.

Over the course of the next few weeks, an Atlantic puffin was brought in with injuries to its feet and beak. It was treated and would spend a few weeks in rehab, but would eventually return to the wild as would the golden eagle. Two peregrine falcon chicks caught in a terrible storm were huddled in the alcove between Pepper's greenhouse and cabin, when Lathen found them. They would be released in Arcadia National Park in a couple months or in the spring depending on their progress, under the watchful eye of the park service.

Dylan Foster brought a gray wolf pup to the rescue. The wolf had been hit by a vehicle in Arcadia National Park, shattered his hind leg and jaw. She pinned the jaw, put a rod in the leg, and neutered him because she felt, even with rehab, the pup wouldn't be suitable for release. Ember watched over the wolf pup, encouraging his recovery. Even after only a few days, Pepper saw a bond forming. After a long discussion, Pepper and Lathen decided the wolf pup would be the first permanent resident of Lobster Cove's Rescue and Rehab Center. They called him Tonk.

Chapter Twenty-Three
If Cursed or Possessed Is the Question, an All
Hallows Eve Celebration Could Be the Answer

In the weeks following the discovery of the dark crystals, Lathen, Pepper, and her parents met for barbecues or pizza at the cabin. Sometimes her parents would bring breakfast from Sweet Bea's all to make sure their discussions regarding Ben and Tom would not be overheard and lessen the chances of another attack. He no longer could access the McKay property, so planned attacks would have to be in town where he'd be more vulnerable. They determined Ben was behind all the attacks, but obtaining undeniable proof was difficult without putting people at risk. Evidence was needed to enlist the participation of Ashling's coven to stop Ben before the attacks escalated or turned fatal.

A couple of weeks before Halloween, a soft knock followed by a slow squeak of Pepper's office door caused her to look up from her computer. Colleen stood in the doorway with a cumbersome book in her hands and a friendly smile.

"I saw Lathen on the path to your cabin. He said you were in the office and to go on in. Is this a bad time?" Colleen asked.

"No, not at all. It's good to see you again. Did you and your family enjoy the rehab celebration? Sorry, I wasn't able to spend much time with you."

Colleen set the book on the desk. "It was fine, dear. We enjoyed ourselves tremendously. I am so happy you are finally where you belong, doing what you love."

"Well—thank you. I'm just sorry you had to…"

"No, it was time. I was unpacking the rest of my boxes and found Ashling's grimoire. McKay's book of magic handed down from generation to generation. I know she meant for you to have it."

"Thank you, Colleen. It may be just what we need."

"Yes. After I heard you'd contacted our coven to help with the Ben situation, I remembered packing the book. Didn't want it left on the property unsupervised, you know. Do you really think he's cursed Tom? Bewitching him to do Ben's dirty work?"

"Yes. After all of Mom's research turned up only benign McKay skeletons in the closet, no evil spirits seeking revenge, it's the only conclusion that makes any sense. According to Ravyn, a minion curse on Tom would enable Ben to control him without being in close proximity."

"I don't understand why he continued when you took over the property. A McKay witch in residence would control the magic of the property. It wasn't up for grabs anymore." She sighed. "Sure wish we'd been aware of the consequences of Ashling's life estate. I never would have stayed."

"Don't worry about it. You aren't responsible. Ben's unstable mind would have brought all this down sooner, had I taken over at her death. Our theory is that he figured Ashling's death would bring Mom and Dad back to the property. He planned to eliminate Dad, take over the property, and have Mom all to himself. Any rational person could see all the holes in his plan. But he's spent forty years pining for Mom and blaming Dad for his loss. Not a stable individual. What he didn't count on was me taking over the property instead of Dad, and the surge in magic with two blood McKay's in residence, even it if was only for a little while."

Colleen nodded. "I could feel the magic pulse even before we turned onto the property. It's much stronger than it was when Ashling and I lived here. Of course, your dad's magic ability was strong. Ashling was good, but Duncan…he was exceptional. Then he married Klaren, a Parker witch, and you were born with the best of both worlds. Anyway, no use rehashing ancient history."

"Did someone mention my name?" Duncan stuck his head in the door and smiled at Pepper. "Your mom and I were passing by and thought we'd stop."

"Nice to see you, Colleen," Klaren said peering over her husband's shoulder.

"Hi, Duncan, Klaren," Colleen said cheerfully.

"Lathen will be over in a minute." He looked from Colleen to Pepper. "We're not interrupting anything?"

"No…no, not at all," Pepper replied. "We were discussing ancient history."

Her dad raised an eyebrow but continued on. "After talking with you and Lathen the other night, I think we've devised a plan to take care of dear old Ben permanently," Duncan said sardonically. "Ravyn has agreed to go along with our plan as long as it culminates in his admission of guilt. Then we are free to move forward with the second part of the plan."

"Ravyn and the other nine witches of the coven have agreed to help us. They'd like to meet here to discuss the plans and look over the area," Klaren said.

"Sure, no problem. Barring any unforeseen events, my schedule is wide open." Pepper glanced up as Lathen strode in the door.

"Did I miss anything important?" He grinned and glanced around the room. "Nope, no unaccounted-for toads or rabbits, so we're good."

Pepper narrowed her eyes at him as her parents let out a simultaneous groan.

"See, this is what happens when you take up with a non-witch," Duncan said, his lips twitching. "You going to be howling at the moon this evening, Lathen?"

"Nope, it's not full until Halloween night, then watch out," Lathen shot back. "Of course you'll be too busy donning pointy hats and flying through the sky on your broomsticks." Lathen roared with laughter.

"Touché," Duncan said with a chuckle.

Pepper rolled her eyes. "The pointy hat thing again. Need to come up with something new. Now, can we get back to more important things." Pepper tilted the book up from the desk. "The McKay's grimoire. Colleen brought it by."

Her dad peered at the book, ran his fingers over the worn leather, and touched the metal clasp. "Been a long time since I've seen this." He rubbed his chin with his hand. "Could be very useful. What do you think, Klaren?"

"I agree. Maybe we should take a look at it now."

"If you've other plans, you could take the book with you," Pepper offered.

"We don't have any plans today," Klaren said. "Besides, I don't think the grimoire should leave the property, now that it's back."

"Sounds good. I'd like to hear your plan, anyway," Pepper said.

****

Traditionally All Hallows Eve or Halloween is when the veil between the spirit world and the mortal world is the thinnest. This allows spirits to cross over and share the mortals' plane of existence for one night ending at midnight. Pepper intended to use that magic to her advantage. She was thankful for the unusually mild weather in Lobster Cove. Halloween evening temperatures would be in the upper forties to lower fifties, a boon to the town celebration and the culmination of the events her family and Ravyn's coven had set in motion last week.

Earlier that morning, Pepper had walked to the pond to make sure everything was ready for tonight and to allow Kaylee to feed. Pepper's insistence that Kaylee return to the cabin aviary had been very unpopular with the osprey. Lathen volunteered to check on the eagle, puffin, and peregrine falcon chicks while she took care of Tonk and Ember, a job he usually handled. But today she had strict instructions for Ember.

After checking on Tonk and giving him and Ember their breakfast, Pepper said, "Ember, stick close. I'll be back to lock you in when we leave this afternoon. After that, I want you to stay in the building with Tonk until I come and get you late tonight." She washed out bowls and filled them with fresh water. "You've plenty of food and water," she said before walking to the barn.

In the old barn now known as the seabird aviary, where they'd set up a table and benches, Pepper sat down and viewed the pumpkins sitting in front of her on the table, picked up the carving knife. Was the plan foolproof? What if Ben didn't react as they expected? The townspeople couldn't be endangered. What if he refused to admit his wrongdoing? What if they were wrong? Not possible. She reviewed the plan in her mind once more and sighed. *Nothing will go wrong. I won't allow it.*

Lathen put his hand on her shoulder. "Where'd you go? Been sitting there, knife extended above the pumpkin, for fifteen minutes. Are you going to carve it or just threaten it?" He guffawed and wrapped his large callused hand around hers holding the knife, brought it to the pumpkin, and made carving motions, then tried to hand her an erasable marker. "Try using this first."

She pushed his hand away and frowned at him. "Oh, stop it. I was thinking about this evening after the celebration. I don't want anything to go wrong."

"It won't. We have a solid plan and several powerful witches to bring it to fruition. So relax and enjoy the festivities of your favorite holiday. But the decorations will be lacking if you don't get to carving. We need twenty-five jack-o-lanterns, by your own count, for the gazebo and surrounding area tables in the town square. I have the candles and holders for each right here." As he swung the bag in front of Pepper, the tinkling sound of glass clinking together had her frowning.

"Careful, or you'll be looking for more holders." Snagging the bag from him, she sat it on the ground under her bench and then spun the pumpkin around searching for the best side to carve a face. "Funny or scary?" she asked, drawing her bottom lip through her teeth as she peered at all of the pumpkins arranged around her. They'd carved several last night but still had eleven to go and would deliver them all to the gazebo by two this afternoon. The sun peeked over the eastern horizon, flooding through the window in warm golden shards of light. *Got plenty of time.* Pepper looked forward to joining with the locals to decorate the center of town for the festivities. It felt good to be a welcome member of the community.

"How about a vampire pumpkin?" Lathen asked.

"I can do that. Do we have red food dye for dripping blood from the fangs?"

"Sure. I'll go find it. Meanwhile, how about just a traditional jack-o-lantern? You know—triangle eyes, nose, and toothy grin. You should be able to knock a couple those out by the time I get back with the blood."

"In other words, you have no idea where the food dye is, and you're a slave driver." She chortled, stabbing the knife into the pumpkin, and began carving out the top.

After a few minutes, Lathen returned with the red food coloring and plopped it in front of Pepper. "See I knew exactly where it was," he said triumphantly and bent down to kiss her.

"Will wonders never cease." She ran her fingers through his tousled blond hair without thinking and returned the kiss. When she glanced at him, she giggled. Several pumpkins seeds were stuck in his hair along with a string of slimy pumpkin guts.

"What?" he asked, his eyes rolling up in his head in an attempt to follow her gaze and combed a hand through his hair. Scrunching his face up, he shook his hair vigorously over her. A few pumpkin seeds went flying, but most the guts remained stuck.

Tears streamed down her face as she laughed

uncontrollably.

Lathen stood staring at her until she sobered, a slight smile curving one corner of his mouth. "You can start loading the pumpkins into the truck, while I go wash this shit out of my hair. It's time to go." He turned on his heel and stalked toward the cabin.

The slight shake of his shoulders gave away his silent laughter as Pepper enjoyed the way he moved up the path and the fit of his jeans on that mighty nice ass. He turned to look at her before entering the cabin. She waved and began putting several jack-o-lanterns into a cart. When Pepper stepped outside, the gentle breeze ruffled through her hair. She drew in a breath of freshly carved pumpkins mingled with brine. She loved the combination.

Clouds obscured the sun, but the day was dry and mild. She couldn't complain and grabbed the handle of the cart and tugged it to the truck. After Lathen returned and took over the loading duties, Pepper gathered up buckets with pumpkin guts and discarded pieces and dumped them in the compost bin. The seeds she'd toss out for the wild birds.

By the time they arrived in the town square, there was already quite a crowd. Pepper's mom and dad were waiting by the gazebo, where the Lobster Cove Wildlife Rescue and Rehab booth would be set up. Lathen parked the truck. Several men greeted them and began unloading the pumpkins. Pepper grabbed the bag of candles and jogged ahead to indicate where the jack-o-lanterns should be placed. She hugged her dad and kissed her mom on the cheek. "Are we all set?"

"Yep, had the conversation with Ben this morning. He ate it up. Almost too easy," her mother whispered, looking around nervously.

Duncan patted her on the shoulder. "You'll do fine."

"Hey, hey, Dad," Pepper whispered. "Remember you two are on the outs. Mom, go wander around, talk with your friends."

Lathen and Duncan set up the booth complete with warming pots and insulated cups for hot chocolate. Pepper took three giant bags of candy from the crate and poured them into a big basket. Hands on hips, Pepper glanced around and nodded to Lathen. "I think we're ready."

Trick or treat stations were set up all over the area with a few adjacent merchants sponsoring costume contests and prizes.

Various organizations set up booths to sell or promote their wares. They doubled as additional trick or treat stops for the kids, handing out alternative treats such as popcorn balls, hot apple cider, and sugar free candy. The high school's booth had bobbing for apples set up.

The Lobster Cove Wildlife Rescue and Rehab Center booth was a popular stop serving mugs of hot chocolate to chase away the autumn chill. Pepper, Lathen, Klaren, and Duncan took turns manning the booth and mingling among friends and acquaintances.

Pepper caught sight of Ben once standing with some of his co-workers from the office and again hanging around the group her mom was talking with. But he moved on pretty quickly when she joined the group for a few minutes. She'd heard rumors that Tom was released on home detention, but she was still relieved that he didn't make an appearance.

Just before dusk, Pepper lit all the pumpkins, and Lathen started the portable propane heater inside the gazebo to act as a warming station for the remainder of the festivities. He stayed close to the gazebo, making sure it didn't turn into a bonfire.

The orange glow of the evil, funny, and traditionally carved jack-o-lanterns completed the Halloween ambiance. As Pepper returned to the booth, she was met by a fairy princess accompanied by a young vampire with plastic pumpkins held in their hands. "Trick or treat," the little princess with sparkly wings said. A chorus of trick or treats echoed by the approaching tiny witch in a pointy hat and black and orange striped stockings. A pair of children dressed as M&M's and a couple of popular movie characters rounded out the group.

Pepper reached into the basket, grabbed a handful of candy, and dropped several pieces in each child's pumpkin. The children laughed and hooted as they scurried off to the next candy station.

She hollered at Lathen and pointed to a dog dressed as a red and gold dragon. "Should have dressed Ember up and brought her." Pepper laughed at Lathen's scowl.

"She'd never forgive you for that, no matter how many dog cookies you gave her."

Once the games were over and prizes awarded, the crowds started to thin. Several families stopped by for a mug of hot chocolate and said their goodbyes. Knots of adults moved on to a warmer location offering adult beverages. As part of the decorating committee, Lathen and Pepper started picking up. The jack-o-lanterns would be the last to go. She offered the pumpkins to anyone who wanted them. Otherwise she'd take them home and add to the compost bin. Off in the distance, the mist was rolling in and the breeze picked up.

"Good turnout," Pepper commented to Lathen watching her father approach. "I guess we better get things picked up if we don't want them wet."

Duncan walked up to the gazebo and slowed, leaning his arm on the stair railing.

Lathen watched the older man for a few minutes. He didn't move. "Hey, Duncan, you okay?"

"Not sure. Lower elevation makes me dizzy sometimes but hasn't bothered me this trip—until now. I think I'll go sit down." When he started to sway, Lathen reached for Duncan's elbow to steady him.

At the LCWRRC booth, Lathen pulled out a chair and eased Duncan into it. "He's not feeling well."

Pepper opened the cooler and grabbed a bottle of water, handed it to her dad. "Mom's over visiting with Maggie and Jill. I'll go get her."

"No, don't bother. I'll sit here and drink the water, be fine shortly." He took a long pull on the bottle of water, then rested his elbows on his knees, leaning over.

Lathen and Pepper exchanged looks.

"Why don't you take Dad back to the cabin in his rental car? Mom and I will follow in your truck as soon as I return the decorations to storage. I've got the key to the unit."

He shook his head, glanced around, and walked up the steps to the gazebo, turned off the heater. "Don't want to leave you two alone. Besides, I need to load this heater and rest of the pumpkins in the truck."

Pepper leaned over and whispered in his ear. "Better two witches than a witch and werewolf, if magic becomes an issue. Know what I mean?"

"Still don't like it." A couple guys from Lathen's crew walked by and waved. "Hey, Bill, Jake, any chance I could get you to help load the heater and the rest of the pumpkins in my truck?

"Yeah, no problem," Jake said, picking up the heater as Bill and Lathen grabbed the remaining pumpkins.

"Be right back," Lathen said.

Before Lathen got back, Klaren's little group broke up, and she walked back to the booth. "Hey, Pep—" Klaren looked at her husband. "Duncan, what's wrong?" she asked.

"Got so busy today, I didn't drink enough water. I feel better now." He glanced sideways, raised an eyebrow, and subtly jerked his chin toward the left side of the gazebo.

Pepper followed his gaze just in time to catch a glimpse of Ben disappearing behind a tree. *Showtime.*

"You're still pretty pale. Maybe we should go back to the cottage."

"And miss Halloween at the cabin? No way. I'll be fine."

With an armful of garland, Pepper reached for the plastic storage bag, stuffing the decorations into the bag. She turned to Lathen. "You know what? If you have a tarp in your truck, we can cover the decorations and put them in storage tomorrow. The bags might be a bit damp, but the decorations will be fine."

"That'll work." He took the bag from Pepper. "I'll throw this in the bed and tie the tarp over the front, that way all you have to do is bungee cord the back to the corners of the bumper."

Klaren stuffed more garland into another bag while

Pepper took the big plastic pumpkin off the railing.

"Go ahead and take Dad to the cabin. We'll be right behind you," Pepper said, shoving the remaining bags of decorations into the bed of the truck. She pulled the cord across and hooked it over the bumper on each end.

Lathen took the car keys from Duncan and helped him to the car. "See you in a few," he called out while giving Pepper a thumbs-up.

Pepper climbed into the truck after her mom, engaged the door locks, then watched the rental car back out of the parking lot and turn up the road. She touched her mom's arm. "All set?"

"I think so."

The truck bounced like weight was being added to the bed, and Pepper smiled. "Off we go."

A short while later, she pulled into the driveway behind the rental car at the back of the cabin. Lathen was waiting on the back porch.

"Let's go inside and warm up. Logs in the fireplace await your arrival." He wrapped an arm around her and held the door open for Klaren, then followed her inside and closed the door.

Pepper snapped her fingers watched the flames race up the wood, then peeked out the window, turned, and nodded to her parents. A few minutes later, loud voices erupted inside the cabin. Duncan and Lathen rushed out of the house, got in the rental car, and drove off.

Dressed in a parka, with a blanket wrapped around her, Klaren stepped out on the deck, hands wrapped around a monster mug of steaming coffee and sat in one of the chairs. Pepper let the door bang closed behind her.

"Mom, I'm going to go check on Ember and Tonk at the mammal habitat. Won't be long." Pepper sprinted down the path, doubled back, and hid behind the greenhouse with a view of the porch. She sucked in a breath when the tarp moved and the bungee cord slipped off the bumper with a zing. Ben emerged from the back of the truck, brushed off his clothes, took several minutes to scan the area, then sauntered up the steps to the porch.

Klaren yelped and nearly spilled her coffee. "What are you doing here?"

"Everyone gone?"

"For the moment. What are you doing here?"

"Making sure you're okay. I told you Duncan would show his real colors one day, and I'd be waiting," Ben said smugly leaning against the porch railing.

"You need to leave. Pepper will be back any minute."

"Not worried about her. I can take care of her just like I did...well, never mind." He reached for her. "Come with me."

"You don't have a vehicle," Klaren said getting to her feet.

"Don't need one." He snapped his fingers, and Klaren was in his arms. "I've learned a trick or two over the years."

Klaren threw her coffee in his face, cup and all, then bolted out of his arms and down the stairs as a huge reddish wolf advanced, snarling, and leaped over the railing knocking Ben down the stairs. He hit the ground and tumbled down the path. He scrambled to get to his feet. But the wolf was too fast. One leap and the animal landed on Ben's back, knocking him forward before he finally landed face down on the ground out cold. In a blink of an eye, the wolf was gone, and witches closed in on all sides.

Pepper ran to her mother and helped her to her feet. "You okay?"

"I'm fine, just sorry I didn't have time to get more information out of the son of a bitch. Did you see what he did? I wasn't about to let him transport me to who knows where." Klaren brushed at the knees of her jeans viciously.

The witches formed a circle around Ben. Wisps of fog trailed along the ground and took shape as spirits floating in the meadow. Duncan stepped forward and cast a spell ensnaring the man in vines of shimmering light.

"Don't make the vines too tight around his neck. We need him to be able to speak," Ravyn said in a calm lilting voice.

"Done," Duncan replied.

Ravyn flicked her fingers. A bucket of water appeared over Ben's head. It tipped and the liquid splashed over him.

Ben sputtered and cursed, his eyes wild.

"Mr. Bonchard. It's come to our attention that you are misusing magic for personal gain. You've called on dark magic to curse an innocent to do harm to your own kind. How do you plead?" Ravyn asked in a commanding tone.

"Bitch," Ben bit out. "I only acted to get back what was mine." He narrowed his eyes at Pepper.

She cast a blindfold on him. "Don't want to take

any chances. Not sure what he's capable of," Pepper said when Ravyn glared at her.

Ravyn nodded. "I'll take that as a guilty plea, Mr. Bonchard. Therefore, you are to be spellbound immediately." She paused. "But first, Pepper, do you have the candle?"

"Yes." Pepper produced a tall thick twisted black candle with beautifully carved moon phases on all sides.

"Step into the circle. Face the full moon depiction north." Raven closed her eyes and murmured several words. The candle ignited in a black flame, flickered, then faded to pure white.

"Perfect. Set the candle down and move back," Ravyn said without explanation.

She turned to Ben, who was cursing loudly, threatening the McKay family and everyone else. "Silence," she commanded. His mouth continued to open and shut but without sound. The coven of ten witches, Klaren, and Duncan joined hands forming a circle as Ravyn chanted quietly at first, then her voice rose with the wind. Suddenly all was quiet.

The vines wrapped around Ben glowed dark red, shifted to black, then fell away. When he took a menacing step forward, Pepper flicked her hand. A chair appeared, slamming behind Ben's knees. He fell backward onto the seat and ropes tied him to the seat.

Ravyn nodded in approval.

"Benjamin Bonchard, the spellbinding is complete. The witches' council will convene within two weeks. By that time, you will have found a way to undo the harm you caused to Mr. Green, or face the wrath of the council and your life will be forfeit. Clear?"

Ben slumped in the chair and nodded.

"Good. Our work here is done." Ravyn raised her arms. A flash of lightning and the ten witches faded into the night. Tendrils of mist crawled along the ground as the spirits floated toward the lake.

"Well, that was an anticlimactic ending to the evening," Pepper said, turning her body in a complete circle. "Anyone seen Lathen?"

"Not in human form," her dad said, raising one eyebrow and wrapping an arm around his wife.

"You guys picked up on that, huh?" Pepper said, starting down the path to the lake.

"Yep," Klaren said.

"Picked up on what?" Lathen appeared in the door of the cabin, dressed in fresh jeans, black sweatshirt, and boots. Kaylee's left wing caught his tousled hair as she winged her way into the night air. Ember and Tonk flanked him. Jogging down the steps from the house, he had rain ponchos slung over his shoulder. When he reached the ground, he tossed each person a hooded poncho. "I'm betting this drizzle is going to be pouring rain soon. How about we go see what Ashling and the ghosts have to say before midnight arrives?"

"We all know your little…" Pepper paused. "…or not so little secret. And it's sexy as hell." She wound her arms around his neck and buried her face in his throat, inhaling deeply. *His scent has changed. More woodsy with a touch of spice and musk, very alluring.*

"Not trying to keep it a secret. Making sure I've got control of the beast, not the other way around." He made a chuffing sound and skidded to a stop, staring across the pond. Its banks were draped in fog with at least fifty spirits rising out of the mist.

Pepper's mom and dad settled onto the older bench near the pond. Lathen and Pepper plopped down on the new bench he'd built from enchanted wood on the property. He leaned back, his arm wrapped tight around her. She snuggled into his shoulder and glanced up at him. She'd never noticed how long and thick his eyelashes were. A woman would kill for those.

Ember lay beside the bench, emitting a low growl once in a while to keep Tonk in line. Ashling occupied her usual place against the pine tree so shrouded in mist Pepper could barely make out Kaylee's form in the lower branches.

"An exhausting night, but all's well that ends well," Pepper said with a sigh. A chorus of soft rustles and murmurs around the pond echoed in agreement. "It's really kind of a shame that Benjamin will spend the rest of his life spellbound. But I think Tom will be relieved to finally figure out what was happening to him."

"I think he'll still feel bad about the things he did, even though he really wasn't responsible," Lathen said.

"Do you believe Aidan really stole Dusty's magic?" Pepper tucked her feet up under her and leaned into her warm werewolf.

"I don't know; seems they were happily married for over sixty years from what I learned of the family history. So apparently, she didn't care," Pepper's mom said, shifting in her seat. "Imagine how traumatic the trials must have been for a seventeen-year-old." Klaren shook her head.

"What a way to start a relationship. But maybe facing death at the witch trials and losing her mother made her glad to be rid of her magic," Pepper's dad suggested.

The waves on the pond slapped noisily against the rocky shore as the mist crawling along the ground and settling over the pond took shape. Out of the fog rose a woman dressed in a simple long indigo skirt and peasant blouse under a firm white bodice. Holding her arm was a man who wore knee-length black breeches with a long dark vest over his peasant shirt. They glided across the pond and stepped onto the shore. An audible gasp came from the ghosts, and they moved closer.

Lathen, Pepper, and her parents sat silent, eyes wide in disbelief.

"Good evening, McKay clan." The man offered a pleasant smile and said in a deep voice reminiscent of Duncan's, "Allow me to introduce my wife, Dusty McKay." He wrapped an arm around her waist and brought her forward. "I am Aidan Duncan McKay. We have taken advantage of this night to set the record straight. 'Tis true, as a young girl Dusty ran away in early 1693, after being found not guilty of witchcraft. Because in fact she was a witch, like her mother, who wasn't so lucky and died at the hands of the Puritans. I had arrived in America from Ireland, with no family or friends. I met her shortly thereafter, we fell in love, and I asked her to be my wife. We were wed a fortnight later and drifted from place to place in what was then Massachusetts and settled in what is now Maine on this land. It looked different in my time."

Duncan cleared his throat, clearly wanting to ask something.

Aidan held up an index finger and continued in a clear firm voice emphasizing each word. "With her permission." He paused, making eye contact with each person and ghost. "We blended our magic to create a safe haven and built a cabin."

Dusty nodded as she surveyed the group gathered at the pond.

He looked toward the cabin. "It was much smaller than the one that sits up there now." He smiled wistfully. "I can still see parts of our beloved cabin still standing. We were happily married for sixty-two years before Dusty became ill and left me alone in this world, again. But it wasn't so bad this time. We were blessed with six children, numerous grandchildren, and great-grandchildren."

"Those were the happiest days of our lives," Dusty said, peering lovingly into her husband's face.

He nodded. "Yes. This is the true family history that should be passed down." His gaze traveled from Pepper and Lathen to Duncan and Klaren, then scanned slowly over the McKay ghosts gathered around. He chuckled, shaking his head slowly. "Never expected to have a werewolf in our lineage."

Lathen raised his hands in surrender and shrugged. "Never expected a witch in mine."

Pepper gave a heavy sigh and grinned. "I knew the tales weren't true. What a wonderful love story. Thank you for sharing it."

Before the questions began, Lathen pushed up from the bench, shoved a hand into his jeans pocket, and pulled out a small green velvet drawstring pouch. He reached for Pepper's hand, turned it over, gently kissed her palm, and placed the pouch in it.

Her gaze traveled to the pouch as she turned it over, then tugged at the strings. "What's this?"

"Open it and find out," he said patiently.

As she turned the bag over, pulled at the strings and shook it, a ring spilled onto her hand and glinted in the moonlight. Lathen went down on one knee. "With all the McKay's present, spirit and living as witness, I ask you, Pepper, to share my life as my wife."

Her eyes brimmed with tears that she wiped away with the back of her hand. "Oh, Lathen…" She drew in a deep breath and blew it out slowly.

"He's waiting for an answer," Aidan prompted.

"Oh, yes—yes, I want to share the rest of my life with you."

Kaylee whistled loudly, swooped in, and landed on the back of the bench.

"Well, I'm glad you approve," Lathen said with a chuckle, giving a quick glance at the bird, then slipped the ring on Pepper's finger. "The ring belonged to your great-great-grandmother McKay. Ashling wanted you to have it."

She tilted her head in confusion and said, "It wasn't with her belongings."

"No. She gave it to your mother for safekeeping. During my conversation with your father about marrying you, Klaren mentioned she had the ring with her."

Klaren shrugged. "When we left home, I had a feeling I should bring it."

"So you all were in on this," Pepper said incredulously, holding out her hand to admire the ring in the light of the full moon.

"I think the Winter Solstice would be the perfect wedding date," Lathen said.

"Perfect." Pepper sighed and closed her eyes. His heart beat steady and true against her as she snuggled beside him, hand held in her lap so the ring winked in the moonlight. She relaxed listening to the breeze rustle through the trees and the frogs' croaky serenade. Kaylee's soft whistle was surrounded by murmurs of human and spirits. Finally, Ember and Tonk's light snoring combined with the scents of brine and rain around her would remain in her memory forever.

A word from the author…

With the majestic Rocky Mountains just outside my window, I sit at my computer with Vampires, Demons, Witches, Faeries, and a variety of paranormal creatures gathered around telling me their stories! I am an author of Paranormal Romance. Always remember the magic to a Happily Every After!

Colorado is home. I share my life with a wonderful husband of many moons, our brilliant Chow Chow, a terribly spoiled companion parrot, and a forty-year-old box turtle. We enjoy hiking, biking, and camping, also love water sports including kayaking and whitewater rafting, especially on the Arkansas River through the Royal Gorge.

Another passion of mine is reading. Any winter evening you can find me curled up in front of a crackling fire with a good book, a mug of hot chocolate, and a big bowl of popcorn.

While growing up if I didn't like the ending of a book, I'd rewrite it, which led to writing my own books.

http://www.tenastetler.com

~*~

Other Tena Stetler titles
available from The Wild Rose Press, Inc.:
A DEMON'S WITCH
CHARM ME—A Candy Hearts Romance